I0770495

The Mystery in Mapleton

C'MON!" EDDIE SHOUTED AS HE TOOK OFF INTO the woods. "If we hurry, we might be able to catch 'em and get the map back!"

Nick and Jo raced after Eddie as he darted down the path, zigzagging between inconveniently placed trees and low-hanging vines. Moments later, they stood at the side of the road, panting. They saw no one. Nothing. No people. And unfortunately, no map.

Nick bent over and rested his hands on his knees, trying to catch his breath.

"Those no-good, low-life jerks!" Jo puffed, then laced her fingers together and rested her hands on top of her head. She looked up and down the road.

Nick stood up. "You think it was Billy and Jack?"

"Of course, it was them." Eddie answered, clenching his fists as he paced back and forth. "No one else knows about our hideout. First, our snacks? Now the map?" He kicked at the loose gravel along the side of the road, scattering pebbles into the tall grass.

Jo gasped. "Guys, what if those coordinates actually *do* mark the location of something important?"

"And they find it first?" Eddie's eyes flashed in anger.

"Exactly."

The Mystery in Mapleton

H.M. LAWSON

Tackle Box Treasure Series
Book One

Wilson Lindberg Books, LLC

ISBN 979-8-9899469-0-7

Printed in the United States of America

Cover art by H.M. Lawson
Illustrations by H.M. Lawson
First edition January 2024

For Elsa and Stig

A Note from the Author

Hi there!

Thanks for reading my book. Hope you enjoy it. Throughout the story, you'll notice I've written some words in **bold**. These words are considered "advanced vocabulary." If you can't figure out their meaning using context clues, check out the definitions in the glossary at the end of the book. Increasing your vocabulary is one way to give your intelligence a boost. By the time you're done reading this story, you'll be a smarter version of yourself.

Happy reading,

H.M. Lawson

H.M. Lawson

P.S. If you're looking for more activities involving the story, check out my website: www.hmlawsonbooks.com

Contents

Nick's sketch of Mapleton

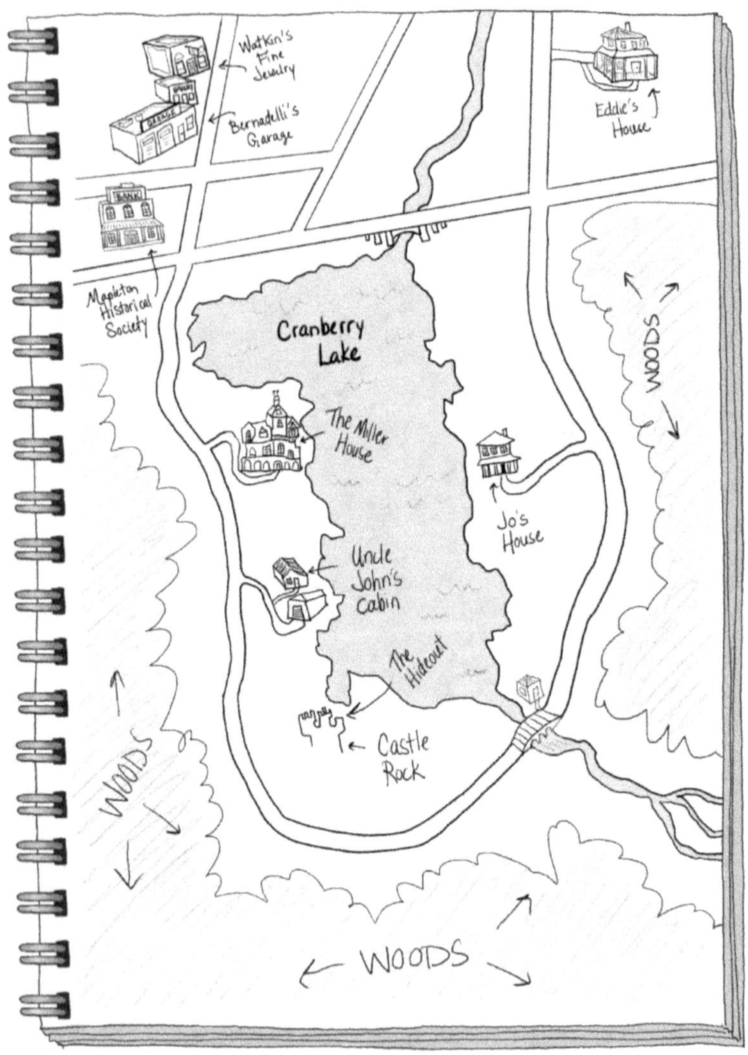

Nick

"DON'T FORGET TO PACK A SWEATSHIRT," NICK'S mom called up the stairs. "It can get pretty cold in the woods at night."

Nick had just closed his duffle bag but quickly opened it again to stuff his gray Pinehurst Pirates hoodie inside. It was one of several new clothing items his parents had recently purchased to help Nick **acclimate** to their new town.

"Got it!"

After a brief struggle with the reluctant zipper, he slung the heavy load over his shoulder and adjusted his baseball hat. As he passed his desk, his eyes lingered on the army green tackle box poking out of a cardboard box. It was nestled between a stack of graphic novels and a few tattered, stuffed animals. He dropped the bag to the ground, pushed aside the comics, then pulled out the tackle box. He ran a finger over the worn wooden handle, flipped the tarnished latch, and opened the lid to admire the contents.

The tackle box was more of a treasure holder than a fishing gear organizer. For as long as he could remember, Nick had taken this dingy, plastic tackle box with him on every family vacation. Each of the treasures represented a memory from a special adventure. Someday, he hoped to become an archaeologist and secretly felt he had a knack for finding things other people overlooked.

He gingerly lifted the snakeskin he'd found on a family vacation to the Grand Canyon. It was delicate and his dad had helped him sandwich it between two pieces of clear packing tape to help keep it intact. Near Mount Rushmore, in South Dakota, he'd discovered a buffalo nickel from 1918 on the edge of the road near a scenic overlook. At a beach in Georgia, he'd nearly stepped on a shark's tooth poking out of the sand. It'd been a particularly exciting addition to the collection. There was a piece of pyrite—also known as Fool's Gold—from a stream in the Smoky Mountains, and his all-time favorite treasure was the small jawbone of a mammal with two teeth still attached; he'd spotted that one while hiking in Wisconsin. He knew it was probably from a raccoon, but when he'd been younger, he'd imagined it was from a previously undiscovered species of dinosaur.

This summer, however, was going to be different. Nick closed the lid, and his shoulders slumped. There wasn't going to be a vacation this year. There would be no road trip, no amusement park, not even an educational summer camp. Instead, his parents had explained, they'd be spending the summer renovating the house his mom inherited. The old, two-story

Victorian house was—as his mom described it—a real "fixer-upper," but Nick recognized it for what it really was—a falling-down, **dilapidated** wreck. To make matters worse, his parents had decided that while the house was under construction, Nick would spend the summer living with his great uncle.

"Nick?" his mom called again. "He should be here any minute."

"Coming," Nick grumbled.

He nudged a bucket on the floor with his toe so it would collect the drips from a new leak in the ceiling. Out of habit, he reached for the tackle box, but when he remembered where he was going, he paused. There was no way he'd find anything interesting at his uncle's house. The town sounded boring, and the only person he knew there was a senior citizen. He left the tackle box where it was next to the stuffed animals.

Nick's tennis shoes clomped down the stairs. As he neared the bottom, he hopped over two strips of plywood covering the missing stair treads on the last two steps. His mom was waiting for him in the foyer.

She met him with a tentative smile. "You ready?"

"No," Nick groaned. "I don't see why I can't just stay here. I could sleep in a tent in the backyard."

"You'll be fine."

"Can't *you* drive me? I can't survive five and a half hours in a car with him."

"It's two and a half hours." She wrapped her arms around him and nestled her cheek into his overgrown mop of brown hair, "and you'll be fine."

Nick pulled away and looked at the pile of plaster on the floor. Deep down, he knew the old house wasn't ready to live in, but he still wasn't happy about his parents' decision to send him away.

"How long until you finish fixing things?"

Nick's mom scratched at a smear of blue paint on her arm. "Hopefully not too long."

Nick groaned, "I don't know anything about this guy, Mom. He's basically a stranger." For emphasis, he added, "A *frail, old* stranger. I'll bet his house smells like moldy cheese."

"Uncle John's place is—rustic." She gave him a wary look. "I'm sure he'll appreciate the company."

"What are we even going to do—play six hours of checkers every day? And he doesn't need company. He's got Judy."

"Judy?" She gave him a skeptical look. "His goldfish?" She walked over to the window. "Listen, he's the only family we have around here."

Nick envisioned himself ladling a spoonful of vegetable broth into the old man's mouth and wiping dribble off his chin. He shuddered.

"You're just lucky John took pity on you and agreed to take you in." She teased, "When I explained that you begged us to let you spend the summer with him, well…"

"Mommm!"

Her eyes twinkled, and she pivoted from playful to practical. "But seriously, John's a really interesting person—once you get to know him. And it'll be good for you to unplug for a change."

Nick cringed as he was reminded about the lack of wi-fi and cell towers in the northern woods. He'd be spending the summer basically off-the-grid, without his laptop, cell phone, or video games.

His mom *tsked* and combed her fingers through his hair. "Agh—I forgot to give you a haircut."

"It's fine, Mom." Nick shook his head and reversed the unwanted styling.

"Did you pack your umbrella?"

Nick was too lost in thought to hear her question. He pictured himself sitting in a cafeteria at a senior center, surrounded by old people playing bingo. Nick couldn't picture John's face but recalled the half-dozen phone calls when he'd been asked to "just say hello." The deep, gravelly voice on the other end had rumbled through the phone's speaker posing boring questions like, *How's the weather by you?*

"I don't want to go."

"Nick, we've already been over this. He's family." She sneezed. "And he has an extra room that isn't covered in sawdust." She called past him up the stairwell, "James? Did you hear from the roofers yet?"

Nick's dad's voice echoed through the second-floor hallway. "Not yet, but the plumber should be stopping by any minute."

She put her hands on Nick's shoulders. "This is only temporary." She glanced up at the exposed ceiling joists and pipes, laced her hands behind her head, and let out a long sigh. Nick followed her gaze to a drop of water glistening at the seam of two overhead pipes. It grew larger and larger, like a blister, until it sagged under its own weight and dropped into the plastic bucket directly underneath.

"If we had known how much work this place needed…" His mom trailed off and rubbed her forehead. "Look, with all the construction going on, it's just not a safe place for a kid."

Nick thought about saying, "*I'm not a kid. I'm twelve,*" but he knew she wouldn't change her mind. The plan was set, and arguing would be **futile**. Nick headed for the door to wait for his great-uncle.

His mom called out, "James? Nick's ready to head out."

"Be right there."

Nick heard a clatter of tools. A moment later, Nick's dad, in his heavy work boots, thumped down the steps.

He stretched his arm out and handed Nick his tacklebox. "You left this upstairs. You never know what kind of treasures you'll stumble upon."

Nick, already feeling deflated, took the tacklebox without arguing. He didn't bother to explain that the chances of finding any treasures in the middle of nowhere were slim to none—not to mention the fact that he'd outgrown the childish keepsakes.

They heard the low thrum of an engine outside. A horn honked twice.

"Late *and* impatient?" Nick's mom raised an eyebrow.

His dad shrugged. "He's a man of contradictions."

A melodic jingle rang out from the phone at the end of the hallway.

"Ooh! I hope that's the roofers, so we can get rid of some of these buckets." She leaned forward and kissed his forehead. "Please call if Uncle John forgets to feed you."

Nick's stomach clenched with worry. He tended to get carsick on an empty stomach. He made a mental note to grab a bag of fruit snacks before he left.

"Kidding," she called over her shoulder as she hurried down the hallway into the living room/painting headquarters.

His dad confirmed, "I'm sure he'll feed you, but don't expect anything gourmet."

"Can I at least take my bike?" Nick's question was drowned out by an ominous clunking sound, followed by a gurgling splash from the next room.

He and his dad rushed into the kitchen, where a geyser of water sprayed out of the sink where the faucet should have been. Brownish water bubbled up from the drain and was filling the sink. Seconds later, it began spilling over the edges onto the floor. As his dad grabbed a plunger and a bucket, the horn honked again.

"Give my best to John." His dad gestured toward the door. "We'll be fine here."

Nick said, "I'll call when I get there." Under his breath, he added, "If the old-timer even has a phone."

His dad didn't respond. He was under the sink, attacking the faucet with a wrench and letting out a series of indistinguishable grunting noises—none of which sounded like an answer to his question about the bike.

When Nick opened the front door, he was surprised to see a rusty, blue pickup truck backing into the driveway. The red taillights glared like angry eyes, and a blue plastic tarp shielded the items in the truck bed from the rain.

"Mom? Dad?" Nick called over his shoulder, "The plumber's here."

Inside, Nick's mom was still talking on the phone. "I really need someone out here today, especially with this rain…"

Over the clanging of tools against metal pipes, Nick heard his dad muttering something about a broken valve.

Nick stood under the overhang of the porch and watched the truck attempt to back into the driveway. Evidently, the blue tarp was making the job difficult. The side mirror on the truck narrowly missed scraping the mailbox, and both left tires were now digging into the grass along the driveway. The driver hooked his tattooed arm over the door and craned his neck out the window. He had a bushy, white beard, and a long, gray ponytail snaked over his shoulder. Despite the warm summer temperature, he wore a knitted winter hat.

The man craned his neck out the window to see where the truck was headed. He asked, "How'm I doin'?"

Nick immediately recognized the deep, gravelly voice. It was his Great-Uncle John, and he was not at all what Nick was expecting.

MAPLETON

THE SOUND OF THE TRUCK DOOR CLOSING JOLTED him awake. Nick pushed his ballcap up and rubbed his eyes. He peered out the windshield at the early evening sky. It was pale gray, with dark clouds hovering ominously on the horizon. His stomach gurgled. He'd forgotten to bring a snack.

The driver's seat was empty. He heard the old man outside muttering as he unscrewed the gas cap. Evidently, Uncle John had more to say to himself than he did to his passenger. Nick's mom hadn't been exaggerating when she said Uncle John was a man of few words. He seemed friendly enough, but after a brief introduction, the ride had been painfully quiet. Nick had fallen asleep out of sheer boredom.

The driver's side door opened. Uncle John leaned in and tossed a small blue and white plastic container onto the seat. "This should hold you 'til dinner."

Printed on the lid of the container were the words *ONE DOZEN Canadian Nightcrawlers.* Horrified, he recalled his mom's words about the old man forgetting to feed him and worried that might be a *best*-case scenario. He was relieved, however, when he looked up to see an outstretched hand holding out a granola bar.

Grateful, Nick took it and mumbled, "Thanks."

Uncle John hopped into the driver's seat and brought with him a wave of humid air and the sickly, sweet scent of gasoline. For such an old man, he moved with surprising agility.

"Tarp's doing a good job," he said.

Nick twisted around in the seat and looked through the back window at the blue tarp protecting the items in the back from the rain.

"Thanks for letting me bring my bike."

The old man nodded once and, with a slight twist of his wrist, brought the engine to life. "You'll need it to get around this summer. I'm not a taxi driver."

"Well, I'm sure it'll just be a week or so."

Uncle John smirked. "Right."

Nick frowned. "You think it'll be longer?"

The old man raised his eyebrows and clarified, "Kid, if you think that house'll be livable before fall, you've got a couple screws loose."

Nick frowned and tried to hide his disappointment about the comment. He tried to convince himself there was nothing to worry about and opened the crinkly granola bar wrapper to take a bite. He usually loved the honey oat flavor, but suddenly his mouth felt very dry, and he wished he had brought a water bottle.

He sincerely hoped he would be back—in his room with a fresh coat of paint on the new drywall—in a week, maybe two, max. Shifting on the uncomfortable bench seat, he tried to stretch his legs out straight, but his feet were jammed against the bag and the cramped area below the glove compartment. His calf muscles ached. He fidgeted, feeling grouchy and thirsty.

Nick stared at the plain-looking dashboard. The truck looked ancient. There was no digital display; just a few silver knobs next to a rectangular **analog** clock. The minute and hour hands hadn't moved since the trip started.

"It'll only be another half-hour 'til we get to Mapleton." Uncle John stared at the road ahead and periodically twitched his lower lip.

Nick tipped his head against the window and watched the trees as they flashed past. Tiny specks of rain spattered across the windshield. His thoughts drifted back home and landed on the **smoldering** resentment he felt about being shipped off for the summer to live with this stranger.

"So," Uncle John looked over and cleared his throat, "what grade are you in now?"

"Eighth—next fall."

Uncle John flipped on the windshield wipers. Minutes ticked by, and he spoke again. "I guess you all are gettin' the same rain as up north. Over two inches in Mapleton last night."

Nick wasn't sure how to respond. *Why do adults always talk about the weather?*

There was a long pause.

Uncle John cleared his throat again. "How're you liking Pinehurst so far? Your mom said something about a new school?"

Nick looked down at his tennis shoes and mumbled, "It's OK, I guess." If his new school was going to be the topic of conversation, he preferred the silence. To avoid further questions about the move, he asked, "Why are you wearing a winter hat in the summer?"

"Change is hard." The old man's throat sounded **phlegmy**. He cleared it again.

Nick wasn't sure if that response was about the hat or the new school. Or perhaps, he realized, it applied to both. They sat in silence. The rain picked up, and Nick listened to the rhythmic beating of the raindrops on the roof of the truck. He watched the droplets navigate jagged paths down the glass—sometimes racing a neighboring drop, sometimes combining efforts with others as their paths converged.

The old man cleared his throat again. "The bass up here only have a taste for leeches, but we'll have to get along with nightcrawlers."

Nick nodded. He'd never been fishing and wasn't sure why they were even talking about it.

Uncle John nodded toward the tacklebox setting on the seat between them.

"Oh," Nick explained, "this isn't a tacklebox. I mean, it is—but—I'm not really into fishing. I use this to organize souvenirs and things I find when I'm—"

He was going to say, "on vacation," but since this summer wasn't going to resemble anything like a fun road trip with fast food and a series of hotel rooms and indoor swimming pools, he chose a different word.

"—traveling."

"It's a treasure box, then." Uncle John gave a nod of approval, giving Nick the impression he thought it was perfectly acceptable to use a tacklebox to organize keep-sakes.

After a pause, Nick asked, "What's all that other stuff in the back of the truck?"

The old man didn't answer immediately. He seemed to be thinking while chewing the inside of his lip. Then, he thumped his heavy palm on the tacklebox, letting it rest on the lid.

"You're not the only one who's a treasure hunter."

Nick's curiosity was piqued.

Uncle John glanced at him with a thoughtful expression in his eyes. After a pause, he said, "Antique furniture, mostly. If it's old enough, or rare enough, it can be pretty valuable. A couple of times a week, I drive over to the big antique mall in Walton—see if they have anything interesting." He made a left-hand turn onto a narrow, paved road.

Nick had been to an antique store once, with his mom. He thought it was strange that people would spend money buying old things when they could buy something brand new for much less. Plus, new things didn't have that weird "old" smell. He wondered if collecting antiques was Uncle John's job, or maybe it was just a hobby. His parents had mentioned Uncle John had lots of interests, but Nick assumed these were things like whittling or working on jigsaw puzzles.

Nick poked at the soft fibers peeking through a rip in the blue, vinyl bench seat. The truck hit a small pothole, and the two passengers bobbed in unison. As they drove, the trees on either side of the road became thicker and thicker until they formed almost a tunnel. The truck flew past a painted, wooden sign. It read: *Welcome to Mapleton.*

A few minutes later, the truck slowed as they approached a red stoplight. It was the first sign of civilization Nick had seen since the gas station. The road here was lined with two strings of small buildings and shops.

As they waited for the light to change, John gave Nick a pensive stare, as if he were calculating something. "Can you swim?"

Before Nick could answer, the door to one of the shops opened and a tall, thin man wearing a wide-brimmed hat and glasses with thick, brown rims walked out. He waved, then headed toward the passenger side of the truck.

Nick cranked the window down all the way and scooted his leg away from the raindrops splattering across the seat.

The man peered over his glasses. The lenses were blurry with water. "Hey there John." He pulled his collar up to barricade the rain. "Big limb down on Harvey Street last night."

"That old aspen?" John asked.

The man nodded. "Couldn't handle the wind. Landed straight right across the road."

"It was only a matter of time." Uncle John glanced up through the windshield. "I'll help you boys clear it once this front moves through."

"Appreciate it. 'Far as I know the back road is clear. You'll have to take the long way around the lake."

"Got it," John replied, then added, "Stan, this here's Nick. He's James's boy."

The man pulled off his glasses and held out a hand.

Nick returned the firm handshake and nodded hello.

"Nick'll be staying with me for a bit, while James and Rachel get the house in Pinehurst fixed up."

"Alice's old place?" Stan tipped his head, letting a small puddle pour off the brim and onto the ground.

Uncle John raised an eyebrow. "They're hoping to be done by the end of summer."

"**Ambitious**." Stan chuckled and shook his head. "The optimism of youth."

John nodded.

"Well, I'll let you two be on your way." Stan thumped the side of the truck. He looked at Nick. "Don't let John force you to do all his chores all summer." He winked.

Nick hoped Stan was joking and rolled up the window. He was curious about who Alice was but was extremely distracted by the comments implying the renovation project might last "all summer."

The truck lurched forward.

Uncle John repeated, "So, can you swim?"

Nick nodded.

John smoothed his beard and added in a satisfied tone, "You're welcome to my canoe then. I'll show it to you when we get to the lake."

Fishing? Canoeing? Lake? Nick was curious. "I thought you lived in the woods."

Uncle John let out a wheezy laugh and rested his elbow on the edge of the window. He adjusted his hat and asked, "Your parents didn't tell you much, did they?"

"They told me a little." Nick didn't include the fact that his parents had simply described Mapleton as frozen in time; a small island surrounded by an ocean of trees. Nick looked down and poked his duffle bag with his foot. "We've had a lot of changes lately, with the move and renovation and everything."

"I've lived in Mapleton most of my life. Got a little place in the woods at the edge of Cranberry Lake. Not far from town." The old man glanced over and added, "I told your parents I'd keep an eye on you, but from the looks of you, I figure you're pretty near old enough to manage yourself. I'm usually out early and back late toting my treasures around. I keep most of 'em in a warehouse outside of town, and I spend a fair amount of time on the road."

The freedom sounded appealing, and Nick felt himself relax a little. The light changed, and they continued along the road. Through the blurry window, Nick saw a large, faded billboard. On it, a man and woman stood back-to-back, arms folded across their chests. Underneath were the words *Cooper Realty.* A shop in a small strip mall caught his eye. It had a green awning with white letters. *Charlie's Comics.* He would definitely be checking out the comic store. Nick had hoped to buy the latest issue of his favorite graphic novel about a pirate, *Captain Kidd*, but there hadn't been time before he left.

The truck lurched forward and a moment later, they were back in the woods. Nick looked into the shadowy trees flanking the road. The blue-gray of the water peeked out beyond a thick fence of evergreens.

That must be Cranberry Lake, he thought.

A gust of wind scattered soggy leaves across the road. The sky darkened, and the clouds began to relinquish heavy droplets onto the windshield. Moments later, rain poured down in diagonal sheets. The windshield wipers struggled to displace the torrents of water sloshing across the bleary glass.

Nick hoped it wouldn't be a rainy summer. Now that he knew a little more about where he was going to be staying, he was curious to explore the woods and the lake. He absentmindedly gripped the handle of the tacklebox setting next to him. If he couldn't go on a real vacation this summer, he hoped he could at least make his own adventure.

Through the trees, Nick watched the lake peek in and out of view between the drooping leaves of the trees. Ahead, a patch of white caught his attention, and he noticed a long driveway leading to a large, old house with a huge porch and sharp peaks in the roofline. It was half-covered by vines and had the same forgotten, forlorn appearance of a **mausoleum** in an overgrown cemetery. Nick glanced at Uncle John and noted the distinct similarity between his disheveled, gray ponytail and the weed-covered yard at the overgrown house. He was struck by a jolt of fear. His parents had described the house as a rustic shack in the woods. Had they been wrong? Was this haunted-looking house where he would be living?

Uncle John explained, "Only three houses on the lake. Mine, the Millers, and a family by the name of

Perkins." He pointed toward the water beyond the house. "Perkins's place is across the lake. The house we just passed is the old Miller place. Gotten pretty run down over the years."

The truck turned onto the next driveway—if it could even be called a driveway. Two, narrow gravel strips sandwiched a mohawk of uncut grass and weeds, currently sagging from the weight of the rain.

In his gravelly voice, Uncle John murmured, "Home sweet home."

They approached a small, one-story log cabin. His parents' description had been accurate. It was literally a shack in the woods. The wood sides of the cabin were dark grayish-brown. A rickety, wooden boardwalk led to the front door. The roof appeared to be covered with green shingles coated with a thick layer of green moss. Nick felt a flutter of anxiety in his stomach, like the first big drop on a roller coaster. He wondered if the cabin even had electricity. If given the option between Uncle John's cabin and the haunted mansion next door, Nick would have been hard-pressed to decide which one seemed like a worse place to stay.

As the truck neared the cabin, a small lamp near the front door clicked on. Seconds later, a lamp on the side of the detached garage did the same.

Electricity. Thank goodness.

"Gets pretty dark out here in the woods. Those motion sensor lights can be real handy."

Uncle John eased the truck toward a small, barn-like building. Nick assumed this was the garage.

He continued. "Stepped into the path of a skunk a few months back and, well—" He shook his head and grimaced. "Took a week to get the smell off my skin. Had to burn my clothes. Haven't been able to find its den, so keep an eye out."

Nick pictured himself walking along the path to the house. In his imagination, he was whistling and carrying a couple of fish he had just caught. The next thing he knew, a blur of black and white was charging toward him and everything became engulfed in a green cloud. He blinked to dispel the vision and suddenly felt a twinge of homesickness.

Uncle John pulled the truck inside the garage. It reeked of damp wood, gasoline, and motor oil. A single, bare bulb hung from the rafters and cast a glowing, yellow perimeter around the truck. The corners were dark with shadows. Along one wall stretched an extensive workshop with various saws and stacks of scrap wood. The opposite wall was packed with shovels, rakes, and hand tools hanging from hooks.

Nick heard a crinkling sound coming from the truck bed. Uncle John was untying a corner of the tarp. "Bone dry." He nodded in satisfaction. "Let's get inside for dinner. Stew's simmering in the crockpot." Without waiting for Nick to reply, he turned and swung a side door open and with long strides, headed toward the cabin. "Keep an eye out for that skunk," he hollered over his shoulder.

As Nick darted across the driveway after the old man, he felt the strange sensation he was being watched. He glanced over his shoulder into the woods. Through a break in the trees, some distance away, he saw the shadowy silhouette of the old house next-door—the Miller place. A light and a movement in one of the second-floor windows caught Nick's eye, but the rain kept him from lingering. When he reached the cabin and looked back, he saw nothing but a soft, yellow glow cascading into the night from the curtainless window. Nick felt a chill creep up his spine.

EXPLORING

Nick stood on the dock. Holding a fishing pole, he watched a red and white bobber float in the water. Suddenly, it disappeared under the surface. His line pulled taut, and the pole doubled over. Nick lifted an enormous small-mouth bass from the water. It glistened in the sunlight, and a round of applause erupted from several nearby fishing boats. Someone handed him a gold trophy and…

NICK WOKE UP WITH A START. THE HOUR CHIME from a clock clanged loudly. During the night, **reverberating** cracks of thunder had awakened him several times, but all was quiet now. The only sound came from the hallway where the pendulum of the grandfather clock tick-tocked a soft, steady cadence. He snuggled into the warm quilt and inhaled the scent; a mixture of an old cedar chest, woodsmoke, and something else…mothballs, maybe. The events from the day before swirled in his head. The drive in the truck. The cabin. And of course, the light in the window next door.

Nick stretched and yawned, then pulled back a corner of the curtain. The gray haze of pre-dawn sunlight filtered in. The storm had passed, and the clear sky promised good weather. Nick threw back the covers, and his bare feet landed on the cool, wood floor. A flash of silvery orange from the fishbowl on the dresser caught his eye.

"Mornin', Judy," Nick said to his silent, aquatic roommate.

Judy stared back.

Nick dressed quickly in the cool morning air and grabbed his brown, canvas backpack. A delicious aroma drew him to the small, tidy kitchen. Uncle John was nowhere in sight. A note was tucked under an old-looking blue, metal lunchbox on the kitchen table.

Apparently, the old man hadn't been exaggerating when he'd told Nick he was usually out before dawn and back after sunset.

Nick lifted the lid of the metal pot on the stove. A billow of steam and the smell of coffee escaped into the room. Scrunching his nose at the scent, he pressed the lid back into place. Nick wasn't usually allowed to drink coffee. However, he was feeling independent since arriving at the cabin yesterday, and this seemed like an appropriate time to try something new.

Nick grabbed a white ceramic mug with a chip on the handle and poured a serving. He took a sip, but after struggling to swallow, he dumped the remaining coffee into the sink and tried to scrape the taste off his tongue with his teeth.

Inside the lunchbox, he found a small bag of trail mix, four slices of bacon wrapped in foil, two buttermilk biscuits with raspberry jam spread on them, and a small thermos of water. The biscuits were wrapped in a thin, red handkerchief and were still warm. He could easily picture Uncle John eating directly out of a can of cold beans with a spoon and had a hard time envisioning the man cooking anything delicious in this cramped kitchen. Nick gobbled the bacon and decided to save the biscuits for later.

He tucked the lunchbox into his backpack next to his notebook, pocketknife, and a plastic bag filled with Band-Aids he'd included at his mom's insistence. All the essentials were there including a sleeve of his favorite chocolate chip cookies and a small minnow net with an extra-long handle. He'd found the cookies and net hidden in his duffle bag. His mom must have snuck them in.

The net would be perfect for shell hunting in the lake, and Nick was excited to try it out. However, he hadn't spent a lot of time in a canoe and was slightly worried about tipping over and losing his tacklebox collection, so he'd left Judy in charge of it. Any treasures found today would be temporarily stashed in one of the pockets in his army green cargo shorts. Nick slung the backpack over his shoulder, pulled on his Pinehurst ball cap, and walked outside. The screen door clapped shut behind him.

Nick glanced toward the neighboring property. The peak of the roof and one narrow window were the only parts of the Miller house he could see from his **vantage point**. Most of it was obscured by trees. Paint was peeling from the siding and the roof sagged, but this morning it didn't look as creepy as it had last night. Actually, the house reminded him of the old Victorian his parents were working on, probably at this very moment. The only difference was no one seemed to be fixing up the Miller house.

The sun was just peeking over the horizon as Nick walked down the grassy path to the shore. Small droplets of dew clung to the toes of his shoes. By the time he reached the water, the dew had soaked through his socks, and his toes now felt chilly and clammy. He kicked off his shoes and peeled off his socks.

The aluminum canoe was stored upside down on the bank. Nick stood awkwardly at one end and rolled it over, immediately checking it for spiders. He didn't mind bees and wasps, but for some reason, spiders made Nick's knees feel weak. He was thorough in his inspection and found only one. Using his shoe, he flicked it onto the sandy beach, and it scurried away. Nick clicked the buckles of the life vest around his chest, then stepped into the beige, sandy mud, pushing the vessel into the chilly water. Nick had never launched a canoe before and was suddenly aware of his lack of knowledge on the subject. He was glad he hadn't brought the tacklebox along. The chances of his day of exploring ending with a **capsized** or sunken boat were fairly high.

Nick took a deep breath to steady his nerves, then held each side of the canoe with his hands. In a swift motion—that was much more graceful in his head—he hopped in with both feet simultaneously. He landed face first in the bottom of the canoe. With a tremendous clatter, his cheek smashed against the cold, metal bottom, and his limbs flailed wildly. The aluminum vessel rocked **precariously**.

Somehow, in a move he couldn't duplicate if he tried, Nick regained his balance. He steadied the vessel then adjusted his ball cap. He hadn't capsized, so overall, he felt things were going pretty well. However, he immediately discovered that the weight of his body caused the canoe to sink slightly, and he was now temporarily beached—stuck in the shallow water next to shore. Using his paddle, Nick pushed against the lake bottom. After a few attempts and some shifting of his weight, he inched away from shore, then finally glided out onto the water.

Let the adventure begin.

For a moment, Nick cruised silently without paddling. The surface of the water had been agitated from his attempts to launch, but the ripples were quickly **dissipating**. A thin mist swirled over the placid surface of the lake. Along the shore, two small, brown birds were flitting in and out of the thicket near the water's edge. Nick didn't realize how quiet it was until a small splash broke the silence. It startled him. Nearby, he saw ripples of water, rolling out in fading, **concentric** circles—evidence of a fish that had jumped the moment before he looked.

It had been only fifteen days since his family moved to the old house in Pinehurst. The move had been abrupt, and since the new house was in a different town, this meant leaving his friends behind. In Pinehurst, Nick had already felt the cold sting of being an outsider. Lonely. It was an unfamiliar state of solitude—one he feared might take a long time to **subside**. But here on the lake, he was content to let those feelings of uncertainty fade from his thoughts.

There was no sign of anyone on the lake this morning. Nick was completely alone, yet he felt comforted by the fact that he was surrounded by so many living things. He realized, for the first time, there was a difference between being alone and being lonely.

With this satisfying insight, Nick inhaled deeply. He looked at the murky water along the shore and observed the evidence of last evening's thunderstorm. Hours earlier, carried by wind gusts and churning waves, shredded leaves now lined the muddy bank and were scattered across the lake. During dinner, Uncle John had described Cranberry Lake as crystal clear, offering visibility of around five feet, but today the lake was **opaque**, dark, and **ominous**.

Bits of dirt and **debris** slowly swirling just beneath the surface of the water obscured the lake bottom. Nick was a good swimmer, and he was wearing a life vest, but not being able to see how deep the water was made him feel uneasy. He hoped it water would clear soon, so he could look for shells. In the meantime, he decided to continue exploring the shoreline. The lake was long and narrow and was completely surrounded by dense woods.

The leaves in the aspen trees over Nick's head rustled, and he looked up to see two squirrels chasing each other around narrow tree trunks. Nick's stomach gurgled again. He was glad Uncle John had packed breakfast for him. For the next few minutes, Nick cruised next to shore looking for a place to eat. He headed for a small inlet just ahead.

As he approached, Nick could see a tree had recently blown into the water, nearly blocking the entrance to the bay. The branches, still full of green leaves, stretched out across the water and into the murky depths. Near the shore, the tangled mass of the tree's roots had broken away from the sandy soil and now reached toward the sky like a fan. Beyond the branches was a secluded bay. It looked like the perfect spot for breakfast.

Nick paddled through a small opening between the limbs of the fallen tree. As the canoe squeezed by, the metal sides let out a low screech. The branches clawed at the sides, and he could feel the **vessel** lift slightly as he barely floated over limbs submerged just below the surface. After he maneuvered past the tree and into the bay, Nick looked around. The high banks were lined with lush, green plants covered with orange flowers. The air was warming in the sun, and several fat bumble bees hummed among the nectar-filled blossoms, packing their hind legs with tangerine-colored pollen. Nick's paddle clunked against the side of the canoe and echoed off the steep shoreline. The racket startled a great blue heron who had been silently fishing in the shallow water. The bird watched Nick with his golden eye as he glided away, inches above the surface of the water.

At the back of the bay, a small rock ledge **cantilevered** over the water. After deciding the rock would make a great spot to eat breakfast, Nick hopped up onto it and used the anchor rope to tie the canoe to a nearby tree trunk. Nick sat down and lifted the metal lid of the lunchbox, releasing a scrumptious aroma. After quickly unwrapping the soft, buttery biscuits, he gobbled them in two bites each, and licked his fingertips.

Nick stood up to explore his new ledge hangout. Behind him, a narrow path meandered up the steep bank into the woods. Using exposed tree roots as hand and foot holds, he scrambled up the **precipitous** trail. After about ten feet, the ground leveled off and Nick found himself in a small, peaceful clearing lined with pine trees. His bare feet padded softly on the carpet of pine needles. Along one side, a huge rock formation towered majestically, like a castle, above his head.

He turned around and admired the scenic view of the bay and the lake beyond. The sunlight glinted off the inside of the silver canoe below. The echo of a woodpecker's beak pounding against a hollow tree ricocheted up through the forest canopy.

A twig snapped behind him. Startled, Nick whirled around. His eyes darted along the edge of the clearing.

I should've asked Uncle John if there are bears around here. He lamented the oversight.

Nick's senses were on high alert. He scanned the thick brushy undergrowth in the woods beyond. Backing up to the edge of the clearing, he looked down at the canoe below. The trail to the rocky ledge was steep, and he wouldn't be able to get there quickly without sliding. He certainly wasn't confident he could launch a canoe quickly.

The odds of me outrunning whatever's out there aren't good, he thought.

He eyed the canoe again, then decided to turn around and face his foe.

"Hey!" a voice shouted from the woods. "What are you doing here?"

Trespasser

SOMEONE WAS SHOUTING AT NICK, BUT THE SOUND echoed off the rock and bounced around the clearing. He couldn't tell which direction it was coming from.

Nick held up his hands. "I—I'm sorry—I didn't—" He stumbled over his words, unsure of what to say, but relieved to be interacting with a human—and not a **ravenous** carnivore. "I was just exploring."

He heard a scrambling sound overhead. Nick looked up just in time to see a girl jump down from the branches of a towering pine tree. She landed as though jumping from trees was an Olympic sport for which she had won several gold medals. She wore cut-off jeans and a lime green T-shirt. A scuffed, black walkie talkie hung from her belt. The girl must have been hiding the whole time, watching him. She was a little taller than Nick and had long, blonde hair hanging over her shoulders in two messy braids.

She walked up to Nick and put her hands on her hips. Her green eyes and freckled nose wrinkled into a scowl. "I asked what you are doing *here*," she motioned to the clearing around them, "in our hideout. This is private property, you know."

A crackle of static hissed from the walkie talkie.

The **tinny** sound of a voice projected from her belt. *"Technically, it's not private prop—"*

The girl clicked a button on her walkie talkie, silencing the other voice, then folded her arms across her chest. She fired off several questions, without pausing to hear the answers. "Why are you here? How did you even get here? Did Billy send you? Or was it Jack?"

Nick stood at the edge of the clearing and tried to make sense of what was happening. The girl squared off her stance and rested both hands, now balled into fists, on her hips. She had a wild look in her green eyes that made Nick think she might take a swing at him.

"I don't know Billy or Jack. I—I'm sorry. I didn't realize I was trespassing."

The boy stifled a laugh and Nick knew he'd said the wrong thing.

The girl scoffed and pointed to a sign hanging from a nail on a nearby tree.

A small rectangle of cardboard hung from a grubby piece of yarn. A confusing message was scrawled in capital letters.

"Spring as notes?" Nick asked.

"That's right," she answered.

Nick squinted at the sign and frowned. "What does that even mean?"

Before she could reply, the leaves in a nearby shrub rustled and someone said, "Ha! I told you no one would understand it!" This was followed by more rustling, then, "Ouch!"

A boy with brown eyes and dark, shaggy hair plucked his way out of the prickly thorns. He appeared slightly younger than Nick and the girl. He wore a faded brown T-shirt and an oversized, camo fishing vest with at least a dozen pockets. His jeans had a gaping hole in one knee, and the frayed threads across the other looked like they might disintegrate in a gentle breeze. A pair of headphones hung around his neck and he, too, had a black walkie talkie hanging from his belt.

He explained, "As I was saying—before I was rudely cut off—" He glanced at the girl. "Technically, this isn't private property. We're on the edge of the forest preserve."

Brushing the comment aside, the girl carefully lifted one of the prickly, purple stalks on the shrub and said, "This was your *best* hiding place?"

The boy sighed as he pulled leaves out of his hair and dusted a few more off his shoulders. "I was looking for raspberries. I was hungry. Then, when you said to hide…well, I assumed Billy and Jack were coming, so I panicked." He gingerly inspected the road map of thin, red scratches on his arms and legs. "It's too early for raspberries anyways. Their thorns are brutal."

Nick—who was feeling like an intruder—said, "Well, I should get going."

"Oh, and report back to Billy and Jack?" the girl accused.

"I really don't know who those people are," Nick replied.

"Oh, I get it," the girl said. "You think if you claim ignorance, we won't suspect they sent you." She poked her index finger twice into Nick's chest. "Well, you can tell Billy and Jack we're fed up with this, and we consider sending in a spy an act of war."

Nick guessed denying his association with these Billy and Jack characters would get him nowhere. Instead, he used a trick he'd learned while dealing with a bully at his old school.

He stared at her with a blank expression and said, "Wanna hear a joke?"

The girl narrowed her eyes at him.

"I wanna hear a joke," the younger boy chimed.

The girl gave the boy a look that clearly meant he should stop talking. Then she looked back at Nick. She scanned him from toe to head, apparently sizing him up. "You really don't know Billy?"

Nick shook his head.

"Or Jack?"

He raised his eyebrows and shrugged. "Nope."

"OK," she said with a sigh. "For some reason, I believe you." She stepped toward him. "I've never seen you around, which obviously means you're new here."

Nick explained, "I'm staying with my uncle for a week or so."

She looked at the boy, who nodded in approval.

"So, you weren't sent here to spy on us?" The accusatory edge was fading from her voice.

Nick shook his head. "I honestly don't know Billy or Jack."

"More like Bully and Jerk," the boy muttered.

The girl explained, "They're two kids from our school."

"Hey." the boy walked across the clearing, "Wanna see something cool?"

"Don't." The girl's tone was one of warning.

With a wave, the boy dismissed her command. Stooping down, he dug his hand into a pile of pine needles. He groped around until he found a short length of rope, which he pulled up. The rope was attached to a square piece of plywood. Concealed by pine needles, Nick would never have guessed it was even there. When the boy moved the plywood to the side, he revealed a hole dug into the dirt. It was a little more than a foot deep and wide enough for the small, red plastic cooler stowed inside. He lifted the lid to reveal the cooler was empty.

"Usually, we have granola bars and some candy in here, but they keep disappearing, and we haven't had a chance to refill it."

The girl gave the boy a scowl. "So much for keeping a secret."

"What?" the boy asked defensively, then looked at Nick. "He seems trustworthy." With a shrug he added, "I'm an excellent judge of character."

Nick wasn't sure what to say, so he just nodded. The boy replaced the plywood, and the girl helped him scoop handfuls of pine needles over the top.

"Nice camouflage," Nick complimented before asking, "Do you ever forget where it's buried?"

The boy piped up, "It's half-way between that tree with the weird branch and our sign."

"Oh. My. Gosh." The girl threw her hands in the air. "You are *terrible* at keeping secrets!"

The boy cringed sheepishly. "Sorry."

"So, what does your sign mean, anyways?" Nick looked again at the wrinkled cardboard. "Spring as notes?"

The boy laced his hands behind his head and looked at the girl. "I'll let you handle this one. You're the one who insisted on a sign that I told you no one would understand."

She scoffed and replied, "Well, *I* think it's pretty obvious." Looking at Nick, she explained, "It means no trespassing."

Nick squinted at the sign, trying to make sense of the translation. "Is it a code?"

The boy groaned and said, "Ever since she came back from summer schoo—"

"It wasn't summer school," the girl interrupted. "It was a regular summer camp—with a focus on English and grammar." She pulled her lime green shirt flat so they could read it.

The shirt read *Camp Mangara.* Under the writing, the letters of the alphabet floated around a campfire and tent.

She asked, "Do you get it?" Without waiting for an answer, she explained, "Mangara is actually an anagram for anagram. An anagram is when you jumble up the letters to make a new word."

"We know what an anagram is," the boy replied, with a slight edge in his voice. He looked at Nick, "Right?"

Nick nodded.

The girl looked at the younger boy, eyes shining. "Hey, you should come with me next year!"

"To Camp Anagram?" the boy replied. "Uh, no offense, but that sounds like school to me."

"Suit yourself. You have to have a certain Lexile score to even be considered for Camp Mangara, so you're probably not even eligible."

"Hey!" The boy frowned.

Looking at Nick, she raised an eyebrow. "What's *your* Lexile score? You know, your reading level?"

Nick shrugged.

"You don't know?"

Nick shook his head. He'd always been a good student but had never heard the term *Lexile score.*

The boy turned to Nick. "Ever since she got back from nerd camp, she's been crazy about making codes."

"An anagram isn't a code," she corrected. "A code involves substituting letters for a letter, or a number, or even a symbol. Our sign is an anagram. It doesn't need a codebreaker to solve it—just pure intellect—common sense, even. I really wouldn't expect you to understand."

The boy looked at Nick. "See what I mean? No one with a normal IQ gets these things."

With a sigh, the girl flipped a braid over her shoulder. "I think it's clever."

"It's confusing, is what it is." The boy stuffed his hands into the side pockets of his vest.

"Please," she scoffed, then flipped the second braid to her back. "Anagrams are easy once you get the hang of 'em."

Nick tipped his head to the side and looked again at the sign. "So, *spring as notes* is a jumbled message?"

"Anagram," the girl corrected. She looked at Nick, clearly disappointed. "If you simply rearrange the letters, you get *no trespassing.*"

While Nick worked on mentally unscrambling the letters, the girl looked over at the boy and said with a sigh, "Your leg is bleeding."

A trail of blood inched down the boy's shin. He unbuttoned one of the pockets in his vest and peeked inside. "Great. I'm out of Band-Aids."

Nick gestured toward the lake. "I have some Band-Aids in my backpack, down in my uncle's canoe." He added, looking at the girl, "Or, as you might call it, my 'no ace,' which, to answer your question from earlier, is how I got here."

The girl arched an eyebrow and replied, "No ace? That's 'canoe' jumbled up, isn't it?"

"Wow!" the boy laughed. "Did you just come up with that?

Nick nodded.

The girl hesitated as she eyed Nick suspiciously. She seemed to be trying to figure out if he was mocking her.

Sensing the hesitation, Nick introduced himself, "I'm Nick, by the way." He looked at the boy. "And I've got trail mix, if you're still hungry."

The girl exchanged a quick look with the boy. Then, for the first time, her scowl melted into a broad smile. She held out her hand and said "I'm Jo. This is Eddie."

Escape

THE SUN WAS WARM, and a gentle breeze swirled along the surface of the glassy water in the bay. Nick and his new friends, Jo and Eddie, sat on the edge of the rock ledge, bare feet dangling. Jo's legs were the longest, and her toes skimmed the surface as she swung them back and forth. The water had begun to clear. Eddie found a long, straight stick and poked it into the clear shallows, trying to pry up a large stone. Nick watched as an orangey-brown crayfish scurried away and scooted under a different rock, leaving a small cloud of disturbed mud in its wake.

Eddie tossed the stick into the water and turned to Nick. "So, what was the joke you were going to tell us?"

"Oh," Nick said. "Why does it take pirates so long to learn the alphabet?"

Jo and Eddie thought silently for a minute before Eddie shook his head. "I don't know."

"Because they always get lost at C."

"Corny," Jo said.

Eddie nodded. "Nice."

"Well, hello there, little guy." Jo held her palm flat against the rock and let a daddy long legs crawl onto the back of her hand.

"Agh!" Nick scooted away from her.

Jo lifted her hand and rotated her wrist as the daddy long legs crawled around.

Nick jumped up. "Are you crazy?"

"What?" she asked, with an amused smirk.

"Wait." Eddie narrowed his eyes into slits. "Are you a *city* kid?"

"What? No."

Jo moved her hand toward Nick.

"Get that thing away from me!" Nick scrambled to his feet and took several steps backwards.

"He's a city kid alright." Jo let the spider climb down onto the rock.

With a look of pity, Eddie nodded.

Nick took a deep breath and tried to relax but didn't take his eye off the unwanted **arachnid**. He wasn't sure if the *city kid* comment was an intended insult.

"I'm from the suburbs, not the city—and I just don't like spiders."

"Well," Jo said, "daddy long legs aren't technically spiders. I actually used to be really afraid of them, too." She pressed her hand down in front of the insect's path, and Nick watched as the leggy creature poked at her skin before deciding to walk across the back of her hand. She continued. "I decided to learn more about spiders, and except for a couple of really dangerous kinds, most are harmless."

"Yeah, but they still bite." Nick shuddered at the thought.

"Not this kind," she justified. "Their mouths are literally too small to puncture our skin." Looking at Nick, she added, "And just because something *can* bite, doesn't mean it will. Daddy longs legs are just looking for food and trying to survive. They're very peaceful creatures."

Nick looked at her skeptically and watched the insect tiptoe away.

Eddie stood up and dramatically recited a poem:

Once Mr. Daddy Long-legs,
Dressed in brown and gray,
Walked about upon the sands
Upon a summer's day…

A smile spread across Jo's face. "What was that?"

"What?" Eddie stood triumphantly, with his hands on his hips. "You haven't heard that before?"

Jo shook her head.

Eddie looked at Nick and explained, "This is a momentous day. This is the day that Eduardo Bernadelli knew something Josephine Perkins didn't." He put his hand over his heart. "I'd like to thank all of the people who have brought me to this moment."

Jo rolled her eyes. "Oh, please."

Eddie continued. "First of all, I'd like to thank Edward Lear for writing that poem. Second, Mrs. Peters, the best sixth-grade teacher—for making me memorize it." With a twinkle in his eye and a poorly suppressed smile, he added, "Third, Jo Perkins, who constantly reminded me how much better she was than me. She motivated me to—"

Jo jumped up and ran towards Eddie, who laughed and darted out of the way. She ran at him a few more times until Eddie almost lost his balance next to the edge of the rock.

"OK, OK." Eddie put up his hands.

"Truce." Jo plopped back down and dug her hand into the bag of trail mix. Eddie sat down next to her and did the same.

"Your last name is Perkins?" Nick asked. Nick remembered Uncle John mentioning a family with the last name of Perkins lived across the lake.

"Josephine Margaret Perkins. Third and youngest child of Gwendolyn and Floyd."

"I think I can see your house from my Uncle John's cabin." Nick said as he sat up and scooped a handful out of the bag.

"Wait." She finished chewing. "Your uncle is John Shaydel?"

Nick nodded. "Great Uncle, technically."

Eddie grinned and said, "I had no idea Big J made such tasty trail mix. I've never had trail mix with pretzels in it before." He dug around in the bag for a pretzel, then popped it into his mouth.

Jo said, "We're neighbors, then."

"I live in town," Eddie said through a full mouth. A projectile piece of food shot out from his mouth, but he either didn't notice or didn't care. He tipped his head back and funneled another handful into his mouth.

"What a **Neanderthal**." Jo rolled her eyes.

Nick asked, "Do you know who lives in the big house next door to Uncle John?"

Jo looked confused, then curious. "Are you talking about the old Miller place?"

"Of course, he is." Eddie scoffed. "Big J's only got one neighbor—sort of."

Jo explained, "The house next to your uncle's cabin is abandoned. No one lives there."

Nick furrowed his brow. "But I saw a light on in one of the windows last night."

"Yeah, right." Eddie poked through the trail mix and picked out a piece of chocolate candy.

Nick felt confused. "I'm sure I saw a light on."

Jo and Eddie exchanged glances.

Eddie snickered. "Must have been Mr. Miller's ghost, because no one's lived there in a long time."

Jo reassured, "Maybe it was the sunset reflecting off the window."

Eddie tossed a pebble into the water. "My grandpa said the Millers used to be the richest people in town. I think Big J's cabin used to be where the servants lived. Maybe one of their ghosts is haunting the place."

"Ghosts aren't real, Eddie." Jo crossed her arms. "There's always an explanation."

"I dunno." Eddie turned to Nick and said, "Our town's had a bunch of weird stuff happen. We had a mine collapse. That was pretty big. A bunch of people died. We also had an invisible bank robber." He shrugged. "Sounds like a ghost to me."

Nick felt a chill creep up his neck. "So, you think a ghost robbed a bank?"

"Just sayin'," Eddie shrugged again.

Jo grinned. "Well, people say it was a ghost because the bank was cleaned out, but the lock wasn't broken, and the banker was out of town with the only key."

"Eddie added, "It's kind of a local mystery. And then the mine collapsed like a week later."

"No, it was like the next day, I think." Jo sighed as she scraped a stick along the rock ledge. "But that was a hundred years ago. They sealed the mine entrance. Mapleton's super boring now."

Nick tossed a pebble into the lake and watched the ripples fade.

"Did you know," Jo laughed, "the guy who used to live next to Big J—his first name was *Archibald*."

"Whoa." Nick grinned. "That's a doozy."

Eddie smirked. "Can you imagine him as a little kid?" He switched to a British accent. "Oh dear, little Archibald. You spilled your porridge all over your britches."

Jo laughed. "He was from the eighteen hundreds, Eddie—not England."

Eddie shrugged.

Jo laughed again. "You'll never guess what good ol' Archibald Miller's business partner's name was."

Nick asked, "What was it?"

Jo giggled. "Cornelius Bennett."

"That's amazing." Eddie chuckled. "Their names were Cornelius Bennett and Archibald Miller?"

"I know." Jo shook her head. "The early settlers of Mapleton had weirdly strange names." Mimicking Eddie's British accent, she mocked, "Hello. I'm Cornelius Bennett. Pardon me, Archibald Miller, could

I trouble you for a spot of tea? We can discuss our evil parents and why they gave us such terrible names."

Nick laughed. Eddie, giggling, gave Jo's shoulder a playful punch, then clutched his sides and tipped over.

Nick squinted as he looked at the water and watched the sunlight shimmering. It felt good to laugh. He hadn't laughed like that in weeks, not since the move—but his smile faded when he thought of the house next door in the woods—the Miller house. He was certain he'd seen a light on.

Could it have been a ghost?

His stomach clenched. The light he'd seen couldn't have been the sunset, because it'd been rainy and overcast. He tried to shake off the chill creeping up his spine.

"Agh." Eddie smoothed the edge of one of the Band-Aids Nick had given him. "Why can't I ever get these things to stick?"

"Because you're **perpetually** covered in a layer of dirt." Jo smirked, then used her fingernail to scratch away some dirt from her own knee. "I'm surprised though. I've literally never seen you run out of First Aid supplies before. You're usually so prepared with that millions-of-pockets-vest of yours."

"It's been a big Band-Aid week. Lucia's nails need to be trimmed."

"My parents won't let me get a pet," Nick lamented. "Is Lucia your cat?"

Eddie looked at Jo and both burst out laughing.

"No." Eddie wiped tears of laughter from a corner of his eye. "She's my sister."

Nick's eyebrows lifted.

"She can be..." Jo squinted, as if searching for the best description.

"Difficult. Manipulative. Evil. You get the picture," Eddie finished. "I'll have to restock when I get home." He patted the empty pocket. With an air of wisdom in his voice, he explained, "When you're the youngest with six older sisters, you *have got* to be prepared for any type of crisis. Zombie apocalypse? Nuclear fallout?" He looked up with a serious expression. "Those are child's play when you have six sisters and only two bathrooms on a Saturday night. My personal motto is: Hope for the best, but plan for a monumental meltdown." Eddie unclipped his water bottle from his belt loop, gulped a mouthful of water, and wiped his mouth with the back of his hand. "Speaking of meltdowns, everyone was walking on eggshells at my house this morning."

Jo crossed her arms. "What did you do?"

Eddie put his hands up and said, "It wasn't me this time. Last night, Angelina used all the hot water, and Isabella was waiting for her hair dye to set, but Lucia didn't unlock the bathroom door until Isabella's hair smelled like it was burning. Unfortunately, Grandpa was in the other bathroom but and was taking forever—as usual—so Isabella's hair was kind of frizzy and smelled like chemicals. Anyways, she was running late for her date with Bryan Henderson and was so upset, she forgot to wear deodorant and sweated through her shirt but didn't notice until he rang the bell.

This morning, everyone tried not to notice her frizzy hair." He drew in a calm breath. "But through it all, I was unscathed. All thanks to these." He un-Velcroed a pocket on his vest and proudly held up two AA batteries. "My survival training has taught me to *always* carry extra batteries." He emphasized "always" like it was a matter of life and death. "I spent the whole time protected by the safety of my headphones... and AC/DC." With that, Eddie played a short, silent air guitar solo.

Jo looked at Nick and asked, "Can you believe they survived a fifteen-hour road trip to Virginia last week?"

Eddie frowned playfully. "I'm glad my life is so amusing to you."

Suddenly, they heard voices in the clearing above.

Someone said, "I'm starving."

They heard a second voice. "Let's see what delicious snacks we can find us today."

Eddie jumped up and looked at Jo. He hissed, "It's them! Let's catch 'em in the act!"

Jo lunged after him and grabbed the back of his vest before he could climb up the trail. "No way, Eddie! They're way bigger than us. They're not just going to run away if we charge up there. Plus, there's nothing in the cooler. You *literally* have nothing to lose by staying down here."

"But if we don't fend them off, they'll just end up coming back, like they always do."

Nick pieced the situation together. "Billy and Jack?"

"Yes," Jo and Eddie whispered in unison.

"We *have* to take them down. C'mon," Eddie whispered, "for once, we've got 'em outnumbered." He nodded towards Nick.

Jo shook her head and said, "We're not fighting anyone."

"Why not? They're trespassing!" Eddie was now standing. He spoke through a clenched jaw.

Jo put her hand up. "Because. First of all, as you said, it's *not* private property; it's a forest preserve. Second, we're better than that." She paused and added, "And third, Billy is on the wrestling team—and they're undefeated."

The first voice sounded angry. "You said there would be candy bars in here!"

The second voice replied, "I said, 'granola bars,' and I said, '*Maybe* there would be granola bars.'"

Eddie looked around and hissed, "So the only hope we have in this scenario is to wait for them to find us?"

Jo replied, "That's *not* going to happen."

Eddie hissed, "Well then, we're sitting ducks down here." He looked at Nick and then at the canoe. "Unless…"

Nick nodded. "Let's go."

They quietly stepped into the canoe and pushed away from the shore, but the paddle made a loud *CLANG* when Nick accidentally banged it against the side.

One of the boys appeared in the open spot between two large shrubs and shouted, "HEY!"

Eddie ordered, "Keep paddling!"

Nick turned around and saw a stocky boy with sandy brown hair and a sneer on his face scrambling down the steep trail. A second boy, scrawny with light blond hair, was already at the bottom and stood with arms crossed across his puffed-up chest. The canoe was moving slowly with triple the weight and only one paddle. Fortunately, they were nearly out of the bay. Nick steered them toward the opening under the fallen tree.

"You. Owe. Us!" the stocky boy bellowed. "Nobody doesn't not give us candy and gets away with it."

Jo rolled her eyes and muttered, "That boy is a grammatical nightmare!"

The canoe squeezed past the tree and into the open water of Cranberry Lake.

Once they were safely out of sight, Nick stopped paddling and looked along the shore. "Think they'll follow us?"

"Nah, knowing how lazy Billy and Jack are, I doubt they'd even try." Eddie eyed the boulders. "Good thing you had this canoe. Otherwise, we'd be swimming!"

"I'll head around the point over there."

Jo reminded Nick, "We can't go too far, because we have to go back and get our bikes."

Nick asked, "If these guys are stealing your snacks, what's stopping them from taking your bikes, too?"

"They won't find mine. I always hide it in the bushes," Jo said. "It's dark green and blends in. Plus, in order to take it, they'd have to leave their bikes behind, which they won't do."

"I'd love it if they'd steal mine," Eddie laughed. "It's a piece of junk."

Jo nodded in agreement, then sighed. "I can't believe those guys."

Shoulders slumped, Eddie complained, "I know. Now we have to move the cooler again. They keep finding it."

Nick thought for a moment. "You should set traps around the clearing."

"We've tried that," Jo sighed, "but they didn't really work."

Eddie snickered, "Remember when we put that garter snake in the cooler?"

Jo's eyes flickered, and she gave a half-smile.

Nick asked, "What happened?"

"Nothing." Eddie tipped his head toward Jo. "*Someone* was worried it would suffocate in there, so she let it go before it could be useful."

"It was going—to die!" Jo defended.

Eddie muttered, "Dead or alive, it would've solved our bully problem."

"It's never OK to be cruel, Eddie."

Nick suggested, "What about just finding a new hideout?"

"No way," Eddie shot back.

"Are you kidding?" Jo folded her arms with a *HUFF*, and Nick could tell this was a sensitive subject.

Eddie added, "We've already done that. Twice. They just keep finding us and stealing our stuff."

"They're not getting this spot so easily." Jo angrily flicked her fingers at the water and watched the spray dimple the surface. "It's our best secret hideout yet."

Eddie's jaw clenched. "Not much of a secret though."

"It *is* pretty nice," Nick agreed. "That huge rock reminds me of a giant, rock castle."

Jo and Eddie looked over in surprise.

"What?" Nick asked, suddenly feeling self-conscious. He looked over his shoulder, expecting to see Billy and Jack paddling after them.

"That's exactly what *we* call it!" Eddie exclaimed. "Castle Rock!"

Jo's eyes glimmered as she added, "I wasn't sure about you at first, but you're alright."

Connecting

Jo lifted her wristwatch and pressed a button to silence an alarm. "I have to get home. Bassoon lesson."

"Me, too," Eddie said, "I told my dad I'd help him mow the lawn. Get this. He said if I mow once a week all summer, I can get a new bike."

Jo laughed and looked at Nick to translate. "When Eddie says 'new bike,' he really means another hand-me-down from one of his six sisters." She grabbed onto a nearby branch hanging out over the water and pulled the canoe towards a narrow animal trail leading up the bank. "Which color do you have to duct tape over this time? Pink or purple?"

Eddie hopped out of the canoe into ankle-deep water, then stepped onto a flat rock on the bank. "Not this time. It'll be a legit, new bike…from the store."

"You're gonna mow all summer?" Jo looked skeptical.

Eddie nodded. "Worth it to get rid of that old bucket of bolts I'm riding around now."

Jo giggled. "That bike has so much duct tape on it."

Eddie sighed, "Well, there were a lot of sparkly unicorns to cover up."

Hopping onto the rock, Jo looked back at Nick with a curious expression. "I don't suppose you have a bike."

He nodded. "Actually, I do."

She gave him a thumbs up. "Cool."

Eddie sloshed back toward the canoe and unclipped his walkie talkie from his belt. "Here," he said. "We're tuned to channel five."

"T-thanks," Nick stammered.

"I need it back eventually, but you can borrow it for a while." Eddie smiled. "This way, we can find each other. I have an extra one at home." Eddie kicked at the water with his big toe, sending a rooster tail of spray along the shore.

Jo explained, "They're long-range, and the signal reaches from my house to Eddie's. It should reach Big J's cabin."

"Maybe we can meet up for ice cream later," Jo suggested.

Nick nodded. "Sure."

Eddie said, "I wanna stop at the comic shop." Looking at Nick, he explained, "The new issue of *Captain Kidd* came out yesterday."

Nick's jaw dropped. He exclaimed, "*Captain Kidd* is my favorite! I'm in."

Eddie said, "I can't wait to see if the Jade Pirate finds out where Calico Jack hid the gold!"

"I know."

"Ugh, pass," Jo said, "I am *not* going to the comic book store."

"Fine," Eddie replied. "Nick'll go with me."

Nick asked, "You don't like graphic novels?"

With an air of superiority, Jo stated, "Some of us don't need pictures to tell the story. I have a **prodigious** vocabulary and an **extraordinarily vivid** imagination." She looked across the lake and held her head high. "I only need words."

Eddie feigned a concerned look. "Jo, I'm so glad you've overcome your **debilitating inferiority complex**." He flashed a smile at Nick.

Jo adjusted her camp T-shirt and ignored the sarcastic remark.

Eddie launched into a debate. "Graphic novels—"

"Comic books," Jo challenged.

Eddie continued. "Are pictures, which are worth a *thousand* words." He smiled triumphantly. "So who has the bigger vocabulary now?"

Jo gave Eddie a sweet smile as she said, "Fifth graders are so **credulous**. C'mon Eddie. Let's go find our bikes." She walked away.

Eddie blurted out, "Takes one to know one."

Jo waved and trotted up the matted trail.

Eddie called after her, "You may think you can trick me by smiling, but I can figure out what *crudge-a-mus* means!" He glanced at Nick with a hopeless expression.

Nick cringed and said, "*Credulous* means easy to fool.'"

Eddie gasped, offended.

"Don't worry, if she really thought you were credulous, I'm sure she wouldn't hang out with you. You must be like a little brother to her."

Eddie muttered, "Just what I need. Another older sister in my life." As he followed Jo up the bank, he called back to Nick, "Remember, channel five. Jo's handle is Anna Graham. Mine is Red Fox. Think about what we should call you, and we'll check in after lunch."

"OK." Nick replied.

He looked at the walkie talkie and turned the knob until it clicked. A hiss of static poured out. Not wanting to waste the batteries, he turned it off again.

Nick took a deep breath and realized he was glowing from the inside out. It felt good to be with friends, even if he had only known them for an hour. He smiled, recalling the graphic novel banter. He knew from experiencc, a true friend allows you to be yourself and respects your opinions, even if they're different from your own. This summer might actually end up being not so bad.

Treasure

As he headed back toward Uncle John's cabin, Nick cruised along shore, looking for shells and brainstorming a cool—yet catchy—walkie talkie name.

Maybe something about my new town, Pinehurst? Or something about being a treasure hunter—wait! Maybe I need a pirate name like Captain Nick? Captain Pinehurst? Nick didn't think any of those ideas seemed very cool or catchy.

He spotted several schools of minnows hovering in the warm water near shore. They were far too quick for the net and scattered the second they saw the shadow of the big canoe. Several clam shell fragments glinted in the sunlight in deep water, but when he tried to scoop them up, he found they were out of reach, even with the long-handled net.

Ahead, the thick trunk of a fallen tree protruded from shore into the water. Two dark domes, the size of dinner plates, glistened in the sunlight along the top of the log. As Nick approached, he realized they were turtles. They held perfectly still, sunning themselves.

As he drifted closer, their heads lifted slightly and revealed their matching green- and yellow-striped necks and the bright orangey-red of their lower shells. The canoe glided close to them. Inches away, Nick held his breath, trying not to move. He was almost close enough to reach out and touch them when he noticed a movement on the shore; a third turtle.

It was much larger and camouflaged among the boulders along the edge of the water. It was a sandy brown color, with black spots on its broad, flat shell. Unlike the blunt noses of the painted turtles, this turtle's nose was like a long snout and came almost to a point.

Suddenly, the painted turtles scuttled along the log and plopped into the water. The larger, flat turtle lingered a few seconds more, then scrambled to the safety of the water. Nick watched them glide under the canoe along the bottom of the lake until they were out of sight in the shadowy depths. He leaned over the edge, watching for movement. The turtles were probably watching from below, waiting for the canoe to float away. Nick wondered what the turtles must think of the giant silver log passing by.

While he waited to see if the turtles would grow tired of waiting and reappear, the gentle waves pushed the canoe onto a sandbar, and he found himself once again beached. Using his trick from earlier, Nick pushed the paddle into the lake bottom at an angle and tried to free the canoe. This time, he wasn't able to launch out into deeper water so easily. The shore here was muddy and sticky, not sandy like the lakebed near Uncle John's cabin. He tried again, this time using **leverage** from a slightly different angle. The paddle sank several inches into the mud until it pushed against something solid.

What do we have here? Nick wondered if the object he'd hit was a clam shell.

Using his new net, Nick dug into the mud until he felt the hidden treasure. He pulled up the mystery object caked with muck, dumped it into his hand, and set down the net. Carefully, he lowered his hand into the water and rinsed away the mud. It was indeed an empty, completely intact, half clam shell, and it was wider than his palm. The outside was a smooth, dark brown, and the inside was a swirl of purple and white, pearly iridescent. As he leaned in for a closer inspection, a large leech frantically wriggled out from underneath and tried to suck onto his finger.

"Aaagh!" Nick exclaimed with a start as he flicked the leech into the water—along with the prized shell. It landed with a splash and immediately sank again. "No!" Nick exclaimed. He watched it tip from side to side as it drifted downward and eventually disappeared in the grassy weeds. Nick wasn't usually squeamish about water creatures, and he was glad Jo and Eddie hadn't witnessed his freak-out.

Leaning carefully over the edge of the canoe, Nick peered into the shallow water. That clam shell would make an impressive addition to his collection.

There it is!

He spotted a glimmering object nestled next to the roots of a plant with striped, green and white leaves.

Nick dipped his arm into the water again, aiming for the shell. His net disturbed the lakebed, and the cloudy plume of mud and dead leaves obscured his view. He blindly probed the soft mud until he felt the net hit something. With anticipation, he scooped up the treasure, along with plenty of muck, and swished the net back and forth in the water to wash away the **loamy** soil. Nick's jaw dropped. Sitting in the net was a small, metal box.

The shell, now forgotten, was no comparison to Nick's new find. The box rested comfortably in his palm. It was silver-colored, and the lid was embossed with the **silhouette** of a bird.

Nick immediately envisioned the box prominently displayed in a compartment in his tacklebox. Only a day ago, he'd been dreading the summer, but now he felt slightly more optimistic.

What a difference a day makes, a comment he had heard often from his parents, echoed in his ears.

He wedged his thumbnail underneath the crusty lip of the box. It was stuck. Nick turned the box over in his hand and heard a *clunk*. He felt the same rush of excitement as the time he found a stash of wrapped birthday presents at the back of his parents' closet. He shook the box. It rattled.

There's something inside!

The Caldwells

NICK PULLED THE CANOE ONTO THE SHORE NEAR Uncle John's cabin. A sense of satisfaction washed over him. This year had been busy—slightly chaotic really—with the recent move and his parents' ambitious house renovation. Here at the lake, the only chaos was the scattered leaves, pine needles, and **indiscriminate** patches of wispy grass covering the ground. It had been less than a day, but Nick was already enjoying the simplicity of life in the woods.

The sound of an ax hitting a log reached his ears.

THA-WACK! THWUNK!

He glanced at the path ahead. The thick underbrush was dappled with sunlight bouncing in rhythm with the swaying boughs over his head. He caught a glimpse of Uncle John's red-and-black checkered flannel shirt through the brush along the trail. He heard the ax again.

THA-WACK! THWUNK!

Nick meandered up the trail and untangled the barbs of an overly-friendly raspberry branch from his shirt. Ahead, he saw the ax swing over Uncle John's head then heave down, forcing the iron wedge into the wood, splitting the stump in half in a single blow.

Uncle John wiped his wrinkled brow with the sleeve of his shirt. "Just in time for lunch. Fish shack's over there."

He pointed to a nearby shed. It was the size of a small closet, and the top half of the walls were screens. Nick noted the dozens of thick cobwebs.

The small shed was designated for preparing fish—a **notoriously** smelly and messy job.

"I wasn't fishing this morning." He grinned, then carefully reached into his mud-splattered cargo shorts to retrieve his finds. "I was exploring. I found a treasure for my collection." Nick theatrically revealed the small box in his hand.

Uncle John drove the ax into a nearby stump. The sharp edge lodged in the **ochre**-colored wood. He turned and inspected the loot.

He ran a finger over the ornate surface of the lid. "I'll be. You weren't kidding. This is a genuine treasure."

The old man inspected the metal container closely. "Now where have I seen this little bird before?" His brow furrowed. "I can't quite place it." His fingernail traced the shallow marks, and he chipped a little of the dried mud away from the hinges.

"I tried opening it, but the lid's stuck closed."

"Hmmm...I'd suggest soaking it in water, but that seems silly, considering it's been in the lake." He chuckled. "Maybe your pocketknife could loosen the lid."

"I tried that, too. Won't budge."

"From one treasure hunter to another, it's still a great find."

Nick was pleased with the compliment. He looked at Uncle John. "What kinds of treasures have you found?"

Uncle John cleared his throat. "Not all treasures are silver and gold." He rubbed his chin. "Mostly old furniture. Early nineteenth century, if I'm lucky." He looked through the trees at the shimmering water beyond. "The lake coughs up a treasure now and then."

Nick looked at him expectantly. "Like this box?"

Uncle John shrugged. "Not exactly, but old, yes. I found an old ceramic bottle once, and of course a fishing lure shows up now and then. Every once in a while, I find a stone the size of a marble on the shore. I keep a collection of them in a jar in the house. It's funny how they turn up every so often. You know, before they built the dam, this lake was a river, so who knows where these things came from before they washed ashore."

Nick looked at the lake, mesmerized momentarily by the sunlight dancing across the rippling water. He thought about all of the plants and animals just below the surface, out of sight, and wondered what other treasures might lay hidden at the bottom of the lake.

"What's that you got there?" Uncle John pointed to the walkie talkie.

"Oh, I met some kids today, and they're letting me borrow this so we can stay in touch."

Uncle John grunted in approval.

"If it's OK with you, they invited me to go into town for ice cream later."

Uncle John lifted the ax handle to remove it from the stump and looked at Nick with a quizzical expression. "When I was a boy, my folks just expected me to stay out of trouble and be home for meals. He propped a stump up position and slammed the ax into it. "'Long as you're home by dinner, we'll get along."

Nick nodded. Uncle John's gravelly voice made it sound like he was scolding him, but his actual words outlined complete trust and freedom.

"If you're stopping at Ginger Sue's for ice cream," Uncle John said, "mind making a delivery for me? I promised her some fresh herbs. It'd save me a trip."

Nick shrugged. "They just said *ice cream* but didn't say where."

A deep laugh rumbled from Uncle John's throat. "Son, this is Mapleton. If you want ice cream, it'll be a scoop from Ginger Sue's."

Before Nick could respond, the sound of voices and a car door slamming echoed through the woods from the road. Nick noted that at home, there were so many doors slamming and cars zooming past his house, he'd learned to tune them out. In the quiet woods, without the constant drone of traffic, individual sounds really stood out.

"Your mom and dad comin' to check on you already?" the old man asked. "Maybe the whole house finally collapsed." He jerked the ax out of the stump and rested it across a strong, bony shoulder. He took a step toward the driveway but stopped and turned to look at Nick. "Best keep that little treasure tucked away."

As Nick and Uncle John walked toward the road, Nick saw a blue sports car parked near the ditch. The car was meticulously shiny. Even from a distance, he could see the whole thing was sparkling clean. Everything from the hubcaps to the gold seagull ornament on the hood glistened.

Two men stood on opposite sides of the vehicle. As he and Uncle John approached, Nick noticed the car was tipped at an odd angle. A spare tire lay on the ground, and a car jack was wedged under the frame. A clean, blue dress shirt lay draped over the side mirror. The shirt's owner, a sweaty, **portly** man stooped down and wrestled with what appeared to be a flat tire. His tight undershirt was covered with grease and dirt. It didn't quite cover his hairy, bulging belly.

On the opposite side of the car, facing away from them, stood a tall, slender man wearing a checkered hat with a feather tucked into the band. He was talking on the phone and was so engrossed in conversation, he didn't seem to notice them.

The kneeling man, and however, stood up and gave a nod. He wiped his hands on a towel and smoothed his thick beard. He pulled his undershirt down and tucked it into a strained belt. He glanced at the tall man. "STEVEN?" He spoke loudly; much louder than necessary.

"Not now, Jake," Steven hissed. He turned his back and continued speaking quietly. "No? Nothing yet?" Steven had a shrill voice; his articulation was precise and punctuated, giving his words a delicate yet sharp sound, like broken bits of **porcelain**. *A pause.* He added in a hushed tone, "We haven't found anything yet…No. Nothing there."

Jake walked over and tapped the slim man on the shoulder, but his hand was cartoonishly slapped.

Jake looked at Uncle John and Nick, then nervously smiled while shrugging his shoulders. The shirt pulled loose, and he tried to tuck it under the belt again. Within seconds it **emancipated** itself.

Steven continued on the phone, "The client is well-funded. I have complete confidence this will be **lucrative**."

With that, he ended the call and turned around, obviously surprised to see Nick and Uncle John standing a few feet from the car. Steven hesitated, then tipped the brim of his hat in greeting. The sunlight glinted across the lenses of his gold, wire-rimmed glasses.

"Eh, ahem...my apologies," he said with a tight smile on his lips. "I didn't hear you walk up."

Uncle John stepped forward and offered a handshake to each of them. "John Shaydel."

"Indeed." Steven looked at Uncle John's dingy boots, clothes, and winter hat before delicately holding his hand out to introduce himself. "Steven Caldwell. This is Jake."

Jake wiped a bead of sweat from his forehead with the back of his hand, which left a second streak of dirt in its wake. "HULLOW," he bellowed.

"Pleased to meet you. This is Nick."

"You fellas need any help?" Uncle John offered gruffly.

"No." The thin man adjusted his glasses. "Thank you." He ran a finger along the inside of his collar and wiped a bead of sweat from his forehead. "My brother here is quite handy."

Nick noted the smudge on Jake's sweaty face and questioned the accuracy of that comment.

Uncle John crossed his arms across his chest. "Haven't seen you two around here before."

"I teach English Literature in Norwich." Steven emphasized *lit-er-a-ture* with deliberate enunciation, as if to give the distinct impression that he possessed a superior intellect. "We're staying in a small cottage for a few weeks near the edge of town. It was *supposed* to be a quiet retreat, so I could work on my own writing." He swatted a mosquito away from his face. "But we ran into a little issue."

Jake nodded. "AIR CONDITIONING'S BUSTED." Again, he was nearly shouting, and his words were garbled, as if his tongue and teeth didn't like working together.

"Clancy at the hardware store'll have the parts you need." Uncle John rubbed his beard. "Writer, eh? Well, I hope you find your muse."

"I find the quiet sanctity of the deep woods most inspiring," Mr. Caldwell said as he swatted another mosquito. He glanced down the long driveway at Uncle John's small log cabin. "I see you live rather…" He seemed to be searching for a polite word. "...primitively."

"I like to keep it simple." Uncle John added, "We are happy in proportion to the things we can do without."

This was the longest string of words Nick had heard from Uncle John. Steven seemed unimpressed.

"If you say so," Caldwell replied dismissively and began barking orders to Jake, who was now struggling to put the flat tire in the small trunk of the car.

Jake placed the shovel on top of the tire and closed the lid. He put his thumbs under his shiny, black leather belt and stepped back to admire his work. He smiled to reveal a row of teeth that glistened like large, yellow, pebbles peeking out from the dark bristles of his overgrown beard.

"OK. Well, we'll leave you to it then. Holler if you need anything. I've got plenty of tools in the garage."

Steven returned the offer with a brisk nod. Jake was busy again, struggling to close the trunk. Uncle John looked at Nick and tipped his head in the direction of the cabin. Nick was relieved to leave these odd newcomers to their tasks. Nick and Uncle John turned and retreated down the driveway. When they had walked about ten steps, Nick glanced behind them. He saw Jake throw his hands in the air as he kicked the tire with his boot. It wobbled noticeably. This was followed by a duet of the soprano and alto voices.

Nick looked up and saw Uncle John trying to suppress a smile. It was the first time Nick had seen Uncle John with a genuine twinkle in his eye.

History Lesson

Back at the cabin, Uncle John flipped on the light in the kitchen. Nick collapsed comfortably onto a worn couch and propped his feet up on the small, brown coffee table. His mother's voice echoed in his head, *Please's and thank you's. Be helpful. Clear the dishes. And keep your feet off the furniture.* She had repeated it a dozen times, reminding him to be a good guest. Nick dropped his feet to the ground.

"Are you sure you don't need any help?" Nick called out over the clatter of pots and pans.

"I'm old, not helpless."

Nick's stomach rumbled. Patience was not his strong suit.

"After lunch, can we take a look at those treasures you were telling me about earlier?" Nick said to the empty doorway.

"Hold your horses," the old man grumbled. "I'll be out in four minutes."

During the drive to Mapleton, Nick thought Uncle John had seemed **cantankerous**, but he was beginning to realize the old man was just quiet. He didn't seem to feel burdened by silence the way most people do. Uncle John seemed content to listen to his own thoughts, and he only said what was necessary. Nick was learning to interpret Uncle John's words separately from his tone.

He was also learning that Uncle John was quite a chef, a fact he suspected even his parents didn't know. He was, as his father had described, a man of contradictions.

Nick listlessly flipped through an old issue of *Captain Kidd* he'd grabbed from his room. He had re-read this issue so many times, the pages were flexible and creased, and he could practically recite each scene by heart. No longer in the mood to read, he tossed the comic onto the coffee table. Nick was looking forward to picking up the newest issue at Charlie's Comics with Eddie.

Just then, Uncle John emerged from the kitchen dabbing a small, dark purple stain splattered across his sleeve. "That apron didn't do me much good." He handed Nick a plate with a turkey sandwich with what looked like the raspberry jam from breakfast, cream cheese, and lettuce on it.

"Thanks," Nick replied.

Mimicking Uncle John's action, Nick took his hat off and hooked it on the empty chair next to him. He looked at the bizarre combination of ingredients on the paper plate. A thick layer of cream cheese and burgundy raspberry jam oozed over the frilly edge of dark green lettuce and several thick slices of turkey between two slices of firm bread.

Nick took a bite. "This is really good."

Uncle John wiped a glob of cream cheese off his mustache. "I've been taking cooking classes. I've got a teriyaki chicken marinade I want to try."

Nick tried to smile, but his mouth was so full, he risked letting some of the meal escape, so he raised his eyebrows and nodded in approval.

"I'll pick up ingredients tomorrow on my way back from Walton. The chicken needs to marinate at least four hours…" He faded off, calculating on his fingers how much time he'd need to prepare.

Nick jumped as the cuckoo clock chimed. He glanced up at the wall to watch the bird peek out of the tiny door. The clock was hidden among the patchwork display of old-looking photos, small paintings, an antique spoon collection, and various framed maps.

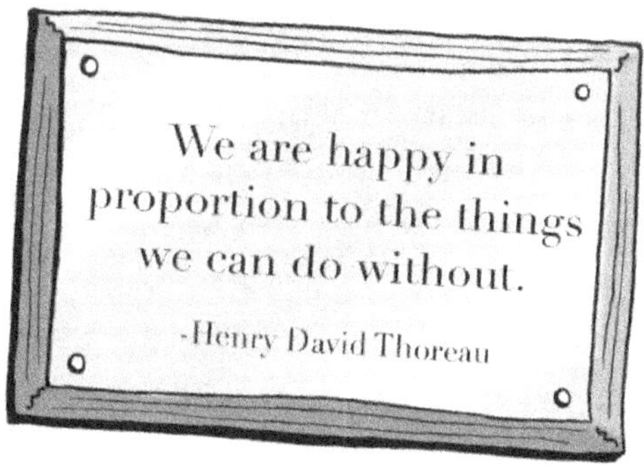

Nick sat up straight when he saw a slightly crooked plaque on the wall.

"Hey—" He recognized the quote. "Isn't that what you said to those guys with the flat tire?"

Uncle John nodded as he replied, "Thoreau? One of my favorites." His expression darkened slightly as he added, "Our new friend, the English professor, didn't seem to recognize it." He scratched his chin and added sarcastically, "Maybe he only knows *English* poets."

The old man took a big bite of his sandwich and wiped his mouth—not with his napkin, but with the back of his hand. Nick recalled his dad's comment about Uncle John being a man of contradictions. Uncle John had made a **gourmet** meal but wasn't concerned with even the most basic etiquette, such as not wiping your face with your hand. He practically lived like a hermit yet was highly educated about poetry and literature.

Never judge a book by its cover, he thought.

Uncle John stood up and disappeared into the hallway. A moment later, he reappeared holding a battered-looking cardboard box and heaved it into the table. Old, yellowed packing tape peeled hung off the sides like the outer layers of an onion.

"Here's the jug I was telling you about. And here are the marbles." He handed a small jar filled with pale blue spheres to Nick. "They stand out in the mud like a sore thumb."

Nick rattled the jar and watched the stones roll and clink against each other. They were a beautiful, opaque color. Some of them had a turquoise swirl snaking through the center. They reminded Nick of marbles.

Uncle John pulled the creased flaps back. A stack of old papers lay at the bottom.

"What's all this other stuff?"

Uncle John explained. "Mostly old newspaper clippings and photographs. They were in the attic when I moved in, and I just left 'em, thinking someone would come looking for them. Been there at least fifty years." He gently flipped through the brittle papers. "Way back before my time, Mapleton was a mining town. The owner lived next door."

"What kind of mine was it?" Nick wondered if it was a gold or silver mine.

Uncle John replied, "Miller and his business partner claimed the bedrock underneath Mapleton contained a rare mineral called neottrite."

"I've never heard of that," Nick replied.

"Well, it's rare—and valuable. Miller had no trouble finding men to work for him." Uncle John smoothed his beard. "Didn't matter in the end though. The main tunnel collapsed, and Miller died alongside his men down there. The town sealed up the entrance and shut down the whole operation."

"And they never found any of the rare mineral?"

"Neottrite?" Uncle John smoothed his beard again. "That's the million-dollar question. That mine was built on scandal and deception. If you ask me, I think those mine owners just made up the story about the neottrite to get people to mine iron ore and work for cheap pay. But people 'round here spin yarns about the old days. They say days before the collapse, one of the miners found a neottrite gemstone as big as his fist. Would've been worth millions of dollars."

"What do you mean *would have been*?"

Uncle John replied, "Well, that's the trouble. Everyone who saw the stone is dead. And stories grow as time passes. Folks started believing neottrite gave people supernatural powers. Others claim it had mystical healing power. Aliens dropped it during a visit to Earth. It contains holy water. There's no shortage of nonsense."

"Which one do you believe?" Nick asked.

Uncle John gave Nick a sharp look. "I don't believe in any of that mumbo jumbo."

Nick crossed his arms, thinking.

Uncle John lifted up an old newspaper article from the box. The headline read *Mapleton's Buried Treasure: Fact or Fiction?* He shook his head. "For a while Mapleton town was full of treasure hunters. Everyone and their grandma wanted to find that gemstone." He returned the other items to the box and folded the flaps along their worn creases, then set the box in the corner of the room. "I suspect most houses around here have a box like this laying around—full of leftover clues from the old treasure hunt."

Nick finished his last bite of sandwich then peered out the window. From the kitchen, he could see just a glimpse of the house in the distance through the trees.

"Does anyone live next door—in the old Miller house?" Nick hoped the answer would be 'Yes. People are over there all the time, turning the lights on and off and there certainly isn't a ghost.' He held his breath, waiting for Uncle John's response.

The old man pulled his wool hat over his gray ponytail and shook his head. "No one's lived there for years."

Nick's stomach dropped like a boulder being pushed off a cliff. He swallowed the nervous lump in his throat. "So, it's abandoned?"

"Yes and no. Miller's grandson owns it now but doesn't live there." Uncle John tucked a loose strand of hair under the hat and smoothed his ponytail with his fingers. "Stops by now and again to check in. Makes sure it doesn't flood when it rains."

Nick felt only slightly relieved to have a plausible explanation for the light he'd seen. It probably had been Archibald Miller's grandson checking for leaks in the old foundation during the rainstorm.

"Haven't seen him lately, come to think of it. I don't think he really wants to deal with the upkeep of an old place like that. He's been sifting through odds and ends for years, and he's barely made a dent. I got some real nice pieces of furniture from him though—maybe six months back."

Nick glanced at the house again and shivered.

Uncle John collected the plates then stood up. "Well? How 'm I doing?" he asked as he combed his fingers through his beard. "This thing collects all sorts of food shrapnel."

Nick gave him a thumbs up. He reached for the dishes on the table. "I'll get these. My mom said I need to earn my keep."

With a nod, Uncle John replied, "I could use your help then, unloading the back of the truck." He hesitated a moment then added, "But let's be clear. I'm letting you help. I don't *need* your help."

He disappeared out the doorway and the screen door slapped shut. Nick followed him outside, and they unloaded several pieces of furniture, including two small desks and several chairs from the truck bed, along with Nick's bike, which he wheeled to the side of the garage and parked under the overhang.

"Thanks," Uncle John grumbled. He set a piece of 2x4 lumber across the base of a compound **mitre** saw. As he adjusted his safety goggles, he said, "Oh, and don't forget, if you stop by Ginger's for ice cream, those herbs are in a paper bag in the fridge." He brought the saw blade down, and it chewed the wood in half.

Back inside the cabin, Nick sat down at the dining room table. He clicked the long-range walkie talkie to *ON*. Holding down the push to talk button, he spoke. "This is—"

He paused and released the button. He hadn't yet decided on a clever name for himself. He looked at the logo on his new ballcap, still hanging on the chair. The single eye of a long-haired man wearing an eye-patch stared back at him. He thought of the perfect walkie talkie name for himself. He pressed the button on the side again and continued.

"This is Pinehurst Pirate. Is anyone there?"

He released the button again and listened to the static. After a moment, he repeated the question and waited again.

This time, the static broke and he heard the muffled sound of a familiar voice. "Hello Pinehurst Pirate! This is Rang Mahana. What's your twenty? Over."

Nick recognized the voice. "Anna Graham? Is that you? Over."

(Static) "Yeah, it's me. Depending on my mood, I go by either Rang Mahana or Anna Graham. Over."

(Static) Nick responded, "Doesn't that get confusing? Over."

(Static) "I like to keep it interesting. I'm kind of addicted to letters. Over."

(Static) "OK. Over."

(Static) "Hey. Red Fox here. I'll be honest, Pinehurst Pirate doesn't suit you. I'm gonna call you C.K., short for City Kid. Over."

Nick sighed and, for a moment, considered pushing back but changed his mind when he realized that even though he was from the suburbs, he wasn't much like a pirate.

(Static) "I'm cool with that."

(Static) "Great timing, C.K., Red Fox and I are headed to the ice cream shop. We're actually just coming down the street now. We'll swing and show you the way. Over and out."

(Static) "OK. Over and out."

Nick wanted to show Jo and Eddie the box he had found, so he put it in his bag next to the brown paper bag for Ginger. He slung it over his shoulder then stuffed his feet into his tennis shoes.

Jo and Eddie were waiting for him at the end of the driveway.

"Ice cream awaits," Eddie raised a fist into the air and called out.

The gravel crunched under his tires while grasshoppers jumped maniacally out of his path as he pulled onto the road and biked toward town with his friends. The afternoon breeze smelled of switchgrass and sunshine.

They hadn't gone far when he saw the driveway to the Miller house ahead. A very old mailbox with a few remaining flakes of green paint hung at a broken angle from its crooked post. It clearly hadn't been used in a long time. Nick stopped to get a better look at the neighboring property. He couldn't see much from the street, but it was enough to understand why Miller's grandson wouldn't want to live there.

Eddie said as he and Jo pulled their bikes up next to Nick's. "The old Miller place."

A black iron gate with an emblem of the letter "M" in the center blocked the entrance. Through the bars, Nick could see parts of the house peeking through the craggy branches of the overgrown trees and plants. Nick craned his neck to see past the curtain of vines hanging from trees across the driveway. Long shadows clawed across the patchy yard.

The house itself was a towering, two-story brick building with two chimneys and a wide, wrap-around porch. The shutters on either side of the many tall, thin windows hung at haphazard angles. Their louvered slats were either broken or missing paint and gave the house a neglected appearance. A combination of arched and rectangular windows all seemed to stare down angrily from under the sharp pitch of the jagged, intersecting roof lines.

"Boo!" Jo said as she nudged Nick's and Eddie's shoulders.

They both jumped.

Jo laughed, then asked Nick, "Do you really think you saw a light on in one of those windows?"

"I know I did." Nick caught her eye and noticed she wore a playful grin. Nick returned the smile but felt his stomach tighten.

"Well, maybe a ghost lives there and wants to make friends," Eddie wiggled his fingers.

"Stop teasing him, Eddie," Jo scolded.

"What?" Eddie deflected. "You were the one who started it. I'm just saying it's your classic haunted house. Every town has one, right?"

Nick pictured his new town and thought of a handful of old houses that were creepy enough to look haunted. He smirked when he realized that at this very moment, inside the creepiest of them all were his parents. He felt a small pang of homesickness when he pictured them working hard to get the stairs fixed, toilets flushing, and walls patched. His desperation to get home as soon as possible had faded a bit, thanks to his new friends, but he really hoped the outside of his house would be repainted by the first day of school. He didn't want to get a reputation at his new school as the kid who lived in a haunted house.

Jo smirked and looked at Eddie. "Dare you to sneak past the gate and knock on the front door."

"Uh, and let the ol' Badger get me?" Eddie replied as he looked at the old house. "No way."

"A badger?" Nick asked.

Jo replied, "Not *A* badger. *THE* Badger—and the Badger was a person," Jo looked warily at the house, "and that's where she lived, a hundred years ago."

Nick felt goosebumps rising on the back of his neck. He swallowed and asked, "Why was she called the Badger?"

Eddie clarified, "Well, the story goes like this. Somewhere around here was the entrance to the old mine."

Nick chimed in. "Uncle John said they boarded it up after the tunnel collapsed."

Eddie nodded. "Did he tell you the cave in trapped a bunch of miners?"

Nick shook his head. He suddenly felt cold and clammy.

Eddie's eyebrows lifted and his tone became **ominous**. "Well, the mom of one of the miners went crazy, and she started digging holes all over town, trying to reach him—"

"Hence the nickname," Jo chimed.

"But she never found him," Eddie continued. "People say she wanders around at night now, digging holes and searching for him."

Nick looked at the lawn, which was pockmarked with small patches of brown dirt where the grass had been dug up. "Wait a minute," he protested. "If The Badger died a hundred years ago, why are there fresh holes all over the yard?"

Eddie replied quietly, "Isn't it obvious?" He widened his eyes, wiggled his fingers. "OooOOooh…"

"You expect me to believe her ghost digs holes?"

Eddie nodded.

Nick looked again at the yard. "Really?"

Eddie nodded again.

Nick looked at the house. “How would a ghost even be able to hold a shovel?”

Jo agreed, “My point exactly. Thank you.”

“Maybe it’s a ghost shovel.” Eddie opened his eyes extra wide, trying to look scary. “If she died holding it, maybe she took it with her to the other side.”

“Whatever, Eddie,” Jo said.

In the daylight, Nick couldn’t tell if any lights were on inside. He shuddered. “That place gives me the creeps.”

“That place gives *everyone* the creeps,” Eddie whispered. This time, Nick could tell he wasn't joking.

“My mom says it’s all just stories,” Jo said. “I don’t believe in ghosts either, Nick. And I’m sure there’s a scientific explanation for the holes. Like, maybe the holes are from a dog.”

“Maybe you’re right,” Eddie said as he started pedaling, “but I’ve never seen a dog in that yard.”

Ginger Sue's

NICK, JO, AND EDDIE PARKED THEIR BIKES OUTSIDE of Ginger Sue's Ice Cream Parlor on Main Street. As they entered the shop, Nick inhaled a breath of the cool, sugary-sweet air. It lingered at the back of his throat, and he suddenly felt very hungry for ice cream. A tall, athletic-looking boy wearing a baseball hat with Ginger Sue's across the front was washing something at a sink behind the counter.

"Be right with you," he droned.

The three kids sat down at a nearby table.

"Oh, I almost forgot!" Nick plopped his backpack down. "I found a something in the lake." He dug inside the pocket for the silver box and set it in the center of the table. "It was buried in the mud near the shore."

Eddie leaned in. "Buried treasure?"

"Wow!" Jo's eyes lit up and she rapid-fired her thoughts. "How do you think it got there? How long do you think it was there? Looks old. Do you think it's worth anything?"

Nick smiled. When Jo had something to say—and she seemed to have something to say about everything—she unleashed a whirlwind of words.

Her finger traced the small contour of the bird on the lid. "My aunt gave me a ring box one year for my birthday. It was about the same size, but this one is so **ornate**."

"This was in the lake?" Eddie asked.

"I thought it was a shell. I scooped it up—just by chance." Nick omitted the incident with the leech.

Jo shook the box lightly. Her eyes flashed to Nick. "Something's inside!"

"Double treasure," Eddie added. "Nice."

Jo tried to open the lid, but it was still stuck. She shook the box again, this time holding it near her ear as she listened to the quiet *clinking* sound. "Think it's a ring?"

"I have no idea. I've tried everything short of a hammer to get it open, but it's stuck tight."

"Do you need a hammer?" Eddie asked. "I can get you a hammer."

Jo rolled her eyes. "That seems a little excessive. It's probably just a puzzle box or something. They sometimes have a hidden button that releases the clasp." She slid her fingernail along the mud-caked edge of the lid and then explored the container on all sides. Nick could see she was getting frustrated as it became evident she was not going to be able to open the lid by "solving it."

Just then, the boy behind the counter announced, "What can I get you?"

The legs of Eddie's chair screeched against the black and white linoleum floor, and he made a beeline for the counter.

Jo smirked. "Eddie doesn't hide his priorities." She handed the box back to Nick, which he pocketed.

Peering into the freezer case, they browsed the options. It was full of cylindrical cardboard cartons loaded with ice cream. A sign on the counter read: *Enjoy a Free Sample.* Underneath, someone had scrawled *Limit 1* in marker.

Nick's eyes roamed across the case from Hokey Pokey Peanut to Exhausted Parent Espresso. A bright, yellow ice cream labeled Birthday Banan-za caught Nick's eye. The description on the label described it as having pieces of banana, birthday cake, and sprinkles generously dispersed throughout.

"Hey Jesse, do you have any more of EnlightenMint?" Eddie asked, pointing to the *Flavor of the Week* label on the glass.

"We're out," came the flat reply.

Eddie's jaw dropped open, and he said crossly, "I have been waiting for the new flavor of the week since—well, since last week."

"Shoulda gotten here earlier, I guess." Jesse didn't sound sympathetic at all.

Nick looked into the carton and saw only a few remnants of light green ice cream against the side of the brown cardboard. The rest had been scraped clean.

"I'll have a scoop of Swiss Raspberry Avalanche with chocolate sprinkles," Jo said, "in a cone, please."

Jesse scooped a generous heap of white chocolate swirled with raspberry vanilla cream onto a sugar cone and handed it to Jo. He wiped the stainless-steel counter, then looked down at the boys.

Eddie mumbled, "I guess I'll try a sample of Moon Mist."

Jesse held out a curved, wooden popsicle stick with a small amount of pale blue ice cream on it. When Eddie reached for it, Jesse withdrew the sample as if holding it hostage. "*One* sample."

"Fine." Eddie agreed as he took the spoon.

While Eddie was deciding, Nick looked around at the mishmash of items displayed on the walls of the shop. Scattered between brightly colored images of delicious looking ice cream, he saw a framed newspaper article from the Mapleton Gazette highlighting the grand opening of Ginger Sue's Ice Cream Parlor. Next to that were several black and white portraits. All of the decorations looked old, giving the ice cream shop a vintage look.

Eddie noticed Nick staring at the pictures. He pointed to one. "That's my favorite." He chuckled and added, "It's like his face is being attacked by a **muskrat**."

Nick smiled at the old-looking photograph of a man staring straight at the camera. He also had the largest mustache Nick had ever seen. A metal label at the base of the photo read *A. Miller*.

"Is that Archibald Miller?" Nick asked.

Eddie nodded and squeezed a wooden sampling spoon between his top lip and nose. "Look, we have the same mustache."

Jo elbowed him. "Honestly, Eddie. Is this your first time in public?"

Nick wondered if Ginger was in the back room. He leaned against the case and craned his neck toward the open doorway behind the counter.

The sound of Jesse's voice shifted his attention. "Do you want anything?" Jesse asked.

"Oh—" Nick faltered. "Yeah—sorry, I was just wondering if Ginger was here today."

"She'll be in later."

"Oh." Nick momentarily wavered on his decision and then ordered a scoop of Birthday Banan-za topped with gummy bears in a waffle cone.

"Thanks," he said, as Jesse handed it to him.

Eddie, still pouting about the sold-out EnlightenMint said, "Moon Mist was pretty good, but I'll have the Peanut Butter Blitz. Two scoops, in a cup, please."

Just then, the bell over the shop door jingled and a woman with mounds of curly red locks walked in. She wore tight blue jeans and a wide belt with a shiny silver buckle, boots with tall heels, and an emerald-green shirt. She was carrying two paper grocery bags.

"Howdy," the woman sang out in a syrupy drawl and used her hip to push past the swinging half-door behind the ice cream case. She set the bags on the counter, then looked toward Nick. "You must be the famous Nick Thornton. I hear you have a delivery for me."

Nick raised his eyebrows and nodded. Jo and Eddie looked at him with surprised expressions.

Eddie murmured, "City Kid's connected."

Nick retrieved the paper sack from his backpack and set it on the counter.

Ginger unrolled the top and inhaled deeply. "Ahh. Fresh mint." She looked at Jesse. "Time to get that next batch going." She returned her attention to Nick and held out a hand. "I'm Ginger. John said you might be stopping by this afternoon." She read his mind and said, "It's a small town. These two troublemakers," she said, winking at Jo and Eddie, "are in here all the time. Y'all enjoy your ice cream." Then she carried the bag into the back room.

Back at the table, Eddie shoveled an impressively massive bite into his mouth, then stabbed his spoon into what remained of the two scoops. He lifted a small flap on his vest and produced a multitool. Through a full, freezing mouth, he asked to see the box again. Had he not also gestured toward Nick's pocket, neither Nick nor Jo would have had any idea what he was talking about because his words were **indecipherable**. Eddie grinned, took the box from Nick, then devoured another enormous bite. With a practiced flip of his thumb, a screwdriver appeared, and he carefully scraped along the edge of the lid. It was difficult to tell exactly where the top and sides met, because the strange buildup at the seam was thick and jagged. A few bits of debris flaked off, but the lid was still stuck.

Jo edged forward. "I'm dying to see what's in there."

Nick pictured himself placing a diamond ring in a prominent compartment in his tacklebox. It would be his most valuable treasure yet.

His mouth finally clear, Eddie licked his lower lip and announced, "You know, my dad would know how to get that gunk off. He's always dealing with rusty bolts and things on the cars people bring in. Maybe he can help us get this tiny treasure chest open."

"Eddie," Nick's eyes lit up, and a smile spread across his face, "That's genius."

Eddie hadn't seemed to hear. He looked off into the distance. "What if it's full of precious gems?"

Jo laughed and reminded him it was a very small box and more than likely stored a cheap ring or pair of rusty earrings.

"Well—" Nick crunched the last bite of his ice cream cone and stood up.

"Wait. I'm not done yet," Eddie mumbled through another oversized mouthful of Peanut Butter Blitz.

"Hurry up," Jo said as she walked to the garbage can and tossed her napkin into the trash.

Nick slung his backpack onto his shoulder, and the three walked outside. They'd only taken a few steps when they heard two familiar voices.

"Great," Jo muttered. She stopped and crossed her arms, staring at the boys near their bikes.

It was Billy and Jack. Nick recognized the pair from the lake. Billy, a stocky boy with sandy brown hair, red cheeks, and freckles, leaned on a bench next to the bike rack. His freckled face wore a **malevolent** grin and stared at them.

Billy's gaze drifted to Eddie's remaining half-scoop of ice cream. "How's your ice cream, Eduardo?"

Eddie lowered his loaded spoon back into the cup. "Hi, Billy."

Billy snarled, "Just one cup? But there's two of us." He stepped closer. "That math don't add up."

Eddie chuckled nervously. "You're just in time. Ginger is making a new batch of mint. Should be almost done."

Perched on Eddie's bike was Jack, a scrawny, blond boy with deep set eyes. He scoffed, "This is one crappy bike, Eddie." He scratched at a loose end of the tape with a stubby fingernail.

"Hey." Billy took a step forward. "You didn't answer my question."

"Your question?"

"I said, 'How's the ice cream, and where's mine?'"

Eddie's voice was at least one **octave** higher than usual as he replied, "It's OK. I—I wanted the mint, but—"

Jack said, "We're hungry, and you didn't leave anything for us in that dumb hideout of yours. Didn't your mother teach you to share, Eddie?"

Jo stepped forward. "Don't you guys have a more productive way to fill your time? These **insipid enterprises** are a total waste of everyone's time."

Jack looked at her and said, "Mind your own business, nerd."

Jo pressed her lips together and an angry flush of crimson crept up the sides of her neck. Eddie took a small step back and Nick watched his eyelids flicker. His gaze fell to the ground, visibly exposing fear.

Don't let them know you're scared. Nick wished he could transmit the thought to Eddie's mind.

Nick watched Eddie's foot shift backward once more. Billy looked down and saw it, too. He looked up with a half-smile smirk and a glint of victory in his eye.

He nodded to the ice cream, which was now shrinking into a puddle in the bottom of the cup.

"Peanut Butter Blitz, huh? Just so happens to be Jack's favorite." Billy turned toward the boy on the bike. "Isn't that right, Jack? Isn't Peanut Butter Blitz your favorite?"

Jack grinned. "It is today."

Nick could tell Eddie was about one second away from handing the cup over to the bully, so he moved between Eddie and Jo and said, "Hey, it sounds like you're hungry."

Billy looked Nick up and down. "Who are you?"

In a calm voice, Nick responded, "You can call me Captain Obvious."

Billy stared at Nick. He narrowed his eyes. Nick stared back and tried not to project any anger or aggression. In his experience, he'd learned that bullies were like cantankerous bears. The smallest thing could cause them to fly into a rampage. Nick took slow, even breaths and made no sudden movements. Jack hopped off Eddie's bike and stood next to Billy. It was a classic move of solidarity. Eddie, slightly behind Nick and Jo, mimicked the move and inched closer to Nick's right side. Then Jo moved in, on the right. The other boys were bigger, but collectively, Nick, Jo, and Eddie made a more **formidable** wall.

Billy crossed his arms but said nothing. He stared at Nick's unflinching gaze. His left eye twitched slightly, and his lips parted. Nick could hear him breathing. His breath stank.

The two groups were in a standoff. Both stared at each other. Then, to everyone's surprise, Billy broke the staring contest with a single, forceful exhale from his chest. Then, he did it again; this time his shoulders lifted, ever so slightly. This strange movement repeated two more times. Jack looked over with a confused expression on his face. Billy's pudgy, freckled cheeks were stretching into—a smile.

"Captain Obvious." He was chuckling now. "That's pretty good."

Taking advantage of the shift in attitude, Jo spoke up. "Ginger's just finishing a batch of mint, and you know she always gives extra big scoops when it's fresh."

Nick nudged Eddie toward the bike rack. "See you guys later."

As they biked away, Nick heard Billy ask Jack, "What the heck just happened? And who's that Captain Obvious guy?"

BERNADELLI'S GARAGE

WHEN THEY WERE OUT OF EARSHOT OF BILLY AND Jack, Eddie asked, "OK, C.K., how'd you do that?" He was riding no-handed while drinking the last of his melted ice cream up from the cup.

"What? Break the bully spell?" Nick looked at him, smiling.

"Yeah," Jo said. "We never get away from them without losing something, even if it's just our dignity."

Nick explained, "I had a bully once. At my old school. His name was Adam Henry—and he was relentless. Every day before science, he would wait for me in the hallway and demand I give him my homework, or a piece of gum, or whatever. It was always something. One day, I'd had enough. I honestly didn't even care what he would do if I refused. I couldn't take any more of it. The situation had become so bad, it was laughable—so, I cracked a joke."

"What?" Eddie looked confused.

"What was the joke?" Jo's eyes lit up. "What did you say?"

"I said, 'Hey Adam—you know why you can't trust an atom?' He got really tense, fist clenched by his shoulder, ready to strike, but I guess he couldn't stand it—you know, not knowing the answer.

"Whad'ya do?" Eddie asked.

"I said, 'You can't trust an atom because they make up everything.' His face got really red, and I explained, 'Get it? As in science class—atoms—A-T-O-M-S—make up everything?'"

Jo grinned, and Eddie nodded.

"It took a few seconds for it to register in his thick, bully brain, but surprisingly, after that, things got better. The other kids started calling me The Bully Whisperer."

Jo chuckled. "Nice."

"So, he stopped waiting for you?" Eddie asked.

"Oh, no, he still waited for me," Nick smiled at the memory. "Every day. But it was because he wanted a new joke." He looked at Eddie. "I mean, we weren't friends or anything, and he still slugged my shoulder if I didn't make him laugh, but it was better than him stealing my lunch."

"You're full of surprises, City Kid." Jo nodded with impressed approval.

"Yeah," Eddie chimed. Then he added, "Thanks."

Nick gave him a knowing nod and smiled. He thought back to how much more confident he felt facing Billy and Jack than when he first dealt with Adam Henry. He wished someone had been there to stick up for him, but he was glad he could help Jo and Eddie.

"My dad's shop isn't far from here."

They continued toward a row of shops and skidded to a stop in front of Ed's Auto where a drilling noise came from the open bay doors. The sweet smell of bread wafted across the parking lot, from the Honey Bun Bakery next door.

Nick and Jo flipped their kickstands down and propped up their bikes on the sidewalk. Eddie's bike fell with a clatter onto the cement.

The two garage doors next to the office of Ed's Auto were open. Nick and his friends walked inside. A white minivan was in the first bay with its hood up. The sound of music came from a TV in the corner. They heard a melodic voice saying, *Join us in celebrating Mapleton's one-hundred-fiftieth Anniversary. We are currently accepting entries for our Brilliant Invention Contest.*

Eddie had clearly memorized the commercial and mimed a broadcaster's voice as he chimed in, "*You could be Mapleton's next brilliant inventor!*" He added, "I'm totally gonna win that contest this year." Eddie stated then hollered, "Pappa!"

"Wha-? Umph!" A muffled reply seemed to come from under the minivan in the first bay.

A worn pair of black work boots peeked out from the van as a wrench tumbled into view on the concrete floor. A large, grease-smudged hand emerged next to the tire and blindly fumbled around until it discovered the mislaid tool. The wrench and hand disappeared momentarily before a burly man dressed in grease-covered coveralls rolled out from under the vehicle.

The man, who Nick assumed was Mr. Bernadelli, smiled and rubbed his forehead.

"What's all the shouting about?"

"Sorry, Pappa. We didn't see you."

Eddie introduced Nick and Nick shook the man's giant, leathery hand. As Eddie explained about the metal box, a familiar blue sports car pulled into the empty bay next to the minivan. Nick recognized the gold seagull affixed to the hood. Steven Caldwell stepped out of the car and answered his phone on the first ring. His shrill but muted voice echoed indistinguishably across the garage.

"I'll be right with you," Mr. Bernadelli's baritone voice boomed. He rubbed his chin for a moment and held the box up to the shop light hanging over one of his workbenches.

Nick cringed as Mr. Bernadelli loudly assessed the box. "That gunk doesn't stand a chance with the butane torch. Just set it on the table, and I'll take a look at it after I finish with these customers. Then, we can see what priceless treasure lies under the hood of that thing."

Nick craned his neck to look past Mr. Bernadelli's towering frame and noticed Caldwell looking in their direction. They briefly made eye contact, and the man quickly looked down and jotted something down on the small pad of paper he was holding. He was still on the phone, but it looked like he might be listening in on their conversation.

"That's OK Mr. Bernadelli," Nick said. Then he added, intentionally projecting his voice as he walked toward the door, "It's probably an old fishhook or some paper clips. I'm sure it's just junk. Thanks anyways." He waved his hand in appreciation and walked through the open bay door.

Eddie and Jo opened their mouths to protest, but Nick gave them a sharp look he hoped they would interpret correctly. To his relief, they said nothing and followed him outside.

As they walked to the front sidewalk to pick up their bikes, Jo asked in a low voice, "Nick, why are you being weird? What's going on?"

Nick explained about his encounter with Steven and Jake Caldwell.

"That's super suspicious!" Eddie paced back and forth.

Jo fired off several frantic questions to Nick. "Did he see you? Maybe he didn't see you? Do you think he noticed us?"

Nick felt worried. "We made eye contact. He seemed pretty interested when Eddie's dad was talking about the box. I saw him write something down on a notepad."

Eddie's eyes lit up. In a low voice, he said, "There's a row of windows at the back of the garage, up near the ceiling. Maybe we can spy on this Caldwell guy and see what he does next!"

The three kids quietly wheeled their bikes into the small alley behind the garage and parked them behind a dumpster. Eddie collected some empty milk crates outside the back door of the neighboring bakery and stacked them up under the **transom** windows on the back wall of the garage.

He pushed up onto his tiptoes but jumped down. "I'm not tall enough. Jo, you try."

Jo climbed the precarious crate tower and reached up to grip the bottom ledge with her fingers. She pulled herself up the last two inches and peered through the pane.

"Can you see him?" Eddie whispered eagerly.

"No. Oh! Wait a minute—there he is." Jo dropped back down and whispered to the boys, "The white van just pulled out, so I have a clear view. He's sitting on a bench near your dad's office. He's still talking on the phone." She hoisted herself back up and took another peek. She gasped and ducked down. With obvious concern in her voice, she rasped, "He's off the phone now. He's headed this way!"

Eddie whispered to Jo, "Did he see you?"

Jo looked panic-stricken. "I don't know."

Their eyes darted to the door at the back entrance.

"Hide," Nick ordered. "Now!"

Jo leaped down from the crates. As she did, the tower clattered to the ground. The three kids leaped behind the dumpster. They crouched down into a squatting position and held their bikes next to them, trying not to move. A gross-looking liquid had **leached** out of the bottom of the dumpster and felt sticky under Nick's shoes. He ignored it and peered around the edge of the huge, metal **receptacle**. The rear door of the garage swung open. Steven Caldwell stepped out into the back alley. Nick could feel his heart beating against his ribcage. Eddie was breathing audibly. Jo aggressively held a finger up to her lips and frowned at Eddie. His breathing lessened, but only slightly.

Nick mouthed, "He's in the alley." He pointed toward the back door of the garage.

Eddie was the farthest away. He craned his neck, trying to see but hissed, "I can't see anything past, Jo's big head."

Jo ignored Eddie's comment and pushed one of Eddie's bike pedals away from her ribcage. "Do you see him, Nick?"

Still crouched, Nick hoped he was out of sight. He watched as Mr. Caldwell walked slowly back and forth around the backyard, looking at the ground. Using his foot, Steven Caldwell pushed one of the milk crates to the side. He adjusted his wire-rimmed glasses, then looked up at the window.

Was he piecing together their movements? Nick wondered if Jo's shoes left footprints on the pavement, and a heat crept up the back of his neck. *Who was this guy?*

Eddie inhaled the aroma wafting out from the neighboring bakery and softly whispered, "A chocolate croissant sounds great right about now."

Jo looked appalled. *What?* she mouthed.

A sharp electronic ringing sound broke the silence, and the kids flinched. Mr. Caldwell pulled his cell phone from his pants pocket, glanced around the yard, and put the phone to his ear.

His metallic voice answered, "Yes?"

The three couldn't hear the voice on the other end of the line, but Mr. Caldwell's forehead creased with worry. He paced back and forth.

"Well, it's important to the client," he replied quietly. "We're close, I can feel it. Keep digging!" With that, he snapped the phone shut and jammed it back into his pocket. He walked back to the door and reached for the door handle.

Precisely at that moment, the piece of duct tape attached to the banana seat of Eddie's bike slipped out of his grip, and the handlebar hit the side of the dumpster with a hollow, metallic thud. Nick and Jo looked at Eddie in horror as all three of them ducked their heads down, trying to become invisible. Nick peered around the corner. They were in the shadows, and he hoped the edge of his face wouldn't be noticeable. He saw Mr. Caldwell's eyes narrow into slits as he took a step in their direction.

Just then, the back door swung open, and Mr. Bernadelli's voice boomed, "Ah! There you are, Mr. Caldwell! I was able to fix your tire." Mr. Bernadelli held the door open, and he motioned to Mr. Caldwell to re-enter the garage.

For a moment, Mr. Caldwell hesitated. He glanced in the direction of the alley again.

Mr. Bernadelli said, "I don't usually service the same car for the same reason twice in one week!" His voice faded. "It was another nail…"

The door slammed shut. A moment later, they heard the rumble of an engine. At the opposite end of the alley, Nick saw a flash of blue as Steven Caldwell's sports car sped past.

Nick breathed a sigh of relief.

Eddie jumped up and stretched. "Oh, man! I was getting a cramp!"

Jo tipped her head against the frame of her bike and exhaled.

"That was close," Nick said.

The three kids walked through the alley to the front of the garage.

"Eddie, you get hungry at the most inappropriate times, and your bike nearly gave us away." Jo rubbed her forehead.

"Ugh…I know. Can't wait to get rid of this thing."

Jo crossed her arms. "Your dad could fix that kickstand in, like, two minutes."

Eddie rolled his eyes. "He says I have to fix it myself, but what's the point now?

"Because it's good for you to learn how to fix things when they break," a deep voice said from behind them.

Startled, the kids whirled around to see Mr. Bernadelli sitting on a bench in front of the garage.

"You have to take care of what you have before you ask for more." Mr. Bernadelli grinned as he wiped his hands on a rag.

"Say, d'ya mind taking another look at that thing?" Nick pulled the box from his backpack and handed it to Mr. Bernadelli.

He scratched his chin. "On second thought, a butane torch would be too hot for the details on the lid. It's a lot more delicate than the things I usually work with. Might melt it completely—not to mention whatever is inside. You'd be better off letting Gordon take a look at it, if he's open today." Mr. Bernadelli thumbed toward a metal sign hanging over a green awning a few doors down.

The sign read: *Watkins Fine Jewelry*. It creaked as it tipped back and forth in the breeze.

Jo and Eddie exchanged a look of concern.

As they walked toward the store, Eddie said, "I'm not sure we should go in there."

Nick asked, "What's wrong with the jewelry shop?"

Jo bit a fingernail, thinking. She looked at Eddie and then back to Nick. "It's not so much the shop that's problematic. It's who's inside." She paused. "Mr. Watkins has a reputation for being—a bit odd."

"That's putting it mildly," Eddie snorted.

Nick crossed his arms.

Eddie whispered, "I heard Mr. Watkins steals jewelry from graves!"

Jo rolled her eyes. "You know those stories are just made up, right? Just local legends—designed to scare kids, so they won't stay out after dark."

Eddie let out an audible sigh. "Yeah, but there's a reason that some stories become legends."

Jo tucked her hair behind her ear and reasoned, "My mom says just because someone is different, doesn't mean we should treat them differently."

"Except Gordon Watkins isn't just different." Eddie crossed his arms. He looked at Nick and said, "My sister Loretta told me his shop is closed most days because he's out digging up graves and stealing rings and watches off dead people." He added, "And, she said he only eats tuna fish."

Jo gave Eddie a skeptical look. "How would she even know that?"

"She works at Shop 'N' Save." Eddie justified. "Apparently that's *all* the body snatcher ever buys; tuna fish—by the case!"

"No, I mean how do you know about the jewelry—and, for the record, what you're describing is graverobbing, not body-snatching."

"Puh-tayto, puh-tahto. Body-snatching, jewelry-snatching. Same level of creepy."

Nick chimed in. "Stealing a body seems much worse."

"Either way," Eddie sounded intense, "his shop is almost always closed. When he opens it after he's been 'gone'" he air-quoted, "the place is packed with new diamond necklaces and ruby-studded—"

"Hang on. How do you even know that? Are you stopping in to keep track of his inventory?" Jo looked skeptical.

Eddie shifted his weight from one foot to the other, then back again. "Well, no."

"He's not a graverobber." Jo sounded confident but chewed on her lip while looking up at the shop sign. "Nick, what do you think?"

Nick considered the situation. He really hoped this Mr. Watkins person could open the box so they could see what was inside, but Eddie's suggestion that the jeweler was a criminal made him feel a little uneasy. However, he had already established himself as a bully conqueror and didn't want to make the impression that he was as nervous as he felt. The decision felt complicated.

"Hello?" Jo put a hand on her hip.

She and Eddie waited for his answer.

Nick replied, "I guess, even if the guy *IS* a graverobber, we should be OK—right? Since we're alive and not corpses." He added, "And there are three of us. Safety in numbers?" He looked at the sign and gulped. "I'm game if you are."

The attention was now on Eddie, who was still clearly conflicted. He sighed. "I'm not sure I agree with your logic, but fine. For the record, I'm *only* going into a store with dead people's jewelry because I'm really, *really* dying to see what's in that box."

The three walked toward the store and stood under the awning. Jo reached for the door handle. Nick and Eddie exchanged uneasy glances. In the window, below the *We're OPEN* sign, a pair of **amber** eyes stared at them. Jo pushed the door open, and they walked inside.

WATKINS FINE JEWELRY

THE BELL OVER THE DOOR JINGLED AS NICK, EDDIE, and Jo walked into the jewelry shop. The overhead lights were off, giving the store a cave-like feel. The afternoon sun streamed in through the large bay windows at the front, sending ribbons of light across the floor. Speckles of dust hung suspended in the air and swirled gently from the movement of the visitors. An amber-eyed cat with sleek, black fur sat motionless near the window and watched the kids as they walked across the worn carpet.

A small desk at the far end of the showroom was illuminated by a single bulb lamp. Behind the counter, a man sat hunched over his work. His wiry, white hair had a wild look, and he reminded Nick of pictures he had seen of Albert Einstein. When the man looked up, his light brown irises looked as large as golf balls as he blinked behind the magnifying lenses attached to his glasses.

Eddie pretended to scratch his nose so he could cover his mouth while discreetly whimpering, "That's him."

Evidently, the old man had excellent hearing because he replied, "Who'd you expect?"

Nick moved forward, a little timidly. Jo was already an entire stride ahead. Eddie stooped down to pet the cat, conveniently allowing him to linger near the door.

"Mr. Watkins," Nick began.

The old man was staring at him and went a long time without blinking. Nick suddenly forgot why they were there.

Jo, fortunately, was more focused. She took a breath as she leaned toward the counter and stated, matter-of-factly, "We have a rusty jewelry box we we're hoping you could fix."

Mr. Watkins was using a tiny screwdriver to adjust something that appeared to be the inner workings of a large clock. Nick wondered if it'd been stolen from a grave. Brass gears of various sizes covered one side, and a series of metal bars crisscrossed the other. The old man laid the screwdriver down and wheeled his creaky chair over a few feet so he could sit in front of them. Mr. Watkins flipped up his magnifying lenses and held an expectant palm over the counter. His hand was old and wrinkled and reminded Nick of Uncle John's. The skin pulled taut at the sides of his outstretched fingers.

"Well, let's have a look, then."

Nick realized none of them had any idea what the box contained, and by asking the jeweler for help, they would be giving him the first peek of its contents. He hoped the old man wouldn't try and steal whatever lay hidden beneath the lid.

Jo seemed to be considering the same **conundrum**. She gave Nick a subtle nod of approval. Nick glanced back at Eddie, to see if he, too, approved, but Eddie was busy playing with his new, feline friend and likely counting the seconds until they could leave. Nick gently dropped the box into the jeweler's hand. Mr. Watkins snapped his magnifying lenses back down and pulled the long arm of his desk lamp in front of his face.

While the jeweler examined the silver box, Nick looked down at the items displayed under the glass countertop. There were a few trays of old-looking rings and necklaces and a long row of gold and silver watches. The sparse inventory was not at all how Eddie had described it.

The old man ran a leathery finger across the delicate raised emblem of the bird. "Beautiful. My grandmother had a ring box like this." He looked up. "Now, let's see why this won't open." He murmured, "Quite a bit of dirt caked into the hinges here. Dirt always proves to be problematic."

Eddie let out a very soft whimper, and Nick knew he was thinking about jewelry with dirt from a grave.

Nick explained, "It's pretty rusty, and as you can see, the lid won't open."

The shop owner gave Eddie a pensive look, then scratched the section of his bushy hair above his right ear and leaned back in his chair. "Your problem isn't rust."

Nick quickly contradicted, "Well, I scraped the seam pretty hard with my pocketknife, but the rust is so thick—"

Mr. Watkins inhaled audibly. "Your pocketknife?" He looked up and grumbled, "Never a pocketknife. That'll likely do more damage than good." His voice trailed off as he repeated, "Never a pocketknife." The jewelry shop owner held the box above the counter and angled the desk lamp closer to them so they could see more clearly. He rotated the box under the bright beam of light. He repeated, "Your problem isn't rust. It's corrosion."

"OK... well, can you open it?" Jo asked.

Eddie stepped up to the counter now, and all three kids looked intently at the jeweler who rubbed the gray stubble on his chin, then blinked his magnified, brown eyes several times. He appeared to be deep in thought.

Mr. Watkins didn't answer the question but continued his analysis, murmuring, "The pitting is fairly uniform across each surface." Using a dull #2 pencil, he pointed to the lumpy seam between the lid and sides of the box. "This thick **crevice corrosion** clearly developed in a damp environment that was entirely deprived of oxygen, and now, the corrosion prevents it from opening." Mr. Watkins paused for a moment and glanced up at them. "I assume it was submerged in water, or possibly mud?"

Nick nodded.

The man scoffed, "An object's failure to function is usually rooted in **systemic** overuse or misuse."

Nick wasn't exactly sure what Mr. Watkins was talking about, but he somehow felt he was being accused of doing something wrong, even though he had been the one to rescue the box. "Uh, no, it was… uh, well…" Nick faltered.

"You didn't have it in a fish tank, did you?"

Nick felt paralyzed.

"No," Jo succinctly answered.

"So, it's corroded. We get it. But can you fix it?" Eddie, who was obviously feeling bolder now, repeated Jo's question.

"Nice of you to join us." Mr. Watkins eyed Eddie, then continued slowly, "I should be able to get it open without much trouble." He added, "Of course, you'll want to store this in a dry place from now on." He gently shook the box. "May I ask what's inside?"

Nick looked down and said, "We don't know."

Mr. Watkins gave him a long stare. Then he blinked and said, "I won't use heat then." He set the jewelry box on the empty shelf behind him and continued his work on the machine with the large, metal gears. "I'll have it ready next week."

The kids exchanged disappointed glances. A week was a long time to wait. Eddie's shoulder slumped, and he trudged to the door. The cat hopped back onto its perch.

The jeweler blew on one of the brass gears and moved his head down so his ear was almost touching the machine, as if he was listening.

"Um, excuse me—sir?" Jo asked in a polite voice.

From the doorway, Eddie cleared his throat. "Ahem!"

Nick looked over to see him discreetly yet frantically waving, beaconing his friends in toward him.

"Let's go!" he hissed. "It's only a week."

Mr. Watkins peered over his glasses, this time not bothering to adjust the lenses. He raised his eyebrows as his giant eyeballs rolled from Nick to Jo to Eddie. He frowned when he looked at Eddie.

When Eddie saw he was drawing attention to himself, he immediately dropped his flailing hand, stood up straight, and held perfectly still.

"Do you need something else?" Mr. Watkins was looking at Jo now.

"Uh, yes. Um—we were wondering, sir, if you might be able to work on the box sooner." She forced a hopeful smile. Nick glanced over his shoulder at Eddie, who looked uneasy.

Mr. Watkins frowned. He glanced over to consult his desktop calendar. Nick noted the empty shelves along the back wall. With the exception of a necklace with a blue pendant and a silver wristwatch, they were empty.

"I might have some time this afternoon," Mr. Watkins said. "I suppose I could work on it then. Come back around three." Again, he rolled over to his workstation.

Jo cleared her throat and gave a sheepish smile. "We don't mean to be pushy or anything, but would you be able to work on it any sooner?"

Mr. Watkins seemed irritated by the question. He absentmindedly scratched the back of his head and muttered something incoherent. Then he looked up.

Nick thought he noticed a twinkle in Mr. Watkins's eye, but as quickly as it appeared, the look vanished. He said, "I don't like to encourage **impudence**. It's a subtle form of impatience." He tapped the gears on the machine. "However, I've been trying for years to get this contraption to work. I suppose a few more minutes won't make a difference one way or the other."

The kids exploded with such energy and excitement; the old man was visibly startled by it.

Nick and Jo high fived. Eddie rushed back to the counter, silently pumping his fist in the air.

Mr. Watkins aimed the beam of the desk lamp at the workbench. The movement of his magnified irises was exaggerated, and they darted left and right as he inspected the box a second time. He then selected a small, electric sander from a pegboard of neatly organized tools next to the empty shelves. He turned on the sander and ran the spinning bit along the corroded seam. It made a high-pitched buzzing sound that reminded Nick of the dentist. Mr. Watkins's hands moved slowly and methodically as he tipped the silver container at various angles. Flecks of debris chipped away as he worked. After a short time, he clicked off the sanding tool.

"Well. That should do it." Testing the hinges, he rocked the lid up and down then opened the lid. His lips parted slightly, and he stared a moment before asking, "Where did you say you found this?"

Nick replied, "I was just out exploring and came across it by accident."

Mr. Watkins closed the lid and placed the box on the counter. Eager to see the contents, Nick, Jo, and Eddie crowded around the small, silver box.

Nick lifted the lid. Inside was a small, silver key.

Revealed

BLACK SPLOTCHES OF TARNISH COVERED THE surface and reminded Nick of an old key he'd seen at a museum once.

"Whoa!" Eddie exclaimed.

Mr. Watkins opened his mouth to say something but was interrupted by the bell over the door. The door shop swung wide. A familiar-looking man carrying a briefcase and wearing a yellow polo shirt and khaki pants strolled in. At first, Nick couldn't remember where he'd seen him before. After all, he'd only been in Mapleton one day and had only met a few people.

The man pushed his sunglasses to the top of his head where his blond hair was gelled into perfect spikes. His suntanned skin accentuated his artificially white teeth when he smiled, and Nick immediately recognized him as one of the realtors whose face he'd seen on the "*For Sale*" sign when he and Uncle John had driven through town.

"Well, well!" the blond man said in an impressed tone as he looked at the group of kids. "Business sure is hoppin' today, eh Gordo?"

"Hello, Ty." Mr. Watkins stood up.

"I'm here for my watch," Ty replied, "and the necklace, if it's ready."

Mr. Watkins rolled his chair a few feet back and retrieved the watch and necklace, then handed them across the counter. "I didn't find any problem with the necklace clasp. You said it was stuck, but it's working fine now. I polished the stone for you, too."

"Great," Ty said as he fastened the watch against the inside of his wrist. He lifted the necklace and inspected the stone. "Looks brand new. Thanks. Dani was worried the clasp was broken. This is a family heirloom, you know." He handed over a wad of folded bills and asked, "Say, mind if I hang a flier in your window? Probably won't get much attention in here, but hey," he added with a pompous smirk, "you never know."

Mr. Watkins responded, "I suppose that would be alright."

"Fantastic." The realtor then moved over to the front window, where the cat had resumed his nap. He set his briefcase down and began rummaging through the contents. He found a roll of tape and tried to pull off a piece, but the roll was empty. "Aw, shucks," he said. He stood up and returned to the counter. "You got some I can borrow? It'd save me a trip back to the office."

Mr. Watkins looked up. He sighed, thinly **veiling** his irritation at being interrupted, and replied, "I think I have a roll in the back."

Ty pointed to Mr. Watkins with both index fingers while making a clicking sound with his mouth and flashed a smile. "You're the best, Gordo."

The shop owner leaned on his cane and hobbled toward a dark blue curtain dividing the showroom from what was probably a storage room. When he didn't immediately return, Nick and his friends distracted themselves by looking around the store. Nick admired a handful of old-looking pocket watches inside a glass case. Eddie wandered over to pet the cat again. Jo looked at a collection of old posters that hung around the store.

Ty looked at Nick. "You know where he gets this stuff, right?"

Nick's stomach dropped. Jo and Eddie overheard the comment and looked panic-stricken. Just then, Mr. Watkins reappeared with a roll of tape in his hand. Ty winked at the kids as he reached for the tape then looked down at the open box and key.

"What's that you got there?" he asked.

Nick opened his mouth to reply, but Mr. Watkins snapped the box shut and said, "Just a trinket these kids brought in."

Ty raised his eyebrows. "Cute." He seemed distracted for a moment, then asked, "Since I'm here, do you have a quick second to talk real estate?" Ty looked at Nick and pointed his thumb at Mr. Watkins. "I've been trying to get this guy to put his house on the market for years, but he won't budge. I know the properties in this town like the back of my hand, and his land is worth a fortune! You know what they say: Location, location, location."

Mr. Watkins looked at the kids. "Excuse us, please." He stood up and led the realtor to the opposite side of the shop.

Eddie eyed Nick and Jo with a curious expression. Nick strained his ears. He knew it wasn't polite to eavesdrop, but the hushed tone of the conversation made it difficult to ignore the audible snippets.

Mr. Watkins sounded agitated. "I'm just not interested..." His voice faded as he turned his back. "...needs too much work…"

"...exactly why I'm bringing it up again…a seller's market, Gordon."

Ty's voice lowered, making it inaudible. A few seconds later, he shook Mr. Watkins's hand and said cheerily, "Well, when you run out of things to sell here, you know where to find me."

The bell over the door jingled again, and the other half of the realtor sign poked her head in the shop and scolded, "Tyson Cooper! There you are! I've been looking for you everywhere! Janice just called. We're gonna be late." Looking at Mr. Watkins, she added, "Hi, Gordy."

Mr. Watkins replied, "Hello, Daniela."

Seeing the kids, Dani paused to comment, "Wow! Full house in here today." She flashed a smile almost identical to her brother's and waved a hand showcasing hot pink fingernails and a half-dozen gold bangle bracelets that clanked together as she moved. "Sorry to break up the party, but I've got to steal this guy." She urged, "Let's move it, Ty! We've got a showing in fifteen minutes at the Kingston farm."

"You're the boss, Dani." Ty lowered his sunglasses and walked out.

Mr. Watkins's gaze lingered on the closing door.

Jo asked, "How much do we owe you?"

"That'll be six dollars."

Nick and Jo dug into their pockets, and each set two dollars on the counter. They looked at Eddie, who was digging around in his shoe. He slapped two sweaty, wrinkled bills on top of the pile.

Seeing the group staring at him, he asked, "What?"

Jo mouthed, *Ew.*

Nick shook his head. Mr. Watkins adjusted his glasses and reluctantly slid the six dollars into the cash register.

The Key

OUTSIDE, THE KIDS WERE JITTERY AND EXCITED. Their imaginations blazed trails through thickets of reality. They hurried their bikes across the street toward a picnic table at the park, chattering as they sat down.

"What if this key opens a treasure chest full of money?" Eddie dreamed. His jaw dropped open, and he let out a long gasp at his own suggestion. "Do you even think that's possible?"

Jo shook her head and rolled her eyes. "Definitely not. It's probably the key to a hidden room where someone is hiding evidence of a deep, dark family secret."

Nick and Eddie looked at her.

Eddie put his hand on her shoulder. "Sometimes I worry about you, Jo."

"What?" She shrugged away his hand. "I read a lot of mysteries."

Nick plopped his backpack onto the picnic table, pulled out the jewelry box, and opened the lid. The untarnished parts of the silver key glinted in the sunlight.

"Check it out." Nick inspected the details.

Eddie and Jo leaned in and looked at the long, narrow shank of the key.

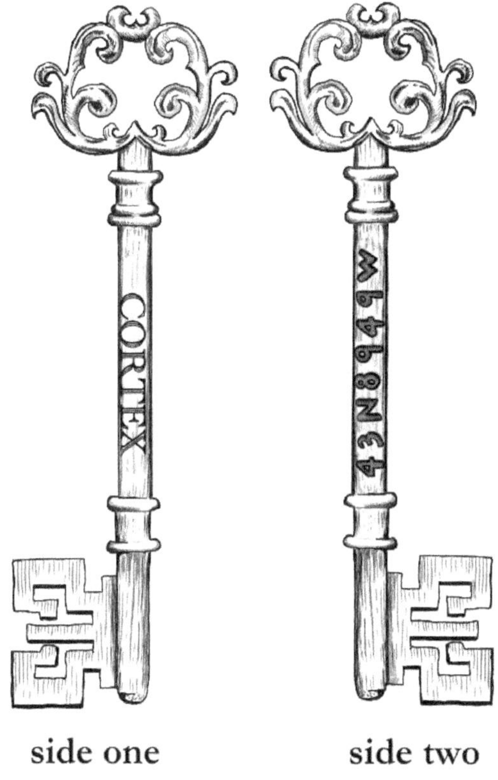

side one **side two**

"There's writing on both sides." Jo grabbed Nick's hand and pulled it closer so she could see the tiny letters.

Nick recited the string of letters. "C-O-R-T-E-X. Cortex?" He flipped the key over and read the other side, "4-3-N-8-9-4-9-W. What do you think that means?"

"Maybe Cortex is the brand," Jo offered, "but the forty-three-whatever? No idea."

Eddie replied, "Maybe it's the combination to a safe."

"That's an awfully long string of numbers," Jo said, rubbing her forehead. "Plus, a combination lock doesn't need a key, just the code."

"How are we going to figure out what this opens?" Eddie asked.

Jo's face brightened. "Hey! My mom had an extra key made at the hardware store. Maybe someone over there could tell us what type of key this is. It looks really old."

Nick looked at his friends. He recalled the scene from the garage, and his stomach clenched. "I think...maybe we should keep this a secret for now."

Eddie asked, "What for?"

"Well—" Nick looked off into the distance. "What if this key actually leads to—I don't know—something amazing—or important?"

"Solid point." Eddie touched his fingers to his forehead in a salute. "No adults."

Jo frowned. "I'm not following."

"Oh, come on," Eddie huffed, "Don't tell me you can't predict what would happen if we showed your parents this key." He paused and nodded toward Nick. "Even Big J would—you know."

Jo asked, "What are you talking about? Why would asking an adult about the key be a problem?"

Eddie gave Nick a knowing look. He rolled his eyes and explained, "Jo isn't used to operating outside of the parameters of parental permission." He looked pleased with his vocabulary choice.

Jo's head jerked toward him. "What is *that* supposed to mean?"

Eddie grinned. "Tell me, Jo—have you ever had an overdue library book?"

"Of course not." She sounded offended.

"You just proved my point." Eddie laced his hands behind his head. "You see, Jo," he spoke as if conveying ancient wisdom, "there are two ways of thinking when it comes to making decisions that parents may—or may not like."

She raised an eyebrow. "Care to enlighten me?"

Eddie held out one of his hands, as if holding an invisible object. "On the one hand, you have people—like you—who always ask permission before they do anything."

"Well," she scoffed, "I'm not a troublemaker, if that's what you mean. I'm not ashamed to admit that my parents trust me."

"Nor should you be," he replied. "But I speak from experience when I say that life can have a little more zest when you live by the second philosophy."

Nick grinned. He knew what Eddie was going to say next. Nick had been in plenty of situations that required weighing the outcome of caution versus boldness. He usually defaulted to the side of caution, since his parents were pretty strict. However, he was guessing Eddie might be the kind of kid who leaned slightly toward the reckless side of decision making. And Nick didn't find that surprising. As the youngest of seven, Eddie probably got away with a lot.

Eddie held out his other palm. "On the other hand—personally, I think it's better to ask for forgiveness than for permission. That's all."

Jo crossed her arms. "And this relates to the key—how exactly?"

Eddie threw his hands in the air and looked at Nick, exasperated. "She's too much of a goody-goody to understand."

Nick translated, "This key is like a project. It's a clue to a mystery, and we're the detectives. If we bring our parents or Big J into the mix, they'll do that thing adults do—you know? Where they say they're helping, but then completely take over?"

Jo crossed her arms. "Alright. I get it. Let's just keep the key between us—for now anyways. But for the record, I don't want to do anything that'll get us into trouble. OK?"

Nick nodded and tucked the box into the front pouch of his backpack.

Eddie put his hand over the bag. "No. No way."

Nick looked at him. "What?"

Eddie pulled a grubby, beige shoelace from one of the pockets of his vest. "Always keep your most valuable assets on your person."

"*On your person*?" Jo mocked.

Eddie frowned. He reached over to the metal box and picked up the key. "Think about it. If, say, a certain couple of bully jerks were to take Nick's bag, they would then also have the key." He threaded the frayed shoelace through the hole at the end of the key and tied the ends in a tight, overhand knot. "Here."

Nick exchanged a glance with Jo and then draped the homemade necklace over his head.

Jo smirked. "And just like that, our mystery key is transformed into a fashion statement." With a gleam in her eye, she added, "And remember, City Kid, at no time is that stylish accessory to be removed from *your person.*"

"Joke all you like, but you know I'm right." Eddie drummed his hands on the table. "And," he added, wiggling his eyebrows, "if the key leads to something incredible, we can take all the credit." Eddie flopped his arms onto the table and said, "Well, are we at least going to talk about the fact that we survived an encounter with Mr. Watkins? What was with that *DIRT* comment, though?"

Nick replied, "About old jewelry covered in dirt?"

Jo corrected, "He said, and I quote, '*Dirt is always problematic.*'"

"Either way," Eddie concluded, "it sounds like he has experience removing dirt from jewelry. I'm just saying, he basically admitted to being a graverobber."

"Whatever." Jo shook her head. "You're being paranoid. We got the box open. We survived." She added, "And sure, Mr. Watkins is a little odd, but he's not so bad."

"It's probably all an act. And you heard what that realtor asked, right?"

Nick countered, "Just because he sells used jewelry doesn't necessarily mean it came from inside a coffin."

"Exactly," Jo agreed. "My mom always says, 'What you get is what you're looking for.' We should be careful about what we assume is true."

Eddie shook his shoulders. "I'm still jittery."

She patted Eddie on the back. "Don't worry, now that we got the key, we won't ever have to go back there again."

Nick grinned.

Jo stood up. "Well, I have to get going. I told my mom I would return a library book for her. Don't unlock anything without me." She swung a leg over her bike and patted the hard, rectangular lump in the bike bag hanging from the handlebars. "I'll see if I can find anything at the library out about old keys." She waved as she pedaled away.

"Wanna head over to the comic shop?" Eddie asked. "I'm dying to get the next issue of *Captain Kidd*."

Nick grinned and pulled a five-dollar bill from his pocket. "I've been saving this for that very reason."

Eddie looked at his sock and said, "Ugh!" He dropped his head onto the table. "Dang it!"

"What's wrong?"

"Thanks to our jewelry bill, now I don't have enough! I knew I should've brought more. I just never know if those jerks are going to steal my cash."

"Well, how far is your house?" Nick asked.

Eddie cringed.

"Is it a long way away?"

"No, it's really close, actually."

"Then what's the problem?"

Eddie exhaled. "It's just that it's my week to clean the bathroom, and, well, let's just say, the shower drain is not going to be a fun project. If my mom sees me, well—she lives by a work-first, play-later mentality."

"My mom's like that, too." Nick wrinkled his nose and said, "It's up to you."

Eddie let out a long sigh. "Fine. Let's go. I just hope we can get in and out without being spotted."

The Gauntlet

Nick followed Eddie's example and leaned his bike against the garage of a two-story yellow house.

"My mom's car is gone. She must be at the store. Let's get in and out."

They jogged up five porch steps and quietly entered through the wide, front door. Eddie silently closed the door behind them.

"Eddie!" A girl wearing a black tank top and jean shorts came clomping down the stairs. Her right earlobe was sandwiched between her fingers as she fastened a large, gold hoop earring. Her eyes were rimmed in black, globby makeup, and her two-inch long fingernails seemed to make fastening the earring difficult.

Two seconds inside, and they'd already been spotted by this girl, whom Nick guessed was one of Eddie's six older sisters.

"Per-fect ti-ming," she said, enunciating the syllables as she spoke. "I'm *sooo* late for work. I need you to get the vegetables cut for dinner tonight."

"No way, Lucia," Eddie said as he shot past her up the stairs. "You're on your own." Looking at Nick, he beckoned, "C'mon. My room's this way."

Lucia—the sister Nick remembered as the reason Eddie was out of Band Aids—looked annoyed and intimidating but hadn't seemed to notice him. He followed Eddie up the stairs, trying to be invisible.

Lucia scoffed. "Come *on,* Eddie. You *owe* me."

Eddie stopped in his tracks. "I don't owe you anything." He turned around slowly. "What about yesterday and the groceries that you 'forgot' to pick up? I looked ridiculous pulling a wagon full of paper bags across town." He crossed his arms. "A community service officer pulled up next to me and asked if I had a place to sleep." Eddie leaned on the railing. "He thought I was *homeless*, Lucia! I had to call Mom to prove I wasn't a runaway. I'm done doing your work for you."

"Give me a break. It's not my fault your messy hair and stupid vest make you look like a **vagabond**. And don't tell me you don't have *five* minutes to chop some stupid potatoes and carrots."

"Nope." Eddie continued up the stairs. "Plus, I helped mom make dinner last night, and I have a friend over, and we don't have time. C'mon, Nick."

As Nick scooted by, Lucia grabbed his arm. He winced from her vise-like grip. Her fingernails pressed into the tender skin of his upper arm. Her eyes bore a hole through his skull. "Nick, was it? You look like a skilled vegetable chopper. If you work together—"

"No."

Nick winced and Lucia released her iron grasp. Her voice lowered an octave, and she sounded genuine. "Come on, please? I do things for you *all* the time." She added in a sweet, higher pitch, "You have no idea how hard it is to be as busy as I am."

When Eddie ignored her and walked away, Lucia let out a melodramatic groan and said, "Fine. But fair warning, I know *exactly* how to make your life miserable."

"Mom said I should never give in to bullies," Eddie sang out from the hallway.

A frustrated shriek echoed through the stairwell.

Eddie pulled Nick through his bedroom doorway and closed the door. "Phew!" he said, leaning against it. "That went *a lot* better than I thought it would."

Nick rubbed the five red, crescent-shaped indentations on his arm and was curious about the scenario Eddie had envisioned. He guessed it involved Band-Aids.

Eddie zigzagged through a maze of dirty clothes toward the window. Muted voices came from the driveway below. He separated two slats in the miniblinds. "I knew it!" he exclaimed in a low voice. "Check this out."

Nick copied Eddie's path through the clothes on the floor and peered down at the driveway. Lucia was leaning against a white Jeep now parked outside the garage. She was smiling and twirling her fingers through her hair.

"I *knew* it," Eddie repeated.

Nick looked at him. "Knew what?"

Eddie pointed at the boy sitting in the Jeep. "That's Jesse Stapleton. Remember him from the ice cream shop? He's Lucia's new boyfriend. And it's *not* Tuesday."

Nick was lost. "Is that important?"

"Yes." Eddie looked at Nick to explain. "Lucia works on Tuesday. It's not Tuesday, so she doesn't have to work, which means she was *lying*—hoping to push her dinner chores off on me, so she could cruise around town with Jesse."

Nick said, "Not cool."

"Not cool at all, but at least I didn't fall for it." Eddie opened the top drawer of the desk in the corner of his room and rifled through an extremely messy pile of crumpled papers and pens until he found what he was looking for—a small plastic cylinder with a yellow lid. He unscrewed it and tapped something into a small bowl. The desk was so full of clutter, Nick hadn't even noticed the fishbowl, or the creature in it.

"That's Jerry, my African dwarf frog," Eddie explained.

Nick peered at the tiny, gray frog, who lay on the multicolored pebbles at the bottom of the bowl near a purple, plastic plant. The frog straightened his long legs to propel himself forward and began attacking the sinking pieces of food.

"What's he eating?" Nick looked at the shriveled, reddish-brown threads.

"Jerry likes frozen blood worms." Eddie reached over the desk to a shelf on the wall. Using both hands, he grabbed a ceramic statue of Snoopy and plopped down on his bed.

While Eddie vigorously shook the bank upside down onto a green and blue plaid bedspread, Nick watched Jerry gobble the soggy, red worms. His thoughts drifted back to the leech and little box—and the key.

"How do you think that key ended up in the lake?"

Eddie sifted through the coins. "Who knows? Could've fallen out of a fisherman's pocket." He plucked the quarters from the pile and looked up. "The important question is: What does the key unlock?"

Nick nodded.

"It's not a diary key, I'm sure of that."

Nick had never seen a diary key, but the confidence in Eddie's tone made it clear to Nick that *he* had. And judging from the fact that Eddie had six sisters, this made sense.

Eddie funneled the unneeded coins back through the slot in the top of Snoopy's head. They landed inside with a cascading *plink-plink-plink-plink* sound. He then dropped a handful of quarters into a large pocket on his vest, zipped it closed, and handed the bank to Nick. "Feel how heavy this is."

"Wow."

Eddie patted his vest pocket. "And that's without two dollars in quarters." Eddie took the statue back and said, "The bathroom scale says three pounds, but it's gotta be more like ten or eleven." He affectionately stroked Snoopy's smooth, shiny head. "This is two years' worth of blood, sweat, and tears."

"Chores?"

Eddie nodded. "Plus, my funds have really added up ever since I got wise to Lucia's 'Sister Tax' scam."

Nick tipped his head to the side. "What's that?"

Eddie smirked. "Lucia tricked me into believing all little brothers had to pay their oldest sister part of their allowance. She called it the 'Sister Tax.' When my mom found out, she was livid. Lucia was grounded for a month. I won that round, but she still holds a grudge."

"Geez," Nick said, "did she have to pay you back?"

"Every nickel, dime, and penny."

As he returned Snoopy to the shelf, Eddie said, "OK, let's get outta here." He opened the door and said quietly, "Don't step on the fourth step—it's got a squeak."

"What?"

But Eddie had already disappeared into the hallway. Nick caught up with him just as they passed a bedroom with strands of beads hanging from the doorframe.

From somewhere beyond the veil of purple and gold, a girl called out, "Eddie, it's your week to clean the bathroom."

Nick took a silent step on the faded, rose-colored carpet, and the floor squeaked when he put down his heel. Eddie's eyes flashed, and he squashed a finger to his lips. They both cringed as the floor squeaked again when Nick lifted his weight.

"Eddie?" The voice called again, "Eddieeee??"

Eddie froze and held a hand up to indicate they should remain still.

"Eddie, I know you can hear me. I can hear you breathing. Mom said that bathroom isn't going to clean itself." The voice faded as they tiptoed down the stairs.

Eddie skipped over the fourth step. Nick, assumed this was the aforementioned squeaky step and braced one hand on the railing while pressing the other against the wall. He lowered himself silently over the tattling tread. As they neared the bottom, Nick heard Lucia's voice through an open window in the living room. She and Jesse were still in the driveway. Eddie made a sharp turn in the entryway and led Nick toward the back of the house. He whispered, "OK, we made it past Gianna. Lucia's outside. Two down, four to go. Try to keep moving. Next—this is what I call 'The Gauntlet.' Stay close."

They slid past the wide doorway to the living room, where two more sisters were sitting on opposite ends of a long couch. One looked a little older than Nick, and a shock of her short, brown hair was dyed bright pink. She wore a pair of metallic blue headphones and bobbed her head to a noiseless beat. The other girl, who looked slightly older, wore her light-brown hair in a ponytail. She sat upside down and backwards on the couch, with her feet dangling over the backrest. Her head hung inches from the ground while she read a paperback book.

Without looking over, the upside-down girl said, "Mom says it's your week to clean the bathroom."

"I KNOWWWW, Angelina."

The headphones-wearing sister noticed Eddie and loudly said, "It's your week—" but the other sister cut her off, saying, "I already reminded him."

"What?" She pulled the left side of her headphones away from her ear.

Angelina shouted so she could hear over the music, "I already told him!"

As Eddie moved past the doorway, Nick watched as the headphones girl casually tipped her head toward her brother and announced loudly, "You're on Lucia's radar."

"I'm not getting stuck doing her chores, Isabella," Eddie muttered as he and Nick approached the next room.

Eddie grabbed a handful of cheddar crackers from a bowl on the counter and weaved around a huge kitchen table that stretched past the wide, arched doorway into the dining room. When they reached the back door, Eddie crammed the crackers into his mouth. Using both hands, he grasped the handle of the sliding glass door and used his body weight to heave it open. Grinning and chewing, he looked at Nick and tipped his head toward the open exit.

They stepped outside onto the back deck, where two more sisters sat at the patio table, facing one another. Apart from the fact that one of them wore purple, thick-rimmed glasses and a sleeveless button-down denim shirt while the other wore heavy, black eye make-up and a black T-shirt with a dragon skeleton on it, they looked identical. A wooden chess set was spread out between them.

"I don't know why you keep using the Sicilian Defense," Nick heard the one with the dragon shirt say. "It never works for you."

"Once again, you're overconfident," the other replied as she pushed her purple glasses up, "and once again, you have underestimated the tactical potential of the lowly pawn fork."

Without taking her eyes off the pieces, the girl with the glasses said, "You know, it's your turn, Eddie."

The girls smiled at each other, then turned their heads in an eerily synchronized motion.

"The bathroom," he replied. "I know."

The girl with the dragon shirt glanced up from the game and asked, "Who's your friend?"

"This is Nick. Nick, Sophia and Loretta."

"Hi, Nick," the girls said, in unison.

Nick forced a smile at them and gave a silent wave as Eddie grabbed his arm and pulled him toward the edge of the deck.

"OK." Eddie glanced at the side yard. "All clear. Let's go."

Their bikes were still leaning against the outside wall of the garage. Nick could hear the voices of Lucia and Jesse coming from the driveway. They were both out of eyesight. Jesse was laughing at something Lucia said.

As he quietly mounted his bike, Eddie whispered, "On my signal, pedal as fast as you can toward the street." He peeked around the corner of the garage with his foot poised on his higher pedal.

"Maybe we should—" Nick began.

"NOW!"

As Eddie sped past the Jeep, Nick heard Lucia shout, "Hey!"

Nick threw a leg over his bike and jammed his foot down toward the pedal, but his foot slipped off, and he scraped his shin on the jagged plastic. *Aghhhh!* Trying to ignore the pain, he jammed his foot down again, this time launching forward.

Eddie was already half-way down the long driveway, and Lucia was pumping her legs and arms like a machine as she closed the gap. Nick knew it would be a struggle to catch up with Eddie, let alone bypass Lucia. He shot past the Jeep, where Jesse gawked at the unfolding scene.

Jesse called out, "Hey, man. I know you."

Nick immediately began closing in on Lucia, who was still sprinting after Eddie. Nick had never seen someone run so fast. Before Lucia could hear Nick approaching, he swung wide and whipped past her, just outside the reach of her fingernails. He then glanced over his shoulder and saw her shift targets. She was now sprinting after *him*. Lucia veered toward Nick and was coming at him from an angle. Her arm stretched out, and she took a swipe at him. She grazed his backpack and nearly knocked him off-balance. Nick heard a metallic clatter, and over his shoulder, he saw Lucia stop running. She doubled back and reached down to the ground. Nick's eyes focused on her outstretched hand as it picked up—the metal box from the lake. It had fallen out of the open pocket of his backpack.

Nick grasped the key through his shirt and was really glad Eddie had insisted on the shoelace. He was disappointed about the box and considered turning around to reclaim it, but remembering Lucia's fingernails sinking into his forearm helped him decide to keep going. He still had the key, at least.

Once he knew the coast was clear, Nick cruised along the sidewalk. A few driveways ahead, he saw Eddie's head poking out from behind a tall hedge. Nick was still out of breath by the time he caught up. Eddie looked down the street in the direction of his house.

Panting, Nick said, "You—don't think—she'll—follow us?" He paused to catch his breath. "Do you?"

"Nah. She's really lazy." Eddie didn't seem to be out of breath at all.

"Except when *(pant)* she's—sprinting."

"Right. I told you she's on the track team, right?"

Nick shook his head. "I must have missed that detail." He looked at Eddie. "I dropped the box."

Eddie gave him a knowing look.

"Good thing I had the key *on my person*," Nick half-joked.

"Exactly." Eddie laughed.

Nick smiled and looked at Eddie's bike. Jo was right. There was an extraordinary amount of duct tape covering every inch of the frame. "That bike is shockingly fast."

Eddie smiled. "As long as the pedals stay attached, it's not bad."

"What was all that about anyways?"

Eddie gave a shrug. "What do you mean?"

"The vegetables? The bathroom? Fleeing for our lives?"

Eddie shrugged again, seeming not to comprehend the questions. Nick couldn't imagine living with six older sisters. He wondered if that was a typical day in the Bernadelli house.

"What do you think would've happened if she'd caught us?"

Eddie shrugged. "I dunno." Then he patted the pocket full of coins. They rattled, softly. "Ready to check out the comic shop?"

"Sure."

The boys spent half an hour in the comic shop, and each purchased the newest issue of *Captain Kidd.*

Nick kneeled down and carefully slid the new issue of *Captain Kidd* into his backpack.

A loud crackle of static blared from boys' walkie talkies.

"Red Fox? City Kid? Does anyone copy? Over."

Eddie unclipped his walkie talkie. "What's up, Anna Graham? Over."

"Guys, I figured something out. Meet me at Castle Rock. Over."

Eddie looked at Nick. "Roger that. We're on our way. Over."

A Map

NICK AND EDDIE RACED ALONG THE ROAD TOWARD Castle Rock. As they rounded the last curve near the hideout, they heard the thrum of an engine approaching from behind. Nick glanced over his shoulder to see a familiar gold seagull, wings outstretched, barreling toward them. The boys immediately hugged the side of the road, narrowly avoiding being clipped by the passenger side mirror.

As the car sped past, Nick caught a glimpse of Steven Caldwell's steely gaze, staring at them through the tinted window. Despite the warm air, he felt a shiver crawl up his spine. The car disappeared around the bend, leaving behind a cloud of dust.

"What was that all about?" Eddie pedaled back onto the road, waving his hand in front of his face to clear a swath of fresh air.

Nick coughed and rubbed the dust out of his eyes. He pulled alongside Eddie and replied, "I don't know. There's something really weird about those guys."

"Seriously." Eddie shot a concerned look to Nick. "People don't usually take this back route. You don't think—they wouldn't be following us, would they?"

Nick shook his head. "I don't know. Uncle John was talking to a guy named Stan about a big tree branch that fell during the storm. He said it's blocking one of the roads. Maybe they're taking a detour."

"Maybe." Eddie slowed his bike. "The hideout's just ahead.

Nick hopped off his bike and steered toward the ditch.

"Wait." Eddie looked up and down the road then said, "All clear." He pushed his bike through the tall grass along the side of the road and dropped it, out of sight, behind a bank of dense, evergreen shrubs. "Ever since Billy and Jack **infiltrated** our hideout, we *always* check to make sure the coast is clear, and no one is following us."

Nick thought this precaution was a little **counterintuitive**, since the boys already knew about the hideout and the cooler, but he felt it was best to keep it to himself. He stashed his bike next to Eddie's, then followed him through a maze of narrow trails through the woods. He was glad Eddie was here to show him the way since he'd only been to Castle Rock once before, and that was by canoe.

The trail was winding as it led through the forest. In the cool shade of the towering trees, Nick inhaled the rich, sweet smell of moss and pine. Their feet crunched against the dry pine needles covering the narrow path. When they came to a massive oak tree, Eddie stopped, cupped his hands around his mouth, and made a strange, squawking noise.

The call was repeated back. "Cuh CAW, Cuh CAW."

Eddie looked at Nick and nodded. "All clear."

A moment later, the trail made a sharp turn around a huge rock formation Nick recognized. It was Castle Rock. They ducked under a low-hanging branch and entered the clearing. Jo was sitting on a red and white striped sheet secured with rope between two trees. Nearby were a black-and-white polka dot sheet and a green checkered sheet, hanging like wide smiles.

"Hammocks? Cool!" Eddie exclaimed as he took a running leap and flopped onto the green and white sheet.

Jo beamed. "My mom's been cleaning the linen closet and said we didn't need these anymore." She held up her hands. "And voilà! Now our shorts won't be wet from sitting on waterlogged stumps."

Nick tested the strength of his hammock before sitting down. The ropes on either end made creaking sounds as they tightened, and the fabric sagged several inches, but the knots held, and he swung, suspended, off the ground. "These are great," he said, sitting sideways. He used his feet to rock back and forth.

Eddie lay on his stomach and was sprawled out like Superman, swinging face down. "So, whad'ya figure out?" He pulled against a handful of tree roots to propel himself forward and backward.

"Well, it's just a hunch, really," she replied, "about the letters and numbers on the key."

Nick looked at her, eyebrows raised.

Eddie let his feet drag and coasted to a stop. His expression dropped. "Is it another code?"

"Not exactly. I think it might be coordinates—to a location." She continued. "Remember learning about latitude and longitude in school?"

"You think they're geographic coordinates on a map?" Nick asked.

Her head bobbled up and down.

"Of course!" Eddie agreed.

Jo's eyes glittered with excitement. "If I'm right, the coordinates just might indicate the location of something."

"Something that can be unlocked." Eddie started swinging again.

Jo asked, "What are the numbers? Forty-three something?"

Nick pulled the key out from under his T-shirt.

Eddie wore a pleased expression on his face. "Notice how convenient that was?"

Nick gave a half-smile.

"Alright, alright." Jo rolled her eyes. "You're a genius."

Nick looked at the tiny numbers and letters on the key. "It says four-three-N-eight-nine-four-nine-W."

"OK, if these are coordinates, the N and W stand for north and west." Eddie stated.

"Right," Jo agreed. "The first number is latitude, which indicates how far north or south the location is from the equator."

"Where's a globe when you need one?" Eddie asked.

Nick kneeled down and brushed away a section of pine needles until he reached the sandy dirt beneath. "Here," he said as he drew a circle on the ground.

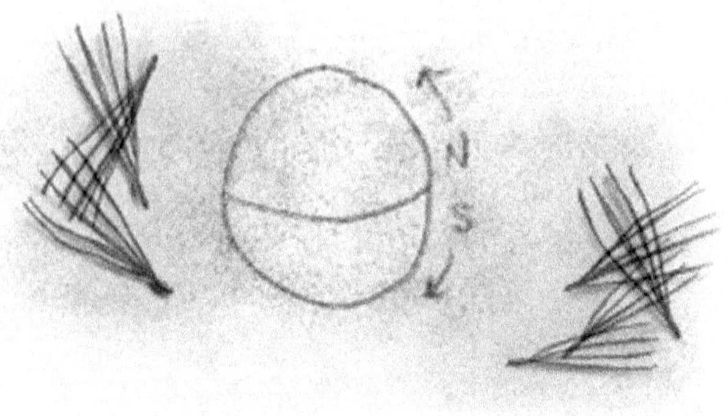

"Pretend this is the Earth. The equator is located here, at zero, and divides the Earth into the northern and southern halves or hemispheres." He drew a line across the middle. "Our first number ends with the letter N, so we know the location on the key is somewhere in the Northern Hemisphere, between the equator and the North Pole." He pointed to the top half of the circle.

"Right," Jo agreed. "For example, the North Pole is ninety degrees north of the equator, and *our* number—" Jo paused. She grasped the key dangling from Nick's neck and pulled it toward her, bringing Nick with it. "Our number is forty-three-N. In other words, forty-three degrees north of the equator."

"About half-way between the equator and the North Pole." Eddie calculated.

Nick regained his balance. "So, if the key unlocks something halfway between the equator and the North Pole—that puts us in North America, right?"

"A, Australia and Antarctica are the only continents *not* found in the Northern Hemisphere," Jo said, "which is where the second coordinate comes into play."

"Longitude." Nick drew a second line on the circle, **perpendicular** to the first.

Eddie leaned in and said in a hushed tone, "I don't usually like social studies, but this is great!"

Jo looked **incensed**. "How can you *not* like social studies?"

He groaned, "Too many facts to memorize—but this is cool. I feel like an actual treasure hunter. Why can't we do stuff like *this* in school?" He looked up and gasped. "Oh, my gosh! Guys—I know I said this before, but—seriously—what if we're on the trail of an actual treasure?" He added, "Was Captain Kidd real?"

"I think Captain Kidd was a real guy, but I'm sure the stories in the comics are made up." Nick grinned. "Treasure or not, we're definitely on the trail of a real-life mystery."

Jo patted his arm and looked impatient. "What's the next coordinate?"

Nick looked back at the key and frowned. "The longitude coordinate is a huge number. Eight thousand-nine hundred-forty-nine degrees west? That can't be right."

Jo scrunched her lips to the side. "No. Latitude and longitude numbers all have to do with degrees of angles in a circle because the Earth is round."

Nick added, "A circle only has three hundred-sixty degrees."

"But coordinates are half of that." Jo crossed her arms. "Coordinates only measure half of the sphere—so one-eighty is the max. Our number is eight-nine-four-nine-W, so—"

"Our number is waaaay too big," Eddie finished her sentence.

"Maybe the extra numbers are leftovers, like fractions," Nick suggested.

Jo's eyes lit up. "That's it! There aren't decimals in latitude and longitude to indicate fractions, but I remember learning that the extra amount *can* be divided up into minutes, and the space between minutes is divided up into seconds. Our longitude coordinate is eighty-nine degrees and forty-nine minutes west of the Prime Meridian."

Nick and Jo looked at Eddie and saw a perplexed expression on his face.

Sensing their gaze, he quickly nodded and burst out, defensively, "Yes, I know what the Primer Indian is." A red flush crept up his cheeks.

Jo opened her mouth, probably to correct him, but Nick interjected, enunciating clearly, "The Prime Murh-id-ee-an. Right." He hoped his clear articulation of the words wasn't too obvious, but he wanted to save Eddie from further humiliation. "That's like the equator, but it runs north and south."

"Exactly," Jo confirmed.

Nick looked at his drawing. "I don't remember exactly how far the Prime Meridian is from the United States. It would help if we had a map."

"Well, that's what I wanted to show you." Jo grinned. "While I was at the library, I did some digging around and—" She reached into her backpack and produced a long, rolled up piece of paper. "I found this."

"What's that?" Eddie asked.

Nick and Jo looked at Eddie.

After a brief pause, Jo rolled her eyes and sighed. "It's a map, Eddie. The thing we were just saying we needed. We were literally just talking about this."

Jo sat down on the ground near her hammock and unfurled the paper across a carpet of dry pine needles. Nick and Eddie secured the edges with stones.

"I mean *where* did you find this?" Eddie asked as he ran a finger along the edge. "It looks old."

"I borrowed it from the library when I realized the numbers on the key were possible coordinates," she said in a self-satisfied tone.

The map looked like an antique.

"I'm surprised they let you take this," Nick commented.

"Don't worry," she said. "I'll take it back when we're done with it. They won't even know it's gone."

A silence hung in the air. Something about the way Jo had phrased that sentence seemed odd.

"Don't you mean you'll *return* it when we're done? And what do you mean they won't know—" Eddie gasped as he connected the dots. "Wait a minute! Did you steal this?"

Nick looked at Jo, unable to hide the concern he felt.

She made eye contact, then looked down at the ground. "I was thinking about what you said earlier, about asking for forgiveness rather than permission and…" She trailed off.

DANBURY
WARRENVILLE
MILLER-BENNETT MINE
CRANBERRY RIVER
MAPLETON
1890
N
E
S

"Yeah, but that doesn't really apply when we're dealing with a rare historical document, Jo." Eddie's arms flew into the air. "You can't steal from a *library*—especially when there's possibly only one of the items in existence!"

She shot an angry look at him. "We have a map that might show us more about the key, OK?"

Eddie held up his hands. "Fine, I'm just surprised, that's all. I mean, if I'm the one calling out irrational, impulsive decisions—I'm just saying we might get in trouble for this."

Jo looked annoyed. She flipped a braid over her shoulder. "Look, I really didn't think it through, OK? If anything happens to the map, I'll assume full responsibility."

Eddie gave a nod. "That's all I wanted to hear. I get myself into enough trouble. The last thing I need is getting blamed for someone else's lack of judgment."

"You know what?" Jo started to curl up the map. "I'll admit, this wasn't my best decision. I just thought we wanted to figure out what the key unlocks. It was right there. I picked it up. I wasn't thinking. I put it in my bag. But if you're so concerned about library property, I think I'll just take it back—"

"No—no." Eddie rested a hand on Jo's arm. "Hold on. What's done is done."

Jo looked at Nick. "Well? Are you going to chastise my bad decision-making skills, too?"

He could tell Jo was embarrassed. Her attitude had quickly plummeted from triumphant victory to guilt-driven, defensiveness.

"Well," he reasoned, "you definitely need to take it back. But—let's at least see what we can find, as long as it's here."

"Fine." Jo spread out the map again.

The map looked different than most Nick had seen. Instead of blue for the water and green for the land, this map was all shades of brown. The cream-colored paper was covered with not only lines, but tiny illustrated clusters of trees and drawings of deer and other wildlife near what appeared to be a river running the entire length of the map.

"It's like a work of art," he murmured.

Eddie nodded and said, "This very old, very important-looking—and possibly priceless—OUCH!" Eddie paused to rub his left shoulder after it received a sharp jab from Jo's fist.

Nick wrote the coordinates on the ground.

Eddie continued. "As I was saying, the Earth is a big place, and well—the map is fairly small."

"And?" Jo asked. "Your point being?" She leaned forward, scanning the document.

"C'mon." Eddie scoffed. "You can't think this tiny part of the world will actually show the random coordinates on the key. This map shows a tiny section of the Cranberry River, and a little bit of land on either side. It doesn't even show the lake which means it's nowhere near where we are."

Nick read a small section of lettering in the corner. "Mapleton 1890."

"We're wasting our time." Eddie sat back and crossed his arms. "If the numbers on the key are, in fact, a geographical location, the odds are pretty slim that this map will show the precise loca—"

"Found it!" Jo said.

Coordinates

"I can't believe it!" Nick exclaimed.

Eddie ran both hands through his hair. His jaw gaped open.

Jo's finger was planted on the exact intersection of the latitude and longitude coordinates from the key. "Forty-three degrees north and eighty-nine degrees forty-nine minutes west." She looked up with a gleam of victory in her eyes.

The intersection was marked with a small star near the edge of the Cranberry River. Jo said. "It *is* like a work of art."

Nick scanned the intricate image. "Looks like the star was drawn on separately. It don't match the ink color on the rest of the map."

"It matches these rectangles," Jo said, observing two shapes above and below the star.

Eddie nodded. "Looks like pen ink." These three shapes are kind of bluish-black, but the rest of the map is more of a dark brown."

All three shapes were drawn a short distance from the edge of the river.

"This mark over here looks like a fortress." Eddie was pointing to a chocolate-colored illustration tucked at the edge of a group of trees.

Jo inspected the unusual, jagged shape and exclaimed, "It's Castle Rock!"

Eddie looked up at the rock formation towering a few feet away.

Nick tipped his head to look at the map from a different angle. "Wow. You're right."

excitedly, planting her finger in the exact center of the latitude and longitude coordinates from the key. "Forty-three degrees north and eighty-nine degrees forty-nine minutes west." She looked up with a gleam of victory in her eyes. Her finger was planted next to a small rectangle near the edge of the Cranberry River. "Someone drew a star at the exact location of the coordinates."

Eddie removed his compass from a pocket in his vest. He balanced it in his outstretched palm and waited for the needle to settle into position. "North is—that way." He pointed toward the woods across the cleaning. "OK, so just for fun, let's assume the rectangle and the square represent a buried treasure and—"

"Hold on," Jo interrupted. "Now *you* need to be realistic. We're looking at two rectangles and a star, not an X-marks-the-spot-and-leads-to-a-buried-treasure wild goose chase."

Eddie made a face, then retorted, "Fine, whatever. But the shapes mark *something*. The key unlocks *something*." He stood up. "Think about it. A buried treasure is a possibility. Those shapes could represent two treasure chests."

Jo blew a loose strand of hair out of her eye. "You've been reading too much *Captain Kidd*," She scoffed. "Anyways, a clever pirate would never make his treasure map that obvious."

"Oh, really?" Eddie asked.

Nick was intrigued to hear what Jo's reasoning would be, considering she had recently and harshly criticized the *Captain Kidd* graphic novels he and Eddie loved.

Jo continued. "Think about it. What kind of pirate would he be if he was super obvious, huh? He would know better than to label the treasure with something as cliché as an 'X,' because if the Jade Pirate found it, he'd know exactly where the loot was buried. Captain Kidd would never leave his treasure that vulnerable."

Eddie's eyes widened. "Uh—hold on." The corners of his mouth curled into a smirk.

Jo ignored him. "So, what could the shapes represent?"

"Wait, wait, wait." Eddie shook his head. He eyed Jo. "Captain Kidd's nemesis—This Jade Pirate you so casually mentioned—didn't show up until this month's issue." The smirk stretched into a wide grin.

"So?"

"So—I think you've moved to the dark side. *You've* been reading comic books!"

She scoffed.

Nick smiled through a cringe. Eddie was right.

"You have! How else would you know about the Jade Pirate?" Eddie walked over to Jo's hammock.

He reached toward a summer math packet it appeared she'd been working on when they arrived. Jo sat up and lunged for his hand. He deflected the attack, but she got ahold of his arm. Eddie's free hand shot toward the packet, and when he lifted it, he gasped. A crisp issue of *Captain Kidd* lay hidden underneath. "Some light reading while you waited for us to get here?" He looked at Nick and reported, "It's this month's issue."

Jo reached over and tried to grab the graphic novel from Eddie, but she missed, and her hammock dumped her on the ground. Nick tried not to laugh.

She shot him a half-angry look. "Don't gang up on me!" She stood up and began picking at the pine needles snagged in the frayed edges of her denim shorts. "OK, so I picked it up to see what all the fuss was about."

Nick joined the banter, "Just admit it. Graphic novels are awesome."

She looked sheepish. "I don't *need* pictures."

"But you like 'em, don't ya?" Eddie beamed and nodded his head.

"Whatever, Eddie. Don't force me to **delve** into my vast **arsenal** of vocabulary and **obliterate** you with another verbal **annihilation**."

Eddie grinned and **deftly** stepped out of the **trajectory** of a pinecone hurtling toward him. "You know, there's a whole section of graphic novels at the library. I heard the comic book club's looking for a new president and—"

"Don't test me." Jo poised her arm, ready for a second launch, and said, "I will show no mercy."

Nick broke the playful tension and said, "C'mon. Let's try and figure out what these mysterious rectangles represent."

The three huddled around the map once again.

"Hmm," Jo said. "I don't mean to burst your bubble, but I actually don't think this is Castle Rock."

"What?" Eddie balked. "Of course it is. Look at the three pointy parts here and the rounded part there. It's an exact match."

"Look," she explained. "If you haven't noticed, Castle Rock is next to the very large Cranberry Lake, not a narrow river."

"But—" Eddie's shoulders slumped. He frowned.

Nick looked back at the map. "If the rectangles are next to the river, how far away do you think they are?"

"Hmmm," Jo replied. "It's really hard to know without any other major landmarks." She looked up at the rock. "Maybe there's another rock formation like this one along the river."

Eddie set his compass on a section of dry earth next to the map and adjusted the paper, so it was aligned with the red, triangular needle hovering over the N. "OK, we know the river feeds into the lake, north of here, and then continues flowing south after the dam."

"Wait." Nick frowned. "If Cranberry Lake was formed by a dam, how does the water get past the dam? Isn't the purpose of a dam to stop water? How can the river continue past the end of the lake?"

Jo answered, "The water is continually flowing into the lake, and the lake would eventually overflow if some of the water wasn't able to continue downstream. The wall of the dam has doors that move up and down, depending on how much water is flowing in. Like, if there's a lot of rain, they adjust the door to let more water out, so the lake doesn't flood." She added, "I did a report on it in sixth grade."

"Hmm," Eddie said. "Our coordinates are along the edge of the river, somewhere north or south of the lake, but some of the woods along the river are really thick, and there definitely aren't roads. Finding another rock formation similar to this one will be like finding a needle in a haystack."

Jo rested her head on her hands. "I wish this map was bigger and newer." She looked at the illustrations. "But even with landmarks to help narrow it down, an square-inch here represents, like, an acre in real life. We could end up looking everywhere and still never find what these shapes mark."

"My guess is it's something underground," Eddie suggested. "I mean, why bother drawing the location on a map if whatever it's marking is in plain sight? Maybe they need to be dug up."

Nick's mind was swirling with ideas. He recalled something Eddie said when they were near the Miller house. "Is it just a coincidence the Badger-lady dug holes all around Mapleton?" He ran a hand through his hair. "Maybe the Badger wasn't digging those holes because she was looking for her son."

"I don't know," Eddie replied. "I mean, everyone talks about how those holes didn't start appearing until the mine collapsed, and she went crazy. I mean, her son was trapped down there, right? What else could she have been looking for?"

"Maybe what she was looking for—" Nick dangled the key out in front of him. It glinted in the light. "—was this."

Stolen

"UGGGHHHHHH! WE'VE BEEN TRYING TO MAKE sense of this map for, like, three hours," Eddie complained.

Jo consulted her watch. "It's only been thirty minutes."

Eddie tipped his head back and let out a groan. "I need a snack." He walked over to his backpack, which was hooked on a broken pine tree limb near his hammock. He rifled through the contents and asked, "You guys want anything? I've got Tootsie Rolls, granola bars, juice boxes, and cheese doodles."

Jo smirked. "Aren't we a little old for juice boxes?"

"Oh, I'm sorry, did you bring anything better? Some ice-cold seltzer water, or perhaps fresh-squeezed lemonade?"

Nick grinned. "I'll take a granola bar and a juice box."

"Tootsie Rolls," Jo said, then added quietly, "and what flavor juice boxes?"

"Apple and fruit punch."

"Fruit punch, please."

Eddie gave her a smug look, tossed the candy and a juice box to her, then walked over to the hidden cooler. After sweeping the pine needles off the hidden lid, he restocked the hidden storage container by upending his backpack and dumping the contents inside.

"Let's see how long those last," Jo scoffed.

Nick asked, "Have you thought about putting some decoy food in there?"

"Like plastic food?" Eddie asked.

"No." Nick leaned forward. "I mean, like putting dirt inside empty granola bar wrappers, or sprinkling some potato chips with cayenne pepper."

Eddie flopped down in his hammock and replied, "We tried that, actually. We squeezed jalapeño peppers on a couple of granola bars, then resealed the wrappers, but it didn't work."

"What do you mean?"

Eddie answered, "We forgot which ones had the jalapeño juice, so we didn't eat any of them."

Jo added, "Billy and Jack raided our stash but must have gotten the only ones without the spice, because it didn't slow them down at all. They just keep coming back."

"Or maybe they really like spicy chocolate." Eddie shrugged.

"Either way, it didn't work."

Nick touched his tongue to his granola bar, testing it to see if his mouth would erupt in flames.

Jo grinned. "Don't worry. The lid got left open, and raccoons or something got the rest of the stash." She shot an accusatory look at Eddie.

His jaw dropped. "It wasn't me. I told you Billy and Jack left it open—and knowing them, they probably did it on purpose." Eddie leaned back in his hammock and jabbed the straw into the top of his apple juice.

Jo looked at Nick and smirked. She thumbed toward Eddie and mouthed, *It was him.*

Nick's shoulders shook as he silently chuckled. He watched Eddie drain the juice box until the cardboard sides collapsed.

They sat in their hammock, swinging in silence and eating. The leaves in the trees overhead fluttered quietly, and the gentle waves splashed against the rocks on the shore below. Nick leaned back and swayed in the hammock.

The shrill cry of a Blue Jay echoed through the forest. It reminded Nick of the bird on the lid of the box. As he chewed a bite of granola bar, he looked up at the trees overhead. A dead tree trunk, covered with holes hammered by woodpeckers. An idea flashed into his mind. He sat forward quickly and nearly flipped the hammock. One leg flailed in the air as he struggled to regain his balance.

Jo smirked at the awkward gracefulness. "Whoa, City Kid."

"You look like you just figured something out," Eddie said.

"Maybe." Nick collected his thoughts. "What if the shapes are markers, like maybe they're carved into the trunk of an old tree or something? Nick suggested. "How far are they from the river?"

Eddie stood up, popped the orange cheese doodle he was holding into his mouth, then kneeled down next to the map. He squinted at the tiny map key in the corner and estimated the distance between the squares. Still chewing, he said, "Well, the woods run all along the river, and the shapes are right at the edge, but you know, over a hundred years have gone by so—"

"Eddie!" Jo scolded, "You're getting cheese doodle dust on the map." She brushed away a faint trail of powdery, orange debris.

"Sheesh!" Eddie stood up and wiped his hands on his shorts. "You're the one who brought an antique map out to the woods. What'd ya expect? That it would stay perfectly clean?"

"I assumed we would be careful—so YES!"

Eddie made a production of licking his fingers one by one. Then he stood up and maneuvered down the steep bank toward the lake.

"Where are you going?" Jo called after him.

"To wash my hands so your precious map doesn't get more snack smears on it." His head disappeared from view.

Jo looked at her own fingers, then dusted her hands on her shorts. She caught Nick's eye and shoved her hands into her pockets.

Nick held up his hands. "I'm not judging." He fished a pencil out of the side pocket of his backpack and carefully made a copy of the map using a pine needle to gauge the distance between objects. He started with the outer edges of the river, then added the woods, and the castle shape. After double checking his proportions, he added the rectangles. "There. Now we can use this map, so the original stays clean."

"Good idea." Jo said as she rolled up the map from the library. When she was done, she held the scroll up to her eye, peering through the tube at the trees overhead.

Nick asked, "What are you doing?"

"Just looking at things from a different perspective." She explained, "When you block out the distractions, you can usually see details you've overlooked. Who knows, maybe I'll find a square carved into the trunk of a tree." She slowly scanned the woods across the clearing, then stopped suddenly and held perfectly still.

"Did you find something?"

"Cardinal nest." She held perfectly still. "They're usually really hard to see, but I just happened to be looking in the right spot when the female landed. I've never seen a nest in real life before. Wanna check it out?"

She handed the scroll to Nick. He panned the circular viewing window back and forth.

"I only see green leaves, no red bird," he admitted.

"Slow down—and female cardinals aren't red, they're mostly light brown, but they have a bright orange beak." She pointed to a cluster of trees just beyond the clearing. "See that "Y"" shape in the branches? She's directly above that."

Nick didn't see the Y-branch or the nest, but he did notice some movement on a narrow tree with light gray bark. "I see a small black and white bird with a black beak," he announced, trying to sound more casual than he felt. The only birds he'd seen back home were boring, sparrows or crows. He held one hand over his eye and watched the bird hop along the side of the tree. "It's got a red splotch on the back of its head."

"Cool," Jo said. "Probably a Downy Woodpecker."

Nick saw a flash of yellow, and a tiny lemon-colored bird landed on a tree several feet beyond the woodpecker. He held his breath, watching the two birds. They both held perfectly still until suddenly, they both flew away. A splash broke his attention.

Eddie shouted from the ledge below, "Hey!"

"Oh my gosh," Jo looked at Nick and giggled. "Did he just fall in?"

Nick carefully laid the map to Jo's hammock. He and Jo darted to the edge of the clearing and stood at the top of the trail. Most of the ledge below was obscured by the leaves of a prickly shrub.

"Eddie?" Jo called again.

There was no sign of their friend. Jo quickly descended the narrow path. Nick followed close behind. When they reached the ledge, they found Eddie leaning against the side of the tall, steep bank. He'd been out of sight from above. Eddie picked a stick up off the ground and glared at them.

"What's wrong with you?" Jo brushed the dirt off the back of her shorts and crossed her arms. "We thought you fell in."

He scowled. "That would've been pretty funny, huh?

"What are you talking about?" Jo asked.

"Well, you missed. You know, I don't appreciate having rocks thrown at me."

"What?" Nick was surprised. "We didn't throw rocks at you."

"Right." Eddie jabbed at the water with the stick. "I suppose it was my imagination."

"Eddie," Jo echoed, "we didn't throw any rocks."

"Then how do you explain why my pants are wet?" He pointed to a wet splotch on his pant leg.

Jo snickered. "That sounds like a personal problem."

Eddie opened his mouth to fire back, but before he could do so, they heard a branch snap in the clearing above.

"The snacks!" Eddie hissed. "It was a trick. This ends now. Come on, Bully Whisperer. Try telling 'em a joke."

Before Nick could protest, Eddie scrambled up the trail. Nick and Jo followed, but when they reached the top, the clearing was empty.

Eddie raced to the snack cooler, which was still uncovered. He pawed through the contents. "Well, I can't believe it, but everything's still here. Your anti-bully magic is amazing."

Nick shook his head. "I don't think that's how it works. Maybe it was a squirrel? Or a tree branch falling?" He glanced up at the branches towering over their heads.

Jo walked across the clearing and disappeared behind the rock formation. She called out, "What we heard was definitely not a squirrel."

Eddie scanned the surrounding understory of the woods. "The only animal large enough to make a branch snap that loudly would be—"

"A bear?" Nick asked.

Eddie let out a loud laugh. "No, City Kid. I thought it was two humans—of the bully-o-saurus subspecies—but since our food is still here, I'm guessing it was a deer."

Jo emerged from behind the rock formation. "All clear. No **troglodytes** back there." As if anticipating their question, she replied, "It means caveman or hermit." She walked two steps then froze.

"It's gone," she said, staring at her empty hammock.

Nick asked, "What's gone?"

She whispered, "The map."

Close Encounter

"C'MON!" EDDIE SHOUTED AS HE TOOK OFF INTO the woods. "If we hurry, we might be able to catch 'em and get the map back!"

Nick and Jo raced after Eddie as he darted down the path, zigzagging between inconveniently placed trees and low-hanging vines. Moments later, they stood at the side of the road, panting. They saw no one. Nothing. No people. And unfortunately, no map.

Nick bent over and rested his hands on his knees, trying to catch his breath.

"Those no-good, low-life jerks!" Jo puffed, then laced her fingers together and rested her hands on top of her head. She looked up and down the road.

Nick stood up. "You think it was Billy and Jack?"

"Of course, it was them." Eddie answered, clenching his fists as he paced back and forth. "No one else knows about our hideout. First, our snacks? Now the map?" He kicked at the loose gravel along the side of the road, scattering pebbles into the tall grass.

Jo gasped. "Guys, what if those coordinates actually *do* mark the location of something important?"

"And they find it first?" Eddie's eyes flashed in anger.

"Exactly."

"OK, let's not get ahead of ourselves here." Nick tried to be the voice of reason, but he was worried about the same thing. If the coordinates were important enough to etch onto a key and draw onto a map, they probably marked something significant. He said, "We don't know what rectangles on the mark represent, but—odds are—Billy and Jack don't either." He pulled the key out from under his shirt. "Plus, even if they do, they don't have this, which hopefully unlocks whatever is located at the rectangle."

"Nick's right." Jo's brow was knitted with concern. "Let's stick with what we know. Getting fixated on a problem has never gotten anyone anywhere. Let's try to stay focused and figure out what to do next."

Suddenly, they heard faint voices and laughter. Two figures on bicycles appeared on the road, in the distance.

"Quick! Hide!" Jo ordered.

The three friends darted into the woods. As the cyclists neared, Nick recognized the voices, and his stomach dropped.

Billy and Jack tipped their bikes into the grass and headed down the trail. They showed no indication they knew they were being watched and every indication they had been on this trail many times before. Crouching motionless from his **clandestine** spot amidst the branches of a dense evergreen tree, Nick's heart was pounding so loudly, he felt the rhythmic pressure pounding in his ears. His eyes darted around as he looked for his friends. Jo was nowhere to be seen, but he had a clear view of Eddie, who stood about thirty feet away, with his back against a wide tree at the edge of the trail. Billy and Jack were approaching from the opposite side. Nick watched Eddie's fingers curl into fists. In a few seconds, the intruders would be within striking distance of Eddie's clenched, white knuckles.

Don't do it, Eddie, he thought. His dad's voice echoed in his head, *Never start a fight you can't win.*

Nick had never been in an actual fight, but he was fairly certain, if provoked, these two boys would obliterate them. He imagined a police detective rubbing tiny particles between his fingers and explaining to his partner the victims had been pulverized into a fine dust. Nick desperately hoped the interaction wouldn't develop into a brawl, especially out here, with no potential intervention from a sympathetic bystander. He glanced again at Eddie, whose eyes looked wild and irrational. The potential for a physical altercation had suddenly gone from **nil** to dangerously probable.

Scarcely daring to breathe, Nick peered through the branches and sized up the competition. Billy was even larger and stockier than he remembered. His feet landed with heavy thuds as he walked. His T-shirt read *Mapleton Wrestling Squad: Only the Strong Survive.* Jack, on the other hand, was thin and gangly, but he looked like the kind of kid people would call "a scrapper" and probably feared no consequences. He had the dark, heartless eyes of a shark, and his eyelids hung low in a perpetual scowl.

Nick felt lightheaded and sweaty.

Billy barked, "I'm starving. Let's see if those dweebs got anything good today."

Jack snickered. "They keep hiding it, and we keep feasting." He picked up a large stick and began taking baseball swings at each tree they passed. *WHACK!* "It's like we have a" *WHACK!* "private vending machine out here." *WHACK! WHACK!*

"Except it's free." Billy stooped down to tie his shoe.

When the sound of footsteps halted, Eddie poked his head around the tree, likely gauging his proximity to see if either boy had moved within arm's length. Fortunately, before Eddie did whatever he'd been planning, he glanced over and caught Nick's eye. Nick shook his head and put a finger to his lips. He reached under his collar and dangled the key in front of his chest, then pointed at it. He hoped Eddie would figure out what he meant. If they started a fight with these bullies, and somehow the key was spotted, they risked losing it, too.

Eddie's nostrils flared, and he shook his head with a grimace. He raised his clenched fishes. Nick shook his head in return. Without blinking, he stared at Eddie. After a moment, his friend relaxed his fists and silently dropped his hands to his sides. Nick's message had been received.

Billy's voice broke the silence. "What do you think happened to all that money?"

"I dunno," Jack replied. "My old man said it's just a rumor and we should all just forget about it, but last night I heard him and his friends talking, and they said the amount of gold stolen during that bank robbery set a world record."

Nick looked at Eddie, whose eyes widened. He mouthed, *Bank robbery!*

Jack swung at another tree. "My dad thinks he found a lead though."

"Yer dad's full of it," Billy snarked.

"Yeah, I know."

At that moment, the intruders moved past Eddie's hiding place. In his camouflage vest, he was barely visible. Jack smacked the stick against Eddie's tree. *WHACK-clunk!* The force caused the stick to break in half. Nick watched a shower of broken pieces cascading around Eddie's feet. Eddie stiffened and pressed against the trunk. Jack chucked the remaining half of the stick into the woods, directly toward the pine tree where Nick was hiding. The stick made a *WHOOSH* sound as it sailed toward him. It **ricocheted** off a tall **stob**, then tangled in the dense, pine branches inches above Nick's head. Holding his breath, he watched Jack glance in his direction. He felt certain those black eyes were looking right at him, but the two boys lumbered down the trail without hesitating.

After the boys were out of sight, Jo popped up from her hiding spot behind a fallen tree and hissed, "Let's get out of here!"

Nick jogged over to Eddie, who was still staring down the trail to the hideout.

Eddie hissed, "I'm so sick of letting them walk all over us." He glared at Nick. "We coulda taken 'em."

Nick grabbed Eddie's shoulder and said, "We have bigger issues than candy and juice boxes."

"I know," Eddie replied. "The map."

"They don't have it." Jo wheeled her bike to the road.

"But you heard what they were saying, right? They were talking about a bank robbery and gold and—"

"Whatever it was they were talking about, it wasn't the map."

"What do you mean?" Eddie hadn't put the pieces together yet.

Nick explained, "Billy and Jack just got here, which means someone else stole the map. The longer we wait to look for it, the less likely it'll be we find it."

Jo's forehead was etched with worry.

Nick guessed she was concerned the map wouldn't turn up, and she would have to decide whether to admit what she did or deal with the guilt of pretending it never happened.

Jo said, "If we leave now, maybe we can track down whoever took it."

Nick nodded.

Reluctantly, Eddie agreed. As Nick hurried to catch up with Jo, he looked over his shoulder to see Eddie crouched over one of the bikes on the ground. Seconds later, he raced to his own bike, then quickly caught up with his friends.

"What were you doing back there?" Nick asked.

Eyes smiling, Eddie scrunched his mouth to the side and wiggled his eyebrows up and down.

Jo looked at him. "You didn't."

"I couldn't help it."

When Eddie didn't elaborate, Nick asked, "Help what?"

Eddie coasted while reaching into one of his pockets. He held up a tiny green tube with a red cap.

"Superglue?" Nick asked.

Eddie grinned. "Kind of hard to ride a bike when your pedals won't spin."

Jo shook her head. "You're asking for trouble."

"Hey, nothing's off limits when people are stealing my snacks!"

They biked the entire perimeter of the lake. Finding neither anything suspicious nor any sign of the map, they circled back and rolled to a stop near Uncle John's driveway.

"Well," Jo said. "Now what?"

Nick suggested, "We can hang out here for a while and figure out a plan."

Eddie asked, "Do you think Uncle John has any more of that trail mix?"

A Different Perspective

NICK SAT WITH HIS FRIENDS AROUND THE SMALL, round table at the edge of Uncle John's living room.

"If Billy and Jack didn't steal the map, what was all that talk about a bank robbery?" Eddie asked through a mouthful of peanuts and pretzels.

"Is it really a surprise those guys spend their free time talking about criminal activity?" Jo scoffed and looked at Eddie. "And can you please chew with your mouth closed? You're spraying soggy—whatever that is—everywhere."

Eddie garbled a noise that sounded like, "Geesh!" then wiped away a semicircle of trail mix debris from the table with the inside of his vest. "But seriously, what if the stolen gold from the bank is buried at the coordinates, and the key unlocks it?" He looked around. "You have to admit, it's a possibility."

Jo shook her head. "Your imagination is totally out of control."

Nick blew out a big breath. "Guys, how are we going to find out who stole the map?"

"I don't know," Jo said, with a heavy sigh. "Billy and Jack certainly aren't the sharpest tools in the shed, but it's *really* unlikely they would steal the map, run away, then come back for candy a few minutes later."

"Unless they're much, *much* smarter than we thought," Eddie said. "Maybe they stashed the map and came back so we wouldn't suspect them."

Jo gave him a look. "Doubtful."

Nick agreed.

"They were our only suspects," Eddie lamented.

"Not necessarily." Nick's thoughts flickered back to the strange encounter he and Eddie had with the Caldwells. He described the scenario to Jo and ended with, "...and then they just sped off. That was just before we got to the hideout. They could've circled back and seen us walking down the trail."

"No way!" Eddie shook his head. "There's *no way* they saw us. I always make sure the coast is clear, and the coast was definitely clear when we ducked into the woods."

"Well, they're weird and creepy, and too many suspicious things involving them have happened." Nick counted on his fingers as he listed the mounting evidence. "One: Steven Caldwell says he's an English professor, but he didn't recognize a quote by a really famous writer. Two: He was eavesdropping on us at your dad's garage." He looked at Eddie, who nodded. "And three: The blue sports car drove past us near the hideout—minutes before the map was stolen."

"You're forgetting number four." Jo looked grim. "Remember Steven Caldwell's conversation behind the garage? He instructed the person on the other end of the line to—"

"Keep *digging,*" Nick finished the sentence. He looked from Eddie to Jo. "Well," he said, "the Caldwells just jumped to the top of our list of suspects."

"They're our *only* suspects," Eddie corrected.

"And," Jo added, "if you think about it, no one was in sight after we ran through the woods, so whoever took the map probably made a quick getaway by car."

"Hmm." Nick nodded. "True."

Eddie groaned and let his head flop backward, as if his neck had turned to spaghetti. "Guys, this is hopeless. Without that map, how are we ever going to know exactly what those coordinates mark, and where to find that spot? We can't just start digging in random places all over town."

"Well, here's some good news." Nick pulled his sketchbook out of his backpack and opened it to his most recent drawing. "I mean, it's really basic, but I made a sketch of the map."

Eddie beamed. "That's not good news, it's *great* news." He leaned in to inspect the sketch. "Pretty decent drawing."

Jo said, "We should at least be able to narrow it down to a general location—even if we have to use a different map. If the Caldwells know what the markings represent and now have the map, we'll just have to beat them to it."

Eddie funneled a handful of trail mix into his mouth and wiped his hand on his shorts. "And if they somehow beat us to it, they don't have the key to unlock—whatever it unlocks."

"Exactly," Nick murmured. He pressed the key against his chest.

The three sat in silence, listening to the ticking of the clock and the crunching noises of the dwindling trail mix.

Jo thumbed through the sketchbook, examining Nick's other drawings. "What's this?"

Nick leaned over to see which sketch she was looking at. It was a section of a pond with a tire swing tied to an enormous willow tree. "That's a sketch of my yard, back home. My mom inherited an old house from her aunt, but it needs a *lot* of work—hence my summer in Mapleton. You two should come visit sometime—when the plumbing gets fixed."

"I'm in," Jo replied. "I've always wanted to swing on a tire swing."

When Jo flipped to the next page, Eddie sat forward. "Wait a sec," he said, "is this what I think it is?"

Nick grinned. "I wondered if you'd recognize that one."

Jo furrowed her brow. She looked from Eddie to Nick and wore an expression of feeling left out. "Tropical island?"

Nick explained, "It's a scene from an issue of *Captain Kidd* from a couple months back." He pointed to a cluster of palm trees on a beach. "See, Captain Kidd drew a map that showed where he hid the treasure he and his men stole. He dug a really deep hole in the sand, near these two palm trees."

Jo rolled her eyes. "This sounds like every pirate story I've ever heard."

"But wait. It's brilliant," Eddie explained. "Captain Kidd filled the bottom of the hole with most of the treasure—all the really valuable things. Then, he filled the hole with a layer of sand and put a smaller portion of the treasure at the top of the hole. Then he drew a map marking the location."

"Ah." Jo nodded slowly. "So, if the Jade Pirate happened to find the map, he'd dig down, find the lesser loot and leave, assuming that was it."

Nick picked around the raisins in the trail mix and plucked out a few pieces of chocolate. "Captain Kidd's pretty smart."

"Speaking of pirates," Eddie eyed the chocolate in Nick's hand. "Stop plundering all the good stuff."

"Oh, my gosh!" Nick suddenly felt brilliant. "That's what you should do with your snacks."

Eddie looked perplexed.

Jo said, "Go on."

Nick explained, "You should dig the hole at the hideout twice as deep and hide the good snacks in a cooler buried below a decoy cooler with inferior snacks."

Eddie grinned. "It'd be more fun to try **laxatives**."

Jo gave Eddie a disapproving look. Then she said to Nick, "That's actually a great idea—the double cooler idea, I mean. We could put an extra piece of plywood down between the coolers and cover it with dirt. They'll never think to look under it."

"Not bad, City Kid." Eddie patted Nick on the shoulder. "Not bad at all."

Jo stood up to get a glass of water from the kitchen. On her way back into the living room, she noticed the cardboard box in the corner of the room.

She read the writing on the side and asked, "Lake Treasures?"

"Uncle John was showing me some things he's found on the shore over the years." Nick pulled the flaps open and rattled the jar of beads.

Jo reached in and pulled out the stack of newspaper clippings. "He certainly didn't find these near the water."

"The rest of this stuff was here when he moved in. It's mostly old newspapers and photographs."

Jo leafed through the articles. She unfolded a sheet of yellowed newspaper. "These are all about the tragedy at the mine."

Nick looked over her shoulder. He read the June 8, 1893 headline. *"Mine Owner and Fifty-two others Trapped in Tunnel Collapse."*

With a mysterious voice, Eddie said, "And they never found the bodies."

Nick replied, "That's creepy."

"He means they didn't find them because no one went to look for them." Jo pulled a clipping from the stack. "Here's another one: *Tragedy in Mapleton: A large group of miners were trapped underground in the town of Mapleton.*" She scanned the rest of the article. "It says here: *Improperly constructed tunnels are to blame for the collapse. Mine co-owner, Archibald Miller, was among the victims.*"

"That's the guy who lived in the creepy house next door," Eddie said.

Jo continued. "*Miller, who designed the mine and has been accused of poor tunnel layout and improper maintenance, is solely responsible for the tragedy.*" She scanned further down and quoted, "*For weeks, the tunnels were too deep and too unstable for volunteer rescue workers to look for survivors.*"

"How terrible." Nick's brow wrinkled. "So, Miller was buried alive by his own bad tunnel design."

Eddie sighed. "I'll bet their skeletons are still down there.

Jo scoffed. "Don't be crude."

He shrugged. "While they waited to be rescued, do you think any of them got hungry enough to eat the weaker ones?"

"Ew, Eddie. Stop!" Jo looked disgusted.

"What?" he defended. "I mean those guys were down there, doing their jobs and KaPOW! Crunch. Trapped—and hungry. The will to survive is very powerful."

Nick pulled another brittle, yellow newspaper clipping from the stack. "Here's an earlier article." He read the headline, "*Cornelius Bennett and Archibald Miller announce discovery of rare mineral.*" He looked up. "My uncle was telling me about that. Somebody supposedly found a big piece of neottrite."

"The Waterstone," Eddie confirmed. "Everyone in Mapleton's heard of it. Makes you live forever or something?"

"I thought it made people psychic." Jo shook her head.

Nick smiled. He wondered how many stories about the Waterstone there were. Jo let out a low whistle. "Apparently it was worth millions in the eighteen-nineties."

Nick's eyebrows raised. "A million dollars is a lot of money now. Imagine what it was worth back then."

Jo pointed to the August 1892 date at the top of the article. "That was written the year before the accident."

Nick scanned the article. "Here's a quote by that Cornelius guy. *Far beneath Mapleton lies the largest vein of neottrite this side of the Mississippi. This valuable mineral will bring great wealth to our community*. And here's a picture of him." Nick held the article up and pointed to a grainy, black and white photograph of a man with a large, handlebar mustache wearing a striped suit and top hat.

"All of these articles are about the mine," Jo said as she sifted through the pile. "Why would someone collect these?"

"My mom always keeps my essays from school," Eddie suggested. "Maybe this cabin belonged to the parent of a newspaper reporter."

"Uncle John said everyone was looking for the Waterstone," Nick reported. "I guess who ever lived here was too."

Jo read another article, "According to this one, Miller and his son were both trapped down there in the mine." She gasped. "Hey. I'll bet the person who used to live here knew them. Maybe they were friends."

Nick guessed, "They were probably keeping track of the rescue mission."

"But there wasn't a rescue mission, remember?" Eddie pointed out. "The tunnels were too unstable."

"Oh, right." A small headline caught Nick's eye. "According to this, they *did* look for them." He read aloud, "*Search for Missing Miners a Dead End.*"

"Well, that's a poor choice of words," Jo mumbled.

Eddie and Nick grimaced.

Nick read, "*After five days of removing debris, the primary tunnel in the Mapleton Mine was structurally reinforced and deemed safe enough for volunteer search and rescue teams to enter. One survivor was rescued from the primary tunnel and is reported to be in fair condition. The other fifty-two are presumed to be trapped further underground beyond a substantial cave-in. Emergency workers hope to remove the debris and add additional supports in time to save the miners, but hope is fading.*"

"Grim," Eddie murmured.

Nick glanced at the rest of the article and read a quote by Cornelius Bennett. "*I warned my former business partner, Archibald Miller about the instability of the tunnels, but sadly, he did not heed my caution. A combination of greed and careless miscalculations caused this avoidable tragedy.*" Nick continued. "The reporter writes: *The blame for the loss of these fifty-two souls has fallen to Mr. Miller, who by an ironic twist of fate and justice was among those who were trapped.*"

Jo looked through the small window in the kitchen toward the Miller house. From this distance, it was entirely obscured by trees. "No wonder no one wants to live there."

Nick looked up and said, "Uncle John said even Archibald Miller's own grandson doesn't want to deal with the old house."

Jo added, "He probably just doesn't want to be associated with his grandfather's reputation."

Eddie made a face and nodded.

"Check these out." Jo flipped through a stack of fliers. "There's stuff in here about the bank robbery, too."

Eddie sat up straight.

Nick recalled the conversation they overheard from Billy and Jack. "I wish my town had an interesting history like yours."

"I'm sure the miners wouldn't agree," Eddie said, slapping Nick on the back.

"Raven Pecoro." Jo held up a wanted poster with a black and white photograph of a grizzly-looking man with greasy hair, parted in the middle. He had a long scar across one cheek. "Adaline Pecoro." The next poster was of a young woman wearing a fancy cowboy hat and a long, light-colored braid hanging in front of one shoulder. The next poster showed the image of a young man wearing a bolo tie around his collar. "Stony Pecoro." The third poster was of a boy who Nick guessed was not much older than they were. He had scruffy light hair and wore an eyepatch on his left eye. "Brud Pecoro."

"Rough-looking group," Eddie said.

"Same hair and eyes—except this guy," Nick pointed to the image of Brud Pecoro, with the eye patch. "Well, his one eye is the same."

"Same last name," Jo observed. "Looks like a family of criminals."

Jo read the writing on the border of the flier. It was the same on each. "*Wanted: Dead or Alive. Five thousand dollars for the capture of the notorious robber of stagecoaches and The Mapleton Bank. Believed to be armed and dangerous.*

Contact Pinkerton's Detective Agency and the Concord Stagecoach Company."

An article in the pile caught Nick's eye. He read the headline. "*Mining tycoon Cornelius Bennett to seal mine entrance and relocate to California.* In an interview with Bennett he said, *I've lost both my mine and all the profits I had stored in the bank vault. Mapleton has nothing more to offer and nothing more to take. Tomorrow, I bid this cursed town farewell.*"

Jo popped a pretzel into her mouth. "How terrible would it be to find out your business partner is a corrupt criminal who caused your mine to collapse? Poor Cornelius."

The cuckoo clock chimed. The group paused to watch the small, wooden bird peek in and out of the tiny door.

Nick was deep in thought as his eyes floated around the framed artwork and miscellaneous items hanging on the wall. He stood up.

Jo and Eddie resumed discussing the newspaper articles. They stopped and stared at Nick.

Jo asked. "Did you figure something out?"

"Jo," Nick asked, "remember what you said about looking at things from a different angle?"

He pointed to a map of the lake tacked to the wall. It was an aerial shot; the kind taken from above.

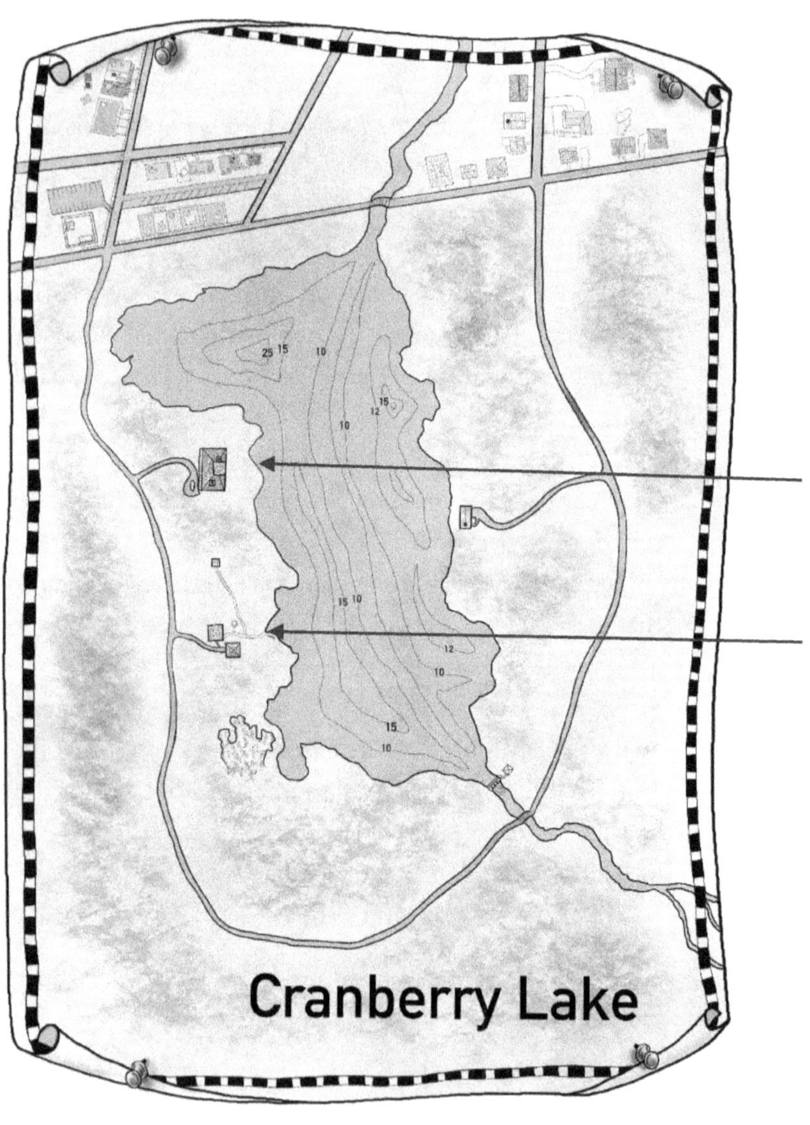
25
15
10
15
12
10
15
10
12
10
15
10
Cranberry Lake

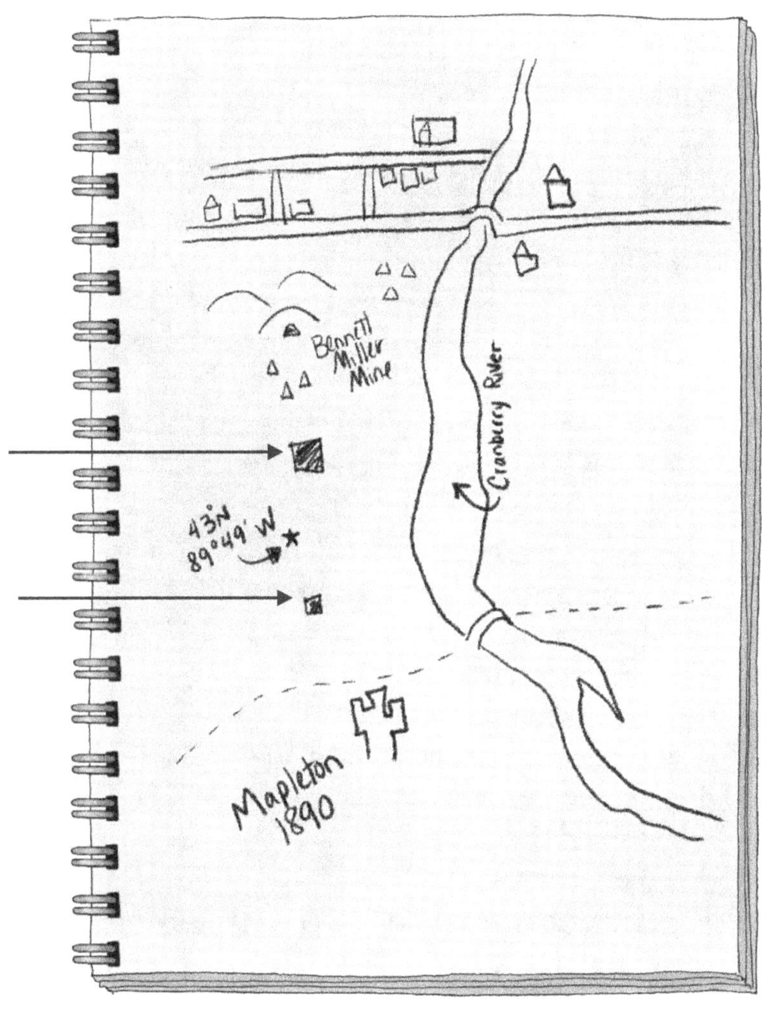
Bennett Miller Mine
Cranberry River
43°N 89°49' W
Mapleton 1890

The colors were faded, and most of the image was filled with an oblong, squiggly, blue shape. It was a bird's-eye view of the lake, with the river feeding in at one end and continuing past the dam at the other.

What caught Nick's eye wasn't the water. It was the shapes along one edge.

"They're not treasure chests. They're rooftops," he said, grabbing his sketchbook.

He held his drawing next to the photograph of the lake. "Look, the shapes in the photograph are clearly the tops of two buildings next to the lake. They correspond perfectly with the two shapes along the river in my sketch."

Eddie's jaw dropped. "Of course. And look—Castle Rock. It's exactly the same distance away. Two houses, near the lake, which used to be a river."

"I thought I saw—" Jo rifled through the contents of the box. "Here it is!" She held up an article with the headline *Mapleton Builds Hydroelectric Dam.* "The town built a dam on the Cranberry River in eighteen-ninety-three, which created Cranberry Lake. The lake wasn't on the map from the library because it didn't exist when that map was made."

Eddie added, "The houses were obviously built when the lake was still just a river."

Nick pointed to the photograph. "This large rectangle must be the Miller house."

"And the small one," Nick concluded, "has to be Big J's cabin.

"That means—" Jo's eyes widened. "Whatever the star marks is buried somewhere in the woods between here and the Miller house next door."

"There's only one way to find out," Eddie stood up and headed for the door. "Let's hope there are three shovels in the garage."

The Trunk

Over the next few days, Nick, Jo, and Eddie dug in various locations in the narrow strip of woods between Uncle John's cabin and the Miller house next door. Uncle John said he didn't mind, as long as they stayed on his property, so they dug at random intervals in the wood chips and pine needles covering the soft, sandy soil near the fish shack.

Nick had been in Mapleton less than a week, but he already knew he'd be sad to leave once his parents called, telling him he could return home. He had secretly begun to wish the renovation would take a month, maybe even two.

Nick drove the point of his shovel into the ground for the thousandth time. His muscles ached as he dumped the dirt next to the slowly widening hole he'd been working on for the past twenty minutes. "I wish we knew what we were at least looking for and how far down to look," he said, leaning on his shovel.

"This feels hopeless." Eddie collapsed dramatically on the ground. "My arms are about to fall off."

Nick spotted a fallen tree trunk that made a perfect natural bench. He sat down to rest and gingerly pressed on the tender, red spots forming on each of his palms. "I think I'm getting blisters."

"Don't tell me you two are giving up." Jo offered a hand to Nick and hoisted him to his feet. "C'mon. I'm sure Uncle John has some work gloves in his garage."

"I'll wait here," Eddie murmured, sprawled out, eyes closed. "Grab that trail mix, would'ya?"

"I'm not your personal assistant," Jo called over her shoulder.

Eddie groaned. He rose to his feet, then trailed behind Nick and Jo as they walked toward the driveway.

The garage bay was empty, and Uncle John's truck was still gone. He'd mentioned another trip to Walton which meant he'd be gone until after dark.

"Let's see what we can find." Nick walked over to the tool bench.

He scanned the side wall, where a collection of long-handled tools was stored in a neat row. An old pair of Uncle John's leather gloves lay at the end of the counter. Nick grabbed them and tried them on for size. They were, of course, too big and fit like crispy baseball gloves.

"Look at all this stuff," Eddie said. He stood with his arms crossed and gazed up at the ceiling. A collection of old boards, ropes, and chains hung from the rafters.

From the back corner of the garage, Jo asked, "Who wants a haircut?"

Nick looked over and saw her holding up an oversized pair of hedge-trimming shears. She opened and closed the blades several times. They made a slicing sound, and she let out an evil chuckle.

"Don't even think about it," Nick cautioned, with a smile.

From the corner, Eddie said, "Now this is the life."

Nick turned around to see Eddie sitting in a rocking chair, hands clasped behind his head, feet propped on the nearby end table.

"What is all this stuff anyways?" Jo asked.

Nick rushed over and yanked Eddie out of the chair. "What are you doing?"

"Geesh. Didn't realize it was a crime to sit in a chair."

"Sorry, it's just that these are antiques," Nick explained.

Jo peeled back the corner of the blue tarp.

"Uncle John collects old furniture so he can fix it up and sell it," Nick explained as he tucked the tarp back into place.

"My mom's into antiques." Jo untucked the tarp and took another peek. "We have a steamer trunk kinda like this at our house."

Nick watched her run a finger across the front of a huge leather-covered box with a hinged lid. The words *Manning & Sons Trunk Co.* were stamped on a brass plate on the side.

"Only rich people had trunks like this one. Just imagine the places it's seen. My mom converted ours into a coffee table." Jo looked to Nick. "Can I look inside?"

"No way."

"Please?"

Nick hesitated for a moment. The trunk looked old and fragile. He bit his lip and pictured the lid crumbling as Jo lifted it. He would feel responsible if the old trunk broke, but he was also curious to see inside.

His friends looked at him with hopeful expressions.

"Come on," Eddie scoffed. "What's the worst that could happen?"

"The hinges could fall off, the whole thing could disintegrate—"

"I'll be careful," Jo assured. "This one is in really great shape compared to the one we have and the hinges on ours have never fallen off."

"OK, but if anything breaks—"

"Nothing will break." Jo carefully lifted the heavy lid and peered inside. "Eddie, hand me your flashlight."

Eddie unhooked his pocket flashlight from a loop on his vest and handed it to Jo. Nick held the lid open, and a musty, stale odor seeped out.

As the three of them leaned forward, Eddie joked, "Smells like my grandpa's room."

Jo clicked the flashlight on and aimed the beam inside the dark cavity. The trunk's interior walls and base were covered with a thin, faded yellow fabric with brown flowers printed on it.

It was empty.

Jo reached inside. Nick immediately envisioned a colony of spiders crawling up her arm and shook his arms to escape the jittery feeling.

She asked, "Do you think Uncle John has a tape measure around here?"

After a brief scan of the workbench, Nick found a small, silver-and-yellow tape measure. He handed it to Jo, then stood next to the trunk and watched her measure the outside height of the trunk. Then she measured the inside.

"Just as I suspected." With her free hand, Jo reached deep inside and moved her arm around."

"What are you doing?" Nick asked.

"You know how I was telling you about puzzle boxes before?" She was now reaching along the sides.

"Yeah," Nick replied.

"Well, this is like the king of all puzzle boxes. My mom told me—" She stopped abruptly, and a smile spread across her face. "*There* it is."

Nick heard a soft, metallic-sounding *CLICK*. "What was that?" He cringed and looked inside. The base of the trunk was now tilted at an odd angle. "Oh my gosh!" His worst fear was realized. The trunk was broken.

Eddie stepped back and held his hands up, palms forward. "Hey, all I did was sit in a chair."

Nick felt nauseous.

"Before you freak out," Jo looked at Nick and assured, "it's supposed to do that."

Jo handed the flashlight to Eddie. "Hold this." She then reached both arms inside the trunk. She wedged her fingertips into the space between the walls and the base of the trunk, then lifted the entire base up, revealing a shallow compartment hidden beneath.

Hidden

"YOU'RE SURE IT'S NOT BROKEN?" NICK ASKED, raking a hand through his hair. He looked at the base of the trunk, now tipped at an odd angle.

"I'm sure."

He asked, "How'd you know that was there?"

"I told you; we have one at our house." Jo explained. "When I measured the inside depth, it was four inches shorter than the outside, so I figured the base was either four inches thick, or—as I suspected—a four-inch compartment was hidden under the panel. There's a tiny lever in the corner. When you press it, it releases the clasp. And don't worry, when we put it back into place, it'll slide right back into position and reset the lever." She leaned the false bottom of the trunk against the back wall.

Eddie aimed the flashlight beam at the compartment. A faded, black, cloth bag lay inside the cavity. "Whoa-ho-ho!" he exclaimed. "Jackpot!"

Nick reached into the trunk and pulled out the bag. The fabric smelled strongly of mothballs and had a drawstring closure. Nick inched it open. Jo and Eddie leaned forward. Inside was a rolled-up piece of leather, tied with a rawhide shoelace. The image of a bird had been stamped into the leather.

"That same bird in on the box you found!" Eddie exclaimed. "That's a weird coincidence."

"Open it," Jo urged.

The lace was tied in a knot and was stiff with age. Nick wrestled with it, but he couldn't loosen the cemented rawhide.

He looked at Eddie. "Any tweezers in your Swiss Army vest?"

Eddie scoffed—as if this was a silly question—and unzipped a side pouch containing a multi-tool.

Before he could open it, Jo boasted, "I've got this one, boys." She took the leather scroll and began wrenching the sides of the knot with her fingers. "Fingernails," she declared, "are nature's tweezers."

A moment later, she had loosened the stubborn lace and unrolled the leather. Inside the scroll were two pieces of yellowed paper. Jo unfurled them and spread them out on the table. One side of each page was ragged, as if they'd been ripped from a book. The first page was written in elegant, cursive penned in brownish-black ink. The other was filled with rows of strange symbols.

Eddie nudged Jo's arm. "Looks like you've got a code to break."

"Nice!" She chewed on her lip. "I don't see a translation code—which means this won't be easy to decipher."

"Someone circled some of the symbols, see?" Eddie pointed to the coded message.

"Hmm," Jo said.

Nick held one of the pieces of paper up to the light. "Maybe they're letters written in reverse."

They weren't. Even from the underside, the symbols were nonsensical.

"You know who loves puzzles? My grandpa," Eddie said. "If you don't mind listening to about an hour of 'back-in-my-day' stories, I'll bet he can help us."

"Hang on." Jo put a hand on her hip. "I said it wouldn't be easy. I wasn't **implying** I couldn't solve it. You guys try to figure out the diary entries. I'll work on the code."

Nick and Eddie stared at the lacey script. Most of the letters were elongated and closely spaced, which made them almost as **cryptic** as the symbols Jo was working on.

"Cursive. Great. I have no idea what any of this says." Eddie squinted at the page. "This looks like a backwards three and these are just a bunch of **curlicues**. Is this even English?"

"It's probably English, but it's cursive, so it may as well be written in a different language." Nick felt skeptical. "Maybe if we break it down by letter—"

"Jo," Eddie sighed like a deflating balloon, "we're not good at reading cursive."

June 5, 1983

Eleanor and I were finally able to get the Telaera running. We made a few alterations and have been able to produce a continuous stream of power.

June 7, 1983

Can't trust anyone. Worried the Telaera will be discovered and stolen. Plan to store it in the vault – away from sluric ore until patent is secured.

I fear the worst.

Beneath Tyme's Face
Dorona's Dusk
Symbols Letters Will Replace

Jo gave a smug half-smile. "Once again, I see I have to do everything."

Nick handed the page to her.

"This bottom section is a poem." Her eyes darted back and forth as she recited it.

Beneath Time's Face,
Dorona's Disk,
Symbols Letters Will Replace.

Eddie groaned, "A poem?"

"I don't think it's just a poem." Nick rubbed his forehead. "It's also a riddle."

The three crowded around the paper.

"Dorona. Any idea who that is?" Jo asked. "Sounds like a character from a fairy tale or a myth."

"I was really into Greek mythology last year, and I don't remember ever reading about someone named Dorona with a disk." Nick frowned. "I don't think it's Greek."

"Well, that's just great," Eddie stated flatly. "So far we've got a key, a map that was stolen, a code, a confusing riddle-poem that's not Greek, a diary entry, and no answers."

They fell silent and continued to observe the symbols and markings on the pages.

Eddie ran a finger along the torn edge of the page with symbols. "I'll bet these were torn from a diary."

Nick offered, "Maybe the key goes to a diary."

"It's too big," Jo replied.

Eddie added, "Did you know every diary key is the same? If you find one key, you're golden."

"They're not all the same, Eddie," Jo said, with a roll of her eyes.

"Well, the kind my sisters get for their birthdays are."

Jo rolled her eyes. "I'm sure your sisters don't appreciate you going through their personal things."

"Hey. I like to know what's coming," he defended, then murmured, "Something's always coming."

Jo pointed to the page with cursive writing. "These do seem like diary entries." She read, "'*Eleanor and I were finally able to get the Telaera running. We made a few alterations and have been able to produce a continuous stream of power.*'"

"Who's Eleanor?" Nick asked.

"And what's a Telaera?" Eddie added.

Jo shook her head and shrugged. "I have no idea." She looked at the page again and said, "Here's another entry from two days later. '*Can't trust anyone. Worried it will be discovered and stolen. Plan to store in the vault— away from slunic ore until patent is secured. I fear the worst.*'" Jo's brow scrunched into a wrinkle.

"Slunic ore?" Eddie asked.

"I've heard of iron ore," Nick thought aloud. "Maybe it's similar."

Jo rubbed a finger along her chin. "This whole entry is strange."

Eddie's eyes lit up. "Guys, what if whoever wrote this put something in the bank vault?"

Nick added, "The very vault the Pecoro's somehow broke into without opening the vault door?"

"The people from the wanted posters?" Jo asked.

Nick and Eddie nodded.

"That seems like a stretch." Jo chewed a fingernail.

"Why?" Eddie asked.

Jo answered, "Because bank robbers steal money."

Eddie folded his arms across his chest. "But think about it. We just saw wanted posters for a family who robbed the Mapleton Bank the same day the mine collapsed. Coincidence?"

"Hmm," Nick said. "Well, the wording is definitely weird, but whatever the message means, we know it has something to do with a bank—but whoever wrote this is talking about putting something *into* a vault, not taking it out."

Nick scratched his neck. "The entry said something about a patent, right? Isn't that what inventors use to protect their idea so no one steals it?"

Eddie held a finger in the air. "I'm actually kind of an expert on inventions right now. I just finished reading a book about patents."

"You?" Jo looked at him and covered her mouth with her hand, not quite in time to cover a laugh. "A book?"

Eddie played along. "Hard to believe, I know. As you know, I'll be entering the inventor's contest this year. The invention is called The Stir Shield. It's a silicone shield that protects your hand while you're stirring something on the stove." He added boastfully, waving his hands as if to ward off immense congratulations, "Hence the non-mandatory reading. The book said patents are really important to inventors, because without one, someone else could potentially steal your idea and claim it as their own."

Jo read the entry again. "The author writes: '*...until patent is secure....*'"

"But why would someone remove these pages?"

"Maybe the coded message explains it all." Eddie looked at Jo. "Any idea what it says?"

She replied, "It's pretty tricky. Without a translation code, we'll have to resort to trial and error. It could take hours to figure out what letter of the alphabet each symbol represents."

Nick walked over to the tool bench and held up the gloves. He looked at Eddie. "Well, while Jo cracks that code, let's back to digging."

"About that," Eddie said, rolling his neck around and stretching his shoulder muscles. "What would you say about using a metal detector?" He bounced his eyebrows up and down.

"I'm not opposed to the idea, but do you *have* a metal detector?" Nick asked.

"Well, no." Eddie looked around. "But I'll bet Uncle John has one. I mean, look at all this stuff."

After a thorough search, they concluded that Uncle John did *not* have a metal detector.

"Well, let's pool our allowances and go buy one." Eddie patted an empty vest pocket. "I'll need to stop at home."

"Sounds expensive." Jo shook her head.

Eddie said. "If whatever is buried out there turns out to be—I don't know—the stolen bank money—and we're lucky enough to actually find it—we can easily reimburse ourselves for a simple, little metal detector."

"We can't spend money we don't have." Nick put his hands in his pockets and added, "I don't have much." He looked at Eddie. "Plus, judging from the fact that your money is all in coin form, I'm thinking a metal detector isn't something we'll be able to afford."

Jo looked at Nick with laughing eyes. "He showed you Snoopy?"

Nick nodded.

She snickered, "Did he tell you about the Sister Tax?"

"OK, OK…" Eddie interrupted. "We all used to be little, and we all used to be naive."

Jo was trying not to laugh. She wasn't succeeding. "You were such a cute widdle kid," she said, reaching over to pinch Eddie's cheek.

Eddie swatted her hand away. "You're only eleven months older than me."

"And look at how much knowledge I've acquired in those additional eleven months. You'll never, ever catch me."

Out of sympathy for Eddie, whose ears were starting to turn red from embarrassment, Nick suggested, "Maybe we can see if the hardware store has a metal detector we can rent."

Jo shrugged. "It's worth a shot."

Eddie beamed.

Divide & Conquer

About thirty seconds after they biked away from Uncle John's driveway, a white Jeep barreled down the road toward them.

Eddie groaned, "Oh great."

The Jeep slowed to a crawl and pulled alongside the three cyclists. Jesse sat behind the wheel.

From the passenger seat, Lucia stood up and called over the open top, "There you are." Her mouth tilted into a smirk as she smacked a piece of pink bubble gum.

"What d'ya want?" Eddie narrowed his eyes.

Lucia sat down and hooked her arm over the door, then paused to blow a gigantic bubble. When it popped, she used her fingers to pull the collapsed gum into a long, stretchy line, gripping the opposite end with her teeth. She coiled it around her finger and popped it back into her mouth, gnashing it a few times before she spoke. In a voice dripping with sarcasm, she droned, "I was *so* worried about you."

"Well—this has been fun." Eddie poised his foot on the pedal of his bike.

"Uh uh uh," she scolded. "Not so fast, little brother."

Eddie looked at Jesse, then back to his sister. "What are you guys doing here?"

"Babysitting, apparently." Lucia's eyes glimmered. "Well, I am. Jesse's just enjoying my company." She reached over and rested her arm on his shoulder.

"Any excuse to drive around." Jesse affectionately ran his hand along the dashboard of the Jeep.

Eddie sighed. "Why are you really here? I don't need a babysitter."

"Well, Mom's paying me, so she must think you do."

"What are you talking about, Lucia?"

"Well," she sighed, then popped another bubble, "*somehow* Mom found out you didn't clean the bathroom this week, so she sent me on a **reconnaissance** mission to find you." Lucia grinned and whispered, "She's furious."

Eddie protested, "I can't believe you—"

"I know," Lucia interrupted, "your chores are none of my business. I just thought Mom would want to know if someone's not earning their keep." She smiled. "Turns out she did. You know, work first, play later and all. Now I'm here to bring you home, so you two can discuss your punishment."

Nick could see Eddie's left eye twitching in anger, and he recalled the vegetable incident with Lucia and subsequent driveway chase sequence.

Jo stepped forward. She lifted her chin and stated, "Actually, we were just heading to your house, so it appears you've driven out of your way for nothing."

Lucia turned her head slowly to look at Jo and gave a tight-lipped smile. She blinked and said, "I don't need anyone managing my time, sweetie. And this is really a private family matter, so Eddie will have to continue," she swirled her finger in the air, "this little playdate later." Lucia pointed to Eddie's bike, then to the back of the Jeep, then snapped her fingers. "Get a move on. I don't have all day."

Eddie huffed, and his nostrils flared, but he said nothing.

As he struggled to hoist his bike into the back of the Jeep, Jesse twisted around in his seat and barked, "Watch the paint, man."

Nick wanted to say something clever to stick up for his friend, but the image of Lucia sprinting down the driveway after him clawed into his mind, and he couldn't think about anything else. He absentmindedly rubbed his forearm. The crescent-shaped fingernail marks had faded, but their imprints still lingered in his thought.

After the bike was loaded, Eddie slouched and walked over to Nick and Jo. "Sorry, guys," he said, looking defeated. "I'm probably going to be grounded for a couple of days."

Lucia snickered. "Well, you can't say I didn't warn you. It was just a few, measly vegetables, Eddie. I hope you've learned your lesson."

Eddie looked at Nick and Jo with sad eyes. He turned to climb into the Jeep, where, like a prisoner locking his own shackles, he buckled his seatbelt. The Jeep rumbled down the road, kicking up dust as it went.

Nick looked at Jo. "Well, now what?"

She shrugged. "We could keep digging."

Nick stretched his arms out in front of him. His muscles were aching from the holes they'd dug already. "Actually," he said, "I'd rather bike over to the hardware store and look into that metal detector option."

Nick and Jo parked their bikes outside of the courthouse, across the street from Clancy's Nuts and Bolts.

As he stepped off the curb onto the crosswalk on Main Street, Nick spotted a blue sports car with a gold seagull on the hood parked a short distance away.

"Jo," he said, halting mid-stride.

She paused and looked at him.

"That's the Caldwells' car." He nodded his head, trying not to draw too much attention.

Jo asked, "Wanna go check it out?"

Nick looked up and down the sidewalk. There was no sign of Steven or Jake Caldwell.

"Let's go."

They jogged across the street and walked briskly toward the parked car.

"I'll keep a lookout," Jo said.

She stepped into the shadow of an awning and leaned against the brick wall. Nick headed for the car but heard a splash. He looked down to see his right foot in a puddle left over from a storm that passed through during the night. Ignoring the damp feeling seeping into his sock, he darted over to the car and landed in a crouched position at the front bumper. Like a hunted prairie dog, he cautiously popped his head up above the hood. The coast was clear. There was still no sign of the brothers.

"Nick!" Jo hissed from a few feet away.

He looked over at her.

She stood with her arms crossed and a scowl on her face. "What are you doing?"

He whispered, "What do you mean?"

Jo rolled her eyes. "You look super suspicious right now. Be cool."

I am being cool, he thought, suddenly doubting his judgment to gauge his own cool-ness.

Jo looked up and down the sidewalk, then enunciated, "Be. Less. Obvious. Stand up."

Nick stood up and casually peered into the front seat of the car. He decided to pretend this was *his* car and he was locked out. A trickle of sweat rolled down his temple as he slowly lifted his head and peeked through the window. He glanced over at Jo, who gave him a subtle nod, a wink, and a thumbs up.

There was a glare on the tinted window, so Nick leaned closer to get a clearer view. He heard Jo quietly whistling and thought, *Now who's being obvious?* Nick's ego still felt a little bruised from her criticism implying he wasn't cool. He heard her whistling louder now. Staying focused, Nick cupped his hands over his eyes and peered through the front passenger window. The car was meticulously clean. His nose touched the glass and left a small smudge that he quickly wiped away with his shirt. Trying his best to look **nonchalant**, Nick took a casual step backwards, scanned the small rear seat, then gasped. There, in the back seat of the car was a long, rolled up piece of paper.

"Jo," he whispered, but when he looked up, Jo had vanished.

Just then, Nick heard another sound. It was the unmistakable, piercing voice of Steven Caldwell, followed by the loud rumble of Jake's. Immediately, he recalled Jo's whistling and realized she must have been trying to get his attention. Instinctively, Nick reverted back to prairie dog mode, and dropped to his hands and knees next to the car. He popped his head up just high enough to peek through the windows to get a view of the sidewalk on the opposite side of the car.

To his horror, Nick saw the Caldwells, a mere twenty feet away, near the entrance of the hardware store. They lingered for a moment, squabbling about something. Nick's thoughts were swirling. He took a breath and tried to focus. He looked again. Jake was juggling several bags and held a slender metal pole with a disk at the end.

A metal detector! Nick's thoughts were surprisingly clear and calm. *I've got to get the map back before they get in the car, or they'll be one step ahead of us!*

Nick lifted the handle of the passenger door. It was locked. He considered waiting for the car doors to unlock with the key fob. He could grab the map, then bolt, but there was no way he would be able to do that without being caught. He didn't have enough leverage for a full-blown confrontation, and his backup was gone.

His only option was to stay hidden. Staying low, he scurried around the minivan in a neighboring parking space. Still out of sight, he dropped to all fours and lowered his cheek to the asphalt, peering under the minivan. Nick's heartbeat pounded in his ears. He heard approaching voices and footsteps.

A pair of shiny, black, leather shoes stepped off the curb in the exact spot he had been only seconds before. One of the shoes took a half-step backward, then poked at something on the ground. A panic crept up his neck as he realized his wet shoe had left what could only be described as a strange **choreography** of footprints next to the car. Nick imagined Steven Caldwell piecing together why the footprints were there and half-expected the thin man to crouch down and discover him. Hardly daring to breathe, Nick squeezed his eyes closed and tried *not* to imagine Steven Caldwell's steely eyes staring back at him from under the minivan.

The nightmarish daydream was broken by a sharp, electronic *bwip BWEEP*, followed by the quiet thump of the doors unlocking. He peered under the minivan and watched one black shoe disappear, followed by the other. Both car doors slammed shut. Nick watched and listened from his hiding spot. He heard the car's engine roar to life. The blue sports car backed out of the parking spot and sped down the street.

Phew! Nick's breath came rushing out of his lungs, and his shoulders relaxed. He sat up and leaned against the side of the minivan and let his head tip back. Taking another deep breath, he closed his eyes, relieved to have avoided the close call but extremely disappointed to have lost the map again when it had been so close.

Ahem. A woman cleared her throat.

Shielding his eyes from the sun, Nick looked up. He was surprised to see Dani Cooper, the realtor he'd seen at Watkins Jewelry. She loomed over him, holding one paper grocery bag in each arm. A set of keys dangled from her index finger. She peered over the groceries and stared at Nick.

"Can I help you?" Dani asked cautiously. "Or is my van just really comfortable to lean on?"

Nick jumped to his feet and tried to sound casual. "Uh, nope." He dusted his hands on his jeans. "Sorry."

Dani paused, frowning, and then to Nick's surprise—she smiled. "I recognize you from Gordon's place. Weren't you there with your friends?"

Nick nodded.

She held his gaze then narrowed her eyes. "I know what you're looking for."

Nick was shocked but tried not to let his expression show it.

"You're looking for a job, right?"

"Uhh…" Nick wasn't sure how to respond.

"Don't be silly. All kids need jobs to keep them out of trouble." She handed off the grocery bags to Nick and said, "Here. Hold these a sec." The bracelets on her wrist jangled as she took her wallet out of her purse. She pulled out a crisp, twenty-dollar bill. "I could use help with some of the properties I'm trying to sell. It'd be general yard work, mowing lawns—you know. How does twenty dollars an hour sound?"

Nick blinked. His jaw gaped open. He really wasn't interested in having a job, since he had no idea how long he would even be in Mapleton. However, metal detectors weren't free, and for a few seconds, he considered taking her up on the offer.

"Thanks, but I'm only here for a little while, and my friends and I are busy with—a project."

"You can think about it and let me know. I have the budget to hire a whole team, so your friends could work too." Dani opened the trunk of her minivan. "Just put the bags there." The back of her minivan was packed with what looked like realtor supplies; a tall stack of yard signs with the smiling faces of Dani and Ty and a big box of flyers. She brushed some dirt onto the ground. "Don't mind the mess here. We've been putting up signs all morning." She looked over at the ice cream shop and asked, "Have you tried Ginger's new flavor?"

"EnlightenMint?" Nick asked.

She nodded.

"I hear it's good."

"I love mint. I'll have to try it."

Nick nodded, then squeezed the bags between a bulky wooden signpost and some gardening tools.

Dani smiled and said, "Think about it."

Nick nodded.

She waved as he trotted across the street to his bike.

Jo popped out from behind a dense shrub next to the bike rack and grinned. "I didn't know you were such a talented grocery delivery boy. Did she tip you?"

Nick furrowed his brow and replied, "No, but she offered us a job."

"What?"

Nick ignored her question. "Where *were* you? I almost got caught."

Jo looked sheepish. "I'm so sorry! I saw the Caldwells coming, and I tried to get your attention, but they were too close and—"

"Jo, listen." Nick looked at her squarely. "The Caldwells just bought a metal detector—and they have the map!"

P.I.F.

"LET'S GO!" JO HOPPED ONTO HER BIKE.

Nick grabbed his handlebars and swung his leg over the seat. Seconds later, he caught up. "Wait—where are we going?"

Jo looked at him and flung a braid over her shoulder. "To follow the Caldwells, obviously." She pedaled furiously, and Nick had to work hard to keep up with her.

"What's the plan?" he panted, still trailing a few feet behind.

She looked back at him, then focused on the road again, loose hair whipping across her forehead. "Find out where they're headed, follow them, sneak into their car, and steal it back."

"Wait a second," Nick matched her speed and they raced along the road. "Even though we don't know what the star on the map marks, we know approximately where it is." We just have to keep digging between Big J's cabin and the old Miller house.

It's just a matter of time before we find something. We don't need the map anymore."

Jo stopped pedaling and coasted to a stop. She looked annoyed. "We don't need the map as much as we need for the Caldwells to *NOT* have it."

Nick chewed his lip. "But they'd be trespassing. You can't just go into someone's yard and dig a bunch of holes." The image of the lumpy yard at the Miller house flashed into his mind.

Jo looked at him. "They'll probably dig during the night." She propelled herself forward. "C'mon. There's dust in the air, which means a car drove this way not too long ago." She picked up speed again.

Nick's mind was racing. Jo's bike was bigger, and she was fast. He struggled to keep up.

They coasted off the main road onto the gravel lane leading to the Miller house, Uncle John's house, and the hideout. The tires on their bikes chewed into the gravel, scattering small stones. There was no sign of the blue sports car—or anyone for that matter—but the trail of dust continued past a curve in the road ahead.

"Dang, I figured they'd be heading right here," Jo said. "Well, I guess we should ride around for a while. Mapleton's a small town, and there aren't many places to hide. We're bound to run into them."

They rounded another curve and Nick spotted a lone cyclist in the distance. The cyclist, moving away from them, erratically zigzagged from one side of the road to the other, intentionally skidding in the loose gravel along the edges and creating plumes of dust.

"Well, there's the eye of the storm." Nick recognized the duct taped bike and the rider wearing a familiar-looking vest.

"Eddie!" Jo shouted.

He didn't seem to hear them. The younger boy was now riding hands-free, playing the air guitar. Finally, when they were almost parallel to him, he pulled his headphones off his ears, looking surprised.

Nick explained what he had seen in the Caldwells' car.

Eddie's shoulders dropped. "Aw man, I'm missing all the action. They just drove by, actually."

Jo asked, "How long ago was that?"

"I don't know—a few minutes. Good thing I was on the edge. They didn't even slow down."

Jo looked down the road. "If we split up, I'll bet we can find them. The road around the lake makes a loop. They may not know exactly where to look, since the map they have only shows the river."

"We shouldn't assume that," Nick said. "Adults always seem to have a lot more resources than kids. They somehow already knew they'd need a metal detector." He looked behind him. "Eddie and I will head this way and—"

"Forget it," Eddie interrupted. "They're long gone."

"Well, let's at least try," Jo urged. "Come on. I'll go this way." She started to pedal.

"It's useless, Jo. Plus, we have Nick's sketch. We don't even need the map anymore."

Jo stopped her bike and looked at Eddie. "That's exactly what Nick said. How are neither of you getting this?" She looked at Nick. "Would you care to explain it this time?"

Nick recited, "We don't need the map, but if we want to find out what's buried, we need to make sure the Caldwells don't get there first. It will help if they don't have the map, which is why we need to take it back."

Jo looked pleased.

"I'm sure they've already seen the markings. They probably know *exactly* where to look, and according to you, they now have a metal detector, which, I might add, was my idea." Eddie sighed. "Let's just forget it."

Nick looked at Eddie. Something seemed off.

"Just *forget it*?" Jo asked, "Why don't you want to follow the Caldwells? What's going on with you today?"

"*Nothing's* going on, that's the problem." Eddie pulled at a piece of duct tape. "Look, if you two want to chase the Caldwells all over town, go ahead. I'm out."

Nick was stunned by Eddie's sudden change of attitude. Then he noticed a pair of yellow, latex gloves tucked into the back pocket of Eddie's jeans. He asked, "Where're you headed? How'd you get out of being grounded?"

Eddie exhaled loudly. "Nowhere, thanks to my evil, nosy sister. I'm grounded."

Jo looked at his bike and frowned. "You don't look grounded."

Eddie scrunched his mouth to the side and lamented. "Look, my mom was mad about the bathroom. Really mad. I'm serving a 'P.I.F.

punishment.'" He looked at Nick to explain. "A 'Pay It Forward punishment.' That's what she calls a punishment for me," he air-quoted, "*that benefits others.* Effective immediately."

Jo looked sympathetic. "What do you have to do this time?"

Eddie held up the yellow gloves. "She's making me clean the bathrooms at my house, but first she's making me clean *other* people's bathrooms." Eddie looked miserable. "Do you have any idea how degrading and disgusting that is?"

Nick grimaced. "That's gross."

He'd been in charge of cleaning the toilets when his family moved to the house in Pinehurst. The musty smell was so bad, he'd had to wear a respirator face mask. Nick was convinced there were few punishments worse than being forced to clean a disgusting toilet.

"It gets worse." Eddie looked forlorn.

Jo cringed. "How?"

"I suppose you're wondering what I'm doing out here by the lake."

Nick and Jo nodded slowly.

"Well," Eddie stated, his voice laced with resentment, "as we previously determined, there are two houses on this side of the lake. I'm not cleaning Uncle John's bathroom."

"No…" Jo looked horrified.

Eddie relinquished a heavy sigh.

Jo clarified, "Your mom's making you clean bathrooms at the old Miller house?"

Nick looked down the road. They were twenty feet from the driveway with the iron gate.

"Yup." Eddie's shoulders slumped.

"How?" Jo asked.

"Why?" Nick shook his head. Haunted toilets seemed like a worse punishment than old, smelly ones.

Eddie tipped his head back, as if he no longer had the strength to hold it up. He heaved another sigh and complained, "Ginger and a bunch of do-gooders from around town are helping clean up the old house so Miller's grandson can sell it." His tone became sarcastic. "And my mom thought that sounded like *such* a good idea, she volunteered—me."

Jo inhaled through clenched teeth. "That's rough."

"I should get going," Eddie grumbled.

"OK. Good luck." Nick poised his foot on his top pedal. He wondered if his friend was worried about being in the old Miller place and was secretly glad Eddie hadn't asked them to help with the chore.

Evidently—and unfortunately—Jo had been thinking the exact opposite. "Maybe we could come with you and help out."

"What?" Nick blurted out.

Jo tipped her head to the side. "That way, Eddie'll finish faster, and we can get back to figuring out what the map is marking and what that key unlocks."

"Seriously?" Eddie sounded hopeful.

Seriously? Nick thought helping his friend clean bathrooms in a haunted house sounded like a terrible idea, but when he saw the dread melting from Eddie's face, he nodded and said, "Sure."

THE MILLER HOUSE

THE DRIVEWAY WAS A JUNGLE OF OVERGROWN weeds. The metal gate with the letter M was open, and they rode downhill, trying to navigate past knee-high, prickly plants and vines stretching down from the trees overhead.

Eddie waved them toward parallel stripes of trampled plants, recently squashed by the tires of a vehicle. "Follow me."

They rode single file along one of the paths of crushed **vegetation**. Nick looked at the **pockmarked** lawn where areas of grass were missing. It really did look like someone had been digging random holes in the yard. He imagined an old woman wearing a ragged, brown dress, grasping a shovel with bony fingers, flitting around the yard and digging with unnatural speed. A chill ran up his spine.

They followed a curve in the driveway, and a shiny, black pickup truck came into view. Behind it towered the old house. Nick had been able to see only half of it from the street. It was evident this dilapidated house was once majestic. Missing boards left gaping holes in the base of the wraparound front porch. Dark, dusty windows stared down at them, giving the house a forlorn and forgotten appearance.

Beyond the house, the lake sparkled as it reflected the afternoon sun. The yard gently sloped toward the shore, and an overgrown path of stepping stones led to a small, brick shed near the shore next to the woods between the Miller house and Uncle John's cabin. On the opposite side of the house sat a large barn and several small buildings in various degrees of collapse.

The three parked their bikes near the truck, then followed a recently mowed path through the grass toward the weathered front porch. A mop with a green handle leaned against the side of the house next to the massive front door.

Eddie marched up to the door. His attitude had made a 180-degree turn. He grinned. "Thanks again, guys. This would be *waaay* worse without you."

Nick forced a tight smile.

Eddie grasped the door knocker, a heavy loop of twisted, black metal. He pulled it back slightly and banged it against the strike plate. The sound of the knocking echoed around the entire eerily quiet yard.

Nick eyed the blanket of dense cobwebs draped between the beams of the ceiling. He really didn't want to go inside.

From the other side of the door, they heard a shuffling sound. After a moment, the door handle rattled. The door creaked loudly as it opened, just a sliver. Then, without warning, it slammed shut again.

The knob jiggled once more, and again the door opened a few inches. This time, a bright blue eye and a lock of curly, red hair appeared in the gap.

"Why, hello there!" Ginger's southern drawl rang out.

Jo pushed Eddie to the front of the group.

"Give me just a sec—" Ginger made a grunting sound. "This old thing sticks a little—"

She slammed the door again. Open—*CRRRREEEEAK*. Shut—*CRRRREAK*. The entire door shook and suddenly swung wide. Ginger stepped into the doorway. Her curly locks poked out around the edges of a faded blue bandana. She shook the **aerosol** can in her hand and aimed the nozzle at the squeaky door hinges, rocking the door open and closed twice more.

"Well, I suppose that's the best I can do." Smiling, she flung a dingy-looking rag over her shoulder and looked from Nick to Jo to Eddie. "You brought your crew. Good. The more, the merrier. Come on in." Her voice faded as she turned away. "Plenty of work to go 'round."

The kids followed her though a large foyer. Nick looked up at a huge crystal chandelier suspended from the high ceiling. Nick expected the old house to be empty, but the rooms on either side of the foyer appeared to be fully furnished although the chairs and couches were draped with white sheets. Straight ahead of them, a wide doorway led to the back of the house.

"Cleaning headquarters are back here in the kitchen." Ginger sang out. She led them along a hallway lined with dark wooden panels.

Suddenly, they heard a fluttering sound coming from the direction of the chandelier overhead. Nick saw a pair of dark wings frantically flapping near the ceiling. Everyone in the group flinched and held their hands protectively over their heads.

"Oh," Ginger said, "and watch out for the bat. I think there's a colony living in the attic, and somehow this little guy got into the main part of the house."

Bats? Nick shuddered, trying to look nonchalant. After the spider incident, he didn't want to invite additional teasing about his status as a *city kid.* He stopped worrying, however, when he saw Jo walking with her hands clasped just below her chin; her tensed shoulders were almost level with her ears. Eddie trailed behind and held the mop handle with a white-knuckled, baseball grip.

Still on high alert for bats, they walked past an elegant staircase with a thick, wooden handrail that followed the curve of the wide stairs leading to the second floor. In the dark hallway, Nick's knee bumped the corner of a long bench that stretched the length of the wall.

"Watch your step," Ginger said, looking back. "Most of the light bulbs are burned out, and there are plenty of dark corners and hallways in this old place." She pointed to an unlit wall sconce and said, "I'll add that bulb to my mile-long to-do list."

At the end of the hallway, Ginger pushed past two swinging doors with horizontal, wooden slats leading to a large, bright kitchen. Several sets of footprints had disturbed the thick layer of dust on the floor, leaving sections of the black and white tiles visible through the dull, gray blanket. Nick immediately noticed the air was warmer, almost stuffy, here at the back of the house. Banners of muted sunlight streamed in through the grimy windows. Outside, Nick saw snippets of golden sunshine reflecting on the sparkling lake.

Ginger walked to the wide counter and rifled through a plastic tub filled with various bottles of cleaning supplies. "A bunch of folks in town have offered to get this old house up to snuff. I'm not sure who's cleaning this afternoon. Maybe Stan? Anyways, the whole town's pitching in to help get the place looking spiffy." She looked at Nick, Jo, and Eddie. "And you might be interested to know I'm offering free ice cream to anyone who helps out." Deep dimples appeared in each of her cheeks as she smiled. "I'm so glad you three volunteered."

Evidently, she didn't realize they weren't all here by choice.

"You'll want these." Ginger pulled three bandanas from the tub and handed one to each of them.

"What are these for?" Eddie asked.

"The dust. There's a crazy amount of dust in this old place. My hair's a magnet for it."

Nick copied Ginger's bandana style by folding the square cloth into a triangle, then securing it around his head by tying a knot at the base of his neck. Jo did the same, then pushed her braids behind her shoulders. Eddie twisted his bandana into a tube and tied it around his forehead, karate style. His dark brown hair was pushed up and fanned across the top of his head like a floppy crown.

"I'm ready," he said.

"That's the spirit," Ginger said, with a grin. She handed a battery-powered headlamp to each of them. "Like I said, a lot of bulbs are out."

Eddie, not surprisingly, declined the offer. He had his own, personal headlamp stashed in a pocket of his vest. "How long has this place been empty?" He tightened the elastic band at the back of his head.

Ginger squinted her eyes, thinking. "My guess is no one's lived here for almost a hundred years." She ran her hand along the banister. "Overall, she's in pretty good shape. Just needs a little TLC, that's all."

"Why is all the furniture covered with sheets?" Nick asked.

"That's kind of an old-fashioned thing to do, I guess. Keeps the dust off. The house hasn't been touched since—well, since the accident." Ginger's eyes moved around the kitchen. "Everything's still here, exactly as it was. The furniture, the dishes, everything. Whoever buys this place probably won't want these old things. We've got to get everything out before it sells."

"Do you actually think anyone will buy this house?" Jo asked. "People say it's haunted, you know."

Ginger replied, "Oh, that's nonsense. With a little elbow grease, this place will make a beautiful home for someone. When we're done with it, I'm sure it'll get snapped right up. It's about time, too. It's a shame to see a big house like this unloved and empty." She gazed around the room, then rubbed her hands together. "But it's not going to clean itself. Let's get to work." She pointed at Eddie. "Now, I'm not sure why, but your mom specified that you'll be doing the bathrooms."

Like a soldier who'd just been assigned to **latrine** duty, Eddie stood up straight, pulled on the yellow gloves, and gave a single, brave nod.

Ginger glanced at Nick and Jo. "Let me get Eddie started. I'll be back in a minute." She escorted Eddie toward the foyer, then out of sight.

"This place is gigantic," Nick said.

"I know. I feel like we should've left a trail of breadcrumbs to find our way back to the front door." Jo chuckled at her own joke.

A mouse poked its head out of the small hole in the wall near the floor. Nick scrambled to sit on the counter.

Jo wrinkled her brow and gave him a look.

"Don't say it."

"Say what?" she grinned.

He narrowed his eyes at her.

She mouthed, *City boy.*

He groaned.

Jo's eyes twinkled mischievously. "Technically, I didn't say it."

From the hallway, Nick and Jo heard the sound of bristles scrubbing a toilet bowl. Ginger re-entered the kitchen. "You'll both be stationed down this way."

She motioned for them to follow, leading them along another dark hallway to a spacious room. A massive fireplace stretched almost the entire length of the wall. Similar to the other rooms near the front door, the furniture in this part of the house was also covered with sheets. It reminded Nick of a campground of strangely-shaped tents.

"The trick is to keep the dust contained." Ginger carefully gathered the edges of a sheet. "Otherwise, you'll end up making a lot more work for yourself later." She collected the cloth into a tidy bundle and revealed a large, wooden desk underneath. The front of the desk was decorated with intricate carvings similar to the ones on the front door. "We need to get all this furniture uncovered. Everything here's going to be put up for auction. Don't forget the artwork."

Nick noticed smaller pieces of fabric covering rectangular objects on the walls.

"Your job is to get everything on the first floor uncovered and get the dust outside without spreading it around everywhere. Collect the sheets and shake 'em out in the yard." She turned and walked down the hallway, calling over her shoulder, "Holler if you need anything."

Jo ran a hand along the top of the desk. "This place is amazing."

Nick yanked a sheet off the desk chair. A plume of dust billowed into the air.

"Geez! Weren't you listening?" Jo pulled the collar of her T-shirt over her nose and mouth. She coughed and said, "We're trying to collect the dust, not spread it around."

"Sorry." Nick opened one of the narrow windows behind the desk. The dust dissipated, and the room breathed in fresh, clean air.

Nick pulled the chair away from the desk and sat down. "It's creepy to think the last person who sat here might've been Archibald Miller."

Jo shook a chill off her shoulders. "Super creepy."

Nick pulled one of the brass handles on one of the desk drawers. It was locked. They were all locked.

Nick met Jo's gaze. She was clearly thinking the same thing he was. He pulled the shoelace from inside his shirt. The silver key dangled from it. Unfortunately, the key didn't match of the locks.

Jo shrugged. "It was worth a shot."

Nick and Jo continued collecting sheets. Once the room was unveiled, it looked almost welcoming. Leather chairs and a coffee table were positioned in front of a fireplace so big Nick could walk right into it without bending down. Over the fireplace was a large painting of a ship. Oil paintings with ornate golden frames hung on every wall.

Near the large desk was a painting of a young boy wearing a white shirt with lots of ruffles around the collar. Next to that painting was a portrait of two young women with matching blue dresses. One of them wore her blonde hair in an enormous pile on top of her head. The other was holding a cat. The next several paintings were landscapes of trees with rolling hills.

"Come on," Jo called from the next room.

He followed the sound of her voice to the **adjacent** room. Jo had already removed sheets from three of the twelve chairs encircling the largest dining room table Nick had ever seen.

He carefully removed the sheet from a large painting at one end of the room. It was a depiction of two dogs running over rocky terrain. An even larger painting hung at the opposite end of the room. Expecting another landscape, or maybe a giant bowl of fruit, Nick was startled to see a group of people staring back at him. It was an enormous, life-sized family portrait.

"Wow." Jo whistled. "How'd ya like to eat dinner with these four staring at you every night?"

Nick and Jo stood side-by-side as they stared back at the stoic faces.

"Think it's the Miller family?" Nick tipped his head, looking at the family.

At the center of the painting sat Archibald Miller, the man with the unforgettable mustache he'd seen at Ginger Sue's. In the painting, he sat in a wooden armchair wearing the same striped suit and a top hat. His dark hair swept across the top of his head like a wave, and the thick mustache blended into bushy sideburns. He wore a gold-rimmed monocle over one eye.

Jo crossed her arms, scrutinizing the image. "Do you think he knew his recklessness would cause such tragedy?"

"He died down in the mine with everyone else, so probably not." Nick looked at the portrait again. "You never really think of bad guys as having families." He pointed to the woman standing slightly behind Archibald Miller. "Do you think she knew?"

"I don't know," Jo said. "She looks nice."

The woman's blonde hair twisted into an elaborate bun on top of her head. Nick recognized her as one of the women with matching dresses in the painting near the desk. In this portrait, she wore a yellow dress with white stripes and a wide, ruffly skirt that reminded Nick of icing on a cake.

Beside the woman stood two children. A boy with wild, curly blond hair wore a dark gray jacket. He stood with one hand gently resting on the man's shoulder.

Next to the boy stood a little girl, about half his height. Her hair was braided and coiled like a golden crown on top of her head. Blonde ringlets of hair formed a halo around her face and wide, light brown eyes. She wore a frilly, light blue dress and held a parasol over one shoulder. A white cat lay curled at her feet.

"I'm so glad we don't have to wear clothes like those." Jo shook her head. "I'm going to go check on Eddie." She disappeared through the doorway.

Nick lingered a moment in front of the painting. The images of the faces were so lifelike, he wouldn't have been surprised to see them blink. He stared into Archibald Miller's dark eyes. It made him feel a little uncomfortable to think that someone who caused such chaos could appear so innocent. He searched for some indication of his **nefarious** nature—perhaps the artist had captured an evil glint in the outlaw's eye—but there was nothing about Archibald Miller's expression that even hinted at that.

"*Psst.*" Jo reappeared in the doorway with a huge grin on her face. She held a finger to her lips and with her other hand beaconed Nick to join her. "You've got to see this."

The Door

NICK FOLLOWED JO UPSTAIRS. THEY TIPTOED toward an open doorway and peeked inside. Jo's shoulders shook as she suppressed a giggle. Inside, Eddie danced around, playing air guitar with the green mop. He was listening to a song through his headphones and belted out, "Dirty knees and the thunder jeep, dirty knees and the thunder Jeep."

"I always tease him about those **mondegreens**." Jo giggled. "They're the wrong lyrics."

Seconds later, Eddie noticed them and pulled the headphones down to his neck. "Oh, hey." He flashed a big smile.

"Wait a minute." Nick looked suspiciously at Eddie. "Are you—having fun?"

Eddie sat on the edge of the tub. "This isn't actually that bad—just a lot of dust from over the years." He stood up and rinsed the mop in the sink.

Nick watched a brown snake of dirt and scum slither off the bristles and coil around the drain before escaping down a black hole.

"The bathrooms at my house are so much worse—especially when the drains have to be unclogged. Did you know humans shed an average of a hundred hairs per day? Multiply that by six sisters, showering seven days a week. You do the math."

Nick pictured Eddie pulling up a giant glob of long, wet hair out of a bathtub drain but quickly looked away when he felt his throat clench.

"Have you seen Ginger?" Jo asked.

Eddie said, "She had to leave. Something about the freezer being on the fritz at the shop. She said we should start replacing light bulbs next."

"Well, the sheets are done," Nick said, "so Jo and I can do that."

Eddie gave a half-laugh and said, "Nice try. Maybe you didn't notice there are, like, ten rooms up here. Lots more sheets, C.K."

Nick stepped out into the hallway and looked down the dark corridor. The house was massive. He walked toward the nearest door, turned the knob, and pushed it open. The hinges let out an echoey creak. Like the rooms on the first floor, the furniture was shrouded in fabric.

Jo leaned her head through the door frame. "Well?"

Nick sighed. "Let's switch to lighting crew for a while. Eddie!" he hollered, "Did Ginger mention where the spares are?"

Eddie didn't reply, and from the sound of it, his headphones were back on.

"My mom keeps light bulbs in the hall closet," Jo suggested. She opened a small cabinet in the wall next to the bathroom. The cabinet was full of old towels and some neatly folded, lacey fabric.

"Anything?" Nick asked.

She shook her head. "If you were a box of light bulbs in an old, creepy house, where would you be?" She opened the door to the room next to the hall cabinet. "Bedroom." She clicked her headlamp on and continued down the dark hallway, opening doors as she went. "Bedroom. Bedroom. Another bedroom. This place is like a hotel!"

Nick put his hand on the curved railing at the top of the stairs and looked over his shoulder. "I'll check the first floor. Maybe Ginger has some in the kitchen, with the cleaning supplies."

Jo gave him a thumbs up.

As he clomped down the stairs, Nick heard Eddie botching more song lyrics. "Take me down to the very nice city…"

In the kitchen, Nick rummaged through Ginger's duffle bag of supplies and found a stack of rags, a screwdriver, hammer, and a box of nails. No bulbs. He checked all the cabinets along the wall and under the countertop. No bulbs. He was just about to leave when he noticed a narrow pantry door on the opposite end of the kitchen.

"Bingo," he said, reaching down to the lowest shelf. From what appeared to be a lifetime supply of old-fashioned lightbulbs, he took two, then shut the door. He cupped his free hand around his mouth and shouted toward the swinging doors. "Found some!"

On his way back through the dim, first floor hallway, Nick jammed his knee—for the second time—on the edge of the long bench. He stifled a whimper and winced as he bent down to rub his throbbing kneecap. He fished the headlamp out of his pocket, tightened the elastic bands around his head, then angled the beam at the small wall sconce above the bench. Like everything else he had seen in the house, the light fixture was ornate. Several glass prisms suspended from short chains and dangled below metal arms that had been formed to look like branches.

Nick threaded a new bulb into the fixture. Then he searched for a switch on the wall. Finding nothing, he looked on the sides of the lamp itself for a toggle lever or anything that looked like it would regulate the power.

One of the prisms caught the beam of Nick's light and cast a frenzy of dancing rainbows along the wall and ceiling. He looked at the collection of cut-glass pieces and noticed one hanging slightly lower than its neighbors. Unlike the others, this prism was attached to a gold chain that fed into a small hole in one of the metal branches. Thinking it was a pull-chain on-switch, Nick tugged it gently. The chain extended about an inch, and he heard a *click*. The light didn't turn on, so Nick pulled again, this time more firmly. When he released the chain, the entire wall shifted.

Nick froze. For a moment, he thought the house was falling down. When it didn't, he curled his fingers around the small opening along the side of the panel and pulled. The brown, wooden panel moved toward him about an inch. Aiming his lamp at the ground, he saw the panel was connected to the bench, which he discovered rolled on tiny casters attached to the legs. Two nearly invisible hinges on the left side of the wall groaned as he swung the secret panel wide to reveal a metal doorknob reflecting the light.

"Guys," Nick shouted up the stairs. "I found a secret door!"

The Laboratory

THE GOLD DOORKNOB GLINTED IN THE LIGHT OF Nick's headlamp. Jo and Eddie huddled beside him.

Nick took a deep breath. "Maybe we should wait for Ginger to get back."

Eddie scoffed. "Oh, come on, City Kid. Don't be scared." He wrapped his hand around the knob but immediately recoiled. "Oh my gosh!" He blew warm air on his palm and rasped, "It's freezing cold." There was genuine concern in his voice.

"Oh, please." Jo reached past both boys. She gripped the metal doorknob.

"See?" Eddie asked.

She rolled her eyes. "It's cold, but not *that* cold. Your hands are probably hot and sweaty because you're scared."

She twisted the knob and pushed open the door. A rush of cool, dank air blew into the hallway. Seconds later, six lights around the perimeter of a hidden room flickered on one at a time. The farthest light immediately sputtered, made a loud *POP,* then went out. The remaining five bulbs flickered and hummed tentatively, then settled into a steady, yellow glow.

"Whoa," Eddie said as they stepped through the doorway onto a small landing at the top of a stone staircase overlooking a large, basement room.

Unlike the **lavishly** furnished rooms in the main part of the house, this room was relatively **sparse**. A rectangular wooden table sat in the center of the room. A stack of books, a large sheet of paper, and some tools the size of screwdrivers lay on top. The wall opposite the staircase was lined with shelves storing rows of glass jars and a collection of what looked like engines or small machines with gears and levers. A large portrait of a woman hung on the wall. Nick recognized her from the family portrait in the dining room. She wore a similar puffy dress. A gold necklace with a blue pendant hung in front of a wide, lacey collar.

"Awwwe-some." Eddie's whisper floated through the dank air. "Hello!" he called, then listened to his echo bounce off the stone walls. *Hello…Hello…Hello…*

Nick's hands felt clammy as he let the heavy door swing close and carefully followed Jo and Eddie down the ancient staircase running diagonally against the length of one of the stone walls. As they descended into the mysterious chamber below. Nick's hand brushed against a hairy root snaking between the stones, and he jerked away. Thick cobwebs in the corners and along the ceiling were evidence that, like the other rooms in the house, no one had been there in a long time.

"What *is* this place?" Eddie asked.

"I have no idea." Jo swiped a finger along the surface of the table. "Looks like the housekeeper hasn't been here in a while." She held up a gray fingertip then wiped it on her shorts.

"No sheets covering things, though." Eddie joined Jo by the table. He tapped a foot on the wood floor. "I would've expected a basement floor to be stone."

Jo scuffed the toe of her shoe across one of the planks. "Maybe old basements only had dirt floors and they got tired of tracking it upstairs."

Nick walked toward the shelves along the wall. The bottom shelf was filled with what resembled small machines. Up close, they reminded Nick of the old-fashioned alarm clocks his science class had disassembled. These machines, however, were covered with a network of copper wires and looked significantly more complex than the ones from school.

A row of large, glass jars with paper labels on them lined the next shelf. The contents were difficult to see due to the accumulation of dust. The edges of the labels were curling away from the glass and were yellowy-brown with age.

Nick wiped the dust off the closest jar and read the label. *Hands.*

The next jar was labeled the same. All of the jars in that row were labeled *Hands.*

Nick gulped. "Guys, this jar is full of severed hands."

Jo, standing near the table, looked over, visibly alarmed.

"Wait, wait, wait." Eddie walked over for a closer look. "If that jar is full of body parts, this has gotta be the secret laboratory of some evil, Frankenstein genius."

Nick's stomach dropped. He blew on the dust to see into the jar, but it was caked with grime. He used the edge of his palm to wipe the surface of the glass. To his relief, the jar contained no grayish, severed hands, no fingers floating in a semi-translucent, brownish liquid. Instead, it held different lengths of flat, metal rods, each with a hole on one end and decorative point on the other.

He looked at the next shelf. The jars were labeled ***Wheels***, ***Pinions***, ***Arbors***, and ***Pivots***. He sighed, relieved. These were words he knew from science class. Looking over his shoulder, he explained, "They're clock parts. *Hands* like hands on a clock."

Eddie patted him on the back and smiled. "For a minute there, I was ready to bolt." Eddie unhooked his water bottle and tipped it toward his mouth.

At that exact moment, Nick heard a faint squeaking noise coming from behind the bookshelf. A fluttering, flapping sound followed. Nick jumped backward and bumped into Eddie, causing water to slosh water down the front of his shirt and onto the floor.

"Hey!" Eddie complained.

Nick continued to back away from the shelf. "I think I heard a bat." He pointed. "Over there."

For a few seconds, they stood frozen, listening.

"I don't hear anything." Jo clicked her headlamp on and tiptoed toward the shelf, then stood perfectly still.

Eddie held his hand up and tipped his head. "I hear something." He dropped to his hands and knees and lowered his ear to the ground.

Nick crouched next to him, and Jo walked over to shine her headlamp on the floor over the spot where Eddie's water bottle had spilled. The water was dripping between two of the wooden planks. Jo's light illuminated something through the crack.

"There's something down there," Nick said.

"Is it alive?" Jo asked.

"No." Nick gripped the floorboard and was surprised to find it pulled up easily. Underneath was a shallow cavity where the dirt under the floor had been dug away. Inside was a small book with a dark brown leather cover.

"No way!" Nick exclaimed as he reached down and lifted the book out of the hole.

Eddie replaced the board, and they gathered around the table to get a closer look.

Nick blew a cloud of dust off the cover and opened to the first page.

"Ugh," Eddie groaned. "More cursive."

Nick handed the book to Jo.

She deciphered the lacey script. "*Intellectual Property of Archibald Miller.*" Looking up with sparkling eyes, she announced, "It's his diary."

Nick raised an eyebrow. "Wow. Archibald Miller kept a diary?"

"Maybe he wrote about the mine." Eddie joked, "Dear Diary, today I have a busy day planned. After I brush my teeth, I'm going to rob a bank and try building an alarm clock, so I can be sure to make it out of the mine before it collapses—" He inhaled through his teeth. "Oops. Guess he didn't quite finish that clock in time."

"Very funny." Jo thumbed through the pages but stopped suddenly. Her jaw dropped. "Wait a second."

"What?" Nick and Eddie said together.

"This is Archibald Miller's house."

"Yeah, and?" Eddie asked.

"This room was obviously his." She turned the book around and held it so they could see what she was looking at. It was opened to a section where one page had clearly been ripped out, leaving a ragged edge against the spine.

Nick looked up. "The message we found in the trunk…"

Jo's eyes widened. "I think it may have been torn from Archibald Miller's diary."

"That makes sense," Nick said. "Uncle John mentioned he bought some furniture from Miller's grandson, so it probably used to be somewhere here in the house."

Jo asked, "I'll bet no one found them because no one knew about the compartment."

"That would make sense." Eddie picked up one of the jars and shook it. The contents clinked against the glass.

"Which compartment are we talking about?" Nick asked. "The one in the trunk, or the one in the floor?"

"Good point." Jo smirked. "Both, I guess."

Nick pulled his sketchbook from his backpack and opened it to the place where he had sandwiched the curled paper. It had already flattened out considerably.

He handed the sheet to Jo and watched as she matched up the jagged edge of the page with the inside of the diary.

She looked up, smiling. "A perfect match, and the handwriting is the same, too. Archibald Miller must be the one who coded the message."

Eddie said, "Maybe this old book explains how to break the code."

Nick walked over to the stack of leather books on the edge of the table. Their covers were identical to the hidden book they'd found. "These are *all* diaries." He thumbed through several. "I wonder what makes that one special enough to hide under the floor."

"I bet it has to do with whatever the coded message says." Eddie studied the symbols from the ripped page.

Jo flipped through the pages. "I don't see anything about a code— just more diary entries. Listen to this," she said, "*April seventeenth: North tunnel nearly complete. If Cornelius's prediction is correct, the neottrite will increase as we dig deeper. He says we're all about to become very rich.*"

"Greedy jerk." Eddie shook his head.

Jo said, "Listen to the next one. *April twenty-sixth: The men have found a vein of neottrite. It's produced many small pieces of the mineral. Yesterday, Matthew found a large* ***ferromagnetic nodule*** *in a naturally occurring pool of brilliant blue water. My tests show it to be solid neottrite. The other men have nicknamed the Waterstone.*"

"The Waterstone?" Nick sat up straight. "That's the huge piece of neottrite the whole town went crazy looking for, right?"

Jo nodded.

"Did Miller write anything else about this Waterstone?" Eddie asked. "And who's this Matthew character?"

"Let's see," Jo continued. "On April twenty-eighth, he wrote: *Considerable* **seismic** *activity in the north tunnel today. Excavation in the deeper passages has become precarious, and I have halted operations while the men increase the number of support beams. April twenty-ninth: Twenty-four additional supports added along the north and northeast tunnels. Operations will continue tomorrow. Eleanor and I resumed work on the Telaera. We should be able to begin testing soon.*

"Eleanor again." Eddie itched his forehead through his bandana. "Her name was on the page from the trunk, too."

"Eleanor could be Archibald Miller's wife." Nick glanced at the woman in the painting on the wall.

Jo looked pensive. "It says they resumed work on the Telaera."

"Maybe the Telaera is a machine." Nick looked at the contraptions on the shelves. "This is clearly a workshop of some sort."

Eddie studied the bizarre tangle of crisscrossing lines on the drawing. "I don't think Archibald Miller was building clocks."

Jo nodded as she looked around. "These parts could all be for the Telaera machine."

Eddie puffed out his cheeks, then released a loud exhale. "Whoa." He looked around. "We've got all these random parts down here. "Does the diary have instructions for this Telaera thing?" He picked up a jar labeled *Pinions.* "If the Telaera is built with clock hands and whatever *pinions* are, *we* could build one ourselves!"

Jo said, "Right, but we have no idea what a Telaera does." She flipped to a new page of the diary and scanned the writing. "Let's see what else ol' Archibald writes about here." Her eyes darted left and right. "Hmm." She murmured. "This entry isn't about the machine, but it might be important. On May first, Miller wrote: *Cornelius is furious about the setback.*"

Eddie scratched his chin. "I wonder why?"

Jo scanned the next few entries. "He doesn't say. The rest is just more about the day-to-day mining operations." She turned the page. "Oh, wait! Listen to this. More about the Telaera. *Eleanor has made a most interesting discovery. Apparently, the problem is not our design—but the power source. The electric current from the copper and zinc batteries creates enough voltage to power a desk clock, yet the amount of power required by our Telaera continues to be significantly more than we predicted. Even our three largest batteries together produce only a fraction of the energy needed. The salt water we've been using as a conductor evaporates almost instantly, giving the machine only seconds of power. However, my brilliant wife, Eleanor—*"

"So, Eleanor *is* his wife," Eddie interjected and smiled at Nick. "C.K., you were right."

Jo nodded. "*My brilliant wife, Eleanor wondered what would happen if she replaced the salt water with the blue water Matthew discovered in the mine.*"

Eddie laced his fingers together and rested them on his head. "Did we find out who Matthew is?"

Nick suggested, "Maybe he's the new mine manager."

"I don't think so," Eddie argued. "His name came up before we heard about the manager."

Jo flipped back through the pages. "You're right." She kept reading. "Here's more about the caves they found. "*Branching off the cave is a network of natural tunnels, many of which have similar pools of blue water. The water appears to be* **laden** *with minerals, including salt, hence the brackish nature of the water. However, according to our tests, the primary mineral in the cave water is neottrite. The neottrite gives the water a bluish tint. When we substituted the salt water with the water from the cave, the effect on the electric current was astronomical! We will resume testing the Telaera once Matthew can retrieve more water. He must do without C.B. finding out.*" Jo looked up. That was from May 8th.

Nick said, "Sounds like the Telaera is some sort of high-powered machine C.B.—was trying to steal!"

Jo added, "And C.B. must stand for Cornelius Bennet."

"Exactly."

Eddie crossed his arms, thinking aloud. "Maybe it's a machine for the mine—to help with the excavation?"

"And the neottrite reacts to water, hence the name *Waterstone*." Nick felt the pieces were falling into place.

Jo gasped. "Oh, my gosh."

"What?" Eddie asked.

She looked up, eyes wide. "Eleanor—Eleanor Miller. She was Archibald Miller's wife, but we've heard of her before."

"I've never heard of Eleanor Miller." Eddie frowned.

"Yes, you have," Jo said, quietly. "*She's* the Badger."

"What?

Nick shuddered, remembering the scene with the old woman he imagined in the front yard.

Eddie's jaw dropped. His hands gestured an explosion above his head. "Whoa!" He looked at the diary in Jo's hands. "From what we just read; it sounds like she was a genius. Why in the world would a genius dig holes everywhere?"

"Her son was a miner, right?" Nick asked. "Maybe she lost her mind when the mine collapsed."

Jo played with the words. "Mine collapse causes *mind* collapse."

Nick nodded firmly.

Jo pointed to the next entry. "This one's from two days later: *I joined Matthew today in the north passage. He showed me a ten-foot wide chamber the men unearthed yesterday. It connects to a large network of naturally formed, underground passageways stretching for more than a mile. These passageways run dangerously close to the tunnels the men have already dug. My map shows the entire area has become a dangerously delicate honeycomb. The mine has yet to produce the large quantities of neottrite Cornelius has boasted about to the press. Since the discovery of the Waterstone, there has been no evidence of additional neottrite deposits, but he insists we keep moving deeper.*"

"Something just doesn't add up," Eddie said.

"I know." Nick shook his head. "Even after he knew the mine had become unstable, Miller let those men keep digging—deeper and deeper."

Jo looked up with sad eyes. "What a horrible tragedy."

"No," Eddie argued, "I mean, yes. It was horrible, but that's not what I'm talking about." He folded his arms across his chest. With a furrowed brow, he asked, "Why did Miller say that Bennett insists they keep going deeper? According to those articles we read, *Bennett* was the one who told Miller to stop."

"That's right." Jo flipped to the next page of the diary, intently scanning the writing. Suddenly, she looked up. "Oh, my gosh." She murmured, "We've got it all wrong. Everything we've heard about the mine tragedy is a lie."

"What are you talking about?" Nick asked.

Jo read the rest of the entry. "*Cornelius has assured the men the tunnels are once again stable. I, however, believe the structural integrity of the mine has been jeopardized. Cornelius keeps pushing the men to dig deeper, despite the obvious instability of the tunnels. When I approached him about it, he became enraged. He said the men can dig until they find the neottrite or die trying. "Because the large piece of neottrite needed to power the machine was found in the mine, Bennett believes his name should be included on the patent. With the men's safety on the line—if I decline, I fear he will stop at nothing and would misuse the power of the Telaera.*"

Nick's eyes widened. "Archibald Miller was—innocent?"

Eddie ran a hand through his hair. "Bennett was the bad guy?"

Nick pointed to the open book in front of Jo. "If what Miller wrote here is true, he was wrongly accused of causing the collapse. With Miller trapped in the mine, he wouldn't have been able to defend himself. Cornelius Bennett framed his business partner, then skipped town before anyone found out the truth."

Jo paced back and forth, thinking. "And if he framed Miller for the mine collapse…"

Eddie finished her sentence, "It's possible he framed Miller for the bank robbery, too!"

Overhead, they heard the front door creak as it opened and shut.

"That must be Ginger." Nick grabbed the diary, tucked it into his backpack, and swung the strap over his shoulder. "Let's see what she thinks about all this."

"Thinks about what?" a man's gruff voice bellowed from the doorway above.

Startled, they looked up and saw Mr. Watkins standing on the landing by the hidden door. He leaned on his cane and glared down at them. Nick's stomach tightened into a knot. As the old man's face turned a deep shade of red, Nick watched Jo's face blanche white. Eddie's jaw dropped.

Jo stammered, "W-what are you doing here?"

Mr. Watkins stepped forward. He did not look pleased to see them. "I think the question is, what are *you* doing here?"

Eddie started explaining. "My mom's forcing me to help clean up this creepy, old house and—"

"You mean *MY* house?" he bellowed. "Where's Ginger?"

"*Your* house?" Eddie blurted out. He eyed the dingy walls in disbelief. "You—live here?"

Mr. Watkins looked flustered. He ignored the question, steadied himself with his cane, and walked back toward the doorway. Turning around, he shook his finger at them. "You shouldn't be in here." His harsh tone deepened to a growl. "Everyone out. *NOW*!"

The kids scurried up the stairs and back through the opening in the panel. Mr. Watkins wore a livid scowl. "GET OUT!"

"Mr. Watkins, wait," Jo began. "We found Archibald Miller's diary and—"

"Ramblings of a madman." Mr. Watkins cut her off and swatted the air, dismissing the words she had spoken. He ushered them toward the front door, nudging the backs of their legs with his cane. He called over his shoulder, "Gin-ger!"

"She had a freezer emergency," Nick explained as they were herded onto the front porch.

"Wait," Jo put her hand on the door. "You *have* to read the diary, Mr. Watkins. It changes things. It changes—*everything*!"

"I want NOTHING to do with any of this— or that room—or this house, for that matter." Mr. Watkins grumbled as he wrestled the heavy door closed. "I *knew* this was a bad idea." The crack in the door was shrinking, and Mr. Watkins scowled at them. "I should've sold this cursed place long ago. The dead are best left buried."

The door slammed. Nick, Jo, and Eddie stood on the front porch, somewhat stunned and entirely confused. They walked down the porch steps toward a maroon sedan parked in the driveway.

Eddie broke the silence. "So, does he live here or not?"

Jo rolled her eyes.

Nick answered, "No one lives here."

"But—" Eddie began.

"Don't you see?" Nick leaned forward. "*He's* the grandson who's been taking care of the house."

Jo nodded slowly. "Of course! Gordon Watkins is Archibald Miller's grandson!"

ENLIGHTENMENT

NICK FELT UNSETTLED ABOUT UPSETTING MR. Watkins when they sat down at a table by the window at Ginger Sue's. Eddie had insisted they cash in their ice cream reward immediately, before Lucia could somehow interfere.

"Free dessert for cleaning toilets?" Eddie scooped a huge bite of green ice cream onto his spoon. "Seems like a pretty fair trade."

Jo leaned forward. "Why don't you think Mr. Watkins wants the diary?"

Nick answered, "I don't know, but I'm surprised he wasn't even remotely interested."

Eddie licked his spoon. "Maybe he's already read the diary."

Just then, they heard Ginger's voice coming from the back room of the shop. She appeared in the doorway, then walked over to the kids' table and sat down. "I wondered if I might find you here," she said, with a smile. "The freezer was acting up, but thankfully

Jesse's a whiz with electronics and was able to fix it. A simple rewiring, and it's good as new."

"Thanks for the ice cream," Nick said.

"Well, thanks for your help today. You finished in half the time I thought you would."

For an uncomfortable few seconds, no one spoke. Nick tried to avoid eye contact with Ginger and poked at his ice cream with his spoon.

"Something wrong with the ice cream?" Ginger's eyebrows lifted, and her forehead mounded into delicate ridges.

"No, it's not that. The ice cream's great," Nick said.

Nick felt guilty about snooping in the old house and upsetting Mr. Watkins. He glanced at Jo, who worriedly chewed on her spoon. Eddie nursed another bite. None of them spoke.

"OK." Ginger crossed her arms. "Wanna tell me what's weighin' on your minds?"

Nick took a deep breath, then confessed, "While you were gone, Mr. Watkins came to the house, and—then he asked us to leave." He conveniently omitted the part about the basement room.

"Oh, gracious." Ginger looked at the ceiling. "He's been in a tizzy all week about all the work that needs to be done before he sells that old place. That's why a bunch of us are pitchin' in to help out." She let out a heavy sigh. "I didn't think he would mind, but I guess I shoulda told him I found some extra helpers. With everything that happened all those years ago, he's understandably very private about his family history. I'm sure it's nothing personal. You just surprised him, that's all."

Nick sucked a breath through his teeth. Eddie glared at him and shook his head. He clearly didn't want Nick to elaborate on *where* Mr. Watkins found them.

Jo, however, didn't see the look. "We surprised him alright," she said. "While we were cleaning—we found a room with a bunch of old clocks, and Mr. Watkins didn't seem to like the fact that we were in there."

Ginger tucked a red lock of hair behind her ear. "I don't remember a room with clocks—although with everything covered up with sheets—"

"You probably didn't see *this* room," Jo explained. "Nick found a hidden door behind a secret panel in the hallway near the kitchen."

"Hidden door?" Ginger's eyebrows lifted. "Secret panel?"

"Please don't tell my mom," Eddie pleaded.

Nick felt the need to justify himself. "I wasn't trying to be nosy or anything. I literally bumped into that bench and just kinda found the door." He absent-mindedly rubbed the bruise on his knee.

With a dramatic tone in his voice, Eddie said, "There was a huge, stone staircase and jars full of hands."

Ginger's eyes widened. "Well, now I'm interested in seeing this so-called secret room."

Nick explained, "It looked like some sort of workshop." He gave Eddie a look before adding, "And the 'hands' were clock hands."

"That's where Mr. Watkins found us," Jo admitted. "He was pretty mad we were down there."

"I see." Ginger rested her hands on the table. "I'll swing by to see him later and see if I can smooth things over. He's probably already back at his shop. He never stays at the house very long."

Eddie grimaced. "Be careful."

"Oh, now. Gordon's usually pretty docile, but he can be a salty old cookie. You can hardly blame him. He's had a rough go of it. I think that's why he keeps to himself. It couldn't have been easy growing up hearing all those ugly rumors about your family. You know, the whole Badger nonsense."

"Why would there be a mysterious room hidden under that old house?" Nick asked.

"I'd guess that secret room you found was his grandparents' workshop. Gordon mentioned they were both brilliant inventors."

Seeing the confusion on their faces, Ginger explained, "Archibald sold part of his land to Cornelius Bennett to get the cash to work on some big invention he and Eleanor wanted to show at the World's Fair in Chicago." Ginger sighed. "Unfortunately, after the accident, with Archibald and Matthew both gone—"

Just then, a group of tall, boisterous boys entered the shop and stood in line behind a gray-haired couple standing at the counter. The couple was clearly annoyed by the new customers. Jesse gave Ginger a desperate look.

Ginger rose to her feet. "Looks like basketball practice just ended."

"Wait." Jo reached for Ginger's arm. "Did you say, 'Matthew?' Was he the mine manager?"

Ginger smiled and replied, "No. Matthew was Archibald and Eleanor's son. Their daughter, Savannah, was Gordon's mother. She was a lovely lady."

"Ginger?" Jesse called from the counter.

"I better give him a hand." She turned and cheerfully greeted the long line of customers.

Jo leaned in and said quietly, "I really feel like we might be onto something big here."

Nick nodded. "Bennett was a criminal. He forced those men to keep digging deeper when Archibald warned him it was too dangerous."

Jo said, "If we can somehow prove Archibald Miller wasn't responsible for the mine collapse, our town's history will be permanently changed, and Mr. Watkins won't have to have people thinking his grandfather was responsible for the mine tragedy."

Nick remembered the large painting in the dining room. The people in the painting had no idea what the future held.

Eddie suggested, "Let's take a look at our inventory. Nick, what do we have so far?"

Nick reached inside the collar of his T-shirt and pulled the key up and over his head. He scratched his neck where the itchy lace had been rubbing against his skin. "We've got the key with the coordinates that unlocks something." He reached into his bag. "We also have a sketch of the stolen map, and the diary including the ripped-out pages.

Nick set the leather book on the table.

"We can't keep it," Jo said. "We'll have to return the diary to Mr. Watkins. He might be mad at us for snooping around, but he deserves to know the truth. His grandfather didn't cause those men to die. He was trying to save them."

Nick frowned as he looked at the sketch he'd made of the map. He'd drawn a star over the location of the coordinates on the key. The star was directly between the Miller house and Uncle John's cabin.

He pressed on one of the blisters on his palm.

Eddie finished the last bite of his ice cream. In a doubtful voice, he said, "I was hoping we'd find a buried treasure, but honestly, I'm starting to think we might just be wasting our time. In all the movies I've seen, the kid detectives find, like, one or two clues, and they're led right to the treasure." He sighed. "We've got a ton of clues here. How do we not have answers? And shouldn't we have found something by now?"

Jo shrugged, "Well, Hollywood makes everything seem easy, and the mystery has to be wrapped up by the end of the movie. This is real life, Eddie. Being a hero takes time. Even if we don't find a buried treasure, I really think we have a chance at clearing Mr. Watkins's family history and the Miller name."

Jo suggested. "Maybe Mr. Watkins can help us fill in some of the missing information."

Eddie shook his head. "Hard pass, thanks."

"I think we should at least show him what the diary says," Jo urged. "If my family was blamed for a horrible tragedy, I'd want everyone to know if they were innocent."

Nick nodded. "Mr. Watkins probably never wants to see us again. Once he realizes we're on his side, he might actually listen to us."

Eddie crossed his arms and sat back against his chair, unconvinced.

Nick added, "These clues must fit together—somehow." He looked at Jo. "It would help if we knew what the coded message says. Is there any hope we'll figure out the symbols?"

"Well, sure," Jo scoffed. "I mean, any code is breakable." She rested her chin on her hand. "Like I said before, it just takes time. If we're lucky, it could be a substitution cipher, where each symbol represents a letter from the English language."

"And if we're unlucky?" Eddie asked.

Jo looked up with a skeptical expression. "Worst case scenario, it's a **polyalphabetic** code, which means each letter equals a different letter, which equals yet a different letter or symbol. If that's the case, it could be a classic **Caesar's Shift** or maybe **Trimethius's Tableau** or…" She trailed off, murmuring to herself.

Nick ran a hand through his hair. "OK, so it's complicated."

Jo looked up. "That's putting it mildly."

"I say we try giving the diary back to Mr. Watkins." Nick suggested. "Maybe he knows how to decipher the code."

Eddie groaned. "I'm still grounded, remember? Technically, I shouldn't even be here." He glanced at the counter where Jesse stood, handing a cone to an elderly man. "I was supposed to come straight home after cleaning the bathrooms. If I'm not back soon, my mom will send my probation officer after me again."

Jo made a face. "Lucia?"

"Exactly." Eddie scrunched his mouth to the side. "Jesse'll probably rat me out anyways."

"Alright," Nick said. "Jo and I'll head over to the jewelry shop. Do you think you can convince your mom to give you the night off?"

Eddie grimaced. "Maybe. No guarantees though."

Nick stood up and set his backpack on his chair. As he tucked his sketchbook inside, Eddie slid back his chair. His courage had returned. His timing, however, was unfortunate because the elderly man with the ice cream cone happened to be walking behind Eddie and collided with the moving chair.

"Agh! My hip!" The man winced. He shook a finger at Eddie. "You should be more careful!"

Eddie immediately apologized. The man dropped the newspaper he'd been holding, and Eddie stooped to pick it up.

"At least you didn't drop your ice cream." Eddie tried to smooth things over.

His smile was met with a scowl.

A gray-haired woman standing next to the old man scolded, "Young man, you should pay attention to what you're doing. Kids these days. So impulsive. Rushing around like that will get you into trouble."

Eddie's gaze fell to the floor. "Sorry," he mumbled.

Nick saw Jesse watching the scene unfold. He had a smirk on his face.

"Would you like to sit down?" Nick asked the couple. "We're just leaving."

The woman answered dryly, "Yes."

Nick and Jo quickly finished gathering the items from the table. The woman had already plopped down in a chair. She wiped up the sticky, green spots where melted ice cream drips had landed.

Jo apologized again, adding, "I like your nail polish."

The woman ignored the compliment and shook her head.

Once they were outside, Eddie said, "Remind me to never be that crabby when I get old."

Nick laughed.

Jo asked, "Eddie, do you still have the bandana Ginger gave you?"

"Eddie checked the pockets of his vest but didn't find a bandana. "I think I left it in the secret laboratory, or whatever that room was. Why?"

"You can use mine." From her back pocket, Jo pulled out her bandana and tied it around Eddie's forehead. Then she messed up his hair, stooped down to rub her hands in the dirt, and started to smudge dirt on Eddie's face.

He pushed her hand away and took a step back. "What the heck?"

"Trust me," she said and smeared a streak of dirt across his cheek. "There," she said. "Now you look like you've been cleaning bathrooms."

"But I *have* been cleaning bathrooms."

Jo smirked. "I know, but this should buy you some sympathy when you ask your mom if you can meet us at Castle Rock later. Keep your walkie talkie on."

Eddie nodded. "Good luck with Mr. Watkins."

JASPER

NICK AND JO ARRIVED at Watkins' Jewelry shop. Through the window, they could see the overhead lights and lamp at the workbench were off. Nick opened the door and poked his head inside.

"Mr. Watkins?"

There was no reply.

He took a step inside and called out, "Hello?"

Jo followed close behind and said, "Nick, look." Jo pointed to the sign in the window. It read: *'We're Closed.'*

They were turning to leave when they heard a *CLUNK* sound from the back room.

"Mr. Watkins?" Nick repeated.

Jo nudged Nick forward, and they walked inside.

From the back of the shop, they heard a scuffling, followed by a soft clatter.

Jo leaned over the glass case and craned her neck, trying to peek past the blue curtain into the back room. "Hello?"

"Mr. Watkins?" Nick moved around the end of the counter and threw back the curtain.

Jo followed Nick into the storage room. It was filled with rows of shelves of cardboard boxes stacked to the ceiling. Several empty boxes lay strewn across the middle of the floor. There was no sign of Gordon Watkins.

"This is weird." Nick picked up an empty shoebox.

One side of the cardboard was covered with clusters of five puncture marks and parallel, diagonal slashes. Three of the flaps were ragged, and the fourth flap was missing altogether. Shredded cardboard pieces were scattered across the cement floor.

"Really weird," he said.

Jo walked behind a row of shelves at the far edge of the room and called out, "Nick, there's something back here."

Nick found Jo standing at a workbench. She was looking at the machine they'd seen Mr. Watkins working on. Dozens of screwdrivers, pliers, and other tools were scattered across the benchtop. The machine itself was not much larger than the shoebox on the ground. Wires poked out the top at odd angles like gangly weeds. On the side was a large lever and a network of gears.

A small movement above Nick's head caught his attention. He looked up to see two yellow eyes staring at him.

"Well, hello, Jasper."

Jo stoked his back. "I wish you could tell us what happened here."

The nimble black feline jumped from the shelf to the table. As he did, a small box clattered out from under his feet and landed next to Nick's foot. Jasper pounced onto it, then jabbed at it with his front paw. The box evaded the attack and slid across the floor. In a flurry of cardboard and fur, the box and cat tumbled end over end into a corner. Jasper leaped onto the cube with a victorious pounce and sunk his claws into one of the sides, leaving diagonal slashes and clusters of tiny holes in the thick, brown cardboard.

"Well, that explains the commotion," Nick said.

"And the massacred box," Jo added.

Jasper darted under the bench. There was a rustling of paper, and a single paw poked out.

"He sure is playful," Jo said. She nudged a nearby box with her foot, and a streak of black shot toward it, curled into a ball, and rolled across the top.

"He's like a furry ninja." Nick laughed.

When Jasper paused, Jo picked him up and cradled him in her arms. She ran her hand across his sleek fur until he jumped down and pressed his curved back and tail against the leg of the bench. After several more box **ambushes**, Jasper strolled across the room. His burst of energy spent, he disappeared behind the blue curtain, presumably to his napping station near the window.

"Do you think Mr. Watkins is still at the old house?" Nick asked.

"He's clearly not here. It's weird, though, that the front door was unlocked." Jo looked around and replied, “I know his store isn’t known for having a lot of valuable items, but I’m surprised he left it open.”

Nick said, “Ginger said lately he’s been—how did she phrase it?”

“*In a tizzy*?” Jo said.

Nick nodded. “Maybe he just forgot.” He pushed Jasper's cardboard “toys” toward the edge of the room and headed for the doorway.

A muffled shout called out from Jo's hip.

Jo turned her volume up. “We’re here, Red Fox. Can you repeat that?”

Static. “We’ve got a problem here at the hideout. How soon can you get here? Over.”

Jo spoke into the speaker of her walkie talkie. “We’re at the jewelry shop. What’s up?”

Static. “I can’t say more—not sure this channel is secure—moving to radio silence—see you when you get here—over. Oh, and hurry.”

DISGUISES

NICK AND JO APPROACHED THE HIDEOUT AT CASTLE Rock. After rounding the last bend before the trailhead, they saw a tan car parked on the side of the road.

"This must be the *problem* Eddie was talking about," Jo said.

They wheeled their bicycles into the tall grass. Eddie's bike was nearby, in its usual spot. For several seconds, they held perfectly still, watching and listening. The only sound was the gentle fluttering of leaves in the trees. There was no movement, no sticks snapping under feet walking through the woods. Cautiously, Nick approached the vehicle. It was empty.

The two darted along the trail into the woods toward the hideout. They ducked under the low branch near the entrance and paused. From behind them a hand clamped over each of their mouths, stifling the shouts rising in their throats. They spun around and stared into a pair of familiar brown eyes.

"Eddie?" Nick asked.

Eddie's nose, cheeks, and forehead were smudged with dark green paint camouflaging him against the **foliage** of the forest.

"Shhh!" he hissed. "Someone's here."

"We know," Nick whispered.

"You saw the car?"

Jo frowned. "How'd you get here so fast? Did you get un-grounded?"

Eddie shook his head. "I was on my way home when I saw that tan car turn toward the lake, so I followed it."

Jo nodded and whispered, "Who was it?"

"I don't know. Some guy. I haven't gotten a good look at his face, but he's been down by the lake this whole time. Eddie ducked low and scurried past the hammocks toward the edge of the clearing and dropped to an army crawl.

Nick and Jo followed. A stranger sat below, facing away from them, on the ledge hanging over the water. From their vantage point, they could only see the back of the individual, who appeared to be an adult man. He wore a black sweatshirt with the sleeves cut off at the shoulders. It was a warm day, but the hood of the sleeveless sweatshirt was up, and they couldn't see his face.

Eddie kept his eyes on the figure and whispered, "He hasn't moved from that spot. Let's get a closer look."

The three stealthily descended the trail along the steep bank. A steady breeze blew toward them from the lake, and the rustling leaves overhead covered the sound of their footsteps. Jo pulled Nick behind a wide tree at the base of the trail. Eddie hid behind a cluster of dense shrubs a few feet away.

Legs swinging casually over the water, the stranger hadn't seemed to notice them. He raised his arm and chucked a pebble into the lake. It landed with a soft *PLUNK.* Now that they were much closer, Nick realized the man was actually more like a high school boy but was significantly larger than them. Judging by the size of his biceps, this boy was no stranger to the weight room at the gym. He raised his arm again and revealed a large tuft of hair in his armpit.

Nick felt worried. Confronting a kid was one thing, but this person had the body of an adult and the muscles to go with it. Their safest bet was to head back up the trail, and leave this person alone. Nick caught Eddie's eye and used hand signals to communicate his idea to retreat. Eddie returned a confusing blur of karate chopping motions. They were still miming at each other when the hooded stranger stood up.

Nick watched Eddie lick his lower lip. After everything that had happened with Billy and Jack, Nick suspected Eddie was gearing up for a showdown. He had a fierce gleam in his eye, which, combined with the face paint, made him look like he was ready for battle. Eddie silently picked up an enormous brown pinecone—the kind with thick, jagged petals with sharp points on the ends.

With a sinking feeling in his stomach, Nick realized the peaceful retreat he'd tried to suggest was going to be overruled. He looked at Jo, who grabbed a handful of pebbles. She gave him a single nod. The confrontation was imminent.

Nick knew he needed something with which to defend himself. His eyes darted around, searching for a large, sturdy branch. Unfortunately, the only thing he could find was a pinecone, but it wasn't spiky like Eddie's. It was oblong, compact, green, and the size of a french fry. It was practically useless. Nevertheless, he grasped it and prepared to chuck it—or at least flick it—at the intruder.

Eddie looked at Nick and Jo. He nodded once. Then, slowly raising his arm, Eddie took aim and fired his pinecone grenade at the mystery person. It whizzed through the air and exploded on contact—a direct hit on the back of the head. Jo discharged the **bombardment** of pebbles. Pinecone **shrapnel** and pebbles rained onto the stone ledge.

The stranger stood up and looked up at the overhanging trees while rubbing his head. Before Nick had a chance to balance his puny, green pinecone in his palm and flick it at the intruder's eyeball, Eddie bolted from his hiding place. He leaped onto the stranger's back and knocked him off-balance. In a movement that very much reminded Nick of Jasper attacking the cardboard box, Eddie wrestled the intruder to the ground. Unfortunately, Eddie did not share Jasper's strength or **agility**, and after a brief struggle, he was tossed aside. In this scenario, Eddie was more like the cardboard box than the stealthy feline predator.

"Dude!" The stranger pulled off his hood.

"Jesse?" Eddie asked.

"What's wrong with you people?" Jesse rotated his right arm, inspecting it for injury, then eyed the tiny pinecone pinched between Nick's thumb and forefinger.

Nick chucked the makeshift "weapon" into the bushes. "Sorry Jesse, we didn't know it was you."

Jesse took a moment to inspect a toothpick he'd been clenching between his teeth during the scuffle. "I coulda choked on this." He repositioned it between his molars and clamped down again. "I've been waiting for you dweebs for half an hour."

Eddie stepped forward. "Hey! Who you callin' dwee—"

Jo put her arm out to restrain Eddie.

"How'd you know where to find us?" Eddie asked suspiciously.

Jesse spoke around the toothpick with ease. "I see you guys biking back here all the time when I'm cruising around. I figured you had some sort of nerdy clubhouse in the woods."

Eddie's jaw dropped in disbelief. He let out a series of incoherent noises, then stood in speechless silence.

Nick asked, "Whose car is parked on the road?"

"That's my cousin's car." He added, "Jeep's getting an upgrade."

Eddie ran a hand through his hair and paced back and forth. From the look on his face, Nick could tell he was hung up on the fact that Jesse not only knew about their hideout, but he'd known about it for quite some time.

"You've been looking for *us*?" Jo flipped a braid over her shoulder and rested a hand on her hip. "Why? Do you need our help with something?"

"Uh…" Jesse gave her a patronizing smile, then smirked. "Definitely no." He glanced around and cleared his throat. "Look. I gotta get going, so I'll make this quick." He looked at Eddie. "You know that old guy you bumped into at the shop earlier?"

Eddie bristled and crossed his arms. "Look, if that old guy's got a problem—"

"Nah, nothing like that."

"Well, I apologized right away and—" Eddie stopped mid-sentence. "Great. My mom's probably going to make me scrub the kitchen floor with a toothbrush."

"Dude, would you just listen?"

Eddie frowned. "What?"

Jesse adjusted his hat and continued. "I just wanted to tell you that while you were talking to that old guy—well, his wife—or whatever—tried to take a book or something off your table. Dude, it was a setup. They were trying to distract you."

"What?" Nick asked, thinking back to the scene. The old woman had pushed him out of the way while she was supposedly wiping the table.

"Are you sure?" Jo asked.

Jesse looked at her and scoffed, "Nah, I just had nothing better to do, so I thought I'd come get jumped by a gang of kindergarteners. Of course, I'm sure."

"For your information, we're in middle school," Jo corrected.

"Whatever." Jesse's tone changed when he added, "Anyways, just as she reached for the book," he looked at Nick, "you turned around—and she didn't take it. At least I don't think she did."

"She didn't," Eddie said. "We still have it."

Jo threw a chastising look.

Eddie winced.

"Whatever. I don't care." Jesse took a step toward the trail. "They left right after you did and didn't even finish their ice cream."

Jo asked, "So, you came all the way out here just to tell us that?"

Jesse scratched his chin, clearly trying to decide what to say next. "Well, there is one more thing." He cracked his neck to the side and scraped the toothpick between two of his bottom teeth, then sighed, as if reluctant to continue. "When they left, I caught the old man's eye. He looked—I dunno—suspicious, so I followed them outside, but when they noticed me, they bolted."

"Bolted?" Nick couldn't quite picture the old couple moving faster than a shuffle.

"Did you see where they headed?" Eddie asked.

"Oh my gosh—did their car have a seagull on the hood?" Jo's eyes widened.

Nick knew she suspected were working for the Caldwells.

Jesse replied, "I was chasing 'em on foot, but…" He trailed off.

"You lost them?" Eddie didn't hide his disappointment. "An old man and an old woman outran *you*?"

Nick glanced at the Track & Field logo on Jesse's sweatshirt and noted the irony.

Jesse, clearly embarrassed, rolled his shoulders back and clenched his jaw. "Well," he justified, "I was gaining on 'em, but I lost them when they turned at the end of the block."

Eddie snickered. "I can't believe you were outrun by two senior citizens."

Jesse stepped forward and grabbed the front of Eddie's T-shirt. "Dude. Watch it. I'm only here because Lucia said I should keep an eye on you."

"I already told you I don't need a babysitter."

Jesse smirked, "Last I checked, you were grounded. And yet, you didn't look grounded eating that ice cream."

"I don't need you keeping tabs on me, OK?"

Jesse's voice softened. "Dude, she told me you're being bullied and—"

"What?" Eddie's cheeks reddened.

Jesse flexed his bicep and adjusted the toothpick between his teeth. "I'm just saying—if you need protection, I'm offering my services."

"Yeah." Eddie stood up straight. "Says the guy who was outrun by two old people. Hard pass on that one, buddy."

Jesse leaned forward and poked Eddie's chest so hard, it knocked him backward. "I didn't get outrun by old people."

Jo put her hand on Eddie's shoulder and winked at Jesse. "OK, we got it."

"No, seriously."

Nick mimed zipping his lips shut. "Mum's the word." He twisted an invisible key and tossed it into the lake.

"Cut it out." Jesse looked frustrated. "I didn't get beat by two old people because they *weren't* 'old' people. That's what I'm trying to tell you." Jesse reached into his sweatshirt pocket and pulled out two gray wigs. "I found these on the ground just after I lost sight of 'em."

Nick, Jo, and Eddie exchanged glances. Quickly piecing together what had happened, they realized whoever those people were, they clearly knew about the diary and had gone as far as disguising themselves to get it.

"Anyways, you three ought to be careful. I have no idea who they were or what they were doing, but it seems like they knew who *you* were, and they definitely knew something about that book."

"What if they heard us talking about the code and—" This time, Eddie cut himself off.

Jesse's eyes narrowed. "Code?" He searched their faces. "What exactly are you mixed up in?"

"Nothing we can't handle," Eddie said confidently.

"Look, I'm really not interested in whatever fifth graders do for fun." Jesse turned to leave. "I just thought you might want to know."

"For your information," Eddie retorted, "I'm in seventh grade, and these two are in eighth."

"Good for you."

Eddie looked down. "Sorry about tackling you."

"I'm over it." Jesse pulled off his hat, ran his hand through his hair, and twisted the brim into place. "No harm to the arm, so we're good." He faked a gut punch toward Eddie—who flinched—then he climbed the rugged path to the clearing above.

When Jesse was out of sight, Eddie grabbed Nick's arm. "Can you believe that?"

Nick gave a nod and replied, "I was totally convinced those people were actually old."

Eddie looked confused. "Oh—right."

Jo smiled. "You're mad that he knows about the hideout, aren't you?"

Eddie shot back, "We were being so careful. I mean, does *everyone* know about this place?"

Jo smirked. She reached out and swiped her finger across Eddie's forehead. "I don't remember putting this much on your face."

"I'm always prepared for the occasional spy operation." He pulled out a small tin of camo face paint from his pocket.

Nick said, "Speaking of disguises, we need to figure out who is after Archibald Miller's diary, and I'm betting it's the Caldwells."

Jo put one arm over Eddie's shoulder and the other over Nick's. "We'll figure it out—as long as we stick together and no one else gets grounded."

"Well, now what?" Nick asked as they biked along the road.

"I say we get the diary back to Mr. Watkins," Jo said.

Eddie added, "Before someone actually steals it."

"The last place we saw him was at the Miller house," Nick recalled.

"Let's go," Jo said as she pedaled.

Sneaking In

"Mr. Watkins's maroon sedan was still parked outside the Miller house when they arrived. They walked across the creaky porch. Nick lifted the iron door knocker and let it fall with a *BANG!* against the metal strike plate. They waited, but no one answered the door. Nick tried the handle, but it was locked.

"I have an idea," Jo said. "Follow me."

She led the way to the back of the house and stopped outside the room where she and Nick gathered dusty sheets. The window Nick had opened earlier was still ajar. Jo pushed the sash up all the way and hoisted herself to a seated position on the window ledge.

"Umm," Eddie said. "What are you doing?"

"Returning the diary. That *was* the plan, wasn't it?" Jo disappeared inside the dark room.

"Right. Go back into the creepy house with the angry owner. Great plan," Eddie grumbled as he climbed headfirst through the window. His legs flailed for a moment before flopping over the ledge, and he landed with a *THUD*. He dusted himself off, then leaned out the window. "You coming?"

Nick still felt uncertain about the old house and entering without permission seemed like a whole new category of bad ideas. He stood on the lawn with his arms crossed. "I'll keep a lookout."

"Suit yourself," Eddie replied.

"Wait," Nick said. He eyed the dark woods flanking the house and thought of the "old" couple at Ginger Sues. His hands suddenly felt sweaty. He asked, "Who do you think those people in disguises were?"

"I don't know," Eddie answered, "but if you stay out here, you might just find out." He flashed a smile, then disappeared inside.

Nick sighed. Sneaking into a creepy, old mansion wasn't the sort of adventure he'd anticipated this summer, but it certainly wasn't one he would forget—that is, if they made it out in one piece. A breeze brushed his cheek, and the leaves in the trees surrounding the house chattered quietly, as if whispering a warning. His instinct told him that helping his friends return the diary was the right thing to do. Taking a deep breath, he put his hands on the windowsill and hoisted himself up, over, and through.

Inside, he stood in the familiar room and felt strangely greeted by the painting of the two women in matching dresses. He listened for footsteps, but the old house was dark and quiet. He tiptoed toward the kitchen and jumped when he felt a hand on his shoulder. He whirled around to see Jo grinning.

She clamped her hand over her mouth to stifle a giggle. "Sorry!" she whispered, then looked past him. "Where's Eddie?"

"What do you mean? He's not with you?"

"No. I thought he was with *you*." A veil of panic shrouded her face. "Eddie?" she called out in a loud whisper.

"What?" Eddie popped his head around the corner.

Nick breathed a sigh of relief. "Where did you go?"

"I was waiting here by the bench."

Jo shot back, "But I was just there—"

Nick interrupted her, "Look, this place is a maze. You probably went circles. From now on, let's stick together and do what we came to do." He opened his backpack and set the diary on the kitchen counter.

Jo picked up the leather book and hugged it to her chest. She whispered, "This might be the only piece of evidence that clears Mr. Watkins's grandfather of wrong-doing. We need to make sure it gets back to him—and *only* him."

Eddie patted the counter where the book had been. "This is his house, Jo. I'm sure he'll find it."

She shook her head. "Ginger said a bunch of people from town have been helping clean this place. We can't assume those people from the ice cream shop aren't pretending to be volunteers just so they can snoop around."

Nick nodded. "I agree with Jo."

"Fine." Eddie spun on his heel and opened the swinging, louvered doors leading to the hallway with the bench.

In the dark hallway, Jo grabbed Eddie's arm. She held a finger to her lips then pointed to a pale, yellow light illuminated the edges of the secret panel.

"Someone's here," Nick pulled the panel back and tiptoed onto the landing at the top of the basement staircase.

In the room below, they saw Mr. Watkins. He was walking slowly next to the shelves, looking at the jars filled with clock parts. His back was turned, and he didn't see them.

Jo cleared her throat to get his attention. With a startled expression on his face, Mr. Watkins looked up toward the landing where they stood.

"You again?" He frowned. "How did you…?"

Eddie stated, "We crawled through an open window."

Jo shot him a critical glare.

He shrugged. "What? There's no use in lying."

"You three are trespassing," the old man snarled. "This house is not a public facility from which you may come and go as you please. Perhaps a call to the authorities will send a clear message to you."

"Let's just give him the diary and go." Nick took the book from Jo and started walking down the steps.

"You couldn't possibly have anything of interest to me. You may show yourselves out in the same manner that you entered."

Jo's shoulders slumped.

"Mr. Watkins, it's kind of important." Nick's voice seemed thin as it echoed against the stone walls.

"Ha!" The old man narrowed his eyes. "I'm certainly not looking at anything from three trespassing kids who broke into my house. Leave now."

"Please," Jo called out. "We've been following clues and—"

The old man waved a hand and scoffed, "I have neither the patience for—nor interest in—digging up the past." He shuffled toward an old-fashioned phone hanging on the wall. "I'm calling Pete Hansen." He lifted the receiver, which was attached to a long, curly cord connecting it to a box on the wall. He used his index finger to spin around on the box. The dial had finger-sized holes around the outside edge and made a whirring sound.

On the landing, Eddie paced back and forth. He ran his hand over his face and rubbed the back of his neck, muttering, "This is definitely going to get back to my mom. I think we should go."

"Mr. Watkins, if you just—" Jo began.

"No." His finger spun the dial around again.

Nick turned and whispered to his friends, "Who's Pete Hansen?"

Eddie's eyes rolled toward Nick, and he muttered. "He's Jesse's dad—the Chief of Police."

Nick knew there must be something he could say, something to convince Mr. Watkins to listen to them. A dozen suggestions raced through his head; none of them worth giving a second thought. He took a deep breath and everything seemed to slow down.

Perhaps it was the mixture of **prolonged** tension and anxiety, blended with the fatigue of being pushed around by bullies and people in wigs and worrying about the Caldwells. Maybe it was the fact that he felt a little tired and hungry—which always made him feel a little reckless—but whatever the reason, Nick felt something inside him snap. He was filled with a strange sense of boldness.

Standing tall, he lifted his chin, and before he knew what he was doing, he took one step down, then another.

Suddenly, his mind felt clear.

Of course.

He knew what to say. The idea glowed in his head, as if illuminated by a spotlight.

Mr. Watkins started talking into the round mouthpiece of the phone. "Pete? It's Gordon Watkins. I've got some kids here causing trouble. Can you send someone over?"

Nick knew the window of opportunity was closing fast.

Mr. Watkins was saying, "...they've been snooping around and—"

Nick blurted out, "We know your grandfather was innocent!"

Mr. Watkins froze. The phone slid to his shoulder. He was still frowning, but his gaze had softened from annoyance to something else. Was it—hopeful?

They heard a faint voice through the receiver. "...Hello?...Hello?..."

Mr. Watkins mumbled, "Pete? I'll call you back." He returned the receiver to its hanger. Through narrow slits in his eyes, he stared at Nick. His jaw bounced slightly, as if he were chewing on the words—trying to decide if he liked the thought enough to accept it. “What did you say?”

Jo crept halfway down the stairs. Eddie followed close behind. Standing next to Nick, Jo replied, “We know Archibald Miller wasn’t responsible for the tunnel collapse that trapped those miners.”

The old man’s eyes darted toward the hallway door. “Who told you that?”

When Nick heard the slight waver in Mr. Watkin’s voice, he immediately knew the old man *wanted* to believe them. “It’s all in here,” he said, holding up the leather book. “This is your grandfather’s diary, and it explains everything.”

The Diary

The floorboards creaked as Nick walked toward Mr. Watkins. "We think you'll want to read this." He flipped to the May 10, 1893 entry and held the diary out.

Mr. Watkins glanced at the book but made no effort to take it.

Nick glanced down at the entry. The loops and curls that just days ago had been foreign to his eyes now read clearly as letters and words. In a voice conveying more confidence than he felt, he began reading. "*I, however, believe the structural integrity of the mine has been jeopardized. Cornelius keeps pushing the men to dig deeper, despite the obvious instability of the tunnels. He said the men can dig until they find neottrite or die trying.*"

Nick glanced up. He had the old man's attention, so he skipped ahead to the next entry. "*Because the large piece of neottrite needed to power the machine was found in the mine, Bennett believes his name should be included on the patent. With the men's safety on the line, if I decline—he knows he has all the leverage. I fear he will stop at nothing to gain power and wealth and would misuse the power of the Telaera."*

Mr. Watkins leaned heavily on his cane, took several steps toward the table, and collapsed onto one of the metal stools. Nick offered the book again. With trembling hands, Mr. Watkins accepted the leather-bound pages. His eyes flickered back and forth as he read, and his wrinkled fingers delicately turned the brittle, yellow pages. After several minutes, he looked up with misty eyes.

"Completely innocent?" he murmured, then scanned the next page and repeated, "*Completely* innocent." Mr. Watkins rubbed his forehead. "I—must apologize. I assumed you came here—like the others did, years ago—to look for the Waterstone or the stolen money."

"We want to help prove your grandfather's innocence," Jo said.

Nick elaborated, "This pages are full of answers, but we were hoping—with your help—we might be able to decipher this." He pointed to the page covered with symbols.

Eddie added, "Maybe it leads to the stolen bank money."

"Ah—" Mr. Watkins's expression darkened, and his tone became crisp. "As I suspected—" He glared at them. "You're not concerned about my grandfather's innocence. You're treasure hunters."

"No, we're not," Jo countered.

"No? Then why, exactly, are you here?" Mr. Watkins wore an expression perfectly blending furious and exhausted. "I have news for you. There is no treasure. There is nothing hidden, nothing to be found."

"Are you sure?" Eddie asked. "Because if you happen to have an idea about where anything valuable might be buried, we already have shovels and—"

"What we're trying to say," Nick interrupted, "is we didn't start out looking for any of this. We just sort of stumbled across a clue and, well…"

He wasn't sure how to regain the old man's trust and convince him to share more about potentially important things like the Telaera or the code. He eyed the frayed edge of the cryptic message, and a sinking feeling crept into his stomach. It dawned on him that even if Mr. Watkins wanted to help them with the secret message—which was doubtful—he simply might not know how.

Eddie leaned forward, about to speak again, and Nick cringed. He hadn't known Eddie for long, but he knew the younger boy was often blunt, and usually didn't think before speaking.

"Look," Eddie began, "like Nick said, we didn't start out looking for these clues. We're not like—professional treasure hunters or anything, and we're not trying to rob you or be sneaky—if that's what you're thinking—so you can relax. If there's no hidden money, fine. I won't say I'm not disappointed, but like it or not, you're already in this with us." Eddie glanced sideways at Nick, then added, "You're the one who helped us find the key, and if the coordinates written on the side of that key lead to a buried treasure, well—"

"Bah!" Mr. Watkins let out an amused scoff. "Buried treasure! My grandmother became consumed with the legend, as did my own parents. They lost everything chasing a phantom promise."

Nick pulled the shoelace out from under his shirt. "There are coordinates stamped onto the side of this key. They mark a location somewhere between this house and the cabin next door."

"We've been digging over there for days," Eddie explained. "We think whatever the key marks is somewhere close by." He pulled his compass out and set it on the table.

Nick expected Mr. Watkins to shuffle back to the phone and call the sheriff again, but to his surprise, the old man lifted his cane an inch off the ground and tapped it twice.

"You know. I believe you," Mr. Watkins said. "I haven't heard those words since my grandmother died." He added, "About my grandfather being innocent." He sniffled and placed his palm face down on the open diary. "My grandmother *insisted* the tunnel collapse at the mine was not my grandfather's fault, but after years of finding no evidence to support her claim, I assumed it was merely wishful thinking. So many years, so many secrets." He looked around the room and shook his head. "I had no idea any of this existed. After the collapse, my grandmother couldn't bear to live in this house with its painful memories. She and my mother moved into the little house next door."

They gave the old man a moment to flip through the diary they'd found.

When he reached the section in the diary where the pages had been torn out, he murmured, "I guess I was wrong about nothing being hidden."

Nick explained, "We found those pages separate from the rest of the book. They were under a secret panel in an old trunk. My uncle said you sold it to him a few months ago."

Mr. Watkins nodded. "Ah, yes. That trunk belonged to my grandmother."

Nick was about to point out the coded message when Mr. Watkins's shoulders stiffened. He asked, "Who else knows about this book?"

Jo pressed her lips together and admitted, "We don't know exactly who it was, but someone stole a map we were looking at. We were trying to pinpoint the coordinates from the key, and then two people tried to steal the diary."

"When was this?"

"A few days ago," Nick answered. "The diary thing happened today, at Ginger Sue's. It was two people dressed in disguises."

Eddie added, "Our friend tried to chase them down, but they got away."

Mr. Watkins took a deep breath, adjusted his glasses, and rubbed his chin. After a moment, he seemed to have decided something. "We all need to be very careful." He tucked the ripped pages into place and closed the book.

"Why is that?" Jo asked.

Mr. Watkins looked up sharply. "Because one of the pages contains a very valuable piece of information."

"The coded message?" Nick suggested.

Mr. Watkins nodded. "Whoever is looking for the diary is probably desperate to find it—and desperation can make people dangerous."

Mr. Watkins stood up and began walking toward the stone steps.

"Wait!" Eddie cried out.

"Where are you going?" Jo asked.

Over his shoulder, Mr. Watkins replied, "I'm going to make some chamomile tea. It helps me focus. And we're going to need to focus if we have any chance at deciphering that message."

Nick looked at his friends and beamed. The old man had decided to help them after all.

Dorona's Disk

Tiny particles of dust sifted between the floorboards overhead as Mr. Watkins moved around the kitchen. Nick heard a faucet running and guessed the old man was filling a teapot with water.

When Mr. Watkins returned, time turned to molasses. Eddie drummed the table impatiently while Mr. Watkins pulled a small tea bag out of a wooden box and ripped open the paper wrapper. He set the bag in an ornate cup with tiny flowers and leaves along the top edge. He poured a stream of hot water into the teacup and methodically dunked the teabag three times.

He set the cup aside and asked, "Shall we begin?"

"Yes," all three said, eagerly leaning forward.

Mr. Watkins opened the diary and looked at the coded message. "When I was little, my grandmother loved hiding little messages for me. She'd leave them in my shoe or under my pillow. They were usually poems or codes; she gave me a decoder tool to decipher them. She explained that she and my grandfather often used a complex coding system to protect their inventions until they were patented."

"A patent," Eddie murmured. "Hmm. I wonder if I'll need one of those for the Stir Shield." He explained to Mr. Watkins, "That's my invention for the contest this year."

Mr. Watkins set the teacup down. "If you have an invention, you must protect not only the thing itself but the idea behind it." Mr. Watkins continued. "Inventing can be a competitive business, and the race for patents can be quite fierce." He set the teabag on the saucer and sipped the steaming beverage. "If Alexander Graham Bell had waited just one extra day to submit his patent application for the telephone, we would all know the name Elisha Gray instead. Gray submitted an application just hours after Bell, for a similar invention."

Eddie raised his eyebrows. "Speaking of inventions," Eddie began, "there's a lot in this diary about something called—a Telaera or something?"

"Have you heard that word before?" Nick asked.

The old man nodded.

"What is it? What does it do?" Eddie asked.

Mr. Watkins lifted his teacup and took a sip. "As far as I understand, the Telaera was some sort of communication device. I have no idea what became of the original. Years ago, I came across the designs my grandparents sketched out, and I've been working on a replica for years, but I can't quite figure out how it works."

Nick scratched his neck. "You said your grandparents used codes to keep their ideas from being stolen, but in the diary, your grandfather said Cornelius Bennett was blackmailing him for it. Maybe he stole the machine when he fled after the tunnel collapsed."

"Unfortunately, that's the part of the story I don't know." Mr. Watkins held the ripped pages in front of him. "But I'm hoping we can find some answers here."

"Ordinarily, you'd be in luck," Eddie put his hand on Jo's shoulder, "because sitting before you is Josephine Perkins, the human code breaker." He scrunched his mouth to the side and continued. "However, even Jo thinks this double alpha blabety-blah-blah code is super hard to crack. We don't have a Dorona's Disk, or whatever the riddle said—"

"What did you just say?" Mr. Watkins leaned forward. His bushy, gray eyebrows pushed up mounded ridges on his forehead.

"Dorona's Disk?" Jo asked.

Nick turned the ripped page over and showed the riddle to Mr. Watkins.

Mr. Watkins read, "*Beneath Time's Face, Dorona's Disk, Symbols Letters Will Replace.*"

"Dorona's Disk?" Mr. Watkins murmured.

Jo's eyes brightened. "Do you know what that is?"

"Indeed, I do." Mr. Watkins lifted his cane and tapped it on the floor again. He reached inside the front edge of his cardigan, into his front shirt pocket, and pulled out a long, gold chain. Attached to the end was an old-looking pocket watch.

The watch had a tarnished cover, worn nearly smooth. The old man's leathery hand cradled the timepiece in his palm. With a practiced motion, he pressed the button inside the loop, and the watch cover popped open, revealing the ornate face of a clock. Evenly spaced Roman numerals, written in fancy script bordered the outer edge. The delicate clock hands were frozen in place.

"This has been in my family for a long time," Mr. Watkins said softly. He paused and gazed at the watch, then blinked away a sentimental expression and looked up. "It no longer works, but it might help us decipher the code."

"Why do you keep a broken watch in your pocket?" Eddie looked doubtful.

"I guess I'm just sentimental. And just because something is old and broken," Mr. Watkins's eyes twinkled, "doesn't make it useless." He pinched the knob between his fingers, and this time, instead of pushing it in—as he had done before—he pulled the knob out. With a soft *CLICK*, the face of the clock hinged forward, bringing with it the gear mechanism beneath, exposing a small, brass disk.

Eddie noted, "Your family sure likes secret compartments."

Mr. Watkins's eyes twinkled.

"Is that—" Nick began.

"A Dorona's Disk!" Jo exclaimed. She stood up and paced back and forth excitedly. "Beneath time's face. The face of time—it's the face of a clock. Of course!"

"Very good!" Mr. Watkins glanced up, impressed. "This is a Dorona's *Cipher* Disk, to be precise—given to me by my grandmother. It's the very one I used to decipher her messages all those years ago. Mr. Watkins delicately ran a finger across the surface. "This disk has been in my family for generations."

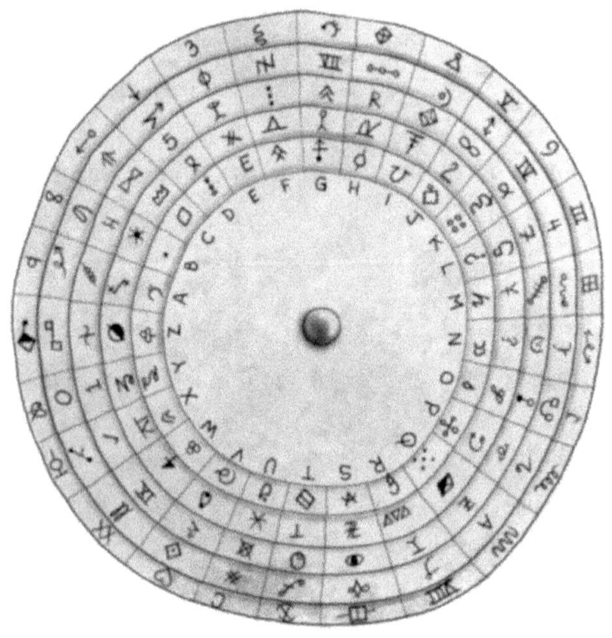

The flat, circular object was made of six thin, metal plates, each one slightly larger than the previous. A string of letters, numbers, and symbols lined the outer edge of each. They were bound at the center with a silver **rivet**. The **concentric** rings fit snugly together, like a miniature bullseye. Mr. Watkins demonstrated how the plates moved. Each one spun separately from the others.

"By rotating the plates and matching the characters along the edges from ring to ring, we should be able to crack the code and decipher the message."

Nick lifted the disk and rotated the largest plate around the outside edge. "How will we know how to match up the characters? There have to be, like, thousands of possible combinations."

"Ah, good question. Each message has a key word. Once we discover what it is, we will be able to properly align the plates and match the symbols to the letter they represent."

Jo scoured the diary entries one-by-one, murmuring, "How are we supposed to know which word is the key word?"

Mr. Watkins sipped again from the teacup. "Judging by the options on the plates, the key word will be a combination of six letters, numbers, or symbols."

Nick let out a sigh and scratched under the collar of his T-shirt. He was feeling frustrated, and the itchy string around his neck wasn't helping matters. He yanked the shoelace over his head and set the key on the table next to Jo.

Eddie glanced at the key, then quickly leaned forward. "How many characters did you say are in the key word?"

"Six," Mr. Watkins replied.

Eddie's eyes widened. "Oh, my gosh—"

Jo's jaw dropped. "No. WAY!"

Mr. Watkins looked confused.

With a hopeful expression on his face, Nick explained, "I think the *key* might have the key word stamped onto it."

Eddie grabbed the shoelace and dangled it in the air.

Mr. Watkins looked at the silver object. He squinted at the tiny letters. "C-O-R-T-E-X."

Jo nodded.

"This key was inside the box I helped you open?"

"Yup," Eddie replied.

Mr. Watkins sat quietly, rubbing his thumb along the rim of the teacup. "My grandmother sometimes spoke of a missing key, although she never said what it opened." He turned the key over and over in his fingers. "Where did you find the box?"

Nick replied, "It was in the lake, buried in the mud."

Mr. Watkins murmured, "The lake…yes, that would explain the crevice corrosion." He looked pensive. "All those years, my grandmother thought it was somewhere in the yard."

Eddie blurted out, "So *that's* why the Badger dug those holes!"

"Eddie! Shhh!" Jo scolded.

Mr. Watkins smiled gently. "It's OK. I'm aware of the rumors."

Nick asked, "Do you know what the coordinates mark?"

Mr. Watkins looked at the symbols on the ripped page. "I'm hoping this message will tell us." He twisted the plates so the letters C-O-R-T-E-X were aligned. "There." Mr. Watkins set the disk in the center of the table so everyone could see. Nick looked skeptically at the coded message.

He opened his sketchbook to a blank page and held his pencil poised and ready.

"Well?" Eddie leaned against the table. "Let's start deciphering."

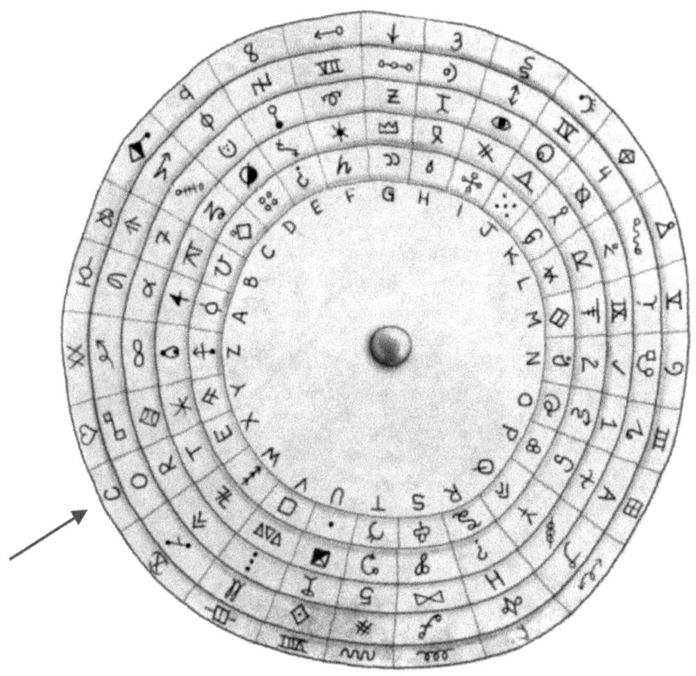

Mr. Watkins began reciting the letters. "T-H-E-S-W-I…" He paused and noticed Jo intently studying the cipher disk. He asked, "Would you like to take a crack at it?"

She nodded eagerly, then continued reading the letters as she matched them up with the correct symbols. "T-C-H-T-H"

The lead of Nick's pencil pressed into the paper as he recorded each letter of the deciphered message.

Jo's eyes ping-ponged back and forth between the message and the disk, her speed increasing as she became more and more familiar with the system. "A-T-T-O…" She fired off the letters in rapid succession.

Eddie rubbed his hands together in anticipation.

Jo announced the last four letters, "...G-A-I-N," then looked up. "That's it. That's the whole message."

"What's it say?" Eddie craned his neck to read the string of letters Nick had recorded.

Nick started to read the words. "The switch…" He trailed off.

Eddie grabbed two fistfuls of his own hair. "What? Why'd you stop?"

Realizing how priceless the next few words would be to a man whose family reputation had been destroyed by the lies of a greedy man like Cornelius Bennett, Nick handed the pad of paper to Mr. Watkins. "You should do the honors. After all, it's your grandfather's message. And we never would have gotten this decoded without your help."

Mr. Watkins gracefully accepted the nomination and cleared his throat and read from the notebook.

"Ugh!" Eddie groaned. "Another riddle?" His head collapsed into his arms as they rested across the table." These word puzzles are driving me *crazy*!"

Jo smirked. "You wouldn't last one day at Camp Mangara."

Eddie rolled his head to one side, just far enough to respond with a sarcastic smile.

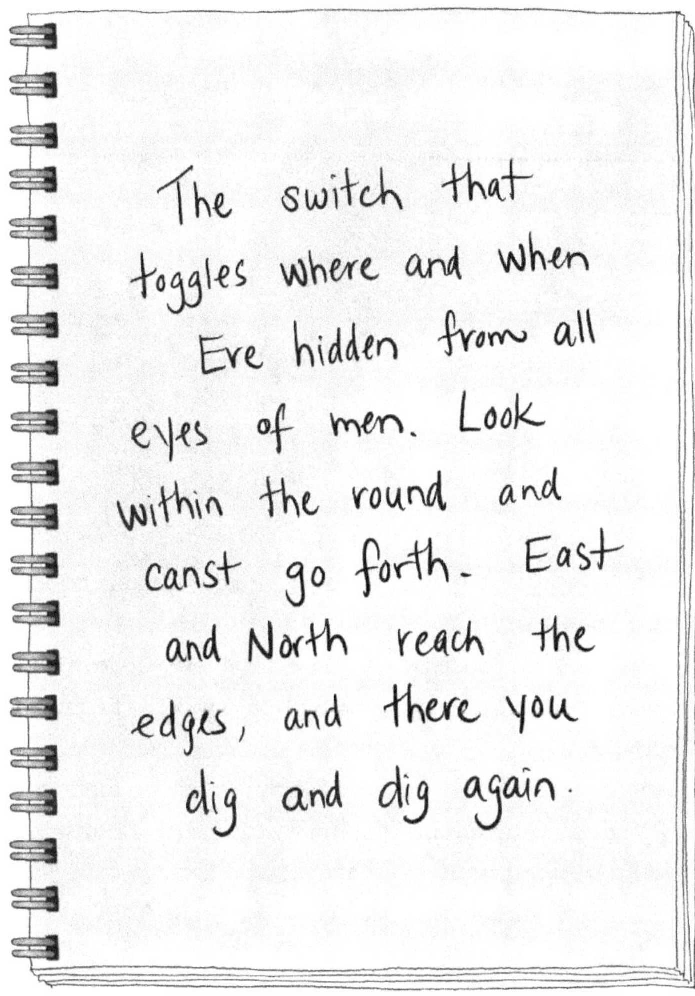

Nick contemplated the wording. "Mr. Watkins, do you have any idea what any of this means?"

"I think I do," he replied.

The Little Wren

The old man's gray eyebrows pinched together. "My grandmother loved leaving coded messages for me. Usually, there were instructions leading to a location of some kind—like a treasure hunt. Sometimes she left a trail of symbols for me to follow."

"Symbols?" Nick flipped through his sketchbook. "We've been finding this image of a bird. Is this the kind of thing she might have left?"

Mr. Watkins' eyes creased as he smiled. "A wren. My grandmother's favorite bird."

He turned the watch over to reveal the image of a bird etched into the back. It matched the drawing Nick had sketched.

"That bird on the box you brought into my shop was a wren."

"You recognized it?" Jo asked.

Mr. Watkins nodded.

Nick frowned. "Did you know the key was inside?"

Mr. Watkins shifted a little. “No. I didn’t.”

Eddie blurted out, “But if you recognized the bird, why didn’t you say something?”

Mr. Watkins inhaled deeply and ran a finger around the edge of his teacup.

“Well?” Eddie scoffed.

“You didn’t want to dig up the past, did you?” Nick searched the old man’s eyes and knew he was right.

Mr. Watkins took a skip of tea and explained, “I’ve worked hard to put my family’s past behind me—to separate myself from the rumors and whisperings.” His gaze flitted to the diary. “Professional treasure hunters have been looking for the stolen bank money for over fifty years. I really didn’t think you would find anything.”

"Well, they obviously didn't have the right clues."

"Do you know what they key unlocks?" Jo asked.

Eddie clasped his hands together and whispered, "*Please say yes. Please say yes.*"

Mr. Watkins pressed his lips together and shook his head. "I'm sorry to say I think this may be a key in the figurative sense."

"Like the key that unlocks the Dorona's Disk code?" Jo asked.

Mr. Watkins nodded. "Yes. My grandmother spent years looking for something extremely important to her. Something she'd lost. And after reading these diary entries, I think it must've been this key."

"That doesn't make sense," Jo chewed her lip. "If she was the one who wrote the code, why would she need the key to decode it?"

"I'm not sure." Mr. Watkins rubbed his chin. "I know my grandparents didn't want Cornelius Bennett to find the Telaera. Perhaps they had other coded documents related to the invention."

Nicd suggested, "And you think she was worried that if Cornelius somehow found the documents, and the key, he'd steal everything."

Jo picked up the torn diary page. "Plan to store in the vault-away from sluic ore..." She thought for a moment. Her eyes lit up and she began mouthing letters. *C-O-R-N-E-L-I-U-S*. She said, "Away from Cornelius. Mr. Watkins, you were right."

Eddie said, "Your grandparents knew Cornelius Bennett wanted to steal their invention, so they put it in a safe place.

"But wait," Nick replied. "The Telaera was locked in the bank vault. Are you saying Cornelius Bennett somehow broke into the bank, stole the Telaera, then framed your grandfather for the robbery?"

Eddie gasped, "Maybe the key opens the vault!"

Mr. Watkins looked at Eddie and shook his head. "Definitely not. The Mapleton Bank had a large safe installed a few days before the mine collapsed. This key is much too small to be a bank vault key."

Disappointed, Eddie's slouched against the back of his chair.

To Nick, he said, "To answer your question, I don't know. That safe was emptied without anyone knowing about it. The town was so distracted by the mine shaft collapsing, they didn't even realize anything was missing until days later. The door didn't appear to be tampered with and the lock was still engaged. No one knows how the vault was breeched."

Nick looked back at the deciphered message. "Mr. Watkins, maybe your grandmother knew about the whole thing."

Jo asked, "What are you talking about, Nick?"

Nick continued. "Think about it. She and your grandfather knew Bennett was bad news." He recited the ripped diary entry, *I fear the worst.* It sounds like they knew Bennett might sabotage the mine and make sure they were out of the picture. They were leaving a backup plan."

"Are you saying Eleanor left this trail of breadcrumbs for Mr. Watkins to find?"

Jo nodded.

All eyes fell to Mr. Watkins. He rubbed his chin, took a sip of tea, then nodded. "I think you may be right." He picked up the diary. "Somewhere in here is the next clue."

Nick pointed to the deciphered message. "I'll bet it's right here. We still haven't figured out what this means."

Eddie leaned over and recited the message. "The switch that toggles where and when Ere hidden from all eyes of men. Look within the round and canst go forth. East and North reach the edges, and there you dig and dig again."

Jo crossed her arms. "It sounds like she's telling us to look for the next clue in a place described as *The Round.*"

Jo asked, "Any ideas what the round thing is?"

"Unfortunately, no." Mr. Watkins shook his head.

Eddie huffed and crossed his arms. "Why can't we get just *one* easy clue?"

Nick joked, "Like, *Start at the old oak tree. Take ten steps south, and dig down four feet to find a million dollars in gold.*"

Eddie threw his hands in the air. "Exactly!"

Jo replied, "Eddie, if the clues were that easy, whatever is buried in *The Round*—whatever that is—would probably have already been discovered."

"That's right." Eddie became thoughtful, adding, "We have to dig to get to the round. Obviously the round thing is buried between here and Big J's cabin."

"Assuming it hasn't already been found," Nick replied. "Remember, Mr. Watkins said a lot of people went looking for some sort of treasure back in the day."

"Nick, why do you always have to be so logical?" Eddie's head tipped back, and he sighed loudly.

The group fell silent.

Mr. Watkins placed the Dorona's Disk in the small, curved compartment in the back of the watch and tucked it into his shirt pocket. "Over the years, I convinced myself there was no buried treasure. No money or valuables." The base of the porcelain cup scraped softly against the saucer as he set it down. "However, this message leaves no question about the fact that my grandparents buried *something*—and guarded it with a coded message they knew only someone with the Dorona's Disk could decipher. If they went to all that trouble, it must have been extremely important."

Jo added, "And, as Nick pointed out, if Cornelius Bennett was threatening them, they must have been worried something might happen to them if they thought it necessary to leave a trail of clues."

"I agree." Mr. Watkins's eyes took on a solemn haze. "As I said, desperation can be a dangerous thing." He closed his eyes and pushed his glasses up to rub the bridge of his nose.

The shrill ring of the telephone made them all jump.

Mr. Watkins stood and leaned on his cane as he shuffled to answer it. "Hello?...yes…no, I'm actually over at the house…no…no." He glanced over at the table. "Turns out they were just offering to help." As he listened to the person on the other end of the line, a deep crease formed between his eyebrows. "Oh, dear.... of course. I'll be right there." He hung up.

"Is everything OK?" Jo asked.

Mr. Watkins replied, "That was Pete Hansen. He said someone at the bakery just reported seeing two suspicious-looking people lurking around the shop."

Nick looked at Jo, and he knew they were both wondering if *they* were the suspicious-looking people, since an hour earlier, they'd been at the shop doing some accidental trespassing.

However, just as Nick opened his mouth to confess, Mr. Watkins added, "They just drove away a moment ago. Pete needs me to stop by to see if anything's missing."

The kids followed Mr. Watkins upstairs. The old man closed the secret door, then pushed the panel until it clicked into place.

He looked at the kids. "That window you climbed through—is it closed?"

Nick answered, "I latched it behind me."

"Good. The last thing I need is someone breaking in here and snooping around." He winked at them over his glasses, then walked down the corridor and heaved the front door open. The sun was setting. The driveway was streaked with dark shadows from the trees. After the group gathered on the front porch, Mr. Watkins pulled the front door closed and locked it.

"Do you want us to come with you to the shop?" Jo asked.

"I'll be fine." Mr. Watkins said as he hobbled down the steps. "You three should get on home. These roads around the lake are black as ink at night." He gave a single nod, closed his car door, and drove away.

Eddie picked his bike up off the ground. "I have to get home for dinner."

"Me, too. Meet back here tomorrow after breakfast?" Nick asked.

"Keep your walkie talkies on until then." Jo led the way as they biked down the driveway and headed in the direction of their respective houses.

Stone Staircase

The motion detector clicked on as Nick coasted toward the garage. The truck was gone, which meant Uncle John was still on his way back from the antique store in the neighboring town, Warrenville. Nick parked next to the garage near the three shovels he and his friends had used in their fruitless search to unearth whatever it was the coordinates marked. Judging by the low sun, he guessed he had about an hour until it was dark and decided to use that time digging. He covered two blisters on his palms with Band-Aids, grabbed a shovel, and headed across the lawn. The soft grass padded under his feet as he walked toward a circle of small boulders marking the perimeter of a campfire ring.

He consulted his sketchbook while scanning the property, noting the dozens of dirt piles they had created along the narrow strip of trees dividing the two properties. Nearly one hundred years earlier, somewhere between the two houses, Archibald and Eleanor

Miller hid something underground. The clue instructed them to *look within the round.*

As he contemplated whether he should dig up the ashes in the *round* firepit, a small movement caught his eye. Camouflaged in the dirt next to the fire ring, a small, black garter snake had begun slithering across a patch of bare earth. Nick froze as he watched the creature staring back at him. He'd never seen a snake this close before. It was shinier than he'd expected. Periodically, the snake's narrow, forked tongue darted in and out of its mouth as it tasted the air.

Suddenly, the snake recoiled and disappeared in the grass. Curious to get another look, Nick darted after it, catching glimpses of the rippling black ribbon here and there amidst a sea of green blades. For a moment, he lost track of the snake and scanned the area for movement. Out of the corner of his eye, he noticed a tiny thread of a tail slipping under the fish shack door. He reached for the handle but hesitated when he eyed the thick cobwebs hanging like curtains from the corners of the door and the screen covered windows. He took an unconscious step back and his foot landed on a slender branch. It let out a loud *SNAP* as it broke in two. Nick nearly jumped out of his skin. Spiders always made him jittery.

The stick, however, looked useful. Nick used the larger half to poke at the webs. The sticky threads clung to the bark, but he didn't see any crawling creatures fleeing the scene. He swished the stick in a circular motion, collecting the cobwebs around the end of it like cotton candy. Above the door, the stick bumped part of the doorframe and knocked it to the ground.

Nick stooped over, expecting to find a piece of loose trim from the doorway.

"Oh, my gosh," he exhaled.

It *wasn't* a piece of trim. It was a small, wooden plaque with two holes—one on each end. He looked up at the spot where it had been hanging from two rusty nails sticking out a piece of wood over the door frame. The weathered wood had been cut into the silhouette of a bird—a wren.

It's the next clue!

Nick paced back and forth. "Oh my gosh, oh my gosh, oh my—" He yanked his walkie talkie off his belt and pressed the side button. "Anna Graham! Red Fox—do you copy?" *(STATIC)* He repeated the message. Nothing. Jo and Eddie were probably getting ready to eat dinner. Either way, it was clear neither had turned on their walkie talkies.

He looked again at the wooden bird.

Maybe it's just a coincidence. Nick began to second guess himself.

The last time he'd seen the box had been at Eddie's house, when it tumbled from his backpack onto the driveway. Lucia had been so close behind him, he'd left it. Whether the birds were identical seemed like a minor detail at this point. The riddle they'd deciphered mentioned a Wren, which Mr. Watkins explained was his grandmother's nickname. Jo said a wren was a small bird. The ring box had a bird on the lid as did the leather wrapped around the torn diary pages. Now he'd found a wooden plaque of a bird. This was no coincidence.

A flush of heat crept up the sides of Nick's neck as a lightning bolt thought slammed into his mind. *The star on the map could mark something hidden in the fish shack.*

Nick eyed the small structure shrouded in a network of arachnid condos.

He tried his walkie talkie again. "Hello? I found something! Do you copy?" The message was answered with the disappointing crackle and hiss of static.

He extended a shaky hand toward the small, metal door latch. The door opened and a long, rusty spring stretched across the inside of the door. It let out a whining *SCREEEECHH* as the coils resisted the movement.

Nick shuddered when he saw thick sheets of cobwebs in the corners. He took a deep breath and looked around the closet-sized space, then stepped inside. Jo's comment about spiders being useful rang in his ears, and he tried to feel less skittish about a potential spider ambush. Nick scanned the room, looking for another clue.

Screen windows wrapped around the upper half of the shack. Alternating warm and cool breezes blew through from the lake, as if it was inhaling and exhaling. Hanging from hooks, he saw a lantern, a wrinkled matchbook, and a short length of hose looped on a wooden peg near a spigot on the wall.

Nick took another step in, positioning his feet carefully on the wide gaps in the floorboards. He'd left his sketchbook on the rocks near the firepit and the only part of the riddle he could recall was the part about The Round. This room certainly wasn't round.

He nudged the *round* metal pail sitting on a stack of newspapers on the floor with his shoe.

Nothing.

As he turned to leave, Nick heard a soft, crinkling sound. He looked back at a loose sheet of newspaper resting on the floor, next to the stack. It was fluttering almost imperceptibly. The thought of the snake flickered into his mind. Remembering facts about garter snakes from a book he'd checked out from the library, he knew garter snakes could bite, but they were shy and non-venomous. He crept toward the newspaper. With lightning speed, he snatched the page off the floor. Underneath, he saw—nothing, only floorboards.

Nick did, however, feel a cool, damp breeze; a gentle flow of air was blowing up between the floorboards. He bent low and peered between the worn planks, but it was too dark to see anything below. He couldn't tell if he was staring at black dirt two inches from his nose or a cavern a mile deep.

Nick pulled the lantern from the shelf and struck a match to light it. The lamp sputtered, then radiated a warm glow against the walls and cast long shadows. Again, he peered between the floorboard, but he couldn't aim the light very well, and the space below was engulfed in flickering shadows.

As he rose to his feet, Nick's gaze fell upon the hose hanging on the wall. He smiled and silently cheered for his new idea. Nick twisted the squeaky spigot handle, and a gentle stream of water flowed into the metal bucket. Then he turned off the water and slowly poured the water between the floorboards. Delighted,

Nick realized he could hear the cavernous echo of splashing water beneath him! The newspapers were getting damp, so he grabbed half of the other stack and set it on the table. When he scooped up the last of the papers, he saw a small, crescent shape on one of the boards.

Nick dropped to his knees and inspected the dark brown, semi-circular shape. It was too perfect to be a natural part of the woodgrain. Nick touched the crescent and his fingertip vanished underneath a layer of mud.

He immediately realized the water had damped a layer of compressed dirt. He traced his finger along the curve and removed enough dirt to reveal a small, metal loop on the floor. It was a handle. The dirt had completely camouflaged it. Uncle John had probably never even noticed it was there and Nick hadn't seen it until the dirt darkened as it became damp.

Nick lifted the metal loop and pulled. A crack appeared between two of the wooden planks beneath Nick's tennis shoes.

It's a trapdoor!

Nick heaved open the trapdoor and lowered the lantern into the space. In the flickering light of the lantern, Nick saw a long, stone staircase leading into the darkness.

The Metal Gate

THE STEPS OF THE STAIRCASE WERE COVERED WITH a thick layer of dirt, the apparent result of debris that had fallen between the boards over the years. The rugged stairs glistened with moisture, and Nick could see a small ribbon of water slowly cascading along the left side of the passage. The glowing lantern illuminated only a few feet in front of him, but Nick could see that each step was more and more damp as they became swallowed up by the shadowy abyss.

A drop of water fell from the arched, stone ceiling and landed on his arm. It was ice cold and sent goosebumps all the way to his fingertips. Nick reached out to touch the stone wall on his right and discovered it was covered with stray roots poking out between the rocks like coarse strands of hair. Each step seemed to reveal more and more of the inky blackness, and the trek seemed to take an eternity. Nick's heart raced as he carefully descended the twelve steps. If he hadn't been counting, Nick would've been sure there were fifty.

Finally, Nick's shoes planted on a narrow landing at the base of the staircase. The air in the stairwell was cool and damp. The insides of his nostrils felt cold. Stretching his arm straight out in front of him, he was able to dispel the darkness only a few inches. The yellow lantern glow cast flickering reflections on something ahead. A towering, metal gate blocked the path. Nick held the lantern up and peered past the thick bars. Through the flickering shadows, he was able to make out very little. The tunnel continued into the darkness.

This gate—or whatever's behind it—has to match the coordinates on the key, he thought.

Nick held the lantern above his head and inspected the arched gate. On the left edge, two massive hinges held the gate in place, and on the right, a large metal lever acted as a latch. He tried to lift it, but it didn't budge; not even a little.

The lantern sputtered, and Nick realized the fuel was almost gone. In a moment, he would be plunged into darkness. Turning quickly, he climbed the stairs. Halfway up, the lantern flickered twice, then went out. Above him, Nick saw daylight and the edges of the trapdoor. He scrambled up the slippery steps. The damp darkness seemed to be gaining on him, ready to swallow him up and drag him back into the dank void. He could almost feel the shadowy fingers curling around his feet and ankles as he scrambled up the last few steps and slammed the trapdoor.

Nick raced back to the cabin, shaking his head and brushing invisible spider webs from his legs and arms. In reality, the only things he was really brushing away were his nerves and the jittery feeling he had in the tunnel. He inhaled deeply, giving his scattered thoughts a chance to settle. Chuckling to himself, he pictured how silly he must have looked sprinting across the grass and running away from invisible shadow-specters. The warm summer air quickly melted away the chill that had crept up his spine. It was replaced with a strange mix of excitement and tension.

"Uncle John?" Nick ran up to the garage. The rusty, blue pickup was still gone. He spoke into the walkie talkie. "This is Pinehurst Pirate—uh City Kid. Anna Graham and Red Fox do you copy? Found a secret passage. Do you copy? Over."

Neither Jo nor Eddie replied.

"This is City Kid. Anna Graham? Red Fox? Do you copy? Over."

(STATIC)

He stared at the walkie talkie in disbelief.

"Keep your walkie talkies on," he mocked Jo's voice.

His eyes landed on an old phone hanging on the wall. A long, coiled cord dangled beneath. A thick book sat on the shelf next to the phone. The words *Mapleton Phone Directory* were printed on the cover.

He dialed Jo's house. A voice he assumed was Jo's mother's said, "Hi. You've reached the Perkins' residence. Gave sesame sale—in other words—leave a message." *Another anagram,* he thought with a smile, but he didn't "gave sesame sale." His instinct told him dinnertime would not be the best time to dial the Bernadelli's house, but he flipped to the Bs in the directory and dialed anyway.

The phone rang twice, and a deep voice answered. "Hello. You have reached the Bernadelli residence. We are unable to—"

A moment later, he dialed the number to Watkins Fine Jewelry.

There was no answer.

He hung up and walked outside. Nick looked at the fish shack, now enshrouded with the evening shadows. A quick mental calculation determined the structure was almost directly between the two houses. Nick couldn't believe they hadn't thought to check there. It was very likely the star on the map marked the location of the underground gate. He felt a chill on the back of his neck.

If the Caldwells had drawn the same conclusion, now that they had the map, they might try to sneak onto Uncle John's property to look around—and, as Jo had predicted, after dark would be the best time to do so.

Nick shuddered.

He didn't feel brave enough to go back and try to open the gate on his own. He grabbed his bike, clicked on his handlebar light and raced down the road to Jo's house.

The Perkins's house was dark, but Nick rang the doorbell anyways. Jo's bike was propped up against an ivy-covered lattice on the side of the garage. Her walkie talkie dangled from the handlebars. It was clear no one was home. Feeling defeated, Nick pulled onto the street and reluctantly pedaled in the direction of Eddie's house.

He was approaching the end of the lake road when two headlights appeared in the distance. The road was pitch black, and his little bike light was about as effective as a jar of fireflies, so he waited on the edge of the road for the car to pass. However, as it neared, the vehicle slowed, then pulled to a stop.

"Kinda dark for a bike ride," a voice with a distinct Southern drawl called out. Ginger illuminated the cabin light of her truck and grinned. "What'cha doin' out here?" She eyed the dark road behind him.

"I was hoping to run into some friends in town. Uncle John's not back yet and—"

"I know. That's why I'm here. Said he tried calling, but you must've been out."

"Oh?"

"He mentioned something about a once-in-a-lifetime, rare Italian cabinet." She shrugged. "Anyways, it's arriving tomorrow, first thing, so he got a hotel room for the night—wants to save himself a trip."

This was not good news. Nick mentally weighed the pros and cons of asking Eddie if he could sleep over.

"You had dinner yet?"

Nick shook his head.

"Didn't think so." She held up a brown paper sack with the Ginger Sue's logo stamped on the side and nodded her head toward the empty passenger seat. "Hop in. You can eat on the way into town."

"Thanks," Nick said. He hadn't eaten in hours, a fact his stomach had begun to grumble about.

He loaded his bike into the back and climbed into the big, black truck.

She handed the bag to him. "It was the best I could scrounge up on short notice."

Nick opened the sack. Nestled inside was a sandwich, a bag of chips, a chocolate chip cookie, and a can of orange soda.

"Thanks," Nick said as he tore into the sandwich.

A few bites later, Ginger was parking her truck behind her shop. She leaned both arms on the steering wheel and looked at Nick. "You gonna be OK in that old cabin all by yourself tonight?"

Nick's stomach knotted at the thought. He was fifty percent sure the front door had a lock on it. He replied, "I'll be fine."

"Let's just hope you don't have any uninvited visitors," Ginger said.

Nick froze, mid-bite.

She laughed. "John told me about the resident skunk."

Nick's shoulders sagged in relief. "Oh, right." He popped the remaining bite of sandwich in his mouth, then rolled the top of the bag down, saving the rest for later.

They both hopped down from the truck, and Ginger dropped the tailgate. Nick pulled his bike down.

"I'll drop by in the morning with some breakfast and to check on you."

Nick smiled. "Thanks."

"You bet." She winked and headed into the shop.

Nick rolled to a stop in front of Charlie's Comics. He was lowering his kickstand when he felt something slam into his backpack. Off-balance and startled, he grabbed the metal rim of the bike rack and whirled around.

Standing with his arms folded across a puffed-out chest, Billy sneered. "Well, if it isn't our new friend, Captain Know-it-All."

"Aye-aye, Matey," Jack chirped and gave a patronizing salute.

Nick held a steady gaze. His previous encounter with these boys had ended in a draw, with no clear winner. Billy wiped the corner of his mouth, clearly hungry for a victory.

Nick knew it was foolish to make the first move with an irrational breed of jerks such as this, but he also knew that letting bullies get creative was even more risky. He lifted his chin and tried to remain as expressionless as possible. "What's up, guys?"

"*What's up, guys*?" Jack mocked in a voice several pitches higher.

The mocking parrot; a classic, brainless response. These boys had no idea what their next move was, and that's what made them dangerous. Nick knew he'd have to let them feel like they were winning if he hoped to come out of this ahead.

"Fine," Nick mumbled, "I'll do it."

The two boys looked at each other, confused by the suggestion they'd been somehow victorious while having no idea how they'd obtained the victory.

Step one: Create confusion. Check.

"Do what?" Billy's upper lip curled into a sneer.

"You want the answer, right?"

More confused looks.

Step two: Deepen the confusion. Check.

"First, I have to tell you the joke." Nick was reusing what he hoped would be a second success with his bully-defeating-joke strategy.

Step three: Buy time.

Billy narrowed his eyes. "I don't like jokes."

Nick's stomach flipped. He'd been banking on a few more back-and-forths with the boys, but Billy shot an arrow through his parachute. Clearly, these boys were members of a subspecies slightly more intelligent than Adam Henry, the bully from his old school.

Billy eyed the paper bag in Nick's hand. "What'cha got there? To-go treat from Ginger Sues?" He looked at Jack. "Wasn't that nice of Captain Obvious to bring us a peace offering?"

"So sweet." Jack laid his hand across his chest. "I'm real hungry."

Billy took a step forward and looked at the bag with the same curious expression a predator wears when looking at its cornered prey.

Nick was out of his league, and they all knew it.

Jack faked a lunge at Nick, then laughed when he flinched. "Hand over the bag, Cap'n."

Nick grimaced and said, "You don't want this. It's just—"

"I'll be the judge of that." Billy held his hand out and repeatedly curled his fingers toward his palm.

Nick took a step backwards. This time, it was Billy who lunged—and he wasn't faking. Nick turned away from him, protectively wrapping his body around the bag from Ginger. He could've easily conceded the food, but Nick knew from experience that giving in to a bully's demands only provides temporary relief. He thought of Eddie and all the stolen snacks. Nick wanted to stand his ground, as long as he could, anyways.

Billy grabbed Nick's free arm and tried to wrench it behind his back. It was clear the boy was on the wrestling team. He was very strong, and Nick's attempts to free himself felt feeble.

Jack made a beeline for Nick's bike and jabbed something into the wheel. "That's for messing with our bikes."

Nick heard a distinct hissing nose and silently cursed Eddie for the stunt he'd pulled with the super glue. This was a revenge situation, and these boys wouldn't be easy to **appease**. An ugly grin smeared across Jack's face as he eyed the bag Nick was trying to shield from Billy. Jack reached over Nick's shoulder and started clawing at the bag.

A blinding light and the deafening blare of a car horn interrupted the scuffle. They all froze. Squinting through the glare of two bright headlights pulling into the parking space in front of them, Nick recognized the outline of a Jeep.

A tall figure jumped over the door and landed with a heavy thud. It was Jesse.

"Problem here, fellas?"

Billy tightened his grip on Nick's arm.

Jack snickered. "We don't got no problem." He stole a glance at Nick then looked back at Jesse. "Not with you anyhow."

Jesse took a few steps forward. Standing in front of the Jeep, he crossed his arms and squared off his stance. His silhouette—backlit by the high beams—looked menacing. Jesse dropped his arms to his sides and moved closer. He was now about four feet away from the younger boys. "You've got a problem alright."

"Nuh-uh," Billy argued.

Jesse stepped closer once more. "See—Nick here's a friend of mine, and you need to take your hands off him."

"Or whut?" Billy squinted into the light and sneered, "You gonna call Daddy to come fix yer problems? When he gets here I'd like to file a complaint about the twerps who messed up our bikes with Super Glue."

Jesse didn't rush his response. He lifted his hat, scratched his head, then replaced it. "Well—we could call him, if that's what you want," he took a step closer and continued, "but that's not really my style."

Billy released his grip on Nick and shoved him toward the ground. Nick stumbled and fell against the window of the shop behind him. Jack **glowered** at him.

Shoulders back, Billy stuck out his chest and swaggered toward Jesse. "You wanna go?" He clenched his fist.

The tension was disrupted when one of the shop doors opened. The sidewalk was flooded with the loud, upbeat rhythm of a pop song. A woman in a white bathrobe waddled out. She was barefoot and walked on her heels—presumably to avoid disturbing the pieces of foam wedged between each of her toes, half of which were painted bright turquoise. A dozen sheets of tin foil stuck out of her hair, and her face was covered with what looked like thick, green frosting.

"William Bennett!" Her voice resonated like a bass drum.

Billy's scowl melted away, and he transformed from a predator to an innocent puppy. "Mama?"

She pointed a finger at him. "You should've been home an hour ago to give Sparky a bath." Casting a disapproving stare at Jack, she added, "And I ran into your father earlier. I happen to know you were *supposed* to be changing the oil in your grandmother's truck this evening. I can't imagine he will be at all pleased to know you're out here causing a ruckus instead of getting your chores done."

"Yes, Ma'am," Jack said, eyes cast to his shoes.

Her attention returned to Billy. "And make sure you give Sparky a good brushing with the blow dryer when you're done, or he'll get all matted, and we'll have to shave him again. You know he looks like a fat possum without his hair."

"Yes, Mama." Billy looked at Jack and tipped his head, indicating they should leave.

They both glared at Nick as they walked away. Nick bit the inside of his lip to keep from smirking.

A young, blonde woman with purple streaks in her hair poked her head out the door. "Time to rinse and condition, Mrs. Bennett."

Billy's mom threw a disapproving stare at Nick and Jesse but said nothing. She turned and waddled back into the salon.

Jesse looked at Nick. "You OK?"

"I had things under control."

Jesse let out a burst of air. "Huh—right." He looked amused, then squeezed the punctured bike tire. "C'mon. I'll give you a ride."

They climbed into the Jeep.

"You can get your bike later, Right now, you can help me test my new turbocharger." Jesse patted the dashboard then pumped the gas. "Listen to that purr." He put the car into gear, then looked at Nick. "Super Glue,

Nick smiled. "That was Eddie."

"Well, it shows real guts you didn't rat him out."

The humiliation of the situation was already beginning to fade, and Nick felt grateful Jesse came along when he did.

"You're staying with Big J, right?"

"Uh—" Nick didn't want to admit he was nervous about staying overnight in the cabin alone. "I was actually hoping to run into Eddie and Jo. We're working on a project together."

"Perfect." Jesse grinned. "I'm on my way to pick up Lucia."

Jesse rang the doorbell, and Nick took a seat on the white porch swing. He couldn't wait to tell Eddie about the trapdoor and hidden staircase.

A moment later, the front door swung open, and Lucia stepped out and stood very close to Jesse. "Hey there," she said, leaning in for a kiss.

Nick cleared his throat to announce his presence.

"What's *he* doing here?" Lucia's expression soured.

Jesse met Nick's gaze briefly, then replied, "I was feeling generous and thought I'd give the kid a lift."

Lucia arched an eyebrow and smacked the gum she always seemed to be chewing. Jaw pumping, she gave Nick a long stare that was hard to read. She blinked, then looked back to Jesse with a sugary smile. "You're, like, such a **philanthropist**."

Nick wasn't exactly sure what that was, but he guessed it had something to do with showing compassion to kids whose bikes were out of commission.

Lucia popped a bubble and tilted her head toward the house. "Kitchen."

"Thanks," Nick said, then bolted inside.

Nick found Eddie standing at the sink next to one of the twin sisters. Her mirror image, minus the glasses, stood nearby, stacking clean cups in a cabinet. Eddie was drying a plate when he noticed Nick.

"Oh, hey. What's up?"

Nick unhooked his walkie talkie and thrust it toward Eddie. In a hushed voice, he hissed, "I've been trying to reach you for an hour!"

Eddie cringed. "Sorry. My mom insists we unplug during dinner so we can 'chat.' What's up?"

Nick pulled Eddie by the arm and took a few steps away from the sink. "I found out what the coordinates mark."

"What?" Eddie's eyes widened. "What is it?" He inhaled. "Is it—the bank money? A treasure? What?"

Nick glanced suspiciously over Eddie's shoulder at his two sisters. They appeared busy with their tasks, so he continued, whispering so softly he was sure Eddie would have to read his lips, "I found a secret staircase under—"

"A secret staircase?" Eddie exclaimed.

Both sisters looked over.

The one at the sink rolled her eyes. "Another one of your treasure hunts?"

The other sister shook her head and scoffed.

Eddie set the plate down and waved Nick into a large pantry, then closed the door.

With his head sandwiched between two boxes of cereal, Nick whispered, "There's a trapdoor in the fish shack that leads to this creepy, stone staircase.

What? Eddie mouthed.

"And there's a big, metal gate at the bottom—but it's locked."

"The key!"

Nick shook his head. "I ran out of light before I could find a keyhole."

"Oh, wow." Eddie ran a hand through his hair. He quoted the riddle, "Look within the round." His eyes flashed. "Did you see anything round?"

"No. Maybe. I-I don't know. It was getting dark, and I tried to get ahold of you guys—"

"The Caldwells! We can't let them get there first!" Eddie grabbed Nick's walkie talkie. "Jo—Anna Graham. Do you copy? Emergency. Over."

After a brief crackle, a tinny version of Jo's voice emitted from the speaker. "Anna Graham here. Red Fox, I copy."

Nick pulled the walkie talkie toward his mouth. "City Kid here. I found something important. Meet us at Uncle John's house. Do you copy? Over."

"Copy that, C.K. See you soon, Over and out."

Eddie bit his lower lip as a huge grin spread across his face. He grabbed Nick's shoulders. "This could be it, Nick—for real. I think we're about to become very, very rich."

The More, the Merrier?

"You really didn't have to give us a ride," Nick said from the back seat of the Jeep.

"It's no problem," Jesse replied. "We have plenty of time."

Lucia glared at her brother and Nick through the rearview mirror. She smacked her gum. "You could've walked."

Jesse replied, "It's not that far out of our way."

Lucia scoffed. "We're going to be late."

"Don't worry. We'll only miss a few previews."

"But I love the previews."

Lucia and Jesse continued debating the pros and cons of arriving late to the theater.

Eddie whispered, "Let's just hope the Caldwells haven't figured out where to look."

"What's the plan if they show up while we're there?" Nick whispered back.

"Way ahead of you." Eddie glanced to the front seat to make sure Jesse and Lucia weren't listening. They were still busy talking about the movie. He unzipped an inside pocket of his vest and showed Nick the small bottle tucked inside. "This outta hold 'em off."

"Hey!" Lucia twisted around and was now looking directly at Eddie. "Is that mine?" She dug around in her bag. "That *IS* mine! Eddie!" She sounded **exacerbated**. "Mom said you're not allowed to go through my stuff—and what do *you* need pepper spray for?"

"What do *you* need pepper spray for?" Eddie shot back.

She fired back. "Jen said she almost got bitten by a raccoon that was under her car, so I figured with pepper spray—I could chase one away if it tried to attack."

"OK." Jesse eyed the back seat through the rearview mirror. "I'm guessing you didn't take Lucia's pepper spray to defend yourselves from varmints. What's *really* going on?"

"Nothing's going on," Nick replied.

Jesse shot him a skeptical look. "Listen—I don't think those jerks will bother you again—not tonight anyways."

"It's not *them* we're worried about." The words slipped out.

"Oh?"

Lucia twisted around. "Spill it."

Nick shrugged and subtly nodded to Eddie.

Eddie nodded. "OK. So—we found this trail of clues that we think leads to something important—maybe a treasure." He added boast-fully, "It might even be the stolen Mapleton Bank money."

Jesse and Lucia exchanged glances, and after a brief silence, they burst into laughter.

Lucia took a moment to catch her breath and said, "Oh—wow! That's hilarious, but you kids are adorable—thinking you're, like, I don't know—little detectives or something."

Jesse pulled into the driveway at Uncle John's place and parked in front of the empty garage bay. "When's your uncle getting home?"

Nick and Eddie hopped out of the Jeep.

"He'll be back at some point. We'll be fine. Thanks for the ride." He left of the fact that Uncle John would be gone until morning. He eyed the woods, and they seemed less spooky now that he wasn't along. Plus, Jo would be arriving any minute.

"Have fun on your treasure hunt." Lucia, still chuckling, rolled her eyes. "If I were you, I wouldn't hold my breath, though. No one knows what happened to that money, which means it's long gone."

Eddie, who clearly did not appreciate her demeaning tone, stepped toward the Jeep. "We have evidence, OK? Actual, real evidence."

Lucia giggled. "Right."

Eddie frowned. "We found a silver key and an old diary—"

"C'mon, now," Nick interrupted. "These two have a movie to get to. They don't want to hear about our wild goose chase."

Eddie didn't take the hint, and instead plowed ahead, full force. "The diary is from, like, a hundred years ago and is basically a map to the stolen bank money."

Nick reached over to put his hand over Eddie's mouth, but the younger boy pushed it away.

"Anyways—we might even know where it's buried."

"Eddie." Nick hissed, but Eddie continued spewing a fountain of information, specifically the clues they'd agreed to keep secret.

Eddie wasn't coming up for air. "And these creepy, rich guys are trying to find it, too—but we're way ahead of 'em because Nick found a secret staircase in Big J's fish shack. It probably leads to the treasure."

"You are *SO* bad at keeping secrets." Nick put his hand on his forehead and sighed. "You literally just told them everything. Every. Single. Thing."

Eddie cringed. "Sorry."

"Uh—" Jesse said, looking at Lucia, "I don't know about you, but I totally want to see this secret staircase."

"But what about *Beyond the Mummy's Tomb*?" Lucia's forehead wrinkled.

Jesse flashed a smile. "We still have a little time."

"Fine." Lucia crossed her arms and shot an irritated look at Eddie.

Nick didn't hesitate and ran to the garage. A moment later, he emerged with a handful of flashlights and distributed them to the group. He grabbed one of the shovels leaning against the garage.

Lucia looked at him quizzically.

"We deciphered a code that mentioned some-thing about digging."

She rolled her eyes.

"Should we wait for Jo?" Nick asked.

Eddie looked at the dark driveway. "I'll bet her mom said no. Let's go."

The four formed a line with Nick in the lead. He led them through the dark yard. The fish shack—which was creepy during the day—now obscured in darkness was terrifying. Nick led the way. Their flashlights cast a myriad of shadows, creating the illusion of movement in the woods.

An owl screeched at them from somewhere overhead. Everyone ducked slightly.

Eddie nervously giggled. "Well, Lucia, you have to admit this is probably scarier than that mummy movie."

Lucia muttered, "You know someone always dies in horror movies, right?"

"This isn't a horror movie," Jesse corrected her. "It's an adventure."

Nick shined his flashlight across the yard, at the fish shack door. "There it is."

They were still twenty yards away when Nick froze. He saw a faint light coming from inside the small building. He signaled for everyone to douse their lights. Then the light in the fish shack went out.

"What should we do?" Nick whispered to Eddie.

Just then, the door opened, and Jo poked her head out. "Nick? Eddie? Is that you?"

The entire group breathed a sigh of relief.

"Jo? What are you doing?" Eddie asked.

"Oh my gosh, my heart is pounding so hard right now." Lucia took a deep breath.

"I thought you said to meet here. My flashlight ran out of batteries, and I was trying to get this lantern started, but it's out of fuel." She eyed the older kids. "What is—*everyone* doing here?" She widened her eyes at Nick and Eddie, hinting that she didn't want to talk about the staircase in front of Lucia and Jesse.

"It's OK." Nick looked at Eddie and sighed. "They know everything."

Jo pressed her lips into a firm line and shook her head.

Eddie inhaled through clenched teeth. "Sorry."

"Is this some kind of joke?" Lucia peered inside the tiny fish shack. "I don't see any stairs."

"Eddie, shine your light right over here." Nick pointed to the metal ring on the trapdoor. He lifted the door and revealed the stone staircase descended into the darkness.

The group let out a collective gasp.

"Totally cool!" Eddie exclaimed.

"Smells like a cave," Jo said, inhaling the cool air seeping up from below.

Jesse leaned forward and shined his light to the landing at the bottom. The metal bars glinted. "And that's the gate you were telling us about?"

Nick nodded.

"Creepy but cool," Lucia said. She pulled Jesse's arm. "I guess we can skip the previews."

NEOTTRITE

NICK WALKED DOWN THE FIRST FOUR STEPS AND looked back. Four concerned faces stared down at him from the opening.

He gave a half-smile. "It's not too bad. There are twelve stone steps leading to a landing and a metal gate at the bottom."

"And you think the key opens the gate?" Jo asked.

Through his shirt, Nick felt the key still hanging around his neck. "We're about to find out."

Everyone filed down the steps after Nick.

"Be careful," he cautioned, "some of these stones are pretty slick."

"Oh, my gosh!" Lucia whimpered. "I just saw a centipede."

"Where?" Jo asked.

"It's slithered into a crack on the wall, but it was enormous and disgusting."

"Aw, I wanted to see it." Jo frowned.

The glow from the flashlights illuminated the stairwell much better than the lantern had. The walls glistened with moisture, and thin, black roots hung from the ceiling. The entire stairwell was constructed from stone, but as they approached the bottom, the stones tapered off, and the walls became solid rock. The landing was about the size of an elevator, and all five of them fit in a huddled group.

"What's a gate doing underneath an old fish shack?" Lucia asked.

"I have no idea," Nick replied. "We found a key with coordinates marking something, and I think this gate might be it."

"Or the gate leads to the coordinates," Jo added.

Nick explained, "When I was here earlier, I couldn't figure out how to get the gate unlocked."

"This smells like that cave we went to at the Grand Canyon, doesn't it?" Eddie asked his sister.

Lucia inhaled the damp, **pungent** air and nodded. "I didn't like that cave, and I'm not sure I like this one either."

"Why didn't Grannie Miller just draw a gate on the map?" Eddie asked. "Or the fish shack? That would've been really helpful."

"She must've thought that'd be too obvious. This way, only someone with *all* the clues could figure it out."

"What did she hide down here?" Nick murmured as he peered through the bars at the dark underground corridor.

"If we can get through these bars," Jo said, "we might start finding some answers."

The thick, vertical bars on the gate seemed to blink at them as they reflected the beams of the flashlights. The blackness beyond the gate was an empty void.

"Well, it's definitely locked." Jo grasped the gate handle and shook it. It didn't budge.

Eddie tried to lift the large metal rod protruding from the wall that appeared to be preventing the latch from moving. Unsuccessful, he found a large rock near the edge of the landing and slammed it against the bars. The sound was deafening, and small chunks of dirt fell from the ceiling overhead.

"Eddie," Lucia scolded. "Stop!" She brushed the dirt out of her hair.

"I don't see a keyhole," Jo observed as she inspected the space with her flashlight.

Nick sighed. "That's what I was afraid of."

"If we can get this metal bar out of the way, I think we can get through," Jesse suggested.

The flashlight beams converged onto the spot where Jesse was shining his light. A metal bar inconveniently blocked the lever and prevented it from lifting.

Nick shined his light around the outline of the metal gate. It nearly reached the ground, but the space underneath was barely large enough for more than the toe of a shoe to squeeze under. The top of the gate reached inches from the ceiling, and again there was not enough space to squeeze through. On the left side of the gate, two huge hinges held the gate bolted to the wall. He scanned the stone walls surrounding the opening, looking for anything out of the ordinary. His light moved across a strange shape in one of the stones.

"I think I found something."

Lucia grimaced and said, "Is it alive? And moving?"

"No." Nick pointed to one of the stones in the wall. It appeared to have a small crevice in it. "I think it's another clue."

Jo shined her flashlight beam on the opening in the stone. Carved into the stone was a cube shape.

"Weird?" Eddie shook his head. "If someone got tired of carrying their Rubik's Cube around, they could stash it in this little cubby."

Nick shined his light into the compartment. At the back, he saw a familiar silhouette. Jo looked over his shoulder.

"It's that bird again!" she gasped.

Eddie explained to the older kids, "We've been tracking this bird image all around town, ever since Nick found a metal box with a key inside in the lake."

"We're definitely on the right track then." Jo said.

Lucia groaned. "If all this leads to a treasure, I want a cut of the riches." She aimed her flashlight at her tennis shoes, which were now speckled with dirt. "And a new pair of shoes."

Eddie chuckled. "Deal."

Jo asked, "Nick, where's the ring box? I think it might fit perfectly into the opening here."

Nick looked at Lucia. "I—um—lost it."

Lucia raised her eyebrows. "Wait. Are you talking about the thing you dropped in the driveway?"

Nick nodded.

Lucia dug around in her bag. A moment later, she pulled out her hand. "Voilà!" she said. In her hand was the box with the bird on the lid. She handed it to Nick.

"Thanks."

The metal box fit into the opening like a missing puzzle piece.

"I think this whole thing turns," Jo said as she traced a circular cut in the stone around the bird.

Nick twisted, and the entire section of stone around the bird turned. When he removed the box, the cavity was much deeper than before.

"There's a secret compartment back there," Nick explained. He thought the cavity looked exactly like the type of cozy hangout a giant spider would love. He brushed away the goosebumps rising on his neck and stepped back. "Someone's going to have to reach inside to find out what's there."

"No way," Lucia said with a shudder.

"I'll do it," Jo offered. She reached inside.

"Don't even think about pretending that something grabs onto your arm," Eddie warned.

"There's something in here!" She pulled out smooth, round stone the size of a golf ball.

"Oh, my gosh!" Eddie exclaimed. "Is it…?"

"It's gotta be a piece of neottrite," Nick said, wide-eyed.

The stone was brilliant blue and a perfect sphere.

Jo whispered, "It's the Waterstone."

Eddie ran a hand through his hair. "Guys, this thing is worth a fortune! But why would it be hidden here? Shouldn't a treasure be hidden *behind* the gate?"

"It's strange," Nick replied, "unless there's something else hidden past this point." He shook the gate, knowing it wouldn't open.

Jo reached back into the opening. Her eyes clenched and she cried, "Oh my gosh!"

"What's wrong?" Eddie took a step back.

Her face melted into a grin. "Gotcha."

"Eddie slugged her shoulder.

"Hey careful." Jo removed her hand and held up a small, circular piece of metal.

"What's that? A soup can lid?" Jesse asked.

"Looks like it," Nick answered. He noticed something on one side. "Turn the lid over, Jo."

The five huddled around the strange, new object and examined the markings on one side.

"Looks like another map," Eddie said.

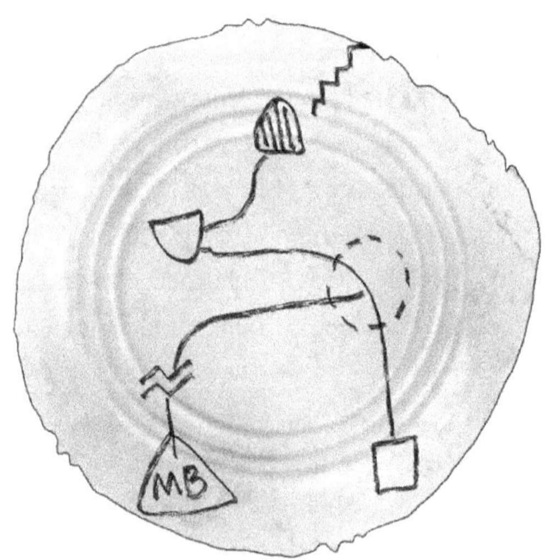

"I'll bet it's a map of the tunnels." She pointed to a small sketch with vertical lines. See, here's the gate."

Her finger traced the line leading away from the gate. "Looks like the tunnel splits up ahead."

"Yeah, but that map is useless if we can't unlock this gate!" Eddie gripped the bars and shook them in frustration.

Nick lightly ran his fingers over the metal latch, scanning it for anything they might have missed. His fingers discovered a strange contour in the otherwise flat surface. He noticed a shallow indentation in the metal. "Hey, guys. What if there *is* a keyhole but the key just isn't the shape we were expecting?"

He carefully took the stone and set it in the rounded hollow. It fit perfectly.

Eddie tried to lift the handle. It didn't move.

Jo unzipped Nick's backpack and pulled out the diary. She knelt down and propped the book open across her knees. "I remember reading something about the light glowing brighter when it comes into contact with liquid." Holding the flashlight in one hand, she flipped through the entries. "Here it is. *When the neottrite is exposed to water, it takes on electromagnetic properties, allowing it to affect light and electricity…and glows.*"

Jo pressed her fingertips against the damp wall, then touched the stone. For a split second, the blue stone appeared to glow, but as quickly as it had begun, the glowing stopped.

"Um…" Lucia said, "did anyone else see that?"

The group nodded.

Jo removed the stone from the cup. She crouched down and rolled the stone across a puddle of water along the edge of the landing. The stone immediately emitted a steady blue light. Jo lifted up the stone. The stone flickered, then faded.

"More water, "Nick said. "We need more water."

"I'm on it." Eddie unclipped his canteen water bottle from his belt and doused the stone with a small splash from the nozzle. The entire orb seemed to glow from within and projected a bright, blue light that illuminated the entire landing.

As she set the stone into the depression, a deep rumbling sound shook the floor, and the walls vibrated. Dirt, dust, and small bits of stone fell from the ceiling, and the floor vibrated. This was followed by the sound of metal scraping against stone. After a moment, the tunnel was silent again.

Nick reached over to the metal bar that blocked the gate latch. This time, it moved easily. He looked at the group with his eyebrows raised.

Eddie said, "Go for it."

The metal lever screeched as the locking mechanism released. The door hinges creaked loudly as Nick pushed the heavy gate open into the tunnel beyond. Jo picked up the Waterstone, which was still glowing faintly, and put it in her pocket.

With Eddie in the lead, the five carefully stepped through the gate. Their flashlight beams illuminated what was clearly the entrance to a cave. Large stalactites hung from the ceiling like glistening, brown teeth. A narrow path meandered between large underground rock formations and stalagmites.

"I can't believe this is here!" Eddie exclaimed excitedly.

"I can't believe *we're* here," Lucia groaned.

Jesse shined his flashlight into the small opening where the stone had been. "If that huge gate behind us swings shut, you realize we'll be trapped down here, right?"

"Good point." Nick looked for something to prop the gate open. He thought about using the shovel to prop the gate open, but then remembered the word *dig* in the coded message and figured it might be useful. Instead, he used a small boulder from the edge of the tunnel and wedged it under the gate. It held.

Lucia continued. "And didn't you say this treasure is linked to a man who, along with fifty-two other people died—in a mine collapse? A *mine collapse!* As in trapped underground—with no hope of rescue." She shook her head. "Eddie, even if you promised to do my chores for a year, there's no way I'd let you go into that tunnel." She crossed her arms. "Mom would never forgive me."

"C'mon." Eddie whined. "Don't you want to know what's down here?"

Lucia frowned. "You said you wanted to check the gate, and we've done that. Now we need to get back up to the surface."

"And let the Caldwells swoop in for the victory?" Eddie threw his arms in the air. "We are probably inches away from finding the treasure of a lifetime, and you're thinking of turning back? Nick? Jo? You're with me, right?"

Nick looked past Eddie into the dark void of the tunnel. "We really don't know what is down here, and all we have is a shovel and some flashlights. Maybe we should get some more supplies first."

"I want to know what's down here, but, Eddie, no one knows we're here." Jo chewed her lip. "It could be dangerous. I think we should wait until—"

"I'm not waiting," Eddie said stubbornly. "We've gotten this far, and I know we can do this." He shined his flashlight into the cavern tunnel and continued into the darkness.

"Eddie!" Jo called after him. "Whatever we find at the end of that tunnel will be worth nothing if we get trapped down here. No one knows we're here. In fact, no one even knows this tunnel exists!"

Now about ten yards away, Eddie stopped and turned to face them. "Mr. Watkins knows where we are."

"N-not really," Nick stumbled.

"Think about it, Eddie, we could *DIE* down here. We have to go back." Nick turned to follow Jo, who was already walking back toward the gate.

Lucia shook her head. "This isn't a negotiation."

"Be reasonable, Eddie," Nick added.

"I'm tired of being reasonable," Eddie fired back. "Everyone is always telling me what to do. This is a cave that's probably been here for hundreds of thousands of years. He slapped his hand on a nearby merged stalactite and stalagmite. This isn't some mine with shaky tunnels. Look, I've got my walkie talkie, so if I need help, I'll radio you. If you want to join me, I'll share the treasure with you." Eddie stormed away from the others, and after a moment, the glow of his flashlight disappeared as the path of the tunnel curved around a bend in the path.

Lucia scoffed. "I don't know how you two put up with him."

Jo took a deep breath. "What now?"

Nick said, "Well, we either head back and wait for help, or we try to catch up to him before he gets lost down here."

Jo nodded. "Eddie doesn't have the tunnel map."

Jesse looked pensive. "We should probably stay together."

Nick rubbed his forehead and stared at the map. "It looks like the tunnel eventually splits. Maybe he'll come back." He looked at Jo.

Suddenly, from ahead in the tunnel, they heard a series of echoing thuds and Eddie's voice crying out, "Aghhhh!"

Trapped

"EDDIE?" JO CALLED OUT. THE DENSE BLACKNESS of the tunnel swallowed up the beams of their flashlights. Nick's flashlight flickered, threatening to run out of batteries.

"Eddie?" Lucia shouted. Her voice cracked with worry. "Eddie!"

They heard a faint voice groaning. "Help. I'm stuck. Help me!"

The tunnel twisted and turned, making it difficult to see very far ahead. The ground was muddy and slick, and the group hurried as fast as they could without losing their footing. What happened next occurred so quickly, it caught everyone off guard. The tunnel sloped downward, and it became even more slippery. Lucia, who was in the lead, halted abruptly. She was standing at the edge of a drop-off.

The rest of the group was following too closely behind her and didn't anticipate the quick stop. By the time they realized they needed to slow down, the domino effect was already taking place. Jesse slammed into Nick and fell sideways against the tunnel wall. He tried to grab hold of Nick, but Nick's tennis shoes skidded, sending him beyond Jesse's grasp. Nick unexpectedly bumped into Jo's leg, knocking her off-balance. Her feet lost traction and slid awkwardly. As Jo scrambled to maintain her balance, she slammed into Lucia.

Only Lucia braced for impact; her hands pressed outward against the sides of the tunnel, but she, too, was sliding, and the path pitched steeply downhill. She groped frantically for something to grasp but found only a few scraggly roots sticking out of the dirt walls. With vise-like strength, she curled her fingers around two clusters of roots. Miraculously, they held her, but Jo both slid past her, followed by Nick, who was still holding the shovel. They both slid over the edge of a drop-off.

Nick and Jo landed in a heap about ten feet down, directly on top of Eddie. Fortunately, he had deployed an emergency life vest he wore under his regular vest, and his ballooned torso created a soft landing for everyone. The shovel blade lodged in the dirt, inches from Eddie's ear.

Their flashlights had ejected from their hands during the fall and were now a few feet away, pointing at awkward angles on the ground. The glowing Waterstone, which Jo pulled from her pocket to inspect for damage, continued to emit a faint light. As they examined their new surroundings, it was clear they'd landed in a pit.

Jesse—who had been behind the collision—called down, “Is everyone OK?”

Lucia shined her flashlight beam at them from above.

“I think so.” Nick pulled a clump of dirt out of his hair.

Jo muttered angrily to herself.

“Phew!” Eddie exhaled. “That was a close one. Good thing I deployed my emergency life vest.” He brushed himself off. “Not a bad landing.” He chuckled. “You’re welcome, by the way.”

Jo, entirely disgusted, said, “Eddie, you are *so* irresponsible! Do you realize what you’ve done?” “We’re trapped down here!” She pulled the shovel blade out of the dirt. “And you almost had a shovel jammed into your skull!”

“Hey, at least I—”

“You can argue about this later.” Lucia interrupted with an authoritative tone. “Are you sure you’re OK?”

Nick patted his torso, inspecting it for damage. Finding nothing out of place, he replied, “I think. Just a little banged up.”

“Maybe we can pull you up.” Jesse reached an arm down.

Jo, the tallest of the three, reached up. Her fingertips barely touched Jesse’s. She jumped up and grasped at his hand, but it was slick from sweat and the moisture of the damp tunnel. Their fingers slipped apart.

Eddie suggested, “Let’s try a human chain. Jo, you step onto my hands, and then Lucia can pull you up.”

He knelt down and clasped his hands together to form a step. "I'll give you a boost."

Jo stepped into Eddie's hands and reached up for Jesse's outstretched hands.

"Wait," Lucia cautioned.

"What?" Eddie asked.

"If you lose your grip and he pulls you in, too, we'll be even worse off." Lucia took a few steps back. "Jesse, I'll hold your feet and try to add some traction."

Jesse reached down again, and Jo stepped onto Eddie's hand-step. Her fingers wrapped around Jesse's hand, but when he started pulling Jo up, his torso began inching over the edge.

"Stop, stop, stop!" Lucia shouted. "We're sliding!"

"I'm letting go." Jesse dropped Jo back down into the pit.

Lucia crept toward the edge and explained, "There's nothing to hold on to up here except these tiny vines and they're not strong enough to hold more than one person."

"What are we going to do?" Nick asked.

"Eddie," Lucia said, "you're always blabbering on about survival skills. Any ideas?"

Eddie thought for a moment and replied, "Resources. We need to use our resources. Look around for anything that might help us. Maybe we can make a rope out of vines or something."

Lucia jerked several long roots from the wall and twisted them together. They split and broke into pieces.

"Next idea?" she asked.

The three kids moved around the pit. Almost immediately, their flashlight beams reflected off a pile of curved, glass objects on the ground.

"Jars?" Jo reached down and picked one up. She used the hem of her shirt to wipe the glass clean. "Anyone hungry?" Jo handed the jar to Nick.

He aimed his flashlight at the jar. It was filled with what looked like hundreds of tiny greenish-brown eyeballs suspended in a translucent, brownish liquid.

"At least we won't starve to death," Eddie joked.

"Gross," Nick replied.

She grinned. "Relax, City Kid, they're just old, canned peas."

Eddie cringed.

Nick stepped on something hard that shifted under his weight. At first, he thought it was a rock, but when he lowered his flashlight to illuminate the ground, he saw part of a ladder half buried in the dirt and mud. Unfortunately, the wood was badly rotted from years of decay. When he tried to pull it out of the ground, it crumbled.

Jo sighed. "I don't think anyone's been down here in a *long* time."

"At least the Caldwells didn't beat us here," Eddie said.

Jesse asked, "Who exactly are these Caldwell people?"

Nick answered, "We think they're treasure hunters who might somehow be connected to the fake-old people at the ice cream shop."

"Mr. Watkins thinks they might be dangerous," Jo added.

"If that old creep thinks they're dangerous, then we're in trouble."

Jo replied, "He's actually really nice, once you get to know him."

"Hey!" Lucia perked up. "Eddie, try radioing Mom. She keeps the spare walkie talkie on in the kitchen so she can keep tabs on you."

"I *knew* someone was listening in…" Eddie muttered before pressing the side button of his walkie talkie, "Mama Bear, do you copy? Mama Bear? Over."

The hum of static filled the pit. Their hope dissolved.

He repeated the message two more times, then shook his head. "Too far below ground. We're out of range."

Jo suggested, "What about some actual rope? You could hoist us up."

Nick looked up at Jesse and Lucia. "There's some in the garage."

"Perfect," Jesse said. "Let's go."

Lucia assured, "We'll be back in two minutes. Don't go wandering off."

"Very funny," Eddie snarked but then smiled.

"Wait!" Jo said. "You should take this." She held up the stone, then carefully tossed it to Lucia. "If that gate locks behind you, and the stone is stuck down here with us, we'll be trapped…for good."

Nick's stomach lurched at the thought.

"Don't worry," Lucia said as she pocketed the stone. "We'll get you out of here."

Nick, Jo, and Eddie watched the glow of their flashlights disappear into the tunnel.

Flashlights

"This should be long enough," Jesse said, holding up a coiled bundle of thick rope.

"Great. Let's go," Lucia replied.

They were about to dart back across the dark yard toward the fish shack when they heard the sound of two car doors slamming. A pair of headlights flickered between the trees beyond the fish shack.

"Looks like someone's at the Miller house." Lucia checked her watch. "Kind of late for the cleaning crew."

"I hope those aren't the people your brother was telling us about." Jesse clicked off his flashlight.

Lucia did the same.

Jesse took one step toward the fish shack, but Lucia grabbed his arm. "Wait a minute."

"Why?" Jesse whispered. "We need to go, like *right now.*"

"Just wait." Lucia's gaze was fastened on the flashlights blinking between the trees. "They're headed the other way, which means—whoever these Caldwell guys are—they obviously aren't interested in the fish shack."

"Or they don't know about it."

"Right. If they spot us heading there, we'll lead them right to it, and we'll all be sitting ducks down there." Lucia bit her fingernail. "No one knows we're here, Jesse. This is turning into a really bad situation."

He looked at her. "I know."

They watched the two flashlights zigzag around the property.

"They're headed toward the lake," Jesse breathed.

"In a minute or so, they'll reach the shore and start heading this way."

"Right."

"Let's split up," Lucia suggested. "When they're out of sight, we'll have about thirty seconds to move. I'll take the rope and try to get the kids out. You take the Jeep into town and get help."

"What if you can't lift them up?" Jesse asked. "Maybe *you* should drive to town."

Lucia frowned. "I won't even make it out of the driveway. The last time I tried to drive stick shift was a total disaster, remember? Plus," she added, "I'm a faster runner than you. I'll get the kids."

"OK," Jesse said.

Lucia added, "Don't start the engine until I get to the shack. No sense in drawing attention over here until I'm out of sight."

"Be careful." Jesse said, then ran toward the Jeep.

When the flashlight beams disappear, Lucia ran around the far side of Big J's cabin, then peered around the back corner. The flashlights were still out of sight. Her eyes had adjusted to the dark, and even without a flashlight, she could see the outline of the shack in the woods.

Lucia's heart was pounding in her ears. She was only about fifty yards from the dark structure. Making a run for it without knowing exactly when the flashlights would reappear felt risky. The path she would navigate to the shack was quite exposed.

Gathering her courage, Lucia took a deep breath and started to make a break for the shack when her shirt snaggled on the branch of a prickly shrub. As she wasted valuable seconds freeing herself, she heard the Jeep roar to life. Jesse must have assumed she'd already made it to the shack. The Caldwells would have been alerted to the activity and were probably already heading this way to investigate. As she predicted, Lucia saw one flashlight appear near the lake followed by the other.

It's now or never.

She dug into the sandy soil and sprinted toward the shack.

STUCK

NICK DISTRIBUTED THE HEADLAMPS HE'D STASHED in his backpack then examined the map again. Jo aimed her light in front of her, inspecting the walls of the pit. Eddie attempted to excavate footholds with the shovel by jabbing at the dirt wall.

The map depicted the staircase and gate with a small illustration. A short, winding line seemed to represent the tunnel that had ejected them into their pit-prison. Beyond the pit, an additional line—presumably another tunnel—led away, in the opposite direction, and eventually forked.

He murmured to himself, "It just doesn't make sense. Why would there be a pit here?" He traced the lines on the map with his finger. "And how do we get to this tunnel over here?" He pointed to the lines that continued beyond the pit before splitting. "Maybe one of these other tunnels leads to the surface."

"There's no way I'm going any deeper underground." Jo tried to pull herself up using a root, but it snapped off in her hand, and she stumbled backward.

Eddie looked around at the dirt floor and added, "I just hope we don't want to find any skeletal remains of old miners down here."

"Eddie! Why would you even suggest that?" Jo sounded exacerbated. A concerned look washed over her face. She murmured, "Now that's all I can think about."

Nick looked around at the rock walls and hoped their surroundings were as solid as they appeared.

Jo pointed her headlamp to the ceiling of the cavern. It was covered with stalactites hanging down in sharp points. "Those mineral deposits up there look really, really old. I'd bet someone found this cave and turned it into a root cellar or something."

"You sound relieved," Nick said.

"Well, yeah." She nodded. "That means, this cave was definitely *NOT* man-made, which means it's not part of the mine."

Eddie jabbed the shovel into the wall to make another foot hold. "Since when do caves have dirt walls, though? The cavern we saw at the Grand Canyon was solid rock. According to the tour guide, that's why it's lasted sixty-five million years. Fun fact, the United States government stashed enough supplies in that cave for two thousand people to use as a shelter during the Cuban Missile Crisis with the Soviet Union."

Nick eyed the jars filled with peas and brownish liquid. "Did they end up needing the supplies?"

"Nope. It ended peacefully."

"Well, cave or not, Mr. Watkins's grandparents must have known about this tunnel, and I doubt some old veggies are what they wrote about in the riddle." Jo crossed her arms.

Nick pulled out his sketchbook and reread the coded message: "*The switch that toggles where and when, Ere hidden from all eyes of men. Look within the round and canst go forth. East and north reach the edges, and there you dig, and dig again.*"

"I wonder if Mr. Watkins figured out the riddle yet," Nick said.

"Well, he'll be the first person we tell when we get out of here," Eddie replied.

"*If* we get out of here," Jo murmured.

The three gazed up at the dark tunnel opening.

Eddie muttered, "What's taking them so long?"

Lucia took three bounds into the woods toward the shack, but each step was accompanied by the loud cracking and snapping of branches under her feet. She instantly slowed and continued slowly and quietly.

Suddenly, she heard a woman's voice behind her. "Hello?"

Lucia whirled around to see two figures coming around the back side of the cabin. She shielded her eyes from their flashlights. As her eyes adjusted, she relaxed and smiled. "Oh, hi! I was worried you were someone else!"

Rotten

"THEY SHOULD'VE BEEN BACK BY NOW." EDDIE combed his hands through his hair as he paced back and forth. "Something's wrong."

Jo glared at Eddie. "If we're stuck down here forever—I will never forgive you."

Eddie looked apologetically at Jo. "You can be mad at me later." He took a deep breath. "Thinking is the key to survival. We have to keep our thoughts moving forward."

"Right," Nick agreed. "There's got to be another way out of here." He looked at the map for the thousandth time. "According to the map, there should be another tunnel right here." He pointed to the dirt wall.

Jo stood next to Nick and examined the map. "What's this long line over here?" She pointed to a meandering line that reached the bottom edge.

Nick explained, "The tunnel that should be *right here*—but isn't—splits further down the line. One of the branches is very short and connects with something nearby with whatever this square represents. This other path," he pointed to the longer line, "continues on for who knows how long—could be miles. See this symbol?"

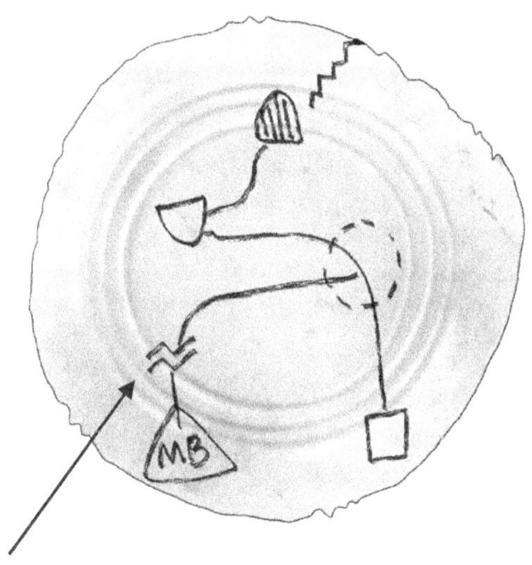

He pointed to parallel zig-zag marks intersecting the long line. "This indicates the length is longer than the edge of the paper and has been shortened for the map. It connects to this triangle shape labeled *M.B.,* but who know what the letters represent."

"Squares? Triangles? This is all starting to feel kind of hopeless." Eddie unsuccessfully tried to pull himself up using the hand- and foot-holds he'd excavated.

"M.B." Jo frowned. "Maybe it stands for Miller and Bennett?"

"Could be the Miller-Bennett Mining Company headquarters," Nick offered. "If this cave connects to the mine, the mining headquarters would connect, too."

"Maybe." Eddie crossed his arms.

Two voices echoed through the passage overhead.

"Finally!" Jo said.

"Don't push me!" A shrill voice echoed toward them. "These stairs are slippery."

Eddie looked at Nick and Jo in alarm. "That doesn't sound like Lucia and Jesse."

"The Caldwells!" Nick whispered.

The sound of the gate rattling against the latch filled the tunnel.

"They won't be able to get through without the stone," Jo whispered.

The gate rattled again—violently.

"Let's hope not." Nick felt a knot of worry tighten in his stomach. He backed up against the wall of the pit. To everyone's surprise and horror, the wall behind him made a creaking sound.

"What. Was. That?" Eddie asked, his voice quivering.

"Oh my gosh, the tunnel's collapsing!" Nick clenched his eyes shut.

"No. It's not," Jo reassured.

Nick opened one eye at a time, then relaxed. The ground wasn't shaking. The ceiling wasn't caving in. Everything seemed fine, but something in the pit had made a noise, and they were curious—and nervous—to find out what it was.

Jo brushed away a curtain of tangled roots to reveal an oddly flat, rectangular section of wall.

In front of them stood a dark brown, wooden door.

"How did we not see this before?" Eddie asked.

Nick wiped the surface and removed a layer of dirt and grime. They quickly discovered a latch holding the door closed, but the wood was far too decayed to withstand any force. Like the ladder, the door was spongy and rotten. When Jo twisted the knob, the wood around it fell apart, and she was left holding the detached metal handle.

"I got this," Eddie announced as he gave the door a mighty karate kick, which successfully created a large hole in the center.

Jo's head momentarily disappeared as she leaned through the opening with her headlamp. "Well," she looked at Nick, "I think we found the missing tunnel."

Into the Cave

THE AIR BEYOND THE OLD DOOR SMELLED EARTHY and chilled Nick's nose with each inhale. The squeaking of tennis shoes on the damp, rock path blended with the trickling of water against the sides of the cave. Aside from an abundance of roots growing into the passageway, the route through the tunnel was mostly clear. The jagged walls glinted against the movement of their headlamps as they moved deeper into the cave. Stalactites hung down from the ceiling and dripped onto their stalagmite opposites, reaching toward each other. Occasionally, the formations met in the middle forming hourglass-shaped columns.

"I feel like we've been walking forever," Eddie rubbed his hands together to warm them.

Jo checked her watch, then rolled her eyes as she exhaled a small cloud of condensation. "It's been seven minutes."

Nick walked at the back of the group. He was worried because he had no idea what happened to Jesse and Lucia. He stopped and listened. Nothing. The silence was slightly reassuring because, although it indicated no sign of help, it also meant the Caldwells hadn't gotten past the gate.

A few steps ahead, Eddie pointed up. "Check out those mini stalactites."

Nick shined his flashlight overhead. "It's like we're walking under a fuzzy, brown canopy." He lifted the blade of the shovel to poke at the lumpy ceiling.

The shovel was about an inch away when Jo hissed, "Wait!" She continued in a whisper, "Those are bats!"

Directly over their heads hung an enormous carpet of hundreds of bats. One of the furry, brown animals stretched a leathery wing. Several other bats shifted and jostled but seemed undisturbed by the visitors.

Eddie whimpered.

"Stay quiet, and *do not* wake them up," Jo whispered.

The group tiptoed past the dangling colony and followed the path as it descended deeper underground. When they were well beyond the bats they stopped to inspect the map.

"How much farther does this go?" Eddie asked.

"It's hard to say," Nick replied. He looked at the short line, and based on the distance they'd come so far, he guessed it stretched less than a half-mile. According to the map, the tunnel would split somewhere ahead, and the long line would branch off and continue for an unknown distance. "The tunnel forks somewhere right around here."

"What should we do when we get there?" Eddie asked.

"We have three options," Jo said. "We either continue on this shorter path, take the longer path toward something labeled "M.B." or go back."

"I'm too cold to think. It's freezing down here!" Eddie nudged a cluster of boards leaning against the wall of the cave. "Maybe we could make a fire to warm up."

"I don't think that's a great idea. There's not much ventilation down here," Nick replied.

"Plus, it would wake up the bats for sure." Jo folded her arms tightly and shivered.

"Seems weird there would be a bunch of rotting wood in a cave though, right?" Nick bent and picked up a small piece of wood cut in the shape of an arrow. "Looks like an old sign."

It was in a state of decomposition, but they could clearly read two words *North Tunnel* carved into the surface.

Eddie rubbed his forehead. "Archibald Miller wrote about a North Tunnel in his diary."

Jo exclaimed, "That's where Matthew found the neottrite!"

"The Waterstone," Nick murmured. "Wait a minute. If this sign pointed to the North Tunnel, that means we're either in the mine, or very close to it."

Jo looked concerned. "But how's that possible? We're definitely in a cave, not a mine—right?"

North
Tunnel

"Look at the ceiling. It's too jagged to be man-made." Eddie rubbed his hands together again. "Plus, all the mine entrances were sealed after the collapse."

"Guys, look." Nick lifted another board leaning against the cave wall.

Hidden behind it was a small opening.

"I'll bet the sign pointed this way." Jo raised her eyebrows. "Which means this passage leads to the North Tunnel."

Through the opening stretched a long, rectangular corridor supported by large, wooden beams spaced at regular intervals.

"Cool." Eddie ducked under the low opening and into the new tunnel. "Now *this* is what a mine looks like." He took another step. "See these supports?" He patted one of the huge, wooden beams lining the passageway.

The air in this tunnel had a dank, musty smell and reminded Nick of a freshly paved road. "Smells like tar," he pulled the collar of his shirt over his nose.

Eddie agreed, "It stinks."

"Guys, look." Jo pointed her beam at an old ax leaning against one of the wooden supports. "Someone chopped away at these beams."

Nick shined his light into the tunnel. At the far end, just before his flashlight beam became swallowed up by the dark, he saw a pile of boulders blocking the way. "Oh my gosh," he said. "The tunnel's caved in." He looked at the ax and the chopped beams. Something didn't add up.

Jo said, "Maybe—do you think—someone *wanted* the tunnel to collapse?"

Simultaneously, they said, "Cornelius Bennett."

Nick was thinking about the articles they'd read when, in the shadows at the far end of the tunnel, something shiny caught his attention. His stomach dropped.

About thirty feet away, two circles glinted between the collapsed boulders. It was a pair of eyes. Animal eyes.

"Guys," Nick warned. "We've got company."

"What do you mean?" Jo added her light to his.

There's something over there, in the rocks. And it's alive."

Eddie whimpered. The eyes stared at them.

"I think," Eddie sniffed the air, "that might be a skunk."

Jo slowly pulled Nick and Eddie away from the tunnel entrance. "Slowly," she whispered. "Skunks have really bad eyesight."

They backed into the wide chamber of the main cave. Nick gently replaced the board over the opening and wondered if this was the same skunk Uncle John had come across.

"Well, we're definitely not going *that* way," Eddie said.

Nick consulted the map again. "Maybe we should try heading back."

"*Toward* the Caldwells?" Eddie scoffed. "Uh—no, thanks. And remember? The gate is locked."

"I think Nick's right," Jo said, chewing her lip.

"Seriously? Eddie scoffed.

Jo replied, "Who knows how much farther this tunnel goes—or if it even connects to anything."

Nick said, "I'm not super excited about going deeper, especially after seeing those chopped beams. This felt risky before, but now it seems really dangerous."

"But we've come this far. We could be just around the corner from finding whatever Eleanor Miller hid." Eddie kicked the dirt. "We've got to be about half-way between the cabin and the Miller house. There's buried treasure down here. I know it."

Nick and Eddie were debating the probability of finding a buried treasure when Jo interrupted. "Hang on," she said, slowly turning 360 degrees. "This part of the cave—is kind of a circle."

"And?" Eddie asked.

Nick scanned the space and quoted the riddle. "Look within *the round*."

"Exactly." Jo beamed.

Nick jabbed the ground with the shovel. Unlike the surrounding tunnel, most of the ground in this section was dirt.

Nick quoted, "*East and North.* That's gotta mean northeast. Eddie, did you bring your compass?"

"Did I bring my compass—" Eddie muttered while fumbling in one of his vest pockets. He quickly oriented himself and pointed at a wall of the cave. "Northeast—is this way."

"Reach the edge." Nick grasped the shovel. "There you dig."

At the northeast edge of the circular cavern, he drove the blade into the earth.

Jo finished the rhyme. "And dig again."

Nick plunged the blade into the dirt a second time. Again and again, he drove the blade of the shovel into the dark, damp earth. The soil here pit was slightly damp, which made it easy to scoop but heavy to lift. Nick took a deep breath and let his cheeks puff out as he exhaled.

The air filled with the pungent scent of disturbed soil mixed with the faint smell of skunk. The **stench** seemed to be **dissipating** a little, but Jo kept an eye on the board covering the opening at the opposite side of the chamber.

Suddenly, a *THUD* echoed in the cavern.

"You hit something?" Jo's eyes lit up.

Nick's jaw dropped. He nodded.

"NO WAY!" Eddie yelped.

All three dropped to their knees and began scraping away dirt with their bare hands.

"Whoa," Eddie squealed like a little kid. "It totally looks like a treasure chest! Are we ready to get rich?"

Nick brushed away more dirt and revealed a large container with a brass latch. It *was* a trunk, with metal rivets lining the edges.

"Oh, my gosh!" Jo exhaled. "It's another steamer trunk."

Eddie grasped one end of the trunk, and Nick wedged the blade of the shovel under the opposite. Using the shovel to create leverage, he leaned on the handle with his entire body weight, and the trunk heaved upward. Jo grabbed the handle on the side and tried to hoist it up to level ground.

"Push!" Jo ordered.

The trunk moved up about two inches but slipped off the shovel and fell back into the hole. They tried again and again, with the same results each time.

"It's too heavy," Eddie panted.

Jo crouched on her knees, brushed dirt off the brass latch. "Look! It's a—"

"Way ahead of you." Nick had already pulled the necklace over his neck and carefully inserted the key into the keyhole.

He jiggled the clasp and pressed a button on the side. The latch released and flopped down.

"I *knew* it!" Eddie smiled.

"On three?" Jo asked.

The boys nodded.

"One—two—three," they chanted, then lifted the heavy lid.

Inside lay a large, black, velvet bag.

A Treasure?

Jo heaved the heavy bag out of the chest and set it on the dirt.

"It weighs a TON." Eddie's eyes glimmered. "Good things come in small packages. This could be the big pay-off; the big payload. We've hit paydirt." He rubbed his hands together. "I've heard gold is heavy!"

Eddie continued to chatter while Nick loosened the drawstring and pulled out a strange-looking contraption roughly the size of his backpack.

It wasn't gold.

Eddie stopped talking. For the first time since they'd walked past the gate, he was silent. Even Jo seemed speechless.

"Well, it's not what we were expecting, but let's not judge it quite yet." Nick was trying hard to be optimistic, but he, too, felt a crushing sense of disappointment.

"What is it?" Jo asked.

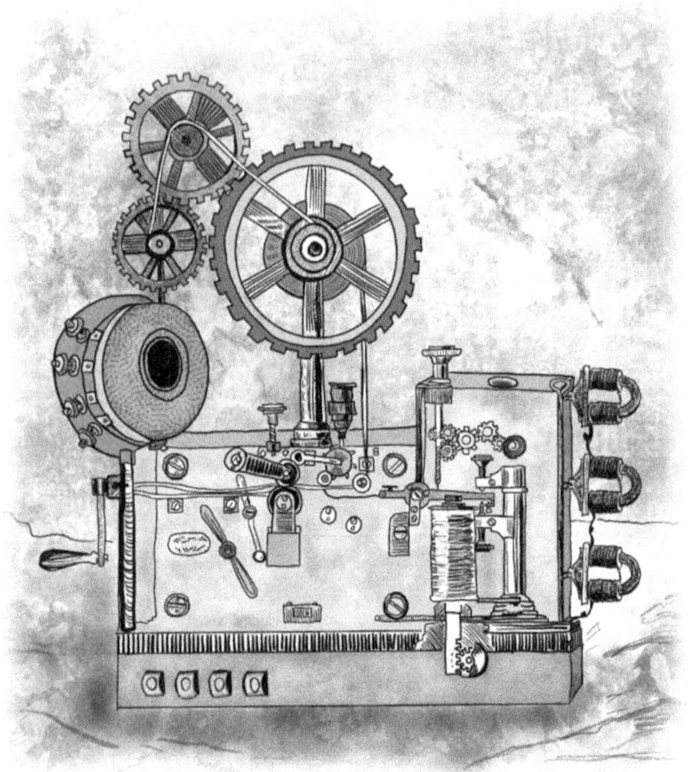

The machine was covered with gears, wires, and tubes. The whole machine was nearly black with **tarnish**. A crank handle was located on the right side. Nick was able to move it a little, but it took some effort.

"This doesn't look like much of a treasure." Eddie let out a sigh.

"Maybe not," Jo looked at Nick, "but it looks just like the machine we saw Mr. Watkins working on at the jewelry store."

"I wonder what this does." Eddie cranked the handle. As he did, the gears rotated. "Maybe this thing controls another secret panel that'll lead us to the gold." He looked around at the cave walls.

Nick asked, "Is anything happening?"

"I don't think so," Jo answered.

"Great." Eddie shook his head and let out a loud sigh. "A broken machine."

"Maybe it needs to generate speed," Jo suggested.

Nick took a turn, cranking faster and faster until he was out of breath. The gears flew into action, spinning and moving smaller parts within the machine. Other than the movement of the gears, nothing appeared to be happening.

"Maybe it's broken." Jo scrunched her mouth to the side.

Eddie frowned. "Trapped in a cave—with a skunk, no treasure, and a hunk of junk." He leaned back against a stalactite column and crossed his arms. "None of this makes any sense."

Nick pulled his sketchbook out of his backpack and re-examined the riddle, hoping to discover a missed clue. He compared it to the original and gasped. "The circled letters! We forgot to circle the letters!" His eyes bounced between the brittle paper they'd found in the trunk and the handwritten message in his sketchbook. Jo pulled out a pen a circled the decoded letters one by one. "T-E-L-A-E-R-A."

"*This* is the Telaera?" Nick asked.

"Think it's worth a million dollars?" Eddie's tone indicated he didn't think so.

The switch that
toggles where and when
Ere hidden from all
eyes of men. Look
within the round and
canst go forth. East
and North reach the
edges, and there you
dig and dig again.

They stared at the small, metal contraption.

"Archibald Miller's diary said the Telaera needs a lot of power to run," Jo said. Jo said, "I think we need the Waterstone to get it running."

Nick pressed his finger along the top edge and noticed the same type of shallow indentation they'd found by the gate. He ran a finger around the indentation at the top of the machine. "I'll bet it fits right in here. When Lucia and Jesse come back, we can give it a try."

A faint, metallic *SCREEEECH* echoed through the cave.

Nick whispered, "The gate."

Eddie looked relieved. "Finally." He stood up and took a step in the direction of the gate.

Jo put her hand in his arm. "Wait. How do we know it's not the Caldwells?"

Eddie scoffed. "How would the Caldwells be able to open the gate unless they somehow got the stone?"

"Jesse and Lucia should've been back right away. Something tells me they're not the ones who just opened the gate."

Nick glanced at the **conspicuous** pile of dirt barely covering the trunk.

"We can worry about that later." Jo looked straight into Eddie's eyes and gave his shoulder an encouraging squeeze. "Right now, we've gotta find a way out of here."

Nick whispered, "If the Caldwells got into the tunnel, we're in big trouble."

Eddie added, "And if they're looking for the Telaera, we've led them right to it! Nick, do you think it'll fit in your backpack?"

"We can't take it with us," Jo reasoned. "If this is what they've been looking for, they'll just keep chasing us deeper into the tunnel. We have to leave it."

Eddie opened his mouth to protest, but Jo continued. "You made the last decision. Look where that got us. Trapped. With a skunk. *I'm* deciding this time. We leave the machine and look for a way outta here."

"Fine," Eddie mumbled.

Jo put the Telaera back into the trunk and closed the lid. Nick grabbed the shovel and frantically began flinging dirt to cover it up.

The trunk was mostly covered when Jo grabbed Nick's arm. She held a finger to her lips and pointed to a dim, yellow glow moving toward them from around a bend in the path. The three frantically searched for places to hide, but the options were limited.

"Over here," Eddie hissed as he ducked into the opening of the North Tunnel. "C'mon."

"But the skunk!" Jo hissed.

Eddie grabbed Jo's arms and pulled her behind the wooden plank. "We're out of time."

Nick squeezed in behind them and crouched on the cold, damp floor. Eddie slid the board over the opening. The skunk was nowhere in sight, but its odor was almost unbearable. All three clicked their headlamps off and held perfectly still. Without their lights, the darkness was **oppressive**.

Nick held his fingers in front of his face but couldn't see them at all. Nick's eyes strained to see the outline of some shape—any shape—in his immediate surroundings. In the absence of his visual sense, his ears became his primary sense of perception.

He heard the drops of water sliding off the stalactites and dripping onto their corresponding stalagmites. Eddie's shallow breathing seemed to fill the cavern. Jo quietly shushed him.

Nick's heart was a drum. He wondered how long it would take for their bodies to be discovered if this didn't end well. He shook away the grim thought.

Parallel lines of light now peeked between the boards covering the opening. The light grew brighter.

Nick craned to see through a small gap between the boards. He saw the shovel leaning against the wall and felt like he'd been punched in the gut.

How did I forget the shovel?

Two shadowy figures moved into the opening.

"How much farther?" a shrill voice hissed.

"I told you. I don't remember!" a deep voice snapped. "Geez, it stinks down here!"

Nick breathed a sigh of relief when he realized the people standing ten feet away in the circular cavern were *not* Steven and Jake Caldwell, but Dani and Ty Cooper.

Thank goodness.

Nick was about to stand up and thank their rescuers, but he froze when Dani hissed, "That money better be here."

Eddie looked at Nick and Jo. He mouthed, *Money?*

Nick gulped. The reality of the situation sank in. The Caldwells and the Coopers must be working together.

Ty kicked the dirt. "Looks like those kids have been poking around down here. Here's their shovel."

Dani replied, "They're probably a mile away by now."

"Well, they're not in the North Tunnel, that's for sure." Ty let out a soft chuckle. "Cornelius made sure of that. When he said he'd fix it, I had no idea he wanted to collapse the whole thing."

Nick shook his head and wondered if he'd heard her correctly. The Coopers were talking as though they knew Cornelius Bennett personally, even though he'd been alive over a hundred years ago. His thoughts were interrupted by the sound of a shovel blade crunching into dirt.

Jo's wristwatch made a deafening chirp as it registered the hour. She clamped a hand over her wrist.

Dani whirled around.

"What?" Ty barked.

"I heard something."

"It's those kids. Think they're hiding around here somewhere?"

The faint glow streaming between the boards suddenly brightened in the beam of an approaching flashlight.

"Yes." Dani's voice took on a sinister tone. An eye appeared between the boards. "Yes, I do."

A Way Out

"DANI KICKED ONE OF THE BOARDS AWAY. SHE pulled Nick into the cavernous room. "Get over here. All of you." She kicked at the pile of loose dirt, exposing a corner of the trunk. "Doing a little archaeology project for homework?"

Jo glared at her.

"That trunk doesn't belong to you," Eddie growled.

Dani walked up to Eddie and leaned forward. Her face was so close to his, their noses almost touched. She snarled, "We've been looking for this for longer than you've been alive."

Jo tipped her chin up and said, "But it's not yours."

"It is now." Dani scoffed and nodded at her brother.

Ty seemed to follow her cue and pulled a rope out of his bag.

"Her necklace," Nick whispered so quietly, only Jo and Eddie could hear. "Look familiar?"

Around her neck, Dani wore the necklace Ty had picked up from Mr. Watkins the day he'd come into the shop. The large blue stone pendant bore a striking resemblance to the Waterstone.

"Think it's neottrite?" Jo breathed, barely speaking.

"Either way, I say we bolt," Eddie whispered.

"Backs against the pillar," Ty barked, nodding toward a section of **accumulated** mineral deposits.

Jo nodded to Nick and Eddie. A split second before they took off, Ty stepped into their path. "Don't be stupid."

"Seriously? You're going to tie up three innocent kids?" Jo took another step but halted when Ty reached into his pocket and pulled out a switchblade. She stepped toward the column.

He flicked the blade open with such ease; it was clear he'd had practice using it. Jo thrust her hands in the air, indicating she wouldn't argue. Nick did the same. Eddie scoffed but didn't argue.

The column was tall, but narrow. Ty wrapped a heavy rope around the kids. He secured the ends in a tight knot, then went to help Dani, who'd already uncovered half of the trunk.

The rope was so tight, Nick couldn't move. The circulation in his hands was being cut off. His fingers tingled and had begun to lose feeling. From his position, he had a clear view of the Coopers and the trunk. Eddie and Jo were facing slightly away, but all their shoulders were touching, and if they tipped their heads toward each other, they could whisper without drawing too much attention.

"Do either of you think you can wiggle free?" Nick asked.

"I can barely breathe." Jo's voice was thin.

Nick felt the rope constrict across his legs and chest when Eddie tested how far he could squirm. One coil of the rope slipped over Nick's shoulder and dug into his neck.

He gasped, "Eddie, can you reach your pocket—"

He paused when Dani looked up sharply. "What are you whispering about over there?"

Ty, who'd taken over shoveling uncovering the trunk heaved the lid open. "Forget about them. Here it is."

Dani's mouth curled into a devilish smile. Her smile faded when she saw the velvet bag. Slowly, she pulled the edges down. To Ty, she said, "Bennett promised to leave it right here. This is the exact location." Then, she looked accusingly at the three kids and hissed, "Where is it? The gold is supposed to be here."

"Bennett?" Eddie craned his neck toward her. "What gold?"

Ty took a step toward Nick and sneered. "Where is it?"

Nick's stammered, "W—we only…"

"That broken machine is the only thing we found." Jo said.

Ty exhaled loudly and looked around, irritated. He glanced at the boards leaning across the opening to the North Tunnel. His eyebrows lifted.

"You don't want to go in there," Eddie warned. "Trust me."

"You expect me to fall for that?" He sneered and rushed past them. "Nice try."

His flashlight glow disappeared and shrank as he investigated the tunnel.

Dani remained next to the trunk, glaring at the kids. "You think you're real smart, don't ya?"

A terrified shriek echoed from the North Tunnel.

"Ty?" Dani left the bag and rushed toward the cries of distress, but she stopped a few feet short of the opening. Her gaze fixed on the ground, and she tiptoed slowly backwards.

A large skunk tottered toward her. She turned to run but wasn't fast enough. The skunk lifted its tail, aimed, and shot a stream of **noxious** fluid directly at her.

"Agh!" Her response was garbled. She rubbed her eyes, staggering toward the direction of the gate.

Ty whimpered and scurried after his sister. "Fresh air," he gagged. "We need fresh air."

He began violently coughing and gasping and pulled his sister toward the gate.

Eddie grinned at Nick. "They should've listened to you."

His smile shrank as the stench from the skunk began to permeate the cave.

"Let's get outta here!" Eddie said while plugging his nose.

The ropes, cut from Eddie's knife, fell to their feet. The smell from the skunk made the air difficult to breathe.

"C'mon. The air is much better this way," Jo called. She led the group deeper into the cave.

Nick felt worried about moving deeper underground and was about to suggest they reconsider when Jo announced, "I see something."

"Please let it be a way out," Eddie said.

They stood in a circle, looking up. Illuminated by the spotlight of Jo's lamp was a shiny, golden doorknob on the edge of a metal door—a welcome sight. At their feet were the crumbled remains of what was once a staircase.

Nick gingerly climbed over the collapsed steps. Eddie and Jo followed. Most of the large stones had fallen off to the sides. He reached up.

Jo eyed the distance. "There's no way we can jump that high."

"It's human chain time again." Eddie laced his hands together and held them out to make a small platform. "Feel like climbing?"

Jo stepped one foot into Eddie's hands. Nick mimicked Eddie's technique and held his hands out for Jo's other foot. She held onto their shoulders, and the three wobbled slightly as she reached up to the door. Her fingers barely brushed the knob.

"I can't reach. Just a little higher."

Nick and Eddie strained to lift her foot another inch.

The sounds coming from Eddie indicated he was exerting a significant amount of energy. He sputtered, "Fingers…slipping!"

Jo retracted her hand and stepped down just as Eddie lost his grip. They landed in a heap.

"Now what?" Nick dusted his hands on his shirt.

"You're lightest, Eddie," Jo offered her hands in the cupped position. "Wanna try?"

"OK," Eddie agreed, stepping into her hands.

Again, Nick offered his hands as additional support. Eddie was light enough to hoist significantly higher than Jo. His fingers floated toward the door. Nick and Jo steadily pressed his feet up until they were level with their chins.

"Almost…almost…got it!" Eddie twisted the door-knob, but it didn't budge. "It's stuck." He pounded the door with his fists. *BANG! BANG!* "Help! HELP!! HELLO? ANYONE?"

His calls were answered by a heavy silence.

Eddie looked down and asked, "What now?"

Nick and Jo lowered Eddie to the ground.

Jo sat on a large stone. Nick and Eddie stood; arms crossed. As they stood in silence, a quiet noise echoed through the tunnels. It was subtle, as if the cave let out a gentle, gentle exhale. If they'd been talking, they wouldn't have noticed.

"Did anyone else hear that?" Nick held his breath, listening.

The three stood perfectly still.

"There it is again. It's like a quiet *shushhh*." Nick looked at his friends. "Do you hear it?"

Jo and Eddie nodded.

The sound quickly grew more distinct, then louder, like quiet cricket chirps leading into a **crescendo** of shrill screams.

"Oh no! It's the bats!" Jo's eyes widened. "Eddie, you woke up the bats!"

Nick looked at the door. "It's our only way out. Try again."

"Hoist me back up!" Eddie grabbed onto Nick's shoulder and poised his foot.

He and Jo launched Eddie up toward the door. A bat flapped frantically around the light on Eddie's head. He swatted at the fluttering creature, nearly losing his balance and grasped the doorknob for support.

The bat brushed against Nick's cheek. "Hurry up!"

Eddie wrestled with the knob. "It's not working!"

The squeaking noises from the bats grew louder. A rush of cool air blew towards them, and Nick's stomach dropped. He caught Jo's eye as they both realized the entire colony was now awake and headed their way.

"OPEN THE DOOR!" Jo cried as a second and third bat began flitting around their heads.

The cries of hundreds more grew louder and louder as they approached.

"I can't get it!" Eddie cried.

"Keep trying!" Jo said, trying to bury her face into her armpit.

"C'mon man!" Nick yelled. "They're swarming! Hurry!"

Eddie yanked the doorknob with such force, he threw his entire weight into the foot Jo held. His other foot flew to the side and Nick lost his grip. Nick hurried to help support the foot Jo was holding. Had it not been for the bats, they could've won a cheerleading competition. Eddie's balance was amazing. Finally, the knob turned. Eddie pulled the door open.

Light spilled into the cave.

Nick and Jo lost grip of Eddie's foot and he dangled above them. His feet bicycled in the air until his toe hooked around the edge of the doorframe and pulled himself into the opening. The entire colony swirled around him. Swarming bats screamed and fluttered against his face, back, and legs.

The bats poured through the doorway. When only a few remained, Nick and Jo pushed Eddie through the bright hole in the wall of the cave.

Eddie reached a hand down, and Nick boosted Jo up through the opening. Jo and Eddie reached down to Nick.

"Jump!" Jo said.

Nick leaped as high as he could toward their outstretched hands. On his second attempt, he caught Jo's hand.

"Whoa." Eddie sighed. "That was close."

As their eyes adjusted to the light, they realized where they were. Nick looked around the familiar stone room lined with shelves and jars of clock parts. The portrait of Eleanor Miller hung on the wall. The door leading to the cave was camouflaged as part of the bookcase. One section of the bookshelf was hinged and rolled on casters to open or close the opening.

"The Miller house?" Jo asked.

"So let me get this straight." Eddie frowned. "The trapdoor in the fish shack leads to another secret door—here?"

"But why?" Nick asked.

Ahem. Someone behind them cleared their throat.

DETECTIVES

THEY WHIRLED AROUND TO SEE MR. WATKINS standing on the landing at the top of the staircase.

"When Pete Hansen called and told me I should keep an eye on the house, I should've known you three were involved." A smile flickered across his face, but he narrowed his eyes. "What's that stench?"

The three stepped aside to reveal the hatch behind the shelves.

"We got stuck in the cave down there and—"

"A cave? That would explain the colony of bats that just escaped out the front door. They just about knocked me over!" Mr. Watkins slowly descended the stairs. "What in the world?" He peered into the opening behind the kids. "It smells awful!"

Explanations from all three came out in **fragmented** bursts.

"That's from the skunk…We solved the riddle…The Coopers were chasing us!...But it sprayed them.…Ty and Dani are working with the Caldwells!…They had a knife and tied us up, but..."

Mr. Watkins raised his hands. "Slow down! Slow down."

Jo stepped forward. "You'll never believe what we found!"

Mr. Watkins looked at the doorway leading to the tunnel. "You found something—in a cave—under my grandparents' house?" He paused and took a deep breath. "What did you find?"

Silence filled the room.

Nick took a deep breath and replied, "We found the Telaera."

The old man's face **contorted**. He blinked several times, evidently trying to decide what to say. A movement at the top of the stairs caught Nick's eye. He nudged Jo. Lucia and Officer Hansen appeared at the top of the stairs.

Lucia, looking bedraggled and weary, hurried down the stairs, limping slightly. "Eddie!"

"Lucia!" He rushed toward her.

"Oh, thank goodness!" Lucia hugged Eddie. "Are you OK?"

He nodded. "Are *you*? Your cheek is bleeding. What happened?

Steven and Jake Caldwell stepped onto the landing.

"Officer!" Eddie pointed to the Caldwells and stammered, "These-these-these guys are criminals!" He pulled Lucia away from them.

"Relax, Eddie. You've got it backwards." Lucia held his shoulders. "I know the Coopers followed you into the tunnel, but Steven and Jake aren't working with them. The Caldwells are the good guys."

"What? Did you hit your head or something?" Eddie's eyes shot toward the brothers. "*They* were the ones looking for the gate. *They've* got the map."

Again, Nick and his friends began talking at once, each trying to add clarity to the obvious mix-up.

Mr. Watkins put his hand in the air to quiet the commotion. He calmly stated, "I see you've already met my friends from the Caldwell Detective Agency." He gestured to the two men descending the stairs.

"Detectives?" Nick asked.

"Friends?" Jo frowned.

Steven Caldwell's face stretched into his characteristic, thin smile. His expression had a kindness Nick hadn't noticed before.

Mr. Watkins explained. "As I mentioned, over the years, there have been dozens of treasure hunters slinking around town. Some come to look for the Waterstone. Others are trying to figure out where the stolen bank money was stashed. Occasionally, one of them tries to break into the house or the shop—thinking something's hidden there."

Steven Caldwell stepped forward. "And when that happens, we get a call.

Jake frowned and bellowed, "THAT'S WHEN GORDON CALLS US."

Steven looked at his brother. "I already told them that."

Jake nodded and replied loudly, "SORRY!"

Steven put his hand on Jake's shoulder. "My apologies. Jake here was trying to remove a nail from our tire when the tire blew, and now he can't hear out of one ear. It's supposedly temporary, but for a few days, he hasn't been able to hear unless I shout."

"PARDON?" Jake asked.

"Nothing," Steven replied, then repeated, "NOTHING. I WAS JUST TELLING THEM ABOUT YOUR EAR."

Jake nodded. "AH. YES. CAN'T HEAR VERY WELL."

Steven continued, "As I was saying, Gordon calls if he sees anyone suspicious hanging around the house or the shop."

Nick looked apologetically at the old man. "Mr. Watkins, we—"

Mr. Watkins winked. "I know about the visit you paid to the store." He explained, "The Caldwells were staked out there while I was gone. We even left the door unlocked, because if someone wanted to get in, they'd probably smash the window. They're expensive to replace. I knew they were keeping an eye out, so I left it open."

Steven adjusted his glasses. "We've always been able to figure out who the hunters are, except for two who always seem to evade us." He added, with an air of dismay, "We've been searching for them for years. Until two weeks ago, we had no idea they live right here in Mapleton, under the alias of Cooper."

Jake explained, "DANI AND TY COOPER ARE THE REAL DEAL"

Steven put his finger to his lips. "YOU'RE SHOUTING AGAIN."

Jake gave a sheepish smile and mouthed *Sorry*.

Nick recalled the shouting he and Uncle John had heard from the driveway. Steven wasn't scolding his brother; he was just trying to speak loud enough to be heard.

Steven continued. "The Coopers are professional treasure hunters and shouldn't be underestimated. They've gone to great lengths to completely erase their history. We can't find any record of them before last year, when they opened Cooper Realty in Mapleton. We think they've been scouring this area the whole time, posing as realtors and until recently were undetected."

Mr. Watkins added, "The Caldwells even had a friend in the FBI trying to dig up some information on those two, but they keep hitting one dead end after another."

Nick recalled the phone calls he'd overheard about "digging up" information.

"If you're not after the money, why did you buy a metal detector to find it?" Jo crossed her arms, unconvinced. "We saw you coming out of the hardware store."

"And the map in the back of your car," Eddie added.

For a moment, Steven looked perplexed. Then, his mouth pulled into its characteristic, thin smile. "Oh, that." He explained, "I think the paper you saw was the property map for our family's cottage. It's been needing some major repairs, and when we're not chasing treasure hunters, we spend our time fixing it up. As for the hardware store purchase, I dropped a box of nails in the driveway, and they went everywhere.

I thought I got them all, but we had two flat tires in as many days. We didn't buy a metal detector. What you saw was a strong magnet with a long handle to help us pick up the rest."

"Hmphf." Eddie looked skeptical.

The walkie talkie on Office Hansen's belt blared a message. "We have a team assembled and ready to move underground. The gate was open when we got here."

Officer Hansen replied, "Copy that. I'm on my way."

"Wait." Nick held out a piece of paper. "Officer, we found this by the gate." He pointed out the line representing the North Tunnel. "We think this is the passageway that connects to the old mine, but it's completely blocked."

"Thanks." Officer Hansen replied.

"Watch out for the skunk down there," Eddie cautioned.

The officer smiled and saluted. "Roger that."

After the officer left, the group turned their attention to Lucia.

Eddie pulled a travel First-Aid kit from his vest and handed her a disinfecting wipe and several Band-Aids. "Wait a minute, how did you know it was the Coopers in the tunnel?"

Lucia winced as she dabbed her cheek, then explained what had happened when she and Jesse went to get the rope. "Dani and Ty showed up and offered to help rescue you from the cave, and—" She inspected a scratch on the back of her arm and added sheepishly, "They tried to trick me into thinking they were helping." Lucia tucked a loose strand of her messy ponytail behind her ear. "I fell for it and told them about the gate, but I got suspicious because they asked if I had the stone. I hadn't mentioned anything about the stone, or the fact that it was the key to the gate, so I made a run for it."

"Good thing you're fast." Eddie's eyebrows arched.

Lucia's eyes dropped. "Fast, but apparently not nimble. I tripped on a root or a branch or something and wiped out." She smoothed the edges of her Band-Aid. "They caught up to me and—"

"They took the stone?" Nick asked. He thought aloud, "That must be how they got into the cave."

Mr. Watkins interrupted. "What's this stone you keep mentioning?"

Eddie slapped his forehead. "I can't believe we forgot to mention the best part! We found the Telaera *AND* we found what might be the Waterstone. They're both mentioned in your grandfather's diary."

Nick explained, "The stone was by the gate."

Lucia pulled the perfectly spherical stone from her pocket and handed it to Mr. Watkins, who blinked and shook his head in disbelief.

Jo said, "Based on the description in your grandfather's journal, we think it might be the same stone your Uncle Matthew found."

"That's—" Mr. Watkins's voice wavered. "That's the Waterstone." His eyes glistened with tears. "So he did find it, after all. To think—after all these years—it was so close. And you found it?"

They all nodded.

"Watch this," Eddie said. He poured a little water from his water bottle over the top of it.

A blue light emanated from within the stone.

Mr. Watkins's eyebrows lifted. "Fascinating."

"So the Coopers didn't take it?" Jo asked.

"Nope," Lucia replied. "After I fell, I tucked the rock under some leaves and threw a pinecone into the woods as a decoy. While they were looking for it, I grabbed the stone and ran into the woods to hide. I saw them run back to the fish shack, and—that was the last I saw of them."

Eddie laced his hands behind his head. "Wait. If *you* had the stone this whole time, then how the heck did the Coopers get past the gate?"

"I don't know," she replied.

"I do," Nick replied. He pointed to the portrait of Eleanor hanging on the wall. "Dani was wearing that *exact* necklace." He held up the stone. "It looks just like the Waterstone, except it's smaller. If the pendant on Dani's necklace is made of neottrite, they could've used it to open the gate."

"Incredible," Mr. Watkins mused. "Dani's necklace was either an exact replica of this one—" Mr. Watkins inspected the painting, "or she somehow has my grandmother's necklace. The ornate **filigree** attached to the **bezel** would be difficult to duplicate." He rubbed his forehead and looked at the group. "It's strange that Ty claimed the necklace needed a repair, but the clasp was in perfect working order."

"That's no surprise." Steven sniffed and wrinkled his nose. "That's right about the time we noticed the Coopers doing other suspicious things. They started driving around late at night, digging holes they claimed were for business signs near this property."

Nick recalled, "I saw a bunch of dirt and some shovels in the back of Dani's minivan!"

Steven added, "We trailed them for three days, and their sneaky activities put them on our radar." He looked at Mr. Watkins. "Gordon, they handed over that necklace *because* it was neottrite—probably hoping you'd lead them to the gate."

"That's foolish because until a few moments ago, I didn't know the gate existed." Mr. Watkins said.

"But *they* didn't know that." Steven inspected the stone. "Working as realtors was a genius way to look for a buried treasure without drawing attention to themselves. They had access to properties all over town."

Nick thought back to the conversation they'd overheard at Watkins Jewelry when Ty had tried to convince Mr. Watkins to list his property for sale. He'd obviously wanted access to look for the gate, the cave, and the Telaera.

"I wonder how Dani ended up with the necklace in the first place." Jo gazed at the portrait.

"After the accident, my grandmother moved into the house next door, but left most of her things here. Ginger mentioned the Coopers were especially eager to help clean out the house." Mr. Watkins shook his head. "We led the fox right into the chicken coop."

Just then, Jesse appeared on the landing.

"Lucia!" He rushed down the steps and inspected her injuries.

"I'm alright," she assured. "I'll fill you in later. Did they find the Coopers?"

He shook his head. "Not yet. They've done a complete sweep of the area around the properties. No sign of either of them. My dad thinks they're still underground." Jesse unfurled a large map of the town. "But the team found this in the Coopers van."

Jo gasped. "That's the map from the library!"

Jesse held up the little map Nick had given to Officer Hansen. "My dad was hoping we could compare these two while they keep searching. Maybe you three can make sense of where that blocked tunnel leads." He laid the small map they'd found with the stone next to the town map. "Dad says he thinks they'll probably head this way looking for an exit." He pointed to the long line.

Eddie said, "We already told them, that's the North Tunnel. It's completely blocked by a cave-in."

"Well, people don't just disappear," Jesse replied. "The team has been guarding the gate the whole time. The Coopers haven't come out yet." He nodded toward the secret bookcase door. "I'm guessing no one but you three came through this passageway."

Mr. Watkins replied, "Just these three."

Jesse continued, "That means, they must be hiding somewhere down there. Dad was hoping you three could make sense of these scribbles, so we can cut them off on the other end."

All eyes fell to the long line on the hand-drawn map.

"Oh my gosh—" Jo inhaled sharply. "Of course! If the North Tunnel continues straight," she traced an invisible line along the map of the town, "it would end here." She jabbed a finger onto the *M.B.* on the map and looked up with a smile. "*M.B.* stands for Mapleton Bank."

Mr. Watkins nodded. "Interesting."

Steven said, "If that's true, this whole situation just got a lot more complicated. The whole mining operation could've been a hoax; a cover-up for what was really going on."

"What do you mean?" Mr. Watkins asked.

Steven replied, "Cornelius Bennett could've had the miners digging a route for him that led them directly under the bank."

Nick added, "Exactly. He could've stolen the money then hidden it in the cave somewhere. That way, he could come back to get it while everyone was busy searching for the trapped workers."

"That's why he sabotaged the North Tunnel!" Eddie combed his fingers through his hair. "He made the tunnel supports weak. W*HACK! WHACK!*" Eddie mimed chopped with an ax.

"He tricked my grandfather and all those men into working for him, thinking they'd find neottrite." Mr. Watkins exhaled slowly.

Jo nodded soberly and opened the journal. "But he didn't count on anyone actually finding any."

Eddie snapped his fingers. "Exactly! What did that journal entry say about keeping something secure from…what was the rest?"

Jo flipped to the correct entry. "Here it is. *Plan to store in the vault—away from sluic ore...*" She looked up. S-l-u-i-c-o-r-e! That's an anagram for Cornelius!"

Nick pieced it together, "When Matthew Miller discovered neottrite in the mine, and his grandparents realized they could use it as a power source for the machine they'd invented, they stored the neottrite and the patent for the Telaera in the bank vault to keep it safe."

"That's right. And Bennett caught wind of the invention, remember?" Eddie asked.

"But remember the wanted posters we saw?" Nick rubbed his temples. "Weren't the Pecoros the ones wanted for the bank robber?"

"I totally called that! Remember?" Eddie asked.

Jo replied, "If that tunnel connects with the bank—"

"Then it wasn't a ghost who robbed the bank after all." Eddie interrupted.

"Nope," Jo replied.

Nick explained, "The vault was locked the whole time. Bennett must have hired the Pecoros to tunnel in from underneath the vault. They could've emptied it during the night, and no one would've noticed until the next day."

Out of Clues

A silence fell over the group. This was an enormous amount of information to digest.

After a moment, Jo spoke. "If Bennett hired the Pecoros to steal the money from the bank and bury it, why wasn't it in the trunk?"

"Right." Eddie scratched his head.

"Someone must've moved the money after they buried it," Nick said.

Eddie shook his head. "It could be anywhere. Bennett probably double-crossed them and took they money with him to California."

Mr. Watkins ran his hand over the leather cover of the journal. "If my grandmother wrote that riddle, she must have known about the buried trunk."

"And its contents," Jo added.

Mr. Watkins nodded.

Nick asked, "Do you think *she* found the money? Maybe she took it or moved it."

"I don't know." The old man rubbed his chin.

"If she did, where would she have hidden it?" Eddie walked around the room gently stomping on the floorboards, presumably looking for another hidden panel or trapdoor. "Maybe it's right here somewhere!" He began frantically jumping up and down along the edges of the room, then fell to his knees, trying to pry up the boards with his fingers.

"Eddie," Jo said.

The younger boy continued to claw at the boards. "We solved the riddle. We found the Telaera. There's *got* to be a treasure somewhere!"

"Eddie," Jo repeated, then added softly, "The gold is long gone. You're probably right about Bennett taking it with him to California. The *treasure* in the riddle has to be the Telaera."

Eddie looked up, eyes brimming with tears. "But that money. It has to be somewhere. It *has* to be. This can't be how our adventure ends, with an old, broken machine. If the Telaera was valuable, Bennett would've taken it with him." His voice trailed off and he crumpled into a ball on the ground. His shoulders shook and Nick could tell he was weeping tears of frustration and exhaustion. "Just once. Just once I want to be the guy who ends up on top."

Nick squeezed his shoulder and said, "I know."

The walkie talkie on Jesse's belt squawked, "Jesse? Do you copy?"

"Copy, Dad."

"We still don't have the Coopers in custody. The cave is clear, and I'm moving the team to search the woods at the south end of the lake. Tell the Caldwells we could use their help out here. They know these two better than any of us. Over."

"Copy that."

Steven nodded and pulled a confused Jake up the stairs to join the search.

"Thanks, Jesse. Would you drive the kids home? I don't want them biking alone. Over."

"Sure, dad," Jesse replied. "Over."

The line crackled, and Officer Hansen continued. "Oh, and Jesse? We found something—in the tunnel." Officer Hansen's voice echoed through the speaker. "Looks like it's the remains of one of the victims of the collapse."

Mr. Watkins's shoulders stiffened noticeably. "Any idea who it was?"

Nick knew he was wondering if the remains were those of his grandfather or Uncle Matthew.

"Were you able to identify them?" Jesse asked.

The radio crackled. "Hard to say. There's a monogram on the belt buckle. Says *C.B.*"

Jo leaned forward. "Cornelius Bennett."

"It has to be!" Nick nodded.

Eddie's brow furrowed. "So, he *didn't* escape to California with the money?"

"Apparently not," Mr. Watkins adjusted his glasses.

"So, there's a chance the gold is still in Mapleton?" Eddie sat up straighter.

"Let's not get our hopes up," Jo replied gently.

"What? Why not?" Eddie cried. "If it's still here, we can still find it!"

Nick reasoned, "We're out of clues, Eddie, but hey, we found the Telaera."

Jo added, "And we got trapped in a cave. We were tied up at knifepoint. It's been a lot. Let's not test our luck."

Mr. Watkins smiled. "Finding the Telaera is a huge accomplishment. Especially for young people like yourselves. You've done what professional treasure hunters couldn't."

Mr. Watkins put his hand on Nick's shoulder. "I was wondering if you all would do something for me."

"Sure," Nick replied. "What do you need?"

Back Underground

Mr. Watkins secured the white sheet tied to a leg of the bookcase. One at a time, Nick, Jo, and Eddie shimmied down the sheet into the cave. Jesse and Lucia followed.

Mr. Watkins peered down from the opening above them. "Be careful."

"Don't' worry Mr. Watkins. We'll bring the Telaera back in one piece."

"I meant *you* be careful." The old man smiled down at them. "Thank you so much for doing this for me. I've been working on a prototype at the shop, but I just can't seem to get it quite right. It'll help if I can see the original design."

With Nick in the lead this time Jo, Eddie, Lucia, and Jesse retraced the passageway to the circular cavern. Bright yellow police tape ran along the edge of one side of the cavern. They'd walked right past the skeleton after Jo noticed the doorknob leading to the basement room.

Eddie leaned over and looked at the remains. "How did we miss *this*?" He shuddered, "Uck! There's hair stuck to his skull."

"Gross, Eddie," Jo said. She shielded her eyes from the scene.

Nick avoided looking too long at the skeleton as well. He was curious, but it was very creepy to think about.

The group continued on to the circular cavern and the uncovered trunk. They expected to find the open trunk just as they'd left it, with the Telaera wrapped in the velvet bag.

But it wasn't.

The Telaera was unwrapped and was on the ground, several feet from the hole.

"That's weird," Eddie said.

"Yeah," Nick agreed.

"What?" Jesse asked.

Jo explained, "This isn't how we left the Telaera." She pointed to the velvet bag lying crumpled in the trunk.

Eddie bent to lift the heavy machine but immediately recoiled his hands. "Aghhh! Ahh haa haaaa!" He began jumping around and blowing on his palms.

"What is it?" Jo asked, rushing over.

"Hot!" Eddie panted. "Very hot."

Nick held his hand so it hovered over the machine. "I think the machine was on—and recently."

Eddie raised his eyebrows.

Jo said, "It had to be the Coopers who used it." As she spoke, something crunched under her foot. She leaned over and picked it up off the ground. A delicate, gold chain dangled from her hand.

Jesse asked, "Isn't this the necklace from the painting?"

Jo shined her light on it and answered, "Yes, but the stone is missing."

"No, it's not," Eddie replied. He shook his burned palms, then cautiously lifted a small, blue stone from a pool of water in the circular indentation on the top of the Telaera. He looked up. "It's like a little Waterstone, and—unlike the rest of the machine— it's perfectly cool."

"I don't get it." Jesse said.

Nick rubbed his temples, thinking. "The Coopers obviously knew about the Telaera, and they knew it was powered with neottrite, but why would they circle back to use it?"

Eddie said, "Mr. Watkins thought it was a communication machine, remember?"

"Maybe they sent a message?" Jesse suggested.

Nick frowned and looked closely at the dials. "This is odd." He pointed to the dials on the base of the Telaera. "Earlier they were turned to two-zero-two-two. Now they're turned to one-eight-nine-three."

"Those are dates." Jo said. "Two thousand-twenty-two and eighteen-ninety-three."

Eddie exclaimed, "Eighteen-ninety-four is a year after the bank was robbed and the mine collapsed."

"True." Jo nodded.

"Wait." Nick pulled out the wanted posters tucked inside his sketchbook. He shined his light on the black and white images. "I knew it! Look."

Lucia shook her head. "Why are we looking at pictures of the Pecoros?"

"See the resemblance?" Nick smiled.

"What?" Eddie's forehead scrunched into a confused wrinkle.

Nick explained, "I *knew* I recognized these two." He held up the posters with Adaline and Stony Pecoro's photographs on them. They were uncanny likenesses of Dani and Ty Cooper.

Jesse leaned in for a closer look. "The resemblance is amazing. The Pecoros must be distant relatives of the Coopers."

"Wait a sec!" Jo squeezed her eyes shut, calculating something. "If you jumble the letters of Daniela and Tyson Cooper, you get—" she gasped, "Adaline and Stony Pecoro!"

"More anagrams?" Eddie murmured. "What a weird coincidence."

Nick felt like a bolt of lightning had just struck his brain. "It's no coincidence," he said, looking at the metal machine on the ground, "and they're not relatives." He looked up at the perplexed faces staring at him. "I think the Coopers *ARE* the Pecoros."

"Yeahhh," Eddie challenged, "except there are these things called time and space," he crisscrossed his fingers in the air, "and they don't bend. If the Pecoros and the Coopers are the same people, they'd be over a hundred years old."

Nick continued, "But think about it. In the tunnel, Ty and Dani were looking for the money *AND* the Telaera."

"So," Eddie gave Nick a sideways look, "you think the Telaera is, what? A time machine?"

"Think about it," Nick said. "The Coopers talked about someone telling them the gold was buried in the trunk. They said he left it there for them." He looked up. "I don't think the Pecoros ever got the money—"

"Because they traveled through time as part of their getaway plan?" Jo didn't look convinced.

Everyone stood in silence, trying to process what Nick was suggesting.

Jesse looked confused. "So, the Pecoros were hired by Cornelius Bennett to steal the Mapleton Bank money—"

Jo added, "Then what? They buried the money and time warped into the future to dig it up and then time warp back again?

Nick nodded. "I think so."

"They traveled back in time," Eddie frowned, "with this machine?"

Jesse scratched his head. "That would explain why my dad can't find them."

"Maybe Mr. Watkins can shed some more light on this," Jo said. "C'mon. Let's get the Telaera back above ground."

"If the Coopers did somehow travel back in time, do you think they took the money with them?" Eddie asked.

"I honestly don't know." Nick rested his arm over Eddie's shoulder. "They seemed surprised the money wasn't in the trunk, which is probably where they left it."

Eddie glanced at the police tape around the remains of Cornelius Bennett. "Too bad he can't tell us."

Nick saw Jo shake her head.

Eddie kneeled down to help Jo put the Telaera into the velvet bag. It was still warm, but cool enough now to touch. As Eddie stood up, his issue of *Captain Kidd* slid from the side pocket of his vest.

Nick picked it up and handed it back.

"Thanks." Eddie sighed. "I bet ol' Cap'n Kidd would've had some good ideas about where to look for that money."

"Yeah," Jo said. "It's weird, because the riddle told us to dig here."

Something didn't quite add up in Nick's head. "Jo," he asked. "What was the date on the coded message?"

Jo opened the journal and replied, "I don't see a date, but the page was torn out just after the last entry in May of eighteen ninety-three.

Nick looked up. "After the collapse?"

Jo nodded. "She moved the money."

Eddie asked, "Why would Eleanor Miller move the money?"

Nick nodded. "The money was stolen, the mine collapsed, the Pecoros hid the money, and then Eleanor dug it up, hid it somewhere else, and wrote the code she hoped her grandson would decipher one day."

"Why wouldn't she keep it?" Eddie asked.

"Because she wasn't a criminal." Nick recalled the face of Eleanor in the family portrait.

"She could've returned it," Eddie countered.

Jo said, "But remember, Bennett framed Archbald Miller for the bank robbery. If Eleanor showed up at the bank to give it back, Archibald would've looked guilty."

"She couldn't keep it and she couldn't give it back," Jo nodded slowly her head. "But she figured out Bennett's deal with the Pecoros and moved the money, so they'd never find it."

"But where would she have put it?" Eddie asked.

Nick inhaled sharply as the words of the riddle flashed into his mind.

And there you dig and dig again.

"Dig again!" He stood up and nearly shouted, "We have to dig again!"

"Dig again," Eddie groaned. "What do you mean? We've been digging."

"I mean," Nick explained, "we have to dig *deeper*. Help me get this trunk out!"

With the help of Lucia and Jesse, the trunk was soon heaved out of the hole. Nick grabbed the shovel and jumped into the cavity where the trunk had been buried. He scooped dirt until he dripped with sweat. Suddenly, the blade hit something. *THUD*.

He looked up to see everyone staring at him with shocked expressions.

The group quickly uncovered an unremarkable-looking, wooden crate buried about two feet directly below the place the trunk had been. Nick wedged the shovel underneath the crate and tried to lift it.

"This is unbelievably heavy," Eddie panted. He was grinning from ear to ear.

Jo used her hand to brush the dirt off the top. "Maybe we can pry these nails up."

She and Nick leaned on the shovel and quickly pried off the lid.

Nick leaned on the edge of the hole.

Jo gasped.

Eddie fell to his knees.

Jesse and Lucia stood with gaping mouths.

Inside were dozens of bags with *Mapleton Bank* stenciled onto the cream-colored fabric. On top lay a piece of rolled up leather.

Nick reached in and unrolled the leather to find two pieces of paper. He carefully turned the first paper over. It was a detailed drawing of a machine. He read the second paper aloud, "United States Patent Office, Archibald and Eleanor Miller, of the town of Mapleton, Wisconsin. United States of America. Telaera Communication Time-Machine. April seventeenth, eighteen-ninety-three."

Jessie inspected the papers. "This is a patent application for the Telaera!"

"And instructions for how to build it," Lucia added.

Nick reached in and opened one of the bags. Jo and Eddie gathered around him. Their headlamps reflected off the mountain of gold coins inside.

"It was here all along," Jo murmured.

"Dig and dig again." Nick grinned.

Famous

News about the gold spread quickly in Mapleton. The mayor scheduled a special press conference, which gave the kids temporary celebrity status. Jo and Eddie were already standing on the steps of City Hall when Nick arrived. He parked his bike next to Jo's and noticed an unfamiliar, shiny, blue bike next to it. He bounded up the steps and joined his friends.

"I'm so nervous, my knees are shaking," Eddie said. He wore the second-place ribbon he'd earned at the invention contest.

"You'll be fine," Nick whispered to Eddie. "Nice bike, by the way."

"Brand new 18-speed—it's got a working kickstand and everything." Eddie grinned. "I see you got a new tire. Hopefully Jack won't stab this one, too."

The mayor spoke into the microphone. "Thank you all for coming! I'd like to introduce three young heroes to you who were able to do what no one in one hundred years has been able to."

Nick scanned the sea of video cameras and microphones covered with fuzz. In the crowd, Nick saw Uncle John. He'd returned from his trip with a very rare Italian cabinet he'd planned to ship to Nick's house once it was restored. He caught Nick's eye and gave him a thumbs up.

The mayor was still talking. "This young trio found not one missing treasure, but two. They corrected a part of Mapleton history and restored the Miller family name in the process—all while making it home by bedtime every night."

The crowd chuckled.

Nick looked at Jo, who rolled her eyes.

"Without further ado, I'll hand this press conference over to Nick Thornton, Josephine Perkins, and Eduardo Bernadelli."

Eddie edged toward the microphone. With a shaky voice, he said, "T-thank you Mayor Barclese. I'd like to ask that the bedtime comment be stricken from the record. First of all, it's summer, and second—"

Jo elbowed him and whispered, "We're not on trial, Eddie. We're being interviewed." She nudged Eddie away. "Hello everyone. I'm sure you've all heard about our adventure, and you probably have lots of questions."

Dozens of reporters' hands shot into the air.

Nick pointed to a reporter with thick-rimmed glasses. The crowd quieted to hear his question.

"Brian Clements, Madison Review. When you were in the tunnel, you found a sort of machine. Can you confirm the rumors that this machine allows time travel?"

Nick replied, "We did find a machine." He glanced at Jo and Eddie, unsure about how much to explain.

Jo chimed in. "It's from the late eighteen hundreds and was invented by Archibald and Eleanor Miller, former residents of Mapleton. The machine is called the Telaera, but it's in disrepair, and unfortunately, it's not currently functioning. We believe it's a sort of communication device."

The desperate hands flew up again and fluttered around.

Nick pointed to a reporter with short brunette hair.

"Sally Jenkins, Mapleton Daily. As a reporter, I'm all too familiar with the idea of having to dig for a story. How did you know digging deeper in the cave would lead to over six million dollars?"

Nick smiled and looked at Eddie. "It's all thanks to a graphic novel about pirates."

The woman rolled her eyes. "Pirates?"

Nick nudged Eddie, who begrudgingly stepped forward.

"Well…" Eddie's voice cracked, and he quickly took a gulp of water from the water bottle in a pocket on his vest. "It's really pretty brilliant." He paused, looking slightly panicked.

Nick nodded in encouragement.

Eddie licked his lips. "You see, Captain Kidd and his men were being chased by Calico Jack, who wanted to steal their treasure. They buried the treasure and marked the location with an X."

The reporter smiled courteously and said, "But that sounds like the plot of every **swashbuckler** tale ever written." She added smugly, "So you followed the line on the map to the X and found the treasure. Are you suggesting a comic book helped you figure that out?"

Jo piped up and corrected her. "Ms. Jenkins, they're called 'graphic novels,' and we couldn't have found the money or the Telaera without the help of Captain Kidd." She smiled at Eddie.

Eddie swallowed and continued. "Captain Kidd was clever because he knew his map was a liability. If it fell into the wrong hands, his treasure would be stolen. But he needed some kind of map to help him remember where he put it. So, instead of being worried about the map, he decided to dig a really, really deep hole, where he buried the most valuable part of the treasure. Then he covered the hole up halfway, buried a less valuable portion of the treasure, and then covered it up the rest of the way."

Nick added, "Any thieves would assume the top treasure was all there was and leave the actual treasure untouched!"

Jo chimed in and said, "There you dig and *dig again.*"

Nick looked at the crowd again and saw the sneering faces of Billy and Jack. He realized he'd just given away their plan to hide their treats at Castle Rock. The boys were flicking pebbles into the hair of a reporter a row in front of them. Nick smiled when he realized they weren't even paying attention.

Mayor Barclese stepped toward the microphone and stated, "Decades after the false reports of negligence on the part of Archibald Miller have been revised. It's been proven the actual culprit of the Bennett-Miller Mine collapse was its co-owner, Cornelius Bennett. Archibald Miller, the grandfather of our very own Gordon Watkins, was innocent of any wrong doing. The mystery of the Mapleton Bank Robbery has finally been solved and the priceless Waterstone has been returned to Gordon Watkins."

The crowd burst into applause.

As the kids were escorted past the throngs of fans waiting on the sides of the crowd, Nick spotted the familiar face of Mr. Watkins. During all of the excitement, they hadn't had a chance to follow up with him about the Telaera.

"I've been trying to track you three down for days!" He greeted them with a crinkly-eyed smile.

"Sorry, Mr. Watkins," Jo replied.

"We've been swamped!" Nick explained.

"Did you have any luck with the—" Eddie started.

Mr. Watkins's eyes darted sideways, and he put a finger to his lips. He interrupted with, "I'd love to have you stop by the shop later. Maybe I can get an autograph?" He winked and disappeared into the sea of admiring faces hoping to have a chance to meet the local treasure hunters.

When Jasper saw them coming, he hopped down from the windowsill. The familiar bell jingled as the door opened. Jasper weaved his way between their shoes, purring.

Mr. Watkins sat behind the counter; his eyes shining with excitement.

He waved his hand, beckoning them closer. "Come, see what I've discovered!"

"Were you able to get the Telaera fixed?" Nick inquired, hopefully.

"Not exactly, but I'm close." The old man pressed a lever at the base of the machine. "When the Coopers—or Pecoros—used the machine, this lever malfunctioned. My grandparents intended the Telaera to tele-communicate between different **eras** in time. However, with the lever working improperly, it didn't turn off automatically. Instead of opening a line of communication to a different time, it opened a portal."

"Like a time machine?" Eddie asked.

Mr. Watkins nodded. "Exactly."

"Can we try it out?" Nick asked.

"Of course." With his thumb, Mr. Watkins rotated a small, circular disk next to each digit and as he did so, the numbers zero through nine flipped into view one number at a time. He asked, "What year should we try to contact?"

Jo and Eddie shrugged but Nick suggested, "How about eighteen ninety-three?"

Mr. Watkins looked surprised. "The year of the accident?"

"And the robbery," Eddie noted.

Nick nodded. "We still have questions. Maybe someone from back then can answer them."

Eddie exclaimed, "We could tell your grandfather and uncle not to go into the mine!"

Mr. Watkins frowned, and his jaw bounced as he thought. "As much as I would love to rewrite history and save my relatives, we need to be extremely careful with this machine. Altering the past—even a tiny bit—could have astronomical effects on the future."

"How about one year after the accident?" Jo suggested. "We could just see if anyone answers."

Mr. Watkins thought for a moment. "OK. Let's give it a try."

He spun the dials one at a time until the numbers on the machine read 1-8-9-4.

"All we need now is the power source."

"The Waterstone!" they said in unison.

"Exactly." The old man nodded. He pulled it from the drawer.

Nick sighed. "Imagine what would have happened if Cornelius Bennett had been able to get his hands on this!"

Mr. Watkins paused and looked up. "I'm sure that's why my grandparents never filed the patent application. If the machine fell into the wrong hands, the world as we know it would be a very different place." He shook his head at the thought, then placed the stone in the tiny basin at the top of the machine. It fit snugly into place. "Are you ready?" he asked the kids.

They nodded in silent anticipation.

Mr. Watkins poured a small amount of water into a funnel at the top of the machine. The liquid quietly trickled through the tubes until it dropped a steady stream onto the surface of the Waterstone. The cup-shaped basin collected the water as it cascaded around the sides of the stone. Just as before, the stone took on a blue glow. The light slowly swirled around the surface of the stone, illuminating different areas of it until the entire stone was shining brightly.

When it was fully glowing, Mr. Watkins began to turn the crank. The crankshaft rotated and engaged the intricate network of gears. After a brief moment, the entire machine was humming.

Jasper jumped into Eddie's lap. The numbers at the top of the machine began to click and shudder. A thin yellow electrical current jumped between the two nodes inside the speaker. The current flickered and sparked. Suddenly, a loud crackling sound filled the room. The line of electricity jumped between the nodes.

Mr. Watkins leaned forward and pressed the speaking lever. "Hello? Can anyone hear me?"

Eddie leaned in, "You should say *Over* when you're done."

Mr. Watkins nodded. "Ah, yes. Over."

The droning hiss of the static filled their ears. Nick thought the *pops* and *crackles* almost sounded like tinny voices. He assumed it was his imagination.

And then, just as suddenly as it started, the static stopped.

A thin voice crept through the speaker. "Hello? Is someone there?"

"Hello!" Mr. Watkins leaned forward. "Who is this?"

There was a pause.

"Hello. This is Eleanor Miller. Did you find it? Did you follow my clues, Gordon?"

Heading Home

Nick stood on the shore of Cranberry Lake and watched the tranquil water ripple against the shore. A small movement near his foot caught his eye. He bent down and watched a small spider maneuver over the grains of sand. Jo had been right. Spiders were peaceful creatures. It crawled toward the woods and disappeared under a leaf.

In Mapleton, Nick had enjoyed a summer of unexpected freedom, friendship, and adventure. He thought of the little Waterstone, the ring box and the key. Such small objects had led to a tremendous adventure and discovery.

During the brief conversation with Eleanor Miller, they'd confirmed the function of the Telaera was originally to link periods of time together—but in communication only. When Archibald and Eleanor discovered that the additional electrical conductors were introduced to the environment, the Telaera opened a portal in time. This portal allowed individuals to jump ahead or behind on the timeline. The risk of the machine's incredible power to disrupt the fabric of time was too great and they agreed to destroy it.

Unfortunately, after Archibald and Matthrew died, Eleanor was overcome by grief. She misplaced the key and lost touch with reality. She spent her remaining years searching for the key to try to bring her husband and son back from the dead. Perhaps a part of her knew doing so would alter the future's history. Nick wondered if she mislaid the key intentionally.

A horn honked, and Nick looked up to see his parents from the driveway. Uncle John handed Nick a newspaper. It was that day's edition of the *Mapleton Review*. The headline read: *Local Sleuths Solve Mapleton Mystery.*

"I picked up an extra copy for you. I already cut out the article and hung it on the fridge." Uncle John smiled. "Amazing thing you kids did, finding all that money."

"You'll be famous at your new school." Jo said with a smile.

Eddie said, "We'll let you know if the Captain Kidd trick works at the hideout."

"Jo and Eddie, you're welcome to visit our house anytime," Nick's mom said.

"Thanks Mrs. Thornton," Jo replied.

After a round of hugs and promises to visit soon, Nick clicked the seatbelt across his chest and waved to Jo, Eddie, and Uncle John through the window.

They drove past a recently repaired mailbox at the end of the driveway next door. The *"FOR SALE"* sign had a *"SOLD"* banner across the font. He saw Ginger's black pickup truck in the driveway and caught a glimpse of her red hair. They'd figured out when the mine collapsed, the dust from the tunnels billowed through the house and coated everything. Now, it was fresh and clean and no longer empty. Ginger waved, then carried a cardboard box inside. He knew she'd make a great neighbor for Uncle John.

Nick opened the bag of trail mix from Uncle John then looked at the newspaper. He gazed at the black and white image of himself standing arm in arm with Eddie and Jo. Their faces were frozen in happy smiles. He carefully ripped out the article, folded up the memory, and tucked it into an empty compartment in his tackle box.

THE END

Glossary

A

Acclimate: to adjust, or get used to
Accumulate: to build up
Adjacent: next to
Aerosol: a fine mist
Agility: ease of movement
Amber: yellow-gold color
Ambitious: having high goals
Ambush: a surprise attack
Analog: a non-digital clock with hands
Annihilation: complete destruction
Appease: to satisfy
Arachnid: a spider
Arbors: a rod attached to gears inside a clock
Arsenal: storage facility for weapons

B

Bezel: the edge of a metal fastener holding a gemstone
Bombardment: heavy attack

C

Caesar's shift cipher: a cipher using letters shifted right or left a specific number of spaces
Cantankerous: grouchy
Cantilevered: extended over a surface
Capsize: to sink
Choreography: prepared dance moves
Cipher: a coded message
Clandestine: secret
Concentric: increasingly larger shapes that share a common mid-point (like a bullseye)
Conspicuous: obvious

Contort: to change shape
Conundrum: a dilemma
Corrosion: erosion of metal
Counterintuitive: opposite of what is logical
Credulous: easy to fool
Crescendo: increase in volume
Crevice: a narrow gap
Curlicues: loops and curls

D

Debilitating: preventing progress
Debris: leftover material, often scattered
Deftly: something done efficiently
Delve: to dive into something
Dilapidated: run down; neglected
Disheveled: Messy, unkempt appearance
Dissipate: to slowly fade away

E

Emancipated: freed from enslavement
Enterprise: a project
Era: period in time
Exacerbate: to irritate
Extraordinary: extreme

F

Ferromagnetic: a substance that remains magnetized after the magnet is removed
Filigree: delicate metal design
Foliate: leaves
Formidable: intimidating; strong
Fragmented: broken into pieces
Futile: pointless

G

Glower: to glare
Gourmet: fancy food or meal

I

Imply: to suggest
Impudent: rude
Incensed: outraged
Indecipherable: impossible to understand
Indiscriminate: random
Inferiority complex: the feeling that one is not as good as others
Infiltrate: to pass into enemy territory, often for the purposes of spying
Insipid: uninteresting

L

Laden: full of
Latrine: toilet
Lavish: luxurious; extravagant
Laxatives: a substance used to speed up digestion of the large intestines (and can cause a bathroom emergency!)
Leach: to seep; to leak
Leverage: using a lever to increase force
Loamy: nutrient-rich soil
Lucrative: profitable; will make money

M

Mausoleum: a tomb
Malevolent: evil
Mondegreen: a misheard song lyric
Muskrat: a rat-like animal that swims
Mitre: an angled cut, often in a piece of wood

N

Neanderthal: a simple-minded creature (used here as an insult)

Nefarious: evil

Nil: none, zero

Nodule: a small lump

Nonchalant: casual

Notorious: having a bad reputation

Noxious: toxic; poisonous

O

Obliterate: to completely destroy

Ochre: a tan color with a yellow-orange tint

Octave: eight notes in a musical scale

Ominous: eerie; threatening

Opaque: not transparent

Oppressive: severe

Ornate: decorative; fancy

P

Perpendicular: forming a right angle

Perpetually: continually

Philanthropist: a charitable person

Phlegm: thick mucous in the throat

Pinions: a gear wheel in a clock

Pivots: the rotating ends of a clock arbor

Pockmarked: scarred with holes

Polyalphabetic cipher: a cipher substituting letters for other letters

Porcelain: a delicate type of pottery

Portly: slightly overweight

Precarious: dangerously unstable

Precipitous: steep

Prodigious: impressive; large

Prolonged: drawn-out

Pungent: strong smell

R

Ravenous: very hungry
Receptacle: a container
Reconnaissance: scouting; searching
Reverberate: echoing
Ricochet: to bounce off something (pronounced: ric-o-shay)
Rivet: a metal faster

S

Seismic: a shaking movement in the ground (i.e. earthquake)
Shrapnel: small shards from an explosion
Silhouette: a shadowy outline
Smolder: steaming hot; angry
Sparse: simple; a few
Stench: a bad smell
Stob: a dead tree, still standing
Subside: to ease
Swashbuckler: an adventurer; a pirate
Systemic: an issue with something as a whole

T

Tarnish: discoloration of metal due to exposure to air
Tinny: a thin, metallic sound
Trajectory: a projected path; the direction something will soon be going
Transom: a long, horizontal window

Trimethius's Tableau: a cipher using letters in a 26 x 26 grid

Troglodyte: a cave dweller (in this case, an insult about lacking manners)

V

Vagabond: having no home

Vantage point: viewpoint or perspective

Vast: wide; broad

Vegetation: plants in a space

Veiling: hiding

Vessel: a container

Vivid: vibrant; lively

W

Wheel: the device in a small clock that keeps time

Special Thanks

To Pete, for being my first fan. Thank you for your constant support and for helping me stay focused on my dream. I'm incredibly lucky to have a partner like you.

To my kids, Elsa and Stig. Thank you for filling my life with light and love. You are always my first choice when it comes to spending my time, but I'm grateful for all the evenings you gave me "just five more minutes."

To Mom and Dad. Thank you for always being supportive of my goals and for always telling me I'm doing a good job. You are both remarkable and inspiring.

To Emmett, Quinn, Caleb, James, Elsa, and Stig for providing priceless feedback on my cover design.

To April Kelly and Jerry Cornille for your support and beta reading. You helped me see my blind spots and were an on-going source of encouragement.

Thank you to the Grayslake Public Library for providing Microsoft Word to patrons who need more than the Chromebook web version for editing.

A huge thank you to E.J. Nickson, who loaned me her personal laptop, after finding out I'd been spending days editing at the library. Thank you for sharing your wisdom on writing and publishing.

To my friends Julie McCarthy and Roiann Baskin for listening to me ramble about "the process," and thank you for never once asking "Is it done yet?" I feel incredibly fortunate to be your friend.

To Zee Lacson, Kari Pohar, and all my friends in the GAA Writers Group and Fremont Writers Group. I'm grateful for the kind and honest feedback. You helped me find my voice while fixing my punctuation.

About the Author

H.M. Lawson is an award-winning author and former middle school art teacher. She is a graduate of the University of Illinois, where she enrolled as an English major, then switched to art education, and later earned an MA in teaching and leadership from St. Xavier University.

What began as a bedtime story for her kids quickly evolved into a full-fledged conquest to write a story for kids with advanced vocabularies who aren't quite ready for the content of YA stories.

Lawson creates worlds where kids run free and find profound things adults have overlooked. She lives in the Midwest with her husband, two children, a red heeler named River, a gecko named Cleopatra, and six chickens.

The Mystery in Mapleton is her debut book.

Leave a review!

www.ingramcontent.com/pod-product-compliance
Lightning Source LLC
Chambersburg PA
CBHW070305310726
48976CB00005B/1572

* 9 7 9 8 9 8 9 9 4 6 9 0 7 *